STITCHING A LIFE IN PERSIMMON HOLLOW

STITCHING
A LIFE IN
PERSIMMON HOLLOW

GERRI BAUER

Franciscan
MEDIA
Cincinnati, Ohio

This is a work of fiction. Names, characters, corporations, institutions, organizations, events, or locales in this novel are either the product of the author's imagination or, if real, used fictitiously. The resemblance of any character to actual persons (living or dead) is entirely coincidental.

Cover illustration and design by Candle Light Studios
Book design by Mark Sullivan

LIBRARY OF CONGRESS CATALOGING-IN-PUBLICATION DATA
Names: Bauer, Gerri, author.
Title: Stitching a life in Persimmon Hollow / Gerri Bauer.
Description: Cincinnati, Ohio : Franciscan Media, [2016] | Series: Persimmon Hollow legacy ; 2 Identifiers: LCCN 2015049800 | ISBN 9781616369637 (softcover : acid-free paper)
Subjects: LCSH: Mexican Americans—Florida--Fiction. | Single women—Fiction. | Mate selection—Fiction. | BISAC: FICTION / Christian / Romance. | FICTION / Christian / Historical. | GSAFD: Love stories. | Historical fiction. | Christian fiction.
Classification: LCC PS3602.A9355 S75 2016 | DDC 813/.6—dc23
LC record available at http://lccn.loc.gov/2015049800

ISBN 978-1-61636-963-7

Published by Franciscan Media
28 W. Liberty St.
Cincinnati, OH 45202
www.FranciscanMedia.org

Printed in the United States of America.
Printed on acid-free paper.
16 17 18 19 20 5 4 3 2 1

To my husband, Peter D. Bauer, and to everyone in the extended Giovanelli and Bauer clans. I love you all.

A special thanks to the Franciscan Media family, for being wonderful to work with and for a deep dedication to bringing people closer to God.

Chapter 1

"Aunt Lupita! You can't mean it!"

Josefa Gomez Rodriguez's breath quickened as she tried to understand her aunt's behavior. Lupita didn't offer any explanation. She had pronounced her decision, and that was that.

Josefa stared at her aunt's solid back as the squat woman moved between the work table, wood stove, counter, and sink. The sizzle and pop of sliced potatoes frying in the cast iron skillet was the only response.

Josefa inhaled a long breath.

"I won't go."

At that, Lupita turned around to face Josefa and pointed the spatula in her direction.

"You will go. It is best for your future."

"But *tia*, I don't want to go all the way to Texas. This is my home. Don't make me leave Persimmon Hollow. I don't want to go so far away. I don't want to work in some stranger's house."

"You don't want this, you don't want that," Lupita chided her. "You forget your place. You are not the lady of the house. You work for the Taylors, just like I do. Just like your Uncle Alfredo does. We are blessed that they treat us as family and that they

1

welcomed you to Taylor Grove when you had no place to go. But we remember our place."

"And you think my place is in some stranger's kitchen and laundry yard in Texas."

The words had slipped out before Josefa had a chance to consider they might be hurtful to her housekeeper aunt, who spent her days on cleaning, laundry, cooking, and other household chores for the Taylors.

Lupita turned back toward the stove. Josefa saw her square her shoulders and could almost see the tenseness in her five-foot-tall frame. Josefa jumped up from her seat at the Taylors' table and went to stand next to her aunt, where her five inches of slender extra height made her feel she towered over her tia. She bent and hugged the smaller woman.

"I'm sorry. I didn't mean that to sound ..."

"You think you are too good for this?" Lupita didn't turn around. Her hands moved quickly as she sliced cabbage and added it to a Dutch oven. "Move aside, before your hair gets into the food. Why is your hair hanging loose like that?"

"It's still drying," Josefa said, and stepped a few paces to the side. "I had to wash it because I did so much sewing today that lint was all over me."

"You sew too much and forget you have other chores. A woman must sew, yes, but to keep her family clothed, not to waste time on fancy garments."

"I like making special clothes for everyone here," Josefa protested. "I want to be a dressmaker. One of the best ever. I want to design expensive gowns for the rich, like Senor Worth does in Paris."

"You like, you want. There you go again. I knew those magazines you get from town were no good. They make you spin those crazy dreams. Playing at fashion is not what it means to be a dressmaker with your head bent over the needle fourteen hours a day. No. You will learn to run a household in a place where you can mingle with our own and find a suitable husband. There are not many Mexicans or even mestizos here. Our relatives in Texas are happy to let you help in the house until you find a husband of good station. I have already written."

Josefa sniffled. She didn't want to cry. She just didn't want this to be happening. "Just because you miss family in Texas since you moved here doesn't mean I do," she said. "I don't even know anybody there. I was born in Florida."

Silence.

"Tia, why can't you understand?" she burst out. The tears trickled out despite her efforts to remain poised.

Lupita sighed, set down her utensils, turned and pulled Josefa into a tight embrace. Then she stepped back, but held onto Josefa's arms. "My bonita Josefa, I have been patient with you this past year because of your grief. I gave you freedom to recover your spirits in this good, heavenly place. I let you play at sewing fancy dresswork as much as you wished. But the time has come. Look at you, a beautiful woman of twenty-two and no suitable marriage prospects yet. It is my duty to make sure you are on the right path in life. Already, I have kept you here too long...yes, because you are family, and because I look at your face and see my beautiful sister in you, God rest her soul. No, it is time. You will go. It is already arranged."

"But..." Josefa started to say.

"Enough. We will discuss this no more," Lupita said, and went back to work. "Now help me prepare the table for supper."

Josefa ran out of the kitchen.

Her first thought was to flee to the chapel at St. Isidore's. The orphanage was one of her favorite retreats on the Taylor Grove homestead. She marveled at the way Seth helped it relocate to his grove when it lost its Northern home and funding. All because he loved Agnes, who had been raised there before coming to Persimmon Hollow to teach.

Josefa slowed her steps as she made her way from the family compound to the orphanage building. She thought of the harmony she saw daily between Seth and Agnes, their adopted older children, and now their baby son. She admired how Agnes even had time to make her special confections, which sold out at the grove's tourist store almost as soon as the shelves were stocked. That's what she wanted: a happy home, husband, and family, and a chance to do her needlework, somewhere in Persimmon Hollow just like the grove. Not a trip to Texas.

She halted at the orphanage doorway, stopped by the shadows that had begun to lengthen. It was almost time for Vespers. She was too agitated to barrel in on the sisters and orphans gathered for prayer. And too upset to bow down her head to the Lord with them. It certainly didn't feel that God was on her side right now, anyway.

She picked up her pace again, dark eyes blinking back tears, and walked deep into the rows of citrus trees that stretched out from the Taylor house in orderly lines. How could Aunt Lupita do this to me, she fumed. Instead of finding peace, she became more agitated as she clomped along the path just wide enough for her to reach out and touch tree foliage on each side. Did they even have orange trees in Texas? Or orphanages like St. Isidore's? People like the Taylors, and her aunt and uncle, and the Sisters of St. Francis at the orphanage, and close neighbors like in Persimmon Hollow, and…? Her resolve grew with every step. She wouldn't go. She would find a way to stay.

The globe-like trees, spaced in precise distance from one another, enfolded her like a fragrant mantle. The grove was always a balm to her spirits. But now, with the trees in full bloom and daylight waning, it was even more magical. She savored being surrounded by the clean, sweet scent of orange blossoms. The small white flowers covered the dark-green foliage like stars, and grew brighter as the daylight dimmed. Josefa inhaled the powerful perfume. The springtime bloom season scented the air for miles around. Everywhere in Florida, right now, citrus was flowering, like a beautiful gift from God.

Josefa slowed her pace again. She didn't know how far she had walked. She'd go just a bit farther, she decided. Then she'd go back and help her aunt with the meal.

Ah, but the trees. They were such inspiration. Josefa imagined the beautiful gown she could make, of dark green silk the exact color of the leaves, and decorated with small white beads sprinkled over it. Such a dress would complement her tawny skin. She could wear it with her hair swept up in one of the latest styles she saw in the Harper's Weekly issues her aunt tut-tutted about. Only her hair would look better than even the magazine etchings. Josefa was proud of her thick, waist-length black hair, and of the way its color matched that of her almond-shaped eyes. She even liked her unfashionably full lips because they fit her face. Hmmm, she thought, her face would show to advantage if she made a matching hat trimmed with delicate new citrus foliage growth instead of feathers.

Josefa stopped, and looked abstractly at the leaves while she thought about how she would pattern her dress design.

The sound of crackling dry undergrowth snapped. Fully present again, Josefa listened to steps that continued in a slow, rhythmical pace. The sound was too heavy to be that of a small animal or bird, and too paced and orderly to be a panther or a bear.

"Hello?" she said, loudly. She looked around for a stick or something to use for protection, just in case. Nothing. Taylor Grove was the neatest acreage in all of Persimmon Hollow. And, really, she reminded herself, she was in Taylor Grove. No one was here who didn't belong, and a shout from her would bring people within minutes. It was probably one of the grove workers who helped her uncle and Seth tend the hundreds of trees. Except she knew that they had worked all day on the far side of the grove, setting out young budded transplants on newly cleared ground.

"Who is it?!" she said, as the footsteps grew closer. Just how far had she walked? She turned to flee back toward the house just as the shape of a person became visible a few feet off the path.

*　*　*

"Wait!" came a soft-spoken voice as a tall young man stepped out from among the trees and into the path in front of Josefa.

"Pardon me, miss, I didn't mean to startle you." He took off his straw hat, gave her a quick, awkward bow, and straightened. She looked into blue eyes as startled as her own dark ones must have appeared to him. A quick grin crossed his face, and she sensed a likability in the stranger that put her more at ease.

"Benjamin Stillman, pleased to meet you," he said, with both hands holding onto the brim of his hat. "I take it I'm no longer on Mr. Heller's land?"

"This is Taylor Grove, owned by Mr. Seth Taylor," Josefa said. She folded her arms across her chest and stayed ready to call for help at a second's notice. But then her aunt would know she had wandered too far, alone, which would add fuel to her newfound zeal to ship Josefa off to Texas.

Josefa made a careful assessment of the young man in front of her. She judged him at close to six feet tall, solid but not fat, and muscled, if she were to guess from his forearms visible from rolled up shirtsleeves. He was clean-shaven, with a strong nose and square jaw. But his eyes – how they enlivened his entire face! They were the kind of bright, bold blue that gave scrub jays their sparkle. His fine-textured brown hair had been lightened in places by the sun and, although clean, was tousled as though combing were an afterthought. Something about his nose and the shape of his face reminded her of people of her own culture, but the hair and eyes didn't fit the picture. Nevertheless, she decided she liked what she saw.

"Shoulda known," he said, and looked around the grove. "These are healthy specimens. A lot healthier than Heller's. Oswald Heller. I work for him, over at the next homestead. I got to studying these trees and kind of ignored everything else. Didn't know I was off his land."

"You grow citrus?"

"No. I mean not for a living. I help out some at Heller's but I'm mainly finishing the carpentry work on his new house. What a place. Largest thing I've seen in a long time. These trees are something else. Look how they're covered with blooms. Heller's aren't half as full." He peered closer at them.

Josefa's initial fright dissipated. Benjamin Stillman had a calming presence about him. She watched as he set his hat on a branch, studied the shape and color of the foliage, and picked apart a few blooms and inspected them. The closer he scrutinized, the less he spoke. It almost seemed he wasn't even aware of her any longer.

She wasn't used to anyone forgetting she was around. She was perplexed until she glanced down at her faded calico work frock. Of course he wasn't as impressed with her as with the grove. She wasn't dressed appropriately to meet a stranger, especially one who had an interesting handsomeness about him. Her face was probably puffy from tears, and her still-damp hair hung loose to her waist and mussed from her walk. No hat, not even a scarf to neaten her appearance. He certainly saw her as her God-given true self. Well, it was too late to matter. What did matter was the passing time. She needed to get back.

She cleared her throat. "I think you should be leaving now," she said.

"Oh. Right." He looked over at her and brushed stray locks off his forehead. Josefa watched they slid right back down again, nearly into his eyes. He grinned again, a friendly, warm smile. "A little overdue on the haircut," he said. "I get busy or involved with something, and forget to tend to it or anything else. You're right. I should be getting on."

He plucked his hat from the branch, but he didn't move. Neither did she. He stood there, looking now at the hat brim as he started to run his fingers along its edge. A silence opened between them.

"Hey, look at that!" he said, and indicated a twig-like, brownish and white lump on the brim of his hat. "C'mon, fellow, back where you belong."

With a firm but gentle hand, Benjamin placed his finger right in front of the globby mass. Josefa leaned forward, scrunched her face and jumped back a few steps when the lump began to move. She stared as the blob inched up and onto Benjamin's finger. When it was fully aboard, he slowly moved his hand over to the foliage of a tree next to him.

"Here, this one looks good," he said, and settled his finger on a thick, glossy leaf. He nudged the lump and it started to inch off his finger and onto the leaf. Soon, it was at rest again and, to Josefa's amazement, it began to chew on the leaf.

Benjamin's face creased in delight. "I must have shook it loose from another tree when I pushed my way through," he said, and with a wave of his hand indicated the trees behind him.

"What on earth is it?" she asked. "Why are you letting it eat the leaf?"

"Because it's a larval caterpillar that will turn into a giant swallowtail butterfly."

"That ugly thing, that looks like something a bird dropped, will become a beautiful butterfly?" Josefa was suspicious.

He nodded. "Yup. Citrus is its larval food. Once it grows to a couple of inches, it will spin a chrysalis, go through metamorphosis, and emerge fully formed."

Josefa had her doubts.

"Can't it eat something else, other than Mr. Taylor's prized trees?" she asked.

"Not around here." He scanned the trees that enclosed them as far as they could see on all sides. "You have to admit, there's more than enough here to spare a few leaves for dinner."

"I guess," she said. "But I must alert Seth. I mean Mr. Taylor. He pays close attention to insects and such. Do you think there are more of them?"

"I hope so."

Josefa opened her eyes wide. Benjamin put up his hand and laughed.

"I mean only a handful. Not enough to do damage."

"Oh, OK," she said, and couldn't suppress a grin of her own.

A silence descended on them again as daylight inched closer to darkness. Josefa unfolded her arms and clasped her hands behind her back. She scuffed at the sandy ground with the toe of her ankle-high boot.

"Do you think the owner would meet with me to talk about these groves?" Benjamin asked. "I know I stumbled where I'm not supposed to be, but I was following the trees. Kept seeing stronger and fuller specimens and wasn't sure why, because I thought they were all on Heller's land. He's been having his grove managed for a while now, long before he started building. These have better care, that's obvious."

He squatted, one knee on the ground, and inspected the graft where the tree's scion met the rootstock. He straightened back up. "You've no idea how exciting it is to see this grove. Do you know what Mr. Taylor fertilizes with? What about cover crops? Does he hoe on a schedule?" His face took on a taut intelligence.

Josefa shook her head. "I know little about grove management. You can ask Seth. I'm fairly certain he won't mind meeting with you. Of course I have to tell him about you being here."

"Yes, yes," he said, again in that quiet tone that made her think he half-spoke to himself. "He may not want to give out any trade secrets. But this is too good to pass up. I'm just going to have to give it a go."

"Josefa! Josefa! Where are you? Josefa!"

The voice carried with it sounds of someone running. Moments later Polly Taylor came crashing through the grove, face flushed and bonnet bouncing on her shoulders, strings loosened.

"Josefa, you better get back right now! Hey! Who are you? What's going on?"

"Polly, I was just telling Mr. Stillman he was trespassing," Josefa said.

"My mistake," Benjamin said to the younger girl, as he gave her a quick bow. "Benjamin Stillman. Ben, is what most people call me."

Polly shrugged, having grown fearless about strange situations now that she was a mature almost-thirteen-year-old. "Well, you better go. We have to get back. Josefa, everybody thought you were at the orphanage. Do you know how late it is? Your aunt is furious at your running off. She's been holding dinner."

Great.

Josefa put out her hand to shake Ben's. "Until next time, Ben," she said, surprised and yet pleased with herself at the smooth farewell. Usually shyness overcame her around strangers. She was curious to learn more about Ben. She felt the strangest pull toward him, as he reached to grab her extended hand, and she hoped they'd meet again.

His face brightened. "Yes!" he said. "Well, goodbye then, for now. Uh, Josefa, right? Josefa Taylor?"

"Oh, no. No, I'm Josefa Gomez Rodriguez. My aunt and uncle are housekeeper and caretaker for Taylor Grove."

Their gazes locked as their hands stayed entwined.

"C'mon." Polly tugged at Josefa's arm and the moment was broken.

"We'll meet again," Ben promised, and started back the way he had come.

The last of dusk's lingering rays faded, but Ben's presence remained with Josefa.

Chapter 2

osefa nibbled on ham and toyed with the cabbage and potatoes. She was caught between surprise at the encounter in the
grove and dismay at the uproar her absence had caused. At least
it had subsided somewhat. She glanced at her aunt through half-
lowered lids, and quickly determined to stay focused on her meal.
She had little appetite, for food or conversation, unlike apparently
everyone else at the table.

"So much news from town is rattling around my head I can't
keep it all straight!" Polly exclaimed as she reached for another
biscuit. "And then to find Josefa in the grove, why, I ..."

"You think everything is news, can't hardly tell one thing from
the other," teased Billy Taylor, Polly's adoptive brother of nearly
the same age. He smirked, and pulled his hand back before Polly
could swat him with her napkin.

"As if you'd be a good judge of anything," Polly declared. She
stuck her tongue out at him.

"Enough, you two," said Agnes Taylor, but her gaze was indul-
gent. "Not at the dinner table."

"To think I call you my brother!" mumbled Polly, her voice low
but her eyes bright with humor.

"You're stuck with me," said Billy in a stage whisper. "Just like

I'm stuck with you for a sister." He made a face at her.

"You heard your mother, you two?" Seth said, more a statement than a question, and Agnes sent him a wry smile while the two youths settled down. But not before Polly got in the last word. "You're still thirteen like me, Billy Taylor, and you won't be a grown up fourteen 'til November, so don't be acting all hoity-toity."

"You're not thirteen yet despite telling everybody you are," said Billy, and got down to the business of eating.

"That's because I think my birth certificate at the orphanage is wrong and I'm months older than anybody says," Polly retorted.

"You'll both be going to the orphanage for prayers of penance if you don't stop this minute," Agnes said in a calm voice that everyone knew overlaid a steely resolve.

Blessed silence reigned for the next several minutes.

A pain had struck Josefa as she witnessed the closeness and sibling banter. It'd been a full year since the accident, and she still felt the loss of her sister and parents as though it had happened yesterday. She was an orphan now, like Polly, Billy, and even Agnes. How did they bear it?

Billy and Polly acted like the siblings they had become by virtue of the love that brought together their adoptive parents: Billy's uncle Seth and Polly's orphanage caretaker Agnes. Now baby Seth Jr. had been added to the fold, all soft and snuggly in the cradle Agnes had set next to the table while they ate. The warmth of the Taylor family circle radiated outward to encompass Josefa and her aunt and uncle, everyone at the orphanage, and friends in town. How she loved them all. She never wanted to leave.

"Polly, do you want to get back to the news you started to share?" Agnes asked. She looked around at the others. "I can almost excuse her rambunctiousness this evening. Even I admit the talk in town has injected a dose of excitement to Persimmon Hollow."

"*Dios Mio*, I can hardly wait to hear," said Lupita. Even normally taciturn Alfredo looked up from his plate.

"Well," said Polly, eager to share, "the president is coming to visit, and some kind of machinery that makes light at night without kerosene or gas is gonna be wired on the street, and a fancy newcomer who everybody says is from a good family is building a huge house, and he's supposed to be the most handsome man ever to—"

"Whoa," Seth said, chuckling as he gestured for her to stop. "Slow down. The president of what is coming?"

"And what is this about street lighting?" Alfredo asked.

"Who is this person of good family?" Lupita wanted to know.

"And how big is that newcomer's house?" Josefa asked.

Agnes laughed. "I told you the news was exciting!" She turned to Polly. "OK, honey, let's try that again. Slowly, and enunciate your words properly. There's no rush. Pretend you're speaking the way you have done at school programs."

"See, the joys of having a former schoolteacher for a mother can be many, you know," Seth said to Polly, sharing a conspiratorial glance of understanding with her. Josefa could almost see the love binding them all together.

Polly sat up a little straighter and started again.

"President Cleveland and his wife are coming to Florida in—"

Josefa swallowed a bite of potato whole.

"Mrs. Cleveland? Frances Cleveland? The most fashionable woman in the country is coming to Florida?" Josefa choked out.

"Do tell," said Seth drily. "I see how much more important she is than her husband."

Agnes raised her hands, palms upturned, and looked at Lupita.

"And we wonder where Billy gets his mischievousness." Lupita just shook her head, but her eyes were merry. Josefa took note, and her chest felt less constricted. Her transgression apparently was forgotten, at least for the moment.

"What I would give to see Mrs. Cleveland in real life, instead of in engravings and photographs," Josefa burst out. "I'm especially curious to know how the first lady dresses for Florida. Maybe she will do some things with women while the men talk politics. Maybe we...hey, Polly, when are they coming?" She twirled to face the girl who was close enough to her to be like a sister.

"Uh, I think in June."

"That's right," Agnes said. "The president is stopping in Florida as part of a campaign tour. We don't know his itinerary yet."

"No matter where he stops, he'll be mobbed with people," Seth said. "It's mighty nice he values the state enough to care about the voters here. All the same, I'll sit out the crowd and read about it afterward in the paper."

"How come only men get to vote?" Polly asked. "It's not fair."

"I could tell you...," Billy started to say until a warning glance from Seth caused him to get busy with the rest of his dinner.

Seth glanced at Alfredo. "The street lights are closer to home for us. What's that all about?"

Agnes and Polly looked at each other. Polly shook her head, and Agnes picked up the thread of conversation.

"Seth, I'm not certain of the details, but Mr. Stetson...you know, the hatmaker—he bought the large grove west of town and built that mansion—is friends with Thomas Edison. Mr. Stetson had his entire house wired for artificial light, and now he's talking about adding some type of lighting to a short stretch of Persimmon Boulevard."

Seth let out a low whistle, and Alfredo nodded approvingly.

"We'd be the first town in the state to have lights on our main street, is what I heard today," Polly said.

"We'd be more than that," Seth said. "What a boon this will be for attracting investors, businesses, and more settlers."

"Maybe a visit by the president and first lady!" Josefa declared.

"Don't get your hopes up," Seth said. "We're a mighty small town still."

"Oooh, that reminds me. I haven't yet told you about the new guy," Polly said. She looked at Josefa. "He's said to be the handsomest man ever, and he's building on land right next to us, and he is from…um…what did they say, Agnes, that he was from 'new money'? What does that mean?"

"It means he's from a family that recently came into its wealth," Agnes said. "His surname is Heller. I forget his first name. He's been the absentee owner of the adjacent grove and now is building a house said to rival the Stetson mansion, although I'm not certain that is possible."

"Oh, the house is almost done. Maybe we could ride over," Josefa said, then clamped her hand over her mouth.

Every person at the table stopped eating and looked at her.

"You have met Mr. Heller?" Lupita kept her voice even, but her eyes wanted to know how such a thing might have happened without her—Lupita—knowing about it.

"No. And I haven't seen the house. I—"

"Oh, darn. I hoped you could tell us if he really does have eyes that make 'ladies swoon,'" said Polly, collapsing into giggles. "Honestly, that is what I heard someone say in town, and it was all I could do to keep from laughing out loud."

The rest of the diners waited for Josefa's explanation, except Billy, who reached for the last biscuit.

"I met the carpenter who is working on the house," Josefa said.

The clatter of dining stilled as she relayed the encounter in the grove. She watched with discomfort as her aunt's eyes grew darker underneath drawn eyebrows. Her uncle pressed his lips together.

"Oh, that's who that guy was," Polly said. "He seemed nice enough."

"He said he'd like to meet with you, Seth, to discuss grove cultivation," Josefa plowed on, ignoring her aunt and uncle.

"Happy to meet with anyone on that subject," Seth said, but his jocularity had morphed into seriousness.

Agnes set down her fork. "Josefa, honey, we were very concerned about your absence and your lateness in returning."

Lupita rose and started to clear the dishes off the table. "Such improper behavior for a young lady. Now you see why I make plans for you."

Josefa closed her eyes. She wouldn't get into this discussion again, not here, and not so soon.

"What kind of plans, Lupita?" asked Agnes. "Anything I can help with?"

"No," said Lupita. But she outlined her idea anyway, down to the smallest detail.

"Do we have to talk about this now?" Josefa asked. Agnes leaned back in her chair in concentration. Polly's eyes had gone large at Lupita's words.

"I'll let you ladies alone now, womanly etiquette not being my strong point," Seth said. He, Alfredo, and Billy rose and retreated in haste, as if afraid they'd be asked for an opinion on so delicate a matter.

Polly drew her brows together in concentration. Then her face brightened. "Josefa, I forgot to say the dressmaker in town is leaving. Fanny mentioned that the lady wants to teach her business to an apprentice before she goes."

It was all the invitation Josefa needed. Before her aunt could persuade Agnes of the merits of the hideous Texas plan, she pounced on the possibility of a dressmaking apprenticeship.

"Aunt Lupita, what an opportunity for me! I can't pass it up. Don't you think so, too, Agnes? What I could learn! Especially now, with ladies probably wishing for new frocks and alterations of old ones to go see the president."

"You traipse around the grove talking to strangers, and now you wish to go be an apprentice off the property?" Lupita asked. She looked at Agnes. "You do know that Josefa does not want to move to Texas."

"I promise to do nothing but sew, sew, sew, for...how long, Polly?"

"I think two months."

"Aunt Lupita, that would give you more time to decide if sending me to Texas is really the best action. Two months won't make a difference out there."

"I don't know, Josefa."

"Please. Just think about it."

"*Si*, all right." But Josefa knew such quick acquiescence from her aunt was an appeasement. If she had to guess, she'd say Lupita had no intention of seriously considering the request. Lupita wasn't known for straying off any course she set for herself or a loved one. In fact, just the opposite. She tended to dig in.

That meant she had to take action herself. Excusing herself from the table, Josefa hurried outside and walked the short distance to the cabin she shared with her aunt and uncle. She lit a kerosene lantern, pulled out a piece of notepaper, pen, and inkwell, and jotted a small note of acceptance to an offer that hadn't been personally extended, but one that Josefa couldn't afford to lose.

She folded the note, slipped it into her pocket, and went back outside. If she walked fast, she could get to the barn in time. She could hear the last of the grove workers there, talking and putting away equipment. One of them lived in town and could carry her note to the dressmaker. As Josefa neared the barn, the very man she sought stepped outside of it and waved hello. She waved back, held up the letter, and ran over and made her request.

That night, as she lay in bed, she felt that she'd already started on her new life. It was too late to stop the apprenticeship now. What a breach of etiquette it would be were she to rescind her offer of acceptance after she'd given her word. Both her aunt and Agnes were sticklers for propriety. Josefa felt a glimmer of hope.

Chapter 3

Polly was right. He was the most handsome man Josefa had ever seen. She sat up straighter in the porch swing, the needle in her hand poised between embroidery stitches, and stared as the man made a practiced dismount from his horse and strode toward the porch. It had to be Oswald Heller. No one else in Persimmon Hollow had caused such a stir over wealth, breeding, youthful good looks, and citified attire. He looked exactly what Josefa imagined such a figure to be.

He paused and assessed her with a quick glance that made her feel undressed before the look in his eyes shifted to a more detached gaze. Josefa blinked. He came closer as though she were the only woman in the entire world that mattered to him.

"Allow me to introduce myself. Your neighbor, Oswald Heller," he said and bowed.

Josefa sat there tongue-tied.

"You are the lady of the house? I heard she was beautiful, but the descriptions don't do you justice." He smiled without warmth. She stiffened, not used to such blatant flattery.

He had such a presence and seemed to fill the space around him. Dark hair, of fashionable cut, blue eyes, even features. His shirt was of fine linen—she had recognized that in a heartbeat, even at a distance. His riding pants were of smooth broadcloth and sewn to fit his figure. So unlike the overalls, denims, or home-made trousers worn by most all the men she knew in Persimmon Hollow, and by Ben Stillman in the grove the other night. Weird, she thought, that Ben had come to mind suddenly.

Agnes pushed aside the mosquito netting draped whenever the door was open, and stepped out, followed by Lupita and Polly.

"Hello! May we help you?" Agnes asked.

"Ah, ladies, good day," Oswald said and bowed again. "Your neighbor, Oswald Heller, come to make your acquaintance."

"Welcome, Mr. Heller." Agnes was quick to step forward. She made introductions, and Josefa felt time stand still when it was her turn.

"May I, señorita?" Oswald asked. Without waiting for an answer, he lifted her hand, kissed the top of it, and laid it back in her lap. He sat down next to her on the swing, prompting a raised eyebrow from Lupita. Even Agnes was slightly put off.

"Ah, well, we'll get some refreshments and send for Mr. Taylor," Agnes said. "Make yourself at home." Polly smirked at Josefa, but Oswald paid no heed. He kept his gaze fixed on Josefa. She bent over her embroidery, unnerved by his bold stare so close beside her.

Lupita tapped Polly. "Go fetch your father while I get some-thing for us to drink." Polly skipped off, Lupita went back inside, and Agnes sat down across from the swing.

"Tell me about yourself, Mr. Heller," she said.

"I'll wait until the man of the house is here. No sense repeating myself. Why don't you tell me about yourself."

Agnes narrowed her eyes. Josefa knew Agnes had reason to be suspicious of strange men, given her traumatic past experi-ence. But surely, she could find nothing wrong in so fine a man as

Oswald appeared to be. He was different from the ruffians who'd harassed and even briefly abducted Agnes.

"And you," Oswald said to Josefa. He leaned forward slightly and turned toward her, using his body language to block out Agnes. "Why are you seated on the front porch of a log cabin when you belong dressed in satin and diamonds and presiding over a ball?" He no sooner spoke the words than Josefa pictured the scene in her mind. How lovely it would be. How well she could see herself in such a setting.

She gave Oswald a shy smile. "We don't have much call for that around here. I fear I'm not versed in such skills."

"Give me time," he said under his breath so that Agnes couldn't hear.

What was that supposed to mean?

He shifted again in the seat, and Josefa was again taken by the quality of his clothing. Only men of class dressed as such, and on a regular workaday, too.

But for no reason, the image of Ben floated again through her mind. She pictured him, standing in the grove as he had when they'd met several days earlier. She remembered his shirt had an old-fashioned cut, with a square-cut neck and drawstrings. Unbleached, rough-weave cotton, for certain. His pants had been faded denim, and his boots scuffed and far from new.

Ben's image was accompanied by the same warm feeling of ease that she'd had in the grove with him. Seated next to Oswald, she felt clammy, uncertain of herself, and afraid to speak or act for fear of doing the wrong thing in front of a man of such quality. She so wanted to impress him.

Lupita returned with mugs and a pitcher of lemonade, and set them down. Agnes prepared to pour just as Seth came bounding up the porch steps two at a time.

Oswald rose and went to meet him, then withdrew his hand at the sight of Seth's grubby, field-stained appearance. Seth nodded hello and stepped around him.

"I'll have some of that lemonade," Seth said, taking a glass and helping himself. He gulped it down, plunked the mug on the table, and wiped sweat from his forehead with his arm. Josefa saw a hint of disdain in Oswald's expression as he watched.

"Have a seat." Seth indicated a chair apart from the swing, while he sat down next to Agnes.

"And do tell us about yourself," said Agnes, who hadn't complied with Oswald's request for information.

Oswald sat, stretched, and crossed his feet at the ankles. "As you probably know, the Heller family corporation is known in Philadelphia, Charleston, and beyond. Manufacturing. Munitions. Banking. Housing. I'm here to assess whether the company should invest in your fast-growing community. Persimmon Hollow has a reputation for itself already."

Seth leaned forward. "An established bank is one thing we need. And a real estate development firm, the kind led by people of your family's stature, would fuel growth. Sawmills would spring up to supply demand for housing, or you could invest in that level of operations, too."

Oswald grinned, but Josefa again noted that his smile lacked warmth.

"I'm aware of the needs. Perhaps some could be rectified."

The grandfather clock inside the house chimed the hour, and Lupita stepped forward from her perch near the doorway. "Come, Josefa. It's time to go to the orphanage for prayer. Where is Polly? Agnes, will you join us as usual?"

Agnes stood up. "Pardon us, Mr. Heller. We ladies say an extra rosary each day as part of our Lenten practice."

"Oh," he said. "Admirable."

He reached for Josefa's hand as she rose. "Allow me." He took her embroidery ring and set it on the small wicker table in front of the swing. He then kissed her hand again. Josefa felt her cheeks flush as her awkwardness transformed into awe. With his smooth actions, Oswald made her feel beautiful and desirable. She imagined what it'd be like to have a man of his station as a beau. He'd be a forceful interference for her aunt's plan. Josefa imagined the possibility. If only she'd be so lucky.

Agnes's voice broke through Josefa's daydream. "Mr. Heller, we'd be honored if you'd join the families for Holy Week devotions, and then Easter Mass and dinner on the first, just a couple of weeks away. What better way to become acquainted than through shared worship of the Lord."

Oswald was out of his chair so fast Josefa almost lost her footing for standing so close to him.

"I'm honored but…must refrain from acceptance until I check my schedule," he said. "Thank you for your hospitality. Now please excuse me. I must attend to business."

Oswald started to make a hasty exit.

"Oh, one thing," Seth called. "Tell your worker Ben Stillman he's welcome here any time to talk citrus. I heard he was asking."

Oswald nodded but gave no verbal acknowledgment. He mounted his horse and rode off.

Josefa felt a relief, a letting go, as though she no longer had to sit poised and anticipate how her next words or actions should be conveyed. She looked forward to the peacefulness of prayer.

*　*　*

Oswald lit a taper in the shadowed house that was already furnished to make a statement even though he had no intention of living there for any length of time. He sat down at his desk in the library and adjusted the wick in his lantern. He pulled out the stationery supplies, dipped his pen in the inkwell, and began to write to his colleagues at the American Protective Association. They had nothing to fear, he told them. He could easily inject himself into town life and help suppress the growing Catholic sentiments among settlers. He'd already made inroads at the leading Catholic homestead. That a lovely señorita was there made the task all the more enjoyable.

She was young and ignorant, he continued, and would be easy to seduce away from her religion and toward his intentions. He would lure her with riches and feigned devotion. Once he had that fracture in place, he'd plant dissent and suspicions among community members. Popery was rampant in the cities, and as an APA leader, he vowed to do his part to prevent Catholicism from gaining a foothold in small new towns in rural country like this. Taylor Grove was the nexus. People appeared comfortable but far from fancy or prosperous. Money, flattery, and material goods were powerful motivators, and he planned to use them all. He'd yet to encounter anyone who couldn't be bought.

Yes, Oswald closed his letter by saying, this assignment wouldn't be as tiresome as first expected.

He rose and saw that one of the servants' hunting dogs had ventured indoors. The lean animal would have felt the brunt of a booted foot if it hadn't moved faster than Oswald, whose face lost its handsomeness when contorted into anger.

Chapter 4

*I*n her room in her aunt and uncle's cabin near the main house, Josefa pulled her sturdiest work dresses from the armoire, stuffed them into her valise and trunk, and went back for more. The sateen with scalloped-edge overdress and shirred yoke? No, too fancy for apprenticing. The brocade with beaded trim and ribbon bows? No, not that one either.

"When are you going to tell your aunt?" Polly was incredulous. "Last I heard, it was an idea being considered, not a done deal. Does Agnes even know?"

Josefa shook her head.

"I've never seen you act this way, Josefa. Where are you going to stay, or are you planning to walk the two miles back and forth every day? I suppose you could. But how will you get back here in time for devotions? What has gotten into you? Holy Week starts in a few days."

Josefa paused as she folded a striped cambric skirt and packed it. She sat down on the bed and smoothed the parallel strips in the log cabin quilt.

"I was going to wait until after Easter. But I don't think my aunt will seriously reconsider her plan for me to move to Texas. So I went ahead and wrote a letter of acceptance to the dressmaker."

Polly put her hands on her hips. "Will somebody tell me what this is about? Why are you going to Texas?" She plopped down on the bed next to Josefa. "I wish everybody would stop treating me like a child."

"I'm not going to Texas," said Josefa with a resolute shake of her head. "My aunt wants to push me into some kind of arranged marriage. First she wants me to improve my domestic skills by boarding with relatives and doing housework for them, as if I don't do or know enough already. It's positively medieval, what she's thinking. I mean, it's almost 1900 now, for goodness' sake!"

"Sounds terrible. But I predict an uproar when she and Agnes find out you accepted the apprenticeship without clearing it with them first. Even your Uncle Alfredo will be mad, and you know almost nothing can get him to lose his temper."

Polly got up and looked at Josefa. "You're acting like me. I can hear Agnes already. She'll say you're supposed to be a role model for me, and here I influenced you." Polly giggled.

Josefa shook her head. "No, you won't take any blame for my actions. This is my own doing. But it's been hard for me."

She wasn't as lighthearted as Polly, who brushed off cares even when things didn't go her way. Josefa's stomach hurt at the thought of moving, even temporarily, even as close as the center of town. But it was better than the alternative. Her shoulders sagged a little. Just where would she stay in town anyway? She hadn't thought that far ahead. She supposed she could sleep in the shop, if it came down to that. She rose and went back to sorting clothes.

"When are you leaving?" Polly asked. She held the kerosene lantern higher so its weak light illuminated the inside of the armoire. The dim rays cast long shadows that coated the room in almost the same gray as the dusk outside.

"Not exactly sure," came the muffled reply from Josefa as she dug deeper into the back of the armoire. She emerged with two more chambray dresses draped over her arm. "I may ask Mr. Heller to escort me to town. I heard he has a barouche that he drives with matched horses. It would be a stylish ride."

"I can see it now, you in fancy outfit, too," Polly said.

"I haven't figured out how to ask him without appearing forward."

"I'll do it! I'll just ask him or say it'd be a fine idea if he offered to help."

"Someday that boldness may trip you up, Polly. Learn to be wise."

Polly shrugged. "I think you should wear the rust-colored walking suit with the velvet trim for the excursion. Depart from here in style and—"

A loud, unfamiliar thud stopped Polly in midsentence. Josefa dropped the dress she had held up against herself in front of the dressing table mirror. A loud clatter rang in the air, then another thud, and then a moan.

Billy ran past the window. "In the barn!" he shouted through the open shutters.

By the time Josefa and Polly reached the barn, the others were already there.

"Uncle Alfredo!" Josefa cried. She knelt down beside her aunt, who leaned in to hear the nearly unconscious Alfredo, who lay on the floor. His face echoed pain, and his leg was twisted at an odd angle and pinned underneath a broken wooden beam. A ladder was nearby, sideways on the ground.

"Was fixing...gave way...," he whispered, then slipped into a fog. Josefa glanced upward and saw how a heavy log beam had partially split. Next to a jagged edge was an empty gap that had held the piece now on the ground.

"Billy, go find any workers still here so we can get him into the house," Seth ordered.

Lupita cradled her husband's head in her lap.

"Polly, get Sister Rose. She knows how to set bones," Agnes said. "Josefa, prepare space for the roll-away bed in…"

Lupita glanced up and finished the sentence. "In the main room, Josefa, not the bedroom."

"Billy will bring the bed over soon as he returns," Agnes said. "I'll get sheets and blankets and will be there momentarily."

Josefa gave her uncle a gentle kiss. His face around his lips was white, and his skin looked waxy in the barn's dim light. Her gaze met her aunt's worried look, and her lips moved automatically in prayer.

Dear God, please help my dear Uncle Alfredo, Josefa prayed as she ran to make preparations. *No more losses. Please, no more losses.* She felt her grip on safety and security tip, even though she knew a broken or sprained leg could easily mend. She couldn't bear to lose anyone else, not anyone at all.

* * *

"Six weeks, most likely, before this fully heals," Sister Rose said to Alfredo after she set a splint on his leg and wrapped it. "It's not as bad as we first thought, thank the Lord. And your arm isn't fractured, just sprained. We'll find you some crutches for that leg, or perhaps Mr. Taylor can make a pair."

"Nothing keeps me down six weeks," Alfredo grumbled.

"Could have been worse," Seth said.

"Indeed," agreed Sister Rose. "Had the bone come through the skin the injury would have far surpassed my limited medical ability to help."

"And way beyond my horse-doctoring skills," Seth added.

Lupita bustled in, carrying a tray containing a teapot and cup. "Drink this sage tea; it's good to keep your strength up," she said and set the tray down on the table next to the bed. Josefa had arranged a sickroom in a corner of the living room in the care-taker cabin. Lupita fussed over Alfredo, tucked his quilt covers just so, propped more pillows behind him to support him in a seated position, and poured the tea.

"Drink, to fortify you," she said. She lifted the cup and helped Alfredo use his uninjured arm so that the liquid didn't spill.

Josefa watched the tenderness between her aunt and uncle. She saw her uncle's glance of thanks and gratefulness to her aunt. As for Lupita, going for tea was the only time she'd left Alfredo's side since they had discovered him two hours earlier.

She studied this aunt and uncle she hadn't know well before the accident that took away her immediate family. Her late mother's sister was much older, almost a generation older, than her sibling, and Alfredo—her late father's cousin—was even older. The fami-lies had never lived close enough for frequent visiting, but their double family ties had kept them connected. Lupita and Alfredo had raced up to Gainesville as soon as they got word about the accident. By then, only Josefa's sister still clung to life. Months of care hadn't helped.

Lupita had embraced Josefa as a daughter and had brought the shocked young woman back to Persimmon Hollow to live at Taylor Grove right after the funeral. Lupita's own two boys were grown and off working as cattlemen, and the Gomezes were happy to be a larger family again. Over the following year, Josefa had gradually risen from her grief, warmed by the love and secu-rity she found in Persimmon Hollow and safe in her haven of Taylor Grove.

As she watched Lupita and Alfredo, she appreciated how they were a strong, unified team. She sometimes heard them talking low and long into the night. But neither was getting any younger. She felt anew a responsibility to always be there for them and to help them when in need, just as they had stepped in to rescue her. She only hoped she, too, would have such a close relationship with her future husband, whoever he might be.

Could she and Oswald ever share such unity, should their budding courtship evolve into something serious? A tiny voice inside her answered no. She brushed it away. She didn't even know the man yet. Oswald was of the modern world, not so old-fashioned as her aunt and uncle. She wondered how a man like Oswald viewed extended families. Did people of his kind all live together, with multiple generations in one place? Surely, as a husband he would allow her to support her aunt and uncle as they aged and welcome them into the Heller home. Wouldn't he?

Josefa sighed. Why was she even thinking about it? Oswald hadn't yet made a formal courtship visit, let alone proposed. At times, Josefa had to admit her aunt spoke truth when she chided her niece's whimsical daydreaming.

Josefa resumed her bedside watch with her aunt. Love or not, Oswald Heller and a two-month dressmaking apprenticeship were strong pillars standing between Josefa and an unwelcome future in Texas. She hoped her little plan worked.

* * *

Josefa twisted the fabric, wrung out the excess water, shook out the material, and hung it on the line. The dye hadn't produced quite the color she sought, and the skirt still needed attention to become good enough for more than workaday wear. She let the second garment sit in the bucket a little longer. That dress was in better shape. If it took the color well, she'd be able to wear it during her apprenticeship and feel as though she were in new garb.

She trotted back to the laundry area of the yard, where she, Lupita, Agnes, and Polly had an efficient system for getting through wash day. Usually, Polly and Josefa heated the water and pounded and swirled the clothing, Agnes rinsed, and Lupita hung the garments on the clothesline and laid some out over bushes and shrubs. The women usually rotated jobs halfway through so no one had sore muscles in only one part of their body. Washday was such a chore, she thought, and not for the first time. She wouldn't miss it a bit when she was an elegant dressmaker. Or when she was rich Mrs. Oswald Heller. Or both. Josefa's lips curved in a small smile as she sank into the daydream.

"I'm almost finished with my second dye bath—I'll help you finish up while it soaks," she called as she reached the other women.

"Good thing. My arms are getting tired," said Polly. She scrubbed the final piece of clothing, a pair of overalls. "And I'm hot."

"Sí, it is warm today," Lupita said. "Spring is moving into summer fast this year."

"Do you know of any other dyestuff to use for red, other than the cherry laurel?" Josefa asked her aunt and Agnes as she reached to take the other end of a sheet and help her aunt secure it to the line with wooden clothespins.

"Ach! Look at your fingers! Don't be touching the clean white sheets!" Lupita said.

Josefa looked at her stained fingertips. "Oops." How could she have forgotten to wear her work gloves?

"Lye soap will take that off, if you do it quickly," Lupita noted. "And, no, I don't know of other plants." Agnes also shook her head.

"I need to find someone who knows," Josefa said. "Surely there's someone." She went to the washday supplies and scrubbed her fingers with the harsh soap, so unlike the gentle soapwort lather she used on her most delicate fabrics.

"The dressmaker in town?" Polly asked in an oh-so-innocent tone.

"Of course!" Josefa said. "Why didn't I think of that?"

"Imagine the many different colored garments I could make with more dyestuff and especially with more and different fabrics," she said, directing her words toward her aunt. "Something other than the usual calico or gingham, and...wouldn't it be wonderful...ah, an apprenticeship with the dressmaker could also give me many new skills. I could make—"

"Slow down," Lupita said. "You and your flyaway dreams, like birds or butterflies flitting all over the place. Appreciate what God has placed in front of you, *si*?"

"Yes, he placed this laundry here so we will appreciate days when we don't have to do it," Polly said. "Either that or washday is God's idea of a joke."

"You're too close to questioning God," Agnes said, and there was no laughter in her voice. "Remember the great commandment: 'You shall love the Lord your God with all your heart, and with all your soul, and with all your might.' You don't question God."

"I wasn't serious!" protested Polly. "Geez. I know the great commandment. Can we change the subject? Josefa, how did the cherry laurel dye work out anyway?"

"I'm still experimenting with it," Josefa said. "I'm not sure I used the bark scrapings the way Tustenuggee instructed. I wish he'd get back from down south so I could ask. It's time enough for today, though. I'm going to go check."

She strode across the courtyard to the shady spot where her small dye vats were set up. She squeezed out the excess water and held up the dress. It really was warm out for March. With one wet, again-stained hand, she pushed aside stray hairs that had escaped her scarf and wiped away perspiration that trickled down her cheek.

"Hey, Josefa, where are you?" Billy hollered.

"Back here, behind the oak," she called.

She heard footsteps and heard Billy say, "Right there. See? There she is. Meet you back at the barn."

As she turned, she saw Ben step past the clusters of wildflowers and plants she tended for dye and walk toward her. She felt her face flush and her heartbeat quicken when she saw the smile open slowly on his serious face.

"Hi!" she said.

"Hello, there," he said. "I thought you might like this." He held out a wooden box with an open top. She peered in. It was filled with citrus leaves, both loose and on branches, and other flora in a rounded, shrub-like clump. A plump caterpillar inched among the citrus, similar to but larger than the one he had shown her the day they met.

"This larva is almost ready to pupate," he said.

She arched her eyebrows in question.

"To spin itself into a chrysalis," he explained. "It's about the right size. Once it spins its cocoon, it will go through what's called 'metamorphosis' and emerge as a butterfly. I provided enough larval food and space for it to latch onto that pile of leaves and branches. You'll be able to observe the whole process."

"Ben, what a thoughtful gift," Josefa exclaimed. "Thank you."

She reached to take the box, but he stepped back in some alarm.

"Uh...your hands," he said.

"Oh!" Josefa still held the wet dress that dripped dye liquid all around her, and her hands were again an unnatural shade of red. She remembered she'd touched her face and hair only moments earlier and realized they, too, were now probably oddly tinted.

For some reason, it all seemed funny. She looked at her hands, lifted a hand to her cheek, and laughed.

Ben grinned. Then he, too, laughed.

"It's a nice color," he said finally. "Looks good on you."

"Hold on," Josefa said, and a bubble of laughter escaped. She hung the dress from the small line strung between two palm trees and then plunged her hands into the bucket of soap and water she'd carried over with her. She scrubbed once again with the lye soap.

"There," she said and dried her hands on a clean corner of her apron. "That's better." She held up her hands, almost back to their natural color.

Her fingers brushed Ben's as he put the box into her arms, and she felt a surge of warmth, a happy, good feeling. Their gazes held, and the warm glow inside her strengthened. Unsure what to do, she dropped her gaze.

They both studied the box again.

"Keep it protected," Ben said. "Inside, with you, not out here unless you are nearby and can keep an eye on it. Make sure there is good ventilation and bright light."

"I will," she said. "I'll send word right away when the butterfly appears. How long do you think that'll be?"

"About ten days to two weeks," he said, and his face fell into its usual earnest lines. "I probably won't be here."

"Oh?" Josefa looked at him questioningly.

"My job at Heller's place is almost finished," he said, indicating the direction of Oswald's property with a nod of his head. "Another week at the most. Not a minute too soon, if I'm truthful about it. I may not get to see this in its final form," he added, looking into the box.

Josefa didn't want Ben to leave. She felt good in his presence: comfortable, alive, and just all-around right. She liked him. She could like him more than as a friend, if she was honest with herself.

"Have you and Seth finished your talks about citrus?" she asked, hoping they hadn't.

He looked puzzled. "Uh, well, he never sent word, so I figured he wasn't interested. I was surprised when your cousin—or is he your brother?—Billy came over just now with a request for me to ride back here with him."

"There must be some mistake," Josefa said. She carefully set down the box on a clean, shaded corner of her worktable. "I distinctly heard Seth ask Mr. Heller to tell you to visit."

Ben regarded her with a solemn but unreadable look. "Heller must have forgotten."

"Why are you here now?" she asked. "Surely you didn't come just to give me this?"

"I had been seeking the right time to visit with the box," Ben admitted. "But I'm here now because, well, I'm not sure. Billy mentioned something about a broken leg and the grove being short of hands."

As if on cue, they heard Billy. "Hey, Ben, you done? My dad wants to talk to you."

As Billy approached, Josefa offered Ben a quick explanation of Taylor Grove's relationship ties. "Billy and I aren't related by blood, but we're kind of like brother and sister. Seth is his uncle, but he adopted Billy and raised him as a son. When Seth married

Agnes, he got Polly, too. She was Agnes's adopted daughter. I'm the niece of the caretakers. It's rather complicated around here."

"Sounds like it! I gotta go. Maybe Mr. Taylor and I can have that talk now," he said with a hopeful look in his eyes. "See you around maybe? I'd like to hear more about how everyone came to be so connected. You seem like one big, happy family. Billy really looks up to Mr. Taylor as a father. I could tell right away."

A glimmer of loss flitted almost imperceptibly across his eyes. Josefa knew the feeling and understood the pain. He had lost someone dear. She wanted to share her own story. Odd. She rarely wanted to talk about it with anyone.

"I'd appreciate if you'd stop by before you leave town and check on our butterfly," she said. "I'll tell you more about our kinships."

"I'd like that." He nodded and left.

"You can come for dinner," she called after him. He turned around, lifted his hat up in salute, plopped it back on his head, and turned back toward the barn. She took that for a yes.

Josefa looked again at the results of the day's dye experiments. The fabric appeared limp, and the color was drab instead of vibrant. She should have asked Ben if he was familiar with plants' dye properties. She expected he knew quite a bit about the natural world. Look how much he had explained about butterflies. *Good*, she thought. Now she had two reasons to make sure she saw him again. Josefa hummed as she hung up the last garment with the other dyed fabric that was already drying and cleaned up her workspace.

"You finished?" She glanced around to see Agnes, with a sleeping baby Seth cradled in her arms, and Lupita and Polly carrying the laundry supplies. "Take a break with us," Agnes suggested. "We all deserve a rest after that mountain of clothes."

"And before we have to take them back inside and iron and fold it," Polly added. "Washday is soooo long."

Josefa picked up her box and looked up into three questioning faces. She grinned, set it down, and called them to stand near and peer inside while she described what was going on. They watched the tiny, plump creature nibble on leaves.

"What a different and interesting gift," Agnes said. She looked quizzically at Josefa. "Do you think he is interested in you? That's quite a bit of work to do for someone he hardly knows...but perhaps wishes to become better acquainted with. He seems to be a nice young man."

Josefa hesitated. How could she explain her fairy-tale picture without sounding shallow? Yet that wasn't her intent. Oswald had the means to give her security from the hardships that snap apart life.

Lupita answered for her. "Interested in my Josefa? Then he better speak to me and Alfredo first if he has intentions," she declared. "So that I can ask about his family and how he earns a living."

She pressed her lips together as though daring anyone to contradict her. For once, Josefa was glad for her aunt's iron determination. It kept her from having to reveal her dream. Especially when she wasn't sure she could fully explain it to herself.

"The same goes for our showy neighbor, Josefa," Lupita added. "I saw him making eyes at you when he was here. And make that exaggerated kiss of your hand. I don't know enough about him yet. Except that he refused to join us in prayer, or even for Easter Mass. Humph. Does he think he's better than God?"

Josefa's gratitude was squelched as quickly as it had arisen. She bit her lip to keep from responding with a tart remark. Men like Oswald Heller played by their own rules, not the guidelines established hundreds of years ago in Aunt Lupita's world.

As the women passed the barn, Seth and Ben walked out, Billy close behind them.

"Keep us in mind when that job ends," Seth said to Ben. "We can use the extra hands until Alfredo is back on his feet, no pun intended. And I'm happy to share what little I know about citrus."

"Sure thing!" Ben said. Enthusiasm flashed in his eyes. "I reckon you know heaps more than a little. This is an impressive grove you have here. I wonder, too, about other crops that could excel in this soil. I've seen some of those ad circulars about Persimmon Hollow over at Heller's place. Sounds like the land here can support all kinds of produce."

"That it can," Seth nodded in acknowledgment. "Talk in town is that a sizeable hotel will go up in the near future. It'll need foodstuffs in season. We've already started to expand acreage for more corn, beans, watermelon, strawberries, and other crops besides citrus. Going to put in a peach orchard, too. I intend to have Taylor Grove ready as a produce supplier when the hotel opens. Down the road a piece, in a year or two, I hope to build a hotel near the spring at the edge of the grove property. We'll need to supply that table, too."

Ben pushed his hat back a little on his head and stopped walking. "You'll be able to offer delicacies the patrons can't get in winter season anywhere else."

Seth looked at Ben as if seeing him anew.

"Even things they're not expecting," Seth said. "Like the fig preserves and persimmon jelly Agnes puts up in late summer. Walk over here. I want to show you the section of ground I'm thinking of clearing for the orchard and additional crops."

Seth steered Ben and Billy on a course away from the women. "We'll be right back," he called to Agnes.

"I wonder if the hotel developers need carpentry help," Ben said to Seth. "The longer I stay in Persimmon Hollow, the more I like it, and the folks in it." The men's voices had started to grow distant, but Josefa heard the comment as though Ben were speaking directly to her.

A sun-rich, languid glow settled on Josefa. The hours of outdoor work on a warm day, the harmony of the family, and the beauty of their ordered homestead in such a wilderness land, lulled her into contentment. The moment held a blissful peace.

Then the dull thud of horse hooves on sand broke the interlude. Oswald yanked on the reins and stopped in front of the house just as Josefa and the others reached it.

"Good day, ladies. Is Seth back yet...oh...I see him over there." Oswald dismounted and brushed imaginary sand off his pants.

Agnes and Lupita were ominously silent. Then Agnes appeared to remember her manners.

"Good day, Mr. Heller. My husband will be here momentarily. Please sit down and make yourself at home." She indicated any of the seats on the porch.

"Ladies," she said and climbed the few steps, walked toward the house, and opened the front door. She looked at Lupita, Josefa, and Polly as though she were back in the classroom and waiting for her pupils to follow her indoors. Lupita took the same route as officiously as did Agnes. Josefa and Polly looked at each other. Josefa shrugged and took a quick look at Oswald before she and Polly followed in the footsteps of the two older women.

Sometimes she couldn't understand Agnes. At twenty-seven, she was only five years older than Josefa. Yet her quiet maturity made Josefa feel almost as young as Polly sometimes. *Did it come with marriage and motherhood?* she wondered. All she really knew, Josefa mused, was that Agnes and Lupita together set some high standards for the younger women to emulate. *They ought to be glad I'm getting enough gumption to move forward with my life after being stuck in misery for almost a year,* she thought. Sooner or later, she would have to tell them of her actions about the apprenticeship. Despite the lack of an answer to her note, she felt confident, for she'd written that she'd take the next step by visiting the shop.

She reached behind her to close the door and darted another glance at her soon-to-be-intended, even if he didn't know it yet. Oswald wasn't paying attention. He hadn't even taken a seat on the porch. He paced back and forth and watched in the direction of the other men. She wanted to ask him for a ride into town. But how? When?

"Help me with this lemonade," Lupita ordered Josefa, who followed her into the spacious new kitchen and dining area at the back of the house. "I give thanks every time I step in here that Seth added all this space," Lupita added.

Polly and Agnes put away the laundry supplies in the cabinet on the cabin's lean-to pantry on the back porch, and came back inside. Agnes settled the baby in the cradle in the parlor.

"Where's Oswald?" Polly whispered to Josefa.

"Pacing on the porch," she said.

"You best busy yourself with packing for Texas instead of making eyes at that man," Lupita said. "He has missed an opportunity to seek my permission for courting."

Josefa herself wondered at the delay. He had seemed so interested in her. Today, he acted as though she were hardly there.

Lupita had opened all the windows wider to let in the breeze. The women had just sat down to slices of pie and lemonade when Seth, Billy, and Ben's voices drifted near. Josefa strained but couldn't make out their words. The quietness of their conversation was drowned by a shout of command as the sound of their voices grew near the house. They heard Oswald's booted feet stomp down the porch steps.

"Benjamin?" he barked in a surprised voice. "What the he... heck are you doing here? I didn't give you leave to stop work. Get back to it."

Not only was the volume loud, the words were brusque.

Josefa bounced from her chair and ran to the front window in the adjoining parlor. She stayed out of the line of sight but peered through the gauzy curtains.

"Good day to you, too," Seth said, as he, Ben, and Billy walked to where Oswald stood by his horse.

Oswald gave Seth a terse nod but kept his focus on Ben. "I don't pay you to make social calls," Oswald said in a lower volume. "The center stairwell needs another coat of varnish. Why aren't you seeing to it?"

"Yes, I know the stairwell needs finishing, sir," Ben said. "I judged the weather held too much humidity for me to—"

"Forget that cra...nonsense," Oswald said. "Get it done or grab your bags and leave my employ. After you return every cent I've paid."

"You haven't paid me yet," Ben said in his firm, quiet voice. He stood tall as he faced Oswald.

Quiet footsteps sounded behind Josefa, and soon Lupita, Agnes, and Polly looked over her shoulder at the unfolding scene. Disapproval darkened her aunt's "tsk-tsking." Josefa worried her chances with Oswald would be ruined before they even started. She couldn't fathom a reason for his behavior. Seth never spoke harshly to anyone who worked for him and always treated them with respect.

After a few long minutes of tension during which Ben and Oswald stared at each other, Ben did a slow backup with a measured step.

"As you wish, Mr. Heller." But he didn't move after that. Oswald continued to stand by his horse.

Agnes took command. She opened the door and stepped out.

"Excuse me, gentlemen. I couldn't help but overhear," she said in the voice she retained for people who tried her patience.

"Mr. Stillman is a guest at our house and, as of a few moments ago, so are you, Mr. Heller. Would you care for refreshments? Please gather on the porch, and I'll see to everyone's comfort."

"I'm fine here," Oswald said, his voice large. Everything about him once again seemed oversized. "May I be so bold as to say you don't need to trouble yourself in men's business."

"Except when it takes place on her property," said Seth. He leaned against the porch railing. Agnes now perched at the edge of the bench that was just outside the door.

"Thank you, ma'am, but I think it's best that I return at a different time," Ben said. He had taken off his hat, and he put it back on now as he moved farther away from Oswald. He was as calm and collected as Oswald was becoming agitated.

"You're da...darn right," Oswald said. Ben's steadfastness seemed to annoy Oswald.

Baby Seth woke up and started wailing.

Josefa bent and picked him up, but his wail turned into a scream. She gave him to Lupita.

"That man needs to be gone," Lupita grumbled. "Now."

A momentary panic descended on Josefa. Oswald was getting back on his horse. She hadn't figured a way to ask for a ride to the dressmaker in town.

Without thinking, she ran outside to Agnes, who gave her a glance of surprise.

"Uh, the baby needs you," she stammered.

Oswald acknowledged Josefa from his horseback position with a nod of his head. "My sweet señorita, forgive my inattentiveness. Until next time."

Lupita had followed Josefa out, and she snorted as she handed the baby to Agnes. "Until you ask permission, señor, is more like it," Lupita muttered.

Josefa stared. There he went. Riding off, before she had a sliver of a chance to even start a conversation. Oh, that she had Polly's brashness. She was sure he would have granted her wish. Now what was she to do? She tried to brush aside the unease she felt over his rude treatment of Ben. Everyone had bad days sometimes, right?

Agnes and Lupita went back into the house, along with Seth and Billy. But Josefa stayed and watched. Oswald galloped down the road, unmindful that the sandy dust he kicked up boiled over the trail Ben walked on foot. Not that Ben noticed either. The last thing she saw before she went inside was Ben squatted on his haunches, examining the cluster of ladies tresses orchids that she knew bloomed only in that section of the grove property, only in spring.

The contrast couldn't be more vivid. She felt a kinship to Ben, who was unabashed about his appreciation of Taylor Grove. But something in her yearned after the man riding the large horse. It was as if her future were riding away. She wanted to soar, not walk.

Chapter 5

$\mathcal{B}$en had been right. That was the first thought that crossed Josefa's mind as she looked at Oswald's house. To think, she might someday live here, if all went according to her plan.

"It's the biggest house I've ever seen," Josefa said. Immediately, she wished Agnes had chosen to ride over in the carriage instead of the plain old work wagon. They were paying a return call on a new neighbor, after all. An impressive new neighbor, even if Agnes and Lupita were slightly put out with him.

Agnes and Lupita, on the wagon's front bench, stayed silent as they looked at the two-and-a-half-story house, so new it still smelled of fresh-sawn pine. Agnes halted the wagon as they stared.

"Why are we here? Remind me," said Lupita drily.

"This is a duty call," Agnes said. "He's visited twice. We have to pay our respects."

"*Si*, I know that," Lupita said.

"One, two, three," Polly counted aloud while kneeling in the wagon bed and looking between the shoulders of Agnes and Lupita. "Three windows on each side of the front door. Three on each side of the door on the second floor. Plus all those windows on that enclosed side porch." She continued her recitation of standout details as though the others were in need of her commentary.

Josefa stayed seated on a blanket in the back of the wagon, legs folded to one side and tucked under her body. Agnes had inched the wagon forward on the U-shaped sand drive as Polly talked. She halted the mule when they reached the front door. The fineness of the house's embellishments came into sharper focus. Etched, beveled glass glinted in the double door's sidelights and transom. The fresh white paint shimmered against the dark green of the shutters.

"The windows are nearly tall enough for a person to walk in and out," Josefa said. "Oh, look, there are latches on them. A person could walk in and out!"

"Quite imposing, this house," Agnes finally said. "The most lavish in all Persimmon Hollow, excepting the Stetson mansion, and that's far west of town. This place is large enough to house quite a family."

"That's the problem," Lupita said. "Where is the family?"

Josefa imagined herself mistress of such an estate. She imagined moon-kissed dances on the enclosed side porch, with breezes blowing through open windows and people strolling in and out, sampling delicacies laid out on silver trays on tables covered with fine lace and linen tablecloths that draped to the floor, and—

"I said, 'Josefa, has Mr. Heller said anything to you about family members joining him here?'" Agnes repeated.

Josefa awoke from her reverie. "No, we haven't talked much yet."

"It just seems so empty, as though it needs warmth," Agnes observed.

Polly gave Josefa a jab with her elbow. "Yeah, as though it needs someone like you," she said.

"The man is too mysterious," Lupita declared. "Why build something this large when he has no family here? No one person needs a house of this size."

"Let's not judge," Agnes cautioned. "We hardly know him."

Lupita crossed her arms over her chest. Josefa lifted her gaze toward the gentle blue of the late morning sky and prayed that Oswald would lower his obvious pride and seek permission to court her.

No one had come to the door at the sound of their arrival, and they sat a few moments longer before Agnes started to get out of the cart.

"For such a gorgeous day, I feel almost as though we shouldn't be here," she said. "There's no welcoming atmosphere. Well, let's drop off the pie and marmalade. It's a rare person who doesn't think that pie tastes like real apples, hard as they are to come by sometimes."

Josefa took the basket of marmalades, and Polly carried the mock apple pie as the four of them climbed the steps to the porch and knocked on the door. A flock of robins swept through the yard and pecked and poked for long minutes before flying off. Still, the women waited. Agnes knocked again. The door opened with a sharp, fast swing.

"Ladies, forgive me, the servants haven't yet been trained," said Oswald, foregoing any niceties of greeting and not in the least surprised to see them. "To what do I owe this honor?" He bowed, stood aside, and beckoned them inside. He was proper, charming, correct, and, Josefa decided, cold. His eyes lacked warmth, that was it.

"No, thank you, we can't stay," Agnes said, to Josefa's bewilderment. She, for one, wanted to see inside.

"We're here to deliver a formal welcome to Persimmon Hollow," Agnes continued and motioned for Josefa and Polly to present the foodstuffs. Polly made a stiff half-curtsy and thrust the pie forward.

"Much appreciated," Oswald said. He stood against the door in the still-open doorway and set down the pie on a sideboard Josefa could see just inside the door.

She dropped into a deep, graceful curtsy, rose, and smiled at him as she presented the woven, palmetto-leaf basket. The contents were covered with a gingham cloth.

"Here you'll find homemade marmalades, candied orange peel, and a loaf of freshly baked bread," she said. "The citrus products are a sample of the types of goods the Taylors offer at their tourist store."

"You can almost see it from here," Agnes said and pointed. "It's right at the edge of our property, near where the railroad laid its new line through last year."

Oswald kept his gaze on Josefa. He took the basket and set it down on the sideboard without breaking the look.

"I'm honored," he said and lifted her hand and kissed it. She felt herself flush from the feel of his lips through her thin glove. Their gazes locked. In his, she saw an assurance that she certainly didn't feel in herself.

"*Tia* Lupita wove the basket from strips of palmetto leaves," explained Polly.

Oswald looked at Polly as though she were an annoying gnat. Josefa saw his muscle work in his jaw and irritation cross his expression. He recovered and arranged his face in a pleasant mask.

"A most useful skill," he said. He scrutinized Josefa again as the five of them stood there. Josefa felt more restless with each passing minute.

"Señora, I'd be honored to have your permission to visit this exquisite young lady," he said to Lupita, while he continued to look at Josefa. She held her breath. She felt there was nothing else in the world but she, Oswald, and his stunning house.

Lupita didn't answer right away. Josefa stared at the slats of wood in the porch floor.

Lupita finally nodded. "Visits only. Chaperoned. No leaving Taylor Grove."

"But then how can he take Josefa to the dressmaker's so she can start working at her apprenticeship...oops!" Polly clasped a hand over her mouth. Josefa groaned and closed her eyes. She opened them to see foxlike interest in Oswald's face, thunder in her aunt's, and questions in Agnes's. Polly crept back a few steps and mouthed the word *sorry* to Josefa. But it was too late.

"I'm most happy to transport the señorita wherever she needs to go, whenever she needs to do so," Oswald said. "Ladies, are you sure you won't step inside?"

Lupita's face grew darker by the second. Agnes shook her head. "Thank you, but no," she said.

"When would you like me to escort you to town?" Oswald asked.

"Tomorrow," Josefa blurted. It was the only thing that came to mind.

"On the first day of Holy Week?" Had they planned it, Agnes, Lupita, and Polly could not have spoken in more perfect unison.

"Just to meet with the dressmaker and review our agreement," Josefa improvised. "I won't start until after Easter." Better to get this out in the open now. Oswald as a buffer could boost her cause.

"What time?" he asked, as though a storm didn't rage around him.

"Josefa, do you really mean to go to town on the Sunday that starts Holy Week?" Agnes asked. "Does the dressmaker even keep hours on Sunday? I doubt it."

"I mean, Monday, eleven o'clock," Josefa said, flustered. She hoped the dressmaker would be there. Eleven o'clock on a Monday. Of course she would.

"My niece will not leave the premises tomorrow, or Monday, or the following day, nor ever, for any such activity," Lupita stated.

"*Tia*, I sent my word to the dressmaker. I can't go back on my word." Josefa forced herself to appear calm. They didn't need to know she hadn't indicated in her letter what day or time she'd be in town.

Oswald looked amused.

Agnes swirled around. "Good day, Mr. Heller. Ladies, we have overstayed our welcome." With each free hand, she grasped Lupita's arm and Josefa's and marched them toward the cart. Polly was already there, having hopped down the steps and into the wagon when Oswald asked what time he should arrive.

Josefa glanced back and saw Oswald full frame in the door, leaning against the doorframe with one arm up for support. He raised the other arm in a farewell gesture.

"Eleven on Monday," he repeated. No one answered.

"It got hot up there," Polly said by way of excuse for not saying a proper goodbye.

They weren't yet to the end of the drive before Lupita spoke up.

"Your impulsive ways are one reason I wish to ship you off to safety with our Texas relatives!"

"Impulsive ideas based on fancy and whim," she continued. "Mr. Heller is not for you. I have a feeling."

"What's wrong with him?" Josefa asked. "If you ask me, he could make a suitable husband."

She saw Agnes glance at Lupita as though considering the same question.

"We don't even know if he is Catholic," Lupita said.

"True," Agnes said. "I meant to invite him again to devotions and Mass."

"I know nothing of his family," Lupita continued.

"Yes, we do," Polly protested. "They're rich and own businesses in Philadelphia and Charleston."

"The outside tells us little about the inside," Lupita said. She had her arms crossed over her chest, but Josefa noted that her hands were relaxed and not clenched.

"We can take time to find out," Josefa said. "I'll learn more as we visit together."

"She has a point," Agnes said. "Like you, Lupita, I have questions about him, but it behooves us to give him a chance."

Josefa seized the momentary ally. "Plus, I really can't go back on my word to the dressmaker. It wouldn't be right. Please, Aunt Lupita. You know what this means to me."

Her aunt shifted so that she could look Josefa in the face. Josefa saw the love in her eyes.

"How many times do I have to tell you I worry over you, Josefa? You went behind my back and didn't ask about this dressmaking because you knew I would likely say no. This pains me."

It pained Josefa, too, for she knew her omission was as bad as an outright lie.

"I need to go to confession," she mumbled.

"That you do," said Lupita.

"So it's OK if I go visit the dressmaker Monday?" Josefa asked, her voice small.

The hope in her voice was poignant.

"*Sí*, very well," Lupita said. "I can see this is so important to you. I don't understand why."

Josefa felt ill-prepared to lay out for the small group her hopes and fears for the coming years. She still held them close to her heart.

She felt a smaller hand grasp hers. "Forgive me, Josefa, I didn't mean…" Polly said.

Josefa squeezed her hand. "It had to come out sometime," she said. She was relieved the plan was no longer a secret.

"Despite your underhanded behavior, I still may insist you decline the apprenticeship, should your uncle and I decide that is best," Lupita continued. "I will speak with him as soon as we return. On the other hand, it may be better for you to stay in Persimmon Hollow while he recovers instead of going to Texas so soon."

She turned toward Agnes. "You can invite our new friend to worship when he comes to escort Josefa. Although I doubt he will accept."

"I can try," said Agnes as they reached the end of Oswald's long drive, crossed the railroad tracks, and rolled onto the grove's property. "Let's give him a chance, Lupita, even though we have reservations. And you know I'm one for saying God helps those who help themselves. Josefa wants to better herself. How about if we send Polly, and Billy too, as chaperones for this trip to the dressmaker on Monday. Surely Mr. Heller won't mind."

Surely he would, Josefa thought to herself.

"I need to make a quick stop at the orphanage," Agnes added as they neared the tidy building that anchored one side of the grove acreage. "I want to find out if Father Kenny sent word about his arrival. He mentioned he might come for all of Holy Week, to teach the children and visit other mission sites. Plus, we're almost in time for noon prayers."

They halted, climbed out of the wagon, and waited until Polly gave the mule some water before walking together toward the orphanage. As they neared the front door, it opened, and a male voice said a hearty goodbye to Sister Rose. Seconds later, Ben exited. He walked forward but still looked behind him as he finished talking to Sister. When he turned face front, he nearly plowed into the four women.

* * *

Ben stopped short, his face open and welcoming. Josefa's mood brightened.

"Morning!" he said and took a quick step back to the door and held it open for them. Sister Rose stepped out. "What is it, Ben… oh, hello! Come in." She held out both her hands to Agnes, who took them and beckoned the others to follow her inside. What had been laborious and awkward at the Heller mansion was natural and warm here.

Rather than make his exit, Ben trailed inside after them.

"How's the caterpillar?" he whispered from behind Josefa.

Josefa always felt like she had to whisper inside the orphanage anteroom, too. The space had a calm, peaceful atmosphere with a hint of incense from the frequent opening and closing of the double doors to the chapel. The myrrh and frankincense mingled with the clean aroma of wood soap. Cast-iron coat pegs above pine wainscoting, a few benches, and a narrow table just inside the doorway were the only pieces of furniture. The hallways that reached out from either side of the room were empty.

"It grows bigger by the day," she whispered back.

"No need to keep your voices down right now," Sister Rose said. "We're not at services yet." She glanced at the clock on the table. "Fifteen minutes. That's why you're here, yes?"

Josefa nodded. Sister Rose looked from one to the other. "Mr. Stillman, perhaps you can delay your next chore until after prayers?" she asked.

Ben nodded yes to Sister Rose but watched Josefa. "I reckon another half hour or so won't matter," he said. "The work there is finished. I'm waiting only for Heller to declare himself satisfied."

"Then what?" asked Josefa, seized by a need to hear that Ben wouldn't leave for who knows where. Not yet.

"I'll help out here at the grove until your uncle is mended. That, plus assist the orphanage caretaker—Mr. Bight, I think is his name—build up his furniture stock."

"His stock?" Agnes jumped into the conversation. "Why does Toby want to stockpile furniture?"

"For the store he's going to open in town," Sister Rose answered for Ben.

"How do you find out such things before anyone at the grove?" Agnes asked. "You'd think I'd know what's going on with my best friend's husband."

Just then, footsteps fast, slow, loud, and soft came down the hallway.

"Could be because Toby is caretaker here, he and his lovely wife and children," Sister Rose said, and her kind face creased in a smile as the anteroom filled with orphans and the entire Bight family, led by Toby and his wife, Sarah.

Agnes ran forward to meet Sarah as the small blond woman entered with a collection of children. Five of them were obviously hers, by appearance and by the varied clothes they wore. Another eight wore the orphanage uniform of gray frock with white apron, or gray pants with suspenders and homespun shirt. The orphans hung back, bashful for the first few minutes of any encounter with the grove residents.

"Sarah, what's this about Toby opening a store?" Agnes asked.

"Not until the end of the year, at the earliest," Sarah said as she hugged Agnes. "I'm happy for him."

"He makes some of the finest furniture I've seen," said Ben. "I'm mighty impressed. The young'uns here have a superb woodworking instructor in him."

"We just settled on the timing last night," Sarah said as she set down her toddler Noah in the care of her eldest, Pansy, who was busy whispering secrets with Polly. "I was just telling sister this morning at breakfast," Sarah said. She began to explain the details to Agnes.

Josefa walked over to Ben, who had stepped back when the room filled.

"If the Bights relocate to town, Agnes will feel responsible for finding new caretakers for the orphanage," she told him. "Toby handles the building's needs, and Sarah does the cooking and helps with housekeeping. She also teaches some needlework. The five children with the reddish-blond hair, the ones who look alike, are the Bight children."

"Ah, I wondered how everybody fit together," Ben said.

"It's going to be a big change," Josefa said.

"Agnes, we'll only be two miles away, not two hundred," Sarah said on the other side of the room and laughed. She had healed, body and soul, during her time at the orphanage. Josefa had heard of Sarah's struggles with melancholy and Toby's business failures until he stopped trying to be the farmer he wasn't meant to be.

"Josefa, maybe you could take over my duties as sewing instructor," Sarah called to her.

"Why, yes, I'd be honored!" Then she gave a saucy look at her aunt. "I'll have many new skills to share from my apprenticeship!"

She batted her eyes in an exaggerated manner toward Lupita, who replied with feigned exasperation.

"Silence, please. The worship hour is upon us," Sister Rose called over the din. The room fell quiet as the group moved into the chapel. Josefa felt a hand at her elbow. It was Ben, escorting her into the chapel.

"Are you Catholic?" she asked, somewhat astonished at his action. She knew every Catholic in Persimmon Hollow. And just what was Ben doing at the orphanage anyway?

"I was baptized Catholic," he said.

But...She opened her mouth then closed it. There was a *but* there, but she didn't know him well enough to ask. Sarah whispered to her four oldest to join the sisters and others for prayer while she took Noah and fixed lunch for everyone. She closed the chapel doors on the hushed gathering seated quietly on benches.

"In the name of the Father, the Son, and the Holy Spirit," Sister Rose began and then led the service of prayers and readings. Josefa tried to stay focused, but her mind wandered to Ben beside her, to how natural it felt to pray with him, to what she had yet to sew on her new Easter outfit and what color trim she should use, the blue or the garnet, to the thought of Oswald and what a fine pair they would make. She tried to picture him here, at prayer beside her, but couldn't grasp the image. No matter, she thought. Many men weren't churchgoing before marriage. She could fix that afterward.

After the service, the Bights and orphans went off for lunch, and Josefa and the others started to say their goodbyes to Sister Rose and Sister Bridget, who had tiptoed in to the chapel a few minutes late.

"When is Father Kenny coming down, have you heard?" Agnes asked.

"We received word this morning," Sister Rose said. "He'll be here Wednesday to hear confessions, and he plans to stay through Easter Sunday. We are so blessed. He'll be here for the stations of the cross and to conduct Maundy Thursday and Good Friday services. He also will instruct Mr. Stillman in his final confirmation studies."

Ben colored slightly as he became the center of attention.

An inexplicable gladness suffused Josefa.

"Is that why you're here today?" she asked him. He nodded. "Partly. Along with the work I'll be doing for Seth, I've been here to shadow Toby and learn his routine."

"So, you'll stay in town a bit longer? That's wonderful!"

"I think so, too," he said.

She turned to see Agnes, Lupita, Sarah, and the sisters all watching them.

"My Josefa, she has big dreams of being a dressmaker," Lupita said.

"Dreams are good," said Ben, with a stout loyalty that Josefa appreciated.

Lupita raised her eyebrows. Agnes smiled.

"Ben, would you like to join us for Holy Week devotions?" Agnes asked.

"Ma'am, I'd be honored," he said. "I'm a bit rusty at all this, but my heart's willing."

"That's what it takes," Lupita told him. "Now, tell us about your family."

It was Josefa's turn to blush. She wanted to run from her aunt's blatant interrogations of any man of marriageable age, as though they all wished to ask for her hand. She loved Lupita dearly, but… she beseeched Agnes with a glance that asked for pity, but Agnes's nonverbal reply made it clear there was no stopping Lupita once started.

"Where are you from?" Lupita peppered him with the first volley.

"Saint Augustine, ma'am," Ben said. "I travel the state on carpentry jobs to help support my mother and sister, who live there in the family house. My father died a number of years ago."

"You support your widowed mother?" Lupita was impressed, Josefa knew. Ben had just jumped up several levels on the Lupita scale of worthiness.

"And my sister. Her health has never been strong," Ben added. "Best mother and sister a man could have, I tell you."

He inched even higher on the worthiness scale. Josefa was glad her aunt liked Ben. Yet, the more he revealed, the more she sensed a touch of sadness in him, a want of some kind. When he turned to go, she saw a hunger in his eyes. Those bright, ocean-blue eyes carried a sadness she longed to wipe away.

Chapter 6

*H*at set at just the right angle? Yes. Gloves wrinkled? No. Josefa smoothed the leather anyway and wriggled her fingers inside their soft casings. She checked her cape, again, for lint or hair from Polly's cat, who was supposed to be a barn cat but who spent more time indoors and ruled everyone's hearts. Even Lupita's.

Everything had to be perfect for this meeting. She had to look the part: fashionable, assured, confident in her ability to learn all aspects of the art of dressmaking.

She gave herself a full-body twirl in front of the dressing table mirror in Agnes and Seth's bedroom. The dark purplish-blue serge cape was impeccable. No wrinkles and no uneven sections where the indigo dye hadn't taken well. She checked her skirt one more time for wrinkles, then blew out a sigh. *Just get out there and go, Josefa. Oswald is waiting. The dressmaker in town is waiting. Polly and Billy are probably already seated in Oswald's barouche.* She glanced out the window. Sure enough, Polly and Billy were perched on one of the facing cushioned seats with...why, it was shy Cornelia from St. Isidore's. Josefa was glad the quiet orphan had ventured out. She was in her late teens and needed to learn how to be at ease in the world.

Josefa stole one more peek in the mirror to make sure every hair was in place. A loud chuckle from the parlor stopped her hand midcheek. Was that her aunt laughing at something Oswald said? That couldn't be. Lupita frowned every time she heard the man's name.

Josefa shook her head and walked toward the parlor.

She stopped in the doorway. Lupita was seated with her hands in her lap and her face alight with mirth. Oswald stood by the mantle leaning on the wood with one arm. He directed the force of his charm toward Lupita.

"So, she finally said to me, 'Master Oswald Heller, if you do that one more time, I will march straight to your parents.' Of course, I begged her, I pleaded, I cried—I was only five, you know—and she relented. Said if I cleaned up the mess, she would think about giving me a reprieve. Wouldn't you know, it took my little arms and legs hours. I say, hours! But I never did it again. Ah, the value of such a housekeeper. I will never forget her. She helped raise me. What a wonderful woman she was. And you remind me so much of her."

Josefa's skirt rustled as she entered the room.

"Here she is!" said Oswald with an expansive sweep of his arm. "You look beautiful as always. I was just telling your aunt about—"

"What a bad little boy he had been and how he taxed the patience of everyone…"

"…especially the saintly housekeeper!" the two said in unison and laughed.

Josefa was speechless.

"Boys will be boys," Lupita said. "I'm glad you have grown into a more upstanding young man and have gotten over your bad ways."

"Oh, yes, ma'am. I have matured." A priest couldn't have sounded more fervent, Josefa thought.

"Hey, you guys ready in there? Let's go!" Billy's voice rang from the barouche.

Oswald held out his arm, and Josefa grasped it. With his other free hand, he made a half bow to Lupita, who gave him a gracious nod. Really? Josefa sensed she had stepped on stage into a bad play. Something was not quite right.

"You be on your way now," Lupita said. She stood and ushered Josefa and Oswald toward the door. "Another beautiful day, it is. Enjoy. But let's not forget it is the week of our Lord's Passion."

Oswald stiffened. They exited and approached the carriage, and Lupita closed the door softly behind them.

"Is the dressmaker expecting you?" He was suddenly distant. It was as though the Oswald of the parlor had changed into a different man. He helped her step up into the barouche and followed.

"Yes, I sent word into town," she said.

They settled themselves, and the driver signaled for the horses to start. She was finally on her way. Josefa embraced the anticipation, the day, the handsome escort, the step toward her dream. Cardinals stirred and chirped as the barouche rolled past holly, pine, and oak trees.

"This is a tight fit," Oswald said. He shifted, and Josefa felt the pressure of his thigh press hard against hers. She inched as far as she could away from him and toward the carriage wall, both uncomfortable and a little excited at his action. She could see across him, and there was space between him and the other side of the carriage.

Next, he lifted his arm and stretched it behind her on the edge of the seat back. Within moments, his fingers brushed her shoulder.

Josefa had no idea what to do. Acknowledge his action? Ignore it? Ask him to move his hand? She met Polly's gaze, and then Billy's. Both fairly gaped at what was taking place. Cornelia had averted her head and watched the scenery they passed.

"Why don't all the ladies sit together," Billy said and then started to move.

"We're fine," Oswald said. Billy sat back.

Josefa swallowed.

She sat still, not moving a muscle, wishing, once again, she knew the etiquette of sophisticated people. This might be how they court, even early in a relationship.

"Speed it up, will you. Let's get this interminable ride over with," Oswald called to the driver.

When the driver turned to acknowledge the request with a nod of his head, Josefa saw that it was Bernie Wade, whose mother, Estelle, cooked for the Alloway House in town. The Wade family, whose roots in Florida went as far back as the Spanish occupation, worshipped at the orphanage chapel with the grove residents.

"Hi, Bernie!" she said. "Do you know which shop I need to go to? And how are plans coming for the school?"

"Hey yourself," he said. "Sure do. And last time I heard, the sisters and my mother were figuring out a good location."

"I believe they've agreed on a piece of property," Cornelia piped in.

Josefa felt, rather than saw, Oswald's stare and felt his hand on her shoulder curl into a fist.

"Riders and drivers do not converse," he said, as if reprimanding a class of recalcitrant children.

"I talk to whoever I want..." Billy started to say before Josefa's head-shaking stopped him. The day suddenly felt warm.

"So, where are the three of you going while we're at the dress-maker's?" Oswald asked.

We? thought Josefa.

"I'm gonna visit my favorite dog pal Lumpy at Clyde's Mercantile and probably go to the livery stable and maybe the firehouse. You know they got some kind of pump truck they can haul out to fires and—"

"And you..." Oswald looked at the girls. His voice was again cooler than it had been when he spoke with Lupita.

Josefa watched Polly's face fold into one of its mutinous moods, but the younger girl kept her temper.

"Cornelia and I will visit with the Alloways. Do you know them yet? Fanny is still an Alloway, but her sister Eunice is now a Williams since she married Clyde. Their father founded Persimmon Hollow. They run the academy where Agnes taught before she had the baby. They use their house as a boarding house, too. They had to start it after their father lost all his money."

"In some foolish venture, no doubt," Oswald muttered. "Starting this place would qualify."

"Hardly!" Josefa said. "He had guaranteed settlers' invest-ments, and when many people gave up after a hard freeze killed their citrus groves, he paid back every last penny to whoever requested it. He went bankrupt and died soon after."

Oswald grunted. "My dear Josefa, you will never have to worry about opening a boarding house after we are married. I will drape you in the finest jewels and clothing, and plant you in elegant surroundings of antique furnishings, fine china, silver, and an army of servants."

Josefa's hand flew to her mouth, and it wasn't because they had just rolled over a dip in the roadway. Her heart beat against her corset, which she had laced so tightly she could hardly breathe.

Had Oswald just asked her to marry him? They weren't even officially courting. And surely, he would seek approval first from her uncle. He would propose the right way, too, not in a jolting carriage. He was speaking generally is all.

But he had distinctly said *married*. She wasn't as elated as she expected to be at hearing the word. And why had Ben's earnest, honest face just darted into her mind?

The riders lapsed into silence. Visions of rooms adorned with plush carpets, velvet drapes, carved furnishings, and fine artwork crowded Josefa's imagination as the barouche rolled beyond the grove's land. The terrain changed as they passed Lake Winnemissett, lined with ancient live oaks shadowed with Spanish moss that hung to the ground. The slight dip gave way to gently rolling sandhills blanketed with longleaf pine trees as they neared the center of town. Profusions of bright pink phlox and yellow coreopsis carpeted the roadsides and empty fields. The overstuffed rooms in her mind felt musty when she drank in the view of the spring blooms.

Finally, they rolled to a halt in front of the dressmaker's shop, sandwiched between the corner druggist and the newspaper office still under construction. The door to Persimmon Hollow Dressmaking was open. "We specialize in cutting and fitting," proclaimed a big sign in the window.

Josefa hardly felt Oswald's hands as he helped her out of the barouche.

"I'll meet you at the Alloway House in about an hour," she said to the youngsters, who had already started to scatter.

"But if you find another ride back to the grove, no need to wait for us," Oswald said before turning to Bernie. "Take this over to the livery and clean it up." Bernie nodded.

"Ready?" Oswald then addressed Josefa.

"There's really no need for you to accompany me," she replied, timid but determined.

"I insist."

"No." She drew in as deep a breath as her corset allowed. She wished she had listened to Agnes and Lupita and loosened it a bit.

Oswald's face darkened, and he took hold of her elbow in a proprietary manner.

Josefa so hated confrontation.

"Mr. Heller, you would be so bored at our talk of fabric and thread and patterns," she said. "I would feel remorse if you were forced to listen to such womanly concerns."

She wasn't Lupita's niece for nothing. If a boulder refuses to move, find a way to go around it. Wasn't that what her aunt had counseled her more than once?

Oswald's lips pressed together. After a few moments, he dropped his hold on her as abruptly as he had first taken it.

"Thirty minutes. Not a moment longer. I will return for you."

He turned on his heel and walked off. Josefa felt reprimanded, again. She needed to figure him out if she were to fit into his world.

Oswald and his peculiarities faded the second she stepped over the threshold into Persimmon Hollow Dressmaking. Rows of shelves filled with beautiful bolts of cloth greeted her. Upright dressmaking forms were off to one side, and display cases of needles, thread, and other notions filled the glass-fronted counter. Behind that counter stood a small woman, who watched her with a tired but assessing gaze.

"Welcome," she said. "You must be Josefa. Please come in." The woman came around to the front of the counter as Josefa introduced herself.

"A beautiful cape," the seamstress said. "Did you make it?"

Josefa nodded, pleased to receive the compliment from a skilled tailor. She had only to take the briefest of looks at the sample dresses to know the quality of the work that took place in the small shop. "I dyed it, too."

The woman's eyes widened with respect.

"I'm Mrs. Penn. Esmeralda Penn. Forgive me, but I have little time for chitchat. Ever since word of the president's visit became known, I haven't had a moment's rest between orders, fittings, and alterations. And here I am trying to tidy up business so I can get home to help my sister and brother-in-law tend our aged parents. Now, you sit at this machine and piece together the sleeve that has been cut. It's right here. That will give me a good look at your seams and stitches, and I'll be able to tell if you can follow a pattern. So many young women can't these days." She pointed out a machine, lifted and set down the sleeve, and smoothed a nearby display.

The woman was a nervous burst of energy. In light of that, Josefa felt a little less like a person on trial. She pulled off her gloves as Esmeralda led her to one of the two treadle sewing machines in the shop. It was similar to the one her aunt and uncle had purchased for her soon after she arrived in Persimmon Hollow. More cause for relief. She sat down but then sprang back up and looked to see what she had sat on.

"A Bloomingdale's catalog!" Josefa grabbed the rare gem of a book. "It must be the only one in all Persimmon Hollow."

"You may well be correct, my dear," Esmeralda said as she took it and placed it on the counter. "I had it shipped on special order from the store. You get to work and let me know when you're finished. I'll be right here, stitching the beadwork on this gown." She indicated a half-finished garment on a dress form. "Brocade, this one is. Ordered by Mrs. Stetson herself for an event she's planning at the Stetson mansion. Oh, but she and the Mister had quite a tussle over that place. He wanted to sink far too much money into it to suit her. 'Just a winter camp, you know,' she said to me. 'I talked him into building only seven thousand square feet instead of ten thousand,' she told me. I had to bite my lip not to laugh outright. This little shop here is only seven hundred square feet, three hundred fifty down here and the same upstairs, where I'm living now that we...oh, that's enough. You get on with your sewing."

"Yes, ma'am." Josefa knew she could feel at home in the tidy shop with the talkative owner.

A half hour later, Josefa snipped off the final thread and gave the sleeve to Esmeralda to inspect. Oswald should have been back by now. Josefa was glad he wasn't.

Esmeralda slipped on a pair of wire-rim spectacles and studied the sleeve construction. Josefa held her breath. This had to work. It had to.

"Tell me a little more about yourself," Esmeralda said. She continued inspecting the stitchery as Josefa explained how she lived at the grove with her aunt and uncle.

"The apprenticeship is rigorous, you understand," Esmeralda said.

Josefa wanted to jump for the joy she felt. She got up in haste.

"Hard work never bothered me. I love to sew, create dresses, and fashion new things, and I can't wait to learn so much more and—"

"Hold on, my dear. You're getting ahead of yourself. This isn't all glamour, not by a long shot. In fact, much of this will be drudgery to you. Hemming, boning of corsets, beadwork, alterations, that sort of thing. Are you willing to do that?" She looked at Josefa over the top of her glasses.

Josefa didn't care if the woman had said she had to spin the cotton for thread or tend silkworms for fabric. She had gotten the apprenticeship! She glanced at the wall clock. Forty-five minutes, and no Oswald. He'd been all in a huff, and now he was late. Josefa couldn't wait to get home and tell everyone about her success. Right this minute, she wanted to skip around the corner to the Alloway House and tell Fanny and then run across to the mercantile to tell Eunice and Clyde, and—

"When can you begin?" Esmeralda asked.

"Is it all right if I wait until next week, this being Holy Week?"

"Of course, dear. The apprenticeship will last two months. I'll be here through the president's visit; it's just too busy otherwise to leave. Plan on long days. At least ten hours."

Not me, thought Josefa. Not ten hours in the shop. No one at the grove would hear of it. She'd take work home. Time enough to discuss that with Esmeralda later, though.

A shadow fell into the room. It was attached to Oswald, who strode in, as usual, as though he owned the establishment.

Josefa glanced at the clock. A full hour had passed.

"I got the apprenticeship," she said, going over to greet him with hands outstretched.

"The what?"

"The apprenticeship. To the dressmaker."

"I thought you came here to be fitted for a gown and to look at fabric."

"No, I came to interview for the apprenticeship." She distinctly remembered how Polly had blurted out information about the apprenticeship when they were gathered on Oswald's porch. He was quite forgetful. "You know my dream is to be a dressmaker of high fashion. Like Charles Worth. You know, the designer? In Paris? Only I want to be here. Based in Persimmon Hollow."

"Don't be silly, Josefa," he said. "You wear the clothes. You don't make them. Furthermore, someone of the stature you indicate resides in the world's top cities, not in a dusty back-water. Let's go. The other three are nowhere to be found. That's fine. They're young and energetic and can make their way back themselves."

"I can't go back alone with you, without anyone there," Josefa said. "Surely you understand the rules of chaperonage. My aunt's a stickler about it. Besides, we agreed to meet the others at the Alloway House."

She mustered back the dignity that had drained under Oswald's words, lifted her skirt hem, and started to walk past him to leave the shop.

"Thank you, Mrs. Penn," she said. She turned and looked back before she stepped outside. "I'll be here bright and early the day after Easter."

Oswald shook his head as she passed him. Josefa noticed it but chose not to acknowledge his mood, which threatened to tinge the lovely day with gloom.

Esmeralda lifted a hand to wave goodbye. Josefa saw that the woman was again in assessment mode, only this time of her and Oswald.

"Wait!" Esmeralda called a moment later and ran out of the shop after them. "Thought you might like to borrow this." She handed Josefa the Bloomingdale's catalog. Josefa clutched it as a lifeline. The catalog would allow her to study what was and wasn't popular. Maybe she could even design clothes from Persimmon Hollow, sew the samples, and send them to Bloomingdale's where they could make more, to order, for clients. Yes, anything was possible.

"You should get in the carriage," Oswald said as Josefa started to walk past the barouche that was again in front of the shop. Bernie looked straight ahead, as though he didn't hear anything.

"Did you forget?" Josefa asked Oswald. "We're going to the Alloway House. We'll meet Billy, Polly, and Cornelia there and ride back to the grove together."

"No, I didn't forget. But it's more important that you learn how to behave like a fashionable lady...if you want to be one."

"Not if it means leaving behind family members and ignoring friends," she said. Her insides churned, and not from delight.

"I thought we might return early so I can give you a tour through my house, which I dare say is preferable to town chitchat."

Josefa actually vacillated for a moment. The idea of seeing his house tempted her mightily.

"I'd love to see your house," she said, "but not right now. I'm committed to visit at the Alloway House."

"My point is, you can break such rules. Are you coming?" He stood next to the carriage, one foot propped up on the floorboard.

Josefa didn't answer. Instead, she turned and walked toward the street corner, half-expecting Oswald to follow.

She heard the squeak of the barouche and the sounds of Oswald climbing in. "Take me home, Bernie," he said.

Josefa twirled around and stared at him. Her mouth started to form the word *but*.

"You'll have to make other arrangements," he said. "Josefa, I'm not a man to be crossed. Especially by an obstinate woman."

As the beautiful carriage glided off with the handsome man inside, Josefa had a premonition her future was riding away. Why was Oswald so cross? She wasn't obstinate. Was she? First, she had crossed Lupita's will. Now Oswald's. But he was the one who had changed plans. Or did he? She realized he'd never actually agreed to visit the Alloway House.

She second-guessed herself all the way to the Alloway House.

There had to be a way to make her dreams fit together. She tried to recover the joy of the apprenticeship news, but it had faded along with her spirits. She didn't want to ruin her chances with Oswald, not when he had already mentioned marriage. To think she might live in that grand house of his, and so close to Taylor Grove. She'd get to stay in Persimmon Hollow. And be a dressmaker of note, if all went well. *Such a beautiful dream,* Josefa thought. All the pieces fit. Was she the only one who could see that?

As she turned up the walkway to the two-story wood-frame house, a cluster of people awaited her on the porch.

"Well, did you get it?" Polly was practically dancing around in excitement.

"She don't look too happy," Billy said.

"Doesn't," said Fanny Alloway. Her silver curls bounced when she talked.

"You were gone long enough, you must have got it," Polly added.

"Hey, where's that Oswald guy?" Billy asked and stepped off the porch to look down the street.

Cornelia hung back a little, watchful of everything. Estelle, the cook, also looked down the street for the carriage.

"He's gone," said Josefa. "He had to go," she amended. She didn't want to explain anything, not just now. "We have to find another way to return home."

"Oh, honey, that's too bad. I was hoping to see my Bernie," Estelle said and then went inside.

"I'll go see if Clyde'll lemme borrow a wagon," Billy said and headed across the street to the mercantile.

"Tell Clyde and Eunice to come over and join us for a bite to eat," Fanny called. "My boarders are out for the day, so I welcome this company. Now, come here, Josefa. Stand up straight. Lord have mercy, I've never seen anyone slump in a corset before." The plump woman shook her head. She looked closer at Josefa.

"Did everything go OK with Mrs. Penn? She's a nice woman, a hard worker. Talks a bit much, but we all have our eccentricities."

Josefa nodded and sat down in the wicker swing. She placed the catalog carefully on the table beside her. "I got the apprenticeship."

"Well, that calls for a celebration! Estelle, do we have any of that pound cake left?" Fanny called ahead as she went indoors. Polly came and sat on one side of Josefa, and Cornelia sat on the other. They swung in silence.

"Was that old rat mean to you?" Polly finally asked.

"Not mean," Josefa said. "Well, maybe a little mean, but he didn't seem to think so. I don't understand everything he says or does. I think it's because he's from a different class of people than I'm used to."

"That doesn't give him an excuse to act weird," said Polly, swinging the chair harder. "Can't say I like him as much as you do."

"You will, once you get to know him," Josefa said. She hoped. She hoped she would, too.

"Cornelia, what do you think of him?" Polly asked.

"I can't tell, not from that short a ride," Cornelia said. "If Miss Josefa likes him, that's fine with me."

"You're getting old enough to just call me Josefa, you know," Josefa said to her. "You're, what, almost seventeen, right?"

"I just turned seventeen last week."

"Now there's a reason to celebrate," said Josefa as Fanny came back outside. "We have a birthday girl here."

"Wonderful! Come in, let's set the table extra special. I love a celebration. You know I sometimes get lonely here with Eunice married and living over at Clyde's now, even if it is only across the street. Even with the boarders here, isn't that silly of me? When the last of the winter folk leave, it'll be far too quiet." The normally bubbly Fanny looked as close to sad as Josefa had ever seen her.

An hour later, they were all seated around the table eating pound cake after a hearty lunch. Josefa now had the catalog on her lap, so nervous was she of forgetting the treasure upon departure.

"Tell us about the apprenticeship," Fanny insisted. "We want to hear all the details."

When Josefa reached the part about the long days, Fanny interrupted.

"My dear, how will you go back and forth to the grove each day after putting in such hours. Have you thought about that?"

"Not exactly," said Josefa. The idea of Ben driving her back and forth popped into her head. And just as quickly left. She couldn't ask for that, even if he was to be working for Seth soon, and even if Seth would allow it. Lupita wouldn't let her travel that much with a single man so close in age.

"That gives me a marvelous idea," Fanny said, reaching for her fan from the sideboard and flipping it open. It fluttered as she spoke. "I'm quite astonished no one thought of it already. You simply must stay here at the house with me, Josefa, for the two months of the apprenticeship."

"I couldn't impose…"

"Impose! Nonsense! It will solve your transportation problem and my wish for more companionship. Do you think your aunt or Agnes would object? I don't think so."

"It's probably the only arrangement they would condone," Josefa said. "I could go back to the grove on weekends. Or at any time needed, really."

"Then it's settled," Fanny said. "Pending their approval, of course."

"That bigwig boyfriend of yours going to be visiting?" Clyde asked as he leaned back his chair onto two legs. "Told me in passing a while back he had something important to discuss with me. I reckon he'll tell me one of these days. Sure ships in enough goods. Like to be furnishing three homes, so many crates have come off the boat and railroad for him in the past few months."

"He rivals Mr. Stetson as the wealthiest personage in Persimmon Hollow," Eunice said. "Quite different than our other settlers, and no one knows just why he chose to come here. Mr. Stetson knew Persimmon Hollow through his long friendship with our father, God rest his soul. And Mr. Stetson has given quite generously to the Academy. Mr. Heller, on the other hand, was impatient the day I extended an invitation to visit the school. Hardly gave me the chance to explain the caliber of our institution. He did, however, indicate he'd consider making a donation."

"He musta known you were the principal and didn't want to get in trouble," Clyde said in an attempt to lighten the mood.

"Well, nothing has come of the lukewarm offer yet," Eunice said.

Josefa had a worrisome thought. Talk of Oswald or being with Oswald often carried a note of darkness. She had to think of a way to change that. To change him. Surely he could be made to see the value of family, friends, and community life. Surely he understood that wealth didn't give a man license to be arrogant. Surely.

* * *

At the grove a few days later, Josefa couldn't shake the idea of seeing the inside of Oswald's house. Seated under the arbor, she tried to sew tiny stitches in the bodice of a new gown she wanted to have ready in case she had a chance to attend a presidential reception. The whole town buzzed about the Florida tour and speculated about receptions and political speechmaking.

She bent her head over the tiny pleats she inserted for their decorative appeal. Little white beads would look stunning atop them. Josefa sewed at a fast clip, for she suspected she'd have little time to devote to her own projects once she started helping Mrs. Penn in town. She ran her hand over the fabric. Such a beautiful green satin. It had been a gift from her mother, so Josefa treasured it and had saved it for a special occasion. She wondered if her mother would have liked Oswald. Or Ben.

A mockingbird trilled from a nearby magnolia. She could see it through the open spaces in the tangle of foliage that covered the arbor. Soon the thick jasmine vine would be in full bloom, and the scent would take prominence as citrus blossoms faded. Now, though, the sweet, calming waves of orange blossom fragrance made her understand why spring was a time for love.

Part of her wished she were stitching her wedding gown. She tried to imagine herself married to Oswald and living as a fine lady. The image faded in and out. She could see fine clothes, jewelry, elegant furniture, and lavish table settings. She just couldn't see Oswald. It was as though she had inserted herself into the etchings of interiors and dinner parties that she studied in the pages of *Harper's Bazaar*. Try as she might, she couldn't quite fit Oswald into the daydream. The image of Ben's face kept intruding. Josefa shook her head. He didn't fit the scene at all. Ben, comfortable in a drawing room? No, she thought not. He was an outdoorsman.

Ben and Oswald were such opposites. Yes, they were both good-looking, each in his own way. Both were intelligent. But Oswald was forceful, opinionated, full of action, and, she had begun to suspect, selfish. But also rich. Ben was quiet, thoughtful, observant, kind. And not rich.

Money shouldn't matter, she told herself. She made a sloppy, irregular stitch and thrust down her sewing in her lap. It did matter. If she didn't find a husband of worth who could support her and her dreams, Lupita would find one for her, in Texas. So Oswald it had to be. Ben could be a dear friend. She would grow to love Oswald and push away any feelings that arose for Ben. Just because she was always happy to see him didn't mean she loved him. She only thought about him now because...because she was still mad at Oswald for his behavior.

Despite her intention to be cool to Oswald for his rudeness in abandoning her in town, she jumped from her arbor seat at the sound of barouche wheels crunching the layers of downed oak leaves that fell from the trees. The Northern people were always surprised when Florida oak trees dropped their leaves in spring, as if the natural world's cycles had gone awry. She never knew exactly how to explain it to them. *Ben would be good at that,* she thought. *Drat! Stop thinking about him!*

She picked up her sewing materials and took her time walking from the yard to the Taylor house. Oswald came only to the main house, never to the smaller cabin she shared with her aunt and uncle. She entered to find him seated with Lupita, Agnes, and Sarah Bight in the parlor. Sarah's toddler, Noah, wobbled back and forth between her chair and Agnes's, where baby Seth appeared an object of fascination to the little fellow. He reached his chubby arms out, touched Seth's bootie, gave a little shriek, and wobbled back to his mother. Sarah picked him up, kissed him, and seated him back on her lap. He fussed, pulled, and pushed until she let him down. This time he toddled over to Oswald, squatted down, patted the black boot he wore, lost his balance, and fell backwards onto his behind. Surprised rather than hurt, he crawled back to Sarah.

The women all cooed and aahed. Oswald sat stone-faced.

A little pang went through Josefa as she looked at the baby and toddler. She wanted a little Seth or Noah of her own. Boy or girl, it didn't matter. She wondered what kind of children she and Oswald might have.

"Mr. Heller, would you like to hold the baby?" Lupita asked. She was testing him, Josefa knew, despite being charmed by him the other day.

"Er, ah, no thank you, ma'am, I fear I might drop him." He stood up and faced Josefa.

"I've come to offer a tour of my house," he said. "You had expressed interest, and I've been remiss in taking action. Would you care to go now?"

He turned and bowed to the others. "Ladies."

"Do stay for some refreshments first, Mr. Heller," Agnes said. "Lupita made a peach pie after hearing how much you liked them as a child."

"I doubt it's as good as the one your family housekeeper makes, but it can hold its own," Lupita said.

Oswald hesitated, and the women seized the opportunity to ply him with slices of sweet, cinnamon-tinged peach pie and cool well water.

"Delicious," he said, and downed his serving in five large bites.

"Do have more," Agnes urged him and started to cut another piece from the pie on the tray Lupita had set on the small, round parlor table.

"Thank you, but no...I know how anxious Josefa is to see the house." He rose and held out his arm to Josefa.

"That leaves more for us then," Agnes teased. "Lupita, I'm sure Father Kenny would appreciate a piece of that pie when he gets here. Especially after the journey."

Lupita nodded in agreement with Agnes's suggestion. "*Dios Mio*, the man is a saint, leaving his parish to come all this way and guide us through Holy Week."

"Is he here yet?" Josefa asked. "What time is confession?"

Agnes shook her head. "No, but he should be soon. Confession will be just before evening prayer at the chapel, I believe."

Oswald halted his march toward the door.

"Your, ah, chaplain has left his own parish to visit here?"

"Isn't it wonderful?" Agnes answered. "Father considers this part of Florida mission territory and is vested in helping us grow. We have the orphanage here now, fundraising for the new church building is progressing, and three more Catholic families have settled in Persimmon Hollow in just the past year."

Oswald cleared his throat but didn't move from where he stood. Josefa inched a little closer to him. His sudden interest in her religion heartened her. She forgot about her decision to stay annoyed over his earlier actions regarding transportation.

"The Holy Spirit is at work, don't you think, Oswald?" she said, and heard the note of hope in her voice that seemed to surface so often in her discussions with him.

He shrugged. "I guess. Where is this fellow's regular parish?"

"Palatka," Josefa answered.

"Interesting," he said. "Well, shall we go? Good day, ladies."

"Who is going with you?" Lupita leaned forward and set down her knitting.

"I have servants at the house, ma'am. All will be proper."

"Take Polly with you," Lupita said before picking up her yarn and resuming knitting.

"I'll get her." Agnes was quick to rise. "She's out with the chickens. One looks different from the others and isn't being accepted by the group. Polly plans to remove it and keep it as a pet."

A small, almost imperceptible puff of air escaped Oswald as he and Josefa walked out front while Agnes went through the kitchen and out the back door.

Oswald helped her into the barouche and sat down heavily beside her. She saw that he had a different driver today, a thin, blond-haired young man she recognized as being from a poor family that lived out in the woods far beyond the settlement. They came to town once in a while on Saturdays.

Agnes and Polly came around the side of the house. Polly carried a plump young chick with feathers that curled instead of lying flat.

"She isn't bringing that ghastly thing with her, I hope," Oswald said. "I understand chaperonage, Josefa, but your family's approach is ossified."

Josefa had no idea what *ossified* meant and no intention of asking. Remembering how Oswald sat too close to her the last time they were in the carriage, she didn't mind one bit that Polly would be with them.

Polly had a glint in her eye and a curve to her lips as she neared the carriage.

"Say hello to Pumpkin," she said, and held the chick out toward Oswald.

Oswald studied the treetops.

"How cute!" Josefa said.

"Pumpkin, you better stay here. I have an idea you wouldn't be welcome with us." Polly was being too innocent. Two spots of color appeared on Oswald's cheeks. He continued to inspect the surroundings.

Polly gave the chick to Agnes, who watched the whole encounter with a keen eye, and scrambled into the carriage as though it were

a citrus cart and she a worker. Josefa was almost certain Polly
made her moves as clumsy and plodding as possible.

"I can't wait to show Pumpkin to Ben," Polly proclaimed. "*He'll*
appreciate him," she said, with the emphasis on the first word.

Josefa tamed the involuntary jump at the name, but Oswald
hadn't missed it.

"He'll soon be gone," Oswald said. "Just as well. Migratory
workers can't be relied upon for long. Never stay in the same
place. And this one seems dimmer than most I've encountered."

"Ben's not dim," Josefa said. "He's quiet, is all."

"And he's not going anywhere," Polly said. "He's staying to
work for my pop while *Tio* Alfredo's leg heals."

"First I've heard," Oswald said. *No, it wasn't,* Josefa said to
herself. She knew he'd been at the grove the day that arrangement
was solidified. Again, Oswald's memory had failed him. He forgot
to tell Ben to visit with Seth about citrus culture. Forgot about her
apprenticeship. Forgot that Ben was to work at the grove. She'd
have to help him remember things once they were married. If they
were married. *No,* when, *not* if, *Josefa. Not if.*

Her tremor of uncertainty faded under Oswald's detailed
description of what they were about to see at his house. By the
time the carriage stopped at the front door, Polly was bored, and
Josefa was wrapped in a daydream of velvet drapes and crystal
chandeliers.

Oswald smiled at her dreamy gaze as he helped her out.

* * *

After the tour, during which Josefa's wonder increased with every
room and Polly sneezed three times in the library full of antique
furnishings, old books, and the smell of cigars, Oswald drove
them to the grove. He refused Josefa's offer of more refreshments.

Instead of returning home, he went to Clyde's Mercantile, which also housed the post office and telegraph station.

"Howdy," said Clyde, seated at the counter in his worn overalls.

"Good day," said Oswald. "I'd like to send a telegram."

Clyde prepared to take down the message. "Ready when you are," he said to Oswald a couple minutes later.

"Prime opportunity in Palatka. Stop. This week only. Stop." Oswald drummed his fingers on the counter.

"That it?"

"No. Add this: 'Inquire at Po…er…' No. Say: 'Close to Catholic church. Stop. Timing critical. Stop.' Now read it back to me, please."

Clyde read, "Prime opportunity in Palatka. This week only. Close to Catholic church. Timing critical."

Oswald nodded and gave Clyde the recipient's information.

"Good thing they're only in Jacksonville. Sounds like they'll need to get a move on to take advantage of this deal you're talking about."

"I certainly hope so," Oswald said as he paid. "And I hope they can read between the lines," he muttered to himself as he walked back out into the bright sunshine.

Clyde sent out the message. "Yup, our Florida keeps growing," he said to Lumpy when he finished. The dog wagged its tail on the floor but didn't get up. "Soon we'll be a right size state and a place to reckon with," Clyde said and then went back to reading the Palatka newspaper that had arrived in the daily mail run.

Chapter 7

*A*nd you should have seen the intricate pattern on the thick carpet in the parlor and library." Josefa continued her litany of what she and Polly had seen to anyone in the kitchen willing to listen. Seth and Alfredo had the construction plans for Persimmon Hollow Catholic Church spread out on the table. Agnes, seated beside Seth, studied the lines and details as Seth pointed them out. Billy stood by her side and added periodic commentary about ground clearing and construction requirements. Lupita sat next to Alfredo and followed the conversation with as close an eye as Agnes. She also held baby Seth, who played with her apron strings except when someone spoke, to which he listened as though he understood the words.

Polly, after a quick glance at the church layout, rummaged in the fruit bin, pulled out a tangerine, and started to peel it. The tangy sweet scent filled the room.

"Smells a lot better than that old library of Oswald's did," she said. "Why'd he go mess up a new room with old stuff?"

"Priceless antiques," said Josefa. "That's what he said they were." She turned to Agnes. "You should have seen it all. The cushions on the sofa and armchair in the parlor were tufted and covered with some of the thickest satin I have ever seen. And the walls! The parlor walls were lined with paper that depicted temples and riverside scenery."

"That's very nice," said Agnes. "Have a look at the layout for the church. See, we'll be able to—"

"It's kind of small," Josefa said after a quick glance. "If we drew the floor plan of Oswald's house atop this, it would swallow it within just the parlor. We'd need more paper to draw out all the rooms.

"Did I mention the brass clock and ornate vases atop the marble mantelpiece in the library?" she continued. "The library and the parlor were truly the most impressive rooms we saw. We didn't go in the bedroom suites, of course. And Oswald wouldn't show us the kitchen. He said I would never have to step foot in a kitchen. All I would have to do is ring for what I wanted."

Her face was animated, her eyes bright, and her cheeks flushed with the memory of the luxury that had surrounded her at Oswald's house. She looked around her now at the large, tidy but spare kitchen. Its pine counters were clean but plain. The cook stove gleamed but was most likely half the size of whatever one Oswald had. Simple homemade curtains framed the window over the sink and the large one behind the thick pine table they sat at. At the end of the table rested items pushed aside to make way for the papers: Agnes's Bible, a kerosene lantern, a few folded homespun napkins, a wooden bowl of grapefruit, and a lopsided ceramic mug filled with late camellias. Why didn't Agnes and her aunt insist on fancier goods? Those flowers, especially, should be in crystal, not in some failed project of Polly's.

"The church will be able to seat sixty people, three times as many as the chapel," Seth said. "That's a good size for starters. Our congregation isn't even half that yet."

"Speaking of seating, we saw the dining room, too," Josefa went on. "The table was massive, mahogany with intricately carved legs and matching chairs with tapestry seats. Oswald said the set could seat sixteen, but of course, that's much too many for a dinner party of style. You wouldn't want more than twelve at the table, he said."

"For all those dinner parties you give?" Billy piped up, and laughed at his own attempt at a joke.

"I'd throw up if I had to eat in that stuffy room," Polly said and popped the last of the tangerine into her mouth. "The whole house was crowded. The furniture was too big, and everything was covered with blankets or throws or drapes. Knickknacks were piled one atop the other: Wardian cases, ugly figurines, a globe, a clock so ornate you had to search to find the time on it—you name it, it was there."

"Oswald was quite proud and considered it all very stylish," Josefa defended. "Don't talk with your mouth full, Polly. Anyway, Oswald told me the most noted designers in Philadelphia drew up the interior décor even before construction. They ordered every-thing and had it shipped so all he had to do was have servants set it up. He said I should start to learn the names of the furniture periods, design styles, and the experts who guide such matters."

"He said, he said," commented Agnes. "I say it's almost time for confession, Josefa. I thought we could walk over together a bit early and prepare ourselves."

Josefa stopped her animated walk around the room. "Oh, that's right, confession is today." She had forgotten in her euphoria over the house.

"Confession of Holy Week," said Lupita with a raised eyebrow. She gave baby Seth a kiss on the cheek and patted and supported his back as he angled to sit upright.

"OK, but just one more thing," Josefa said. "Important artwork covered the walls in the parlor. Oswald said there were some Old Masters among them, but our tour was so fast we didn't have time to study any of the works individually. But he said the wealth encapsulated in such a collection far surpassed anything in the entire state if not the Southeast!"

Even Seth and Alfredo looked at her. Josefa thought it was because they were impressed with all she had relayed. But their faces registered concern, not enthusiasm. Seth gave a half glance toward Agnes, who nodded, rose, and reached for her Bible. She gave him and Lupita a small nod as she sat back down and searched through the thin pages.

"What do you say we start our preparation here?" she asked but didn't wait for an answer.

"Amen," said Lupita.

"A few words from Proverbs," Agnes said.

Do not wear yourself out to get rich;
  be wise enough to desist.
When your eyes light upon it, it is gone;
for suddenly it takes wings to itself,
flying like an eagle toward heaven.
Do not eat the bread of the stingy;
  do not desire their delicacies;
for like a hair in the throat, so
    are they.
  "Eat and drink!" they say to you;
  but they do not mean it.

The room grew quiet. Seth wordlessly rolled up the church plans. Lupita busied herself with the baby. Billy stuck his hands in his trouser pockets and studied his brogans. Alfredo looked out the window. Polly inspected the contents of the pie safe. Agnes kept her gaze on the printed page in her lap.

Josefa looked from one to the other. She felt as if she'd been slapped. "I, uh, you, I…" She took a step, then another, then stopped in front of one of the cane-seat chairs at the table and gripped the top rail. The day's happy taste crumbled like stale cornbread in her mouth. She shrugged, lifted her shoulders, raised her arms, and lowered them to her sides. No one understood. She stumbled quickly out the door and into the yard.

"Sometimes God has to hit a person over the head," said Seth. "I know he did me."

"Or he could let me help by sending her to Texas," said Lupita as she got up. She gave the baby Seth to Polly. "Hold him for a minute while I go find my stationery. It is time for another letter to our relatives out there."

"Not yet, Lupita," cautioned Alfredo. "You don't want to send her away any more than I do or anyone else here does. Let's give it more time."

Lupita put her hands on her hips. "More time for her to run head-first into ruin? We need to act now."

Alfredo shook his head as he scooted his chair back from the table and reached for crutches that leaned against the wall nearby. "No. At least not until I can escort her and you on the journey and we can stay until she is settled."

"Ah, si, smart words," said Lupita. She took the baby back from Polly. "Go to confession with your mother. When you return, maybe you can help with dinner while I go. You need to learn more about cooking."

"My favorite pastime," said Polly, and stepped beyond Lupita's reach.

"Josefa gets wrapped up in dreams of what if," Alfredo said to Lupita. "She would do the same away from us. Better that she do it where we can step in and help her. Agnes, too, who always knows what Bible verse to use. Like she just did."

Agnes gave Alfredo a quick hug. "I always knew you were a wise man," she said. The room's tension lightened.

"Come, Polly. I see Josefa out back waiting for us," Agnes said.

* * *

Josefa lagged a few steps behind Agnes and Polly and refused to keep pace with them. She was upset that she'd forgotten about confession in the glare of the crystal drops hanging off lamp-shades and the carpets so thick her shoes sunk into them. Worse, the scripture passage had stung.

She didn't covet riches. She just wanted to look out for herself. Life grabbed loved ones and things and snatched them away whether a person was ready or not. There was nothing wrong with trying to cushion oneself. But it had to be the right cushion. Her aunt's belief that the best nest rested with faraway relatives and an arranged marriage was just plain wrong.

She trailed Agnes and Polly into the orphanage. The peace and tranquility of the chapel anteroom soothed her, as it always did.

"Wow, am I glad to see you!"

Ben had come out of the chapel when he heard them enter the anteroom. His sunny smile lifted the shadow over her heart.

"Do you know how long it has been since I've been to confession?" he asked. "I'm talking years. Since I was a little kid. I've forgotten what to do." He paced a small circle in front of her.

Josefa reached out and touched his arm and gave him a smile she hoped conveyed reassurance. She drew him over to the bench farthest from where Agnes and Polly waited.

"Relax," she said to Ben. "Confession isn't a test. It's a sacrament. A chance to review your heart. To see where you've strayed away from living right, to see if you've followed the Gospel message, kept the sacraments, and paid attention to the Church's teachings."

"How can one person do all that, all the time?"

"It's not about check marks on a list," she said. "It's more about a way of life, a perspective, and about how you treat others. No one is perfect, only God. The rest of us stumble and fall."

He still appeared doubtful. It was the first time she'd seen Ben anything other than fueled by quiet assurance.

"You go into the confessional and talk to the priest about any missteps. He will guide you from there. The sacrament is cleansing. You feel good afterward, like a burden has been lifted."

And I have my own missteps to discuss, she thought.

"What?" he asked at her sudden silence. "Anything else I need to know?"

"I need to follow my own advice, is all," Josefa said. "I got a little carried away today after seeing the inside of Oswald's house."

"A monstrosity, if you ask me," he said.

"Polly said the same thing."

"But not you?" A hint of sadness tinged his expression.

"I, ah, did find it a bit grand, but really, it was magnificent."

He held her gaze.

"Although, and I didn't tell this to the others, I was afraid to move around in there," she added. "Afraid I'd break something or trip over the furniture."

She decided not to share the words from Proverbs that Agnes had so pointedly read to her. They still resonated.

"Is Father Kenny ready to hear confessions?" she asked.

Ben shrugged. "No idea. I just knew to be here early evening. Tell me what to do one more time."

They sat together on the bench as Josefa reviewed the simple procedure. "You start with this prayer: 'Bless me, Father, for I have sinned. It has been a month since my last confession'— or a year. Or years. Whatever the amount of time is. Then after that, you talk about where you went wrong."

His smile was warm. "You ease a man's heart, Josefa. I'm back to my normal self, almost."

"Just a messenger, is all," she said, but his words were a balm. His fingers reached and intertwined with hers on the seat between them. The rough warmth of his hands sent a ripple of pleasure through her. She held her breath, as if that would capture the moment and make it last.

It was as though they were the only ones in the room. Agnes and Polly were on the far side, looking over some paperwork with Sister Rose. None of the orphans had come down the hall yet. She didn't expect to see anyone from the Bight family. She wondered if people of other faiths like the Bights had confession, or how they came right with the Lord if they didn't. Thoughts flitted in and out of her mind as her senses were consumed by the man next to her and the urge to lean in to him. She wondered how his arms would feel around her.

Was Ben extending a simple hand of friendship? Or something more? Josefa wanted, yet didn't want, more than friendship. Ben seemed content to move casually through life, from job to job, without settling down. She needed a home and a family and a community.

"I'll never be a man of rich tastes, even if I had more money than Heller," Ben said. "Which I sure don't." His fingers tightened over hers.

She turned toward him, eyes wide. She reached for his other hand, and he shifted, so that they sat knee-to-knee, face-to-face. The movement helped Josefa regain some of her equilibrium.

"Ben," she said. "My first reaction was to say money doesn't matter, that only love does. But one needs enough money to live on, to have in case...I've seen with my own two eyes. My family..." She stopped and took a breath. "You have to be ready to survive anything life throws at you. You have to be able to provide necessities for yourself if the need arises, and to do for others should hard times fall."

His face revealed an understanding that touched her.

"I'm no stranger to life's struggles, Josefa," he said. "Hard work has been my companion for a long time. Always will be. A man has to support himself and his family, and that's a duty I take as seriously as anyone on this earth. But to spend hard-earned money on frills you don't need, just to show off? Nah, not me."

With a gentle movement, he disengaged his hands and placed hers softly in her lap. When Josefa didn't reply, he gazed at her for a few moments before continuing.

"I see how you sparkle with all that fancy sewing and material. Even I notice how nice your everyday stuff looks on you. A man couldn't miss it. I don't mean to make light of all frills. There's a heap of difference between you and your finery, and a man's greed and need to grab everything. I mean, I guess I'm saying, of course people want some extras—sure, I do, too—but not..." He blew out a breath. "This isn't coming out right."

He stood up with abruptness, ran his fingers through his hair, and then let his arms hang with stiff formality at his sides.

"I'm not good at this kind of talk."

The doors to the chapel creaked open, and Sister Bridget stepped in from behind them.

"Father is ready," she said in a soft voice. "Mr. Stillman, you were here first. Would you like to go in?"

Ben's and Josefa's gaze locked. She nodded with encouragement and a half smile that spoke the thoughts she couldn't form into words because everything inside her was a jumble. Her heart did a little skip at the boyish, nearly lopsided, Ben-is-back grin she received in return.

"Ready as I'm gonna be," he said to Sister as he turned toward the chapel entrance. He grabbed his hat from the side table, crunched it in his hands, and walked with solemnity toward his first confession in a long time.

"Such a nice young man," Sister Rose said as the doors closed behind him.

"Unlike another we've seen lately," Polly cracked. "Oops, sorry, Josefa." But her tone indicated no remorse.

Josefa stayed seated. She had her head bent in prayer a while later when she heard the chapel doors open, Ben's footsteps come out, and the soft swish of Agnes's dress as she crossed the room and entered the chapel. Josefa tried to keep her mind focused on prayer but was too aware of confident steps as they neared the front door, the click of the latch opening, a slight squeak, the light thud of the closing door, and the quiet in the wake of Ben's departure.

* * *

Easter dawned a pastel mix of rose, pale orange, and a hint of midnight gray-blue. Soft breezes carried promises of warmth and hints of the fruity spice of the Louis Philippe roses that grew against the fence of the kitchen garden. Josefa drank in the beauty from the window of her small bedroom. The Gomez cabin anchored the far side of the household's courtyard workspace. Josefa pushed up the window sash and stretched out. She sensed

God's presence everywhere, from the sunrise painted across the sky to the rooster who crowed in the coop. Her anxieties of the previous days slid away. Easter brought with it new hope, new beginnings, new life.

Humming, she closed the window and dressed. She twisted her braid into a smooth bun, draped a lace mantilla over her hair just as her aunt called out that it was time to leave, and then went outside.

"Happy Easter! Everyone's coming! See!" Agnes said as she stepped out of the Taylor cabin to meet the Gomezes. With the arm that didn't hold the baby, she pointed toward the row of carts and people coming down the entry drive and turning off toward the lane to the orphanage.

"Someday Persimmon Hollow will be filled with churches so all can worship in their own faith," she said. "But there's something special about how everyone joins us here today to celebrate. I pray they feel the beauty and holiness of our rituals."

She gave Seth a half hug as he exited the house. Even morning-averse Polly, when she appeared, was scrubbed and shiny in a new dress and hat, and Billy was stiffly uncomfortable in a suit jacket, tie, and pressed pants.

Josefa waved when she saw Ben with the sisters and Cornelia, who along with Ben would receive the sacrament of confirmation this day. He waved back, his eyes alight and expectant. He was handsome in his suit, despite its plainness and lack of a tie. He returned to his conversation with Cornelia. Josefa felt an odd prick. Envy? To have one of the seven deadly sins prod her on Easter morning was uncomfortable.

She searched around. No Oswald. They still had a few minutes before Mass. Time enough for him to get here, if he got here. It was a big *if*.

She couldn't resist one more peek at Ben and Cornelia. They stood, heads close together, with Sister Rose.

"I'm so happy the bishop in St. Augustine gave special permission for Father Kenny to perform the rite of confirmation," Agnes told Josefa. "The Holy Spirit is at work today! Look how many people are here. I hope we all fit. Come, let's go inside. Mass will begin soon." Baby Seth slept quietly in her arms, undisturbed by the greetings and hellos going on around him. Love suffused Agnes's face as she adjusted the edge of his blanket.

"I see the Alloways," Josefa said and waved. Like many, she still referred to Fanny and Eunice as the Alloways. As soon as Fanny saw the Taylor and Gomez families, she hurried over, out of breath and flushed.

"My dear, I am so sorry," she said to Agnes. "On Easter Sunday, Lord have mercy. It's just awful. Clyde got word from his cousin who lives up there."

Josefa and the rest of the two families stopped in midstep while others milled around them and flowed into the chapel.

"What's happened?" Agnes asked. She held the baby tighter.

"Father hasn't said anything? Oh, mercy, he may not know. Oh dear, this is horrible."

Chapter 8

I thought Clyde said a telegram came in for Father yesterday," Fanny said. "Yes, I'm sure of it. Clyde's cousin said someone broke into the Catholic Church in Palatka and tore apart things and defaced the, what do you call it, the place where you keep the Communion wafers."

"The tabernacle," Agnes said. She paled.

"Yes, I think that's what he said. They also destroyed the—"

The opening bars of "Puer Nobis" on the orphanage melodeon rose above the murmur of talk.

"Fanny, we got some room on a bench back here by the door," Clyde called from inside the chapel.

The choir began to sing the medieval hymn: "Joy has dawned again on Easter Day…"

Josefa heard the words and the music but was so jarred by Fanny's news that joy fled from her heart. Who desecrated a church on Holy Week?

She saw the shock on other faces, too. Lupita took her arm with a firm hand.

"We praise the Lord now and worry about the evils of men later," she commanded. "Come, Agnes, you, too."

Fanny put a hand on Agnes's arm. "We'll talk more after the service. Just know how sorry I am. The Lord carried his cross, and so we must do the same. Keep heart."

She hurried off to find her seat. Seth, Alfredo, and Billy ushered Josefa, Agnes, Lupita, and Polly into the chapel, where they squeezed into the few remaining spaces on the benches. Josefa saw Ben a few rows ahead, beside the sisters and next to Cornelia.

Josefa wondered what else had happened at St. Monica's in Palatka. She, her aunt and uncle, and the Taylors had visited Father Kenny there a couple of times when Agnes sought counsel about organizing a parish in Persimmon Hollow. Josefa couldn't bear to think someone had been hateful enough to do harm to the little wooden church. Perhaps Fanny heard it wrong. Josefa had noted that, recently, Fanny sometimes had to ask a speaker to repeat words to her. Maybe a tree fell, or winds from a storm knocked something down. But Fanny had distinctly referred to the tabernacle, and she wasn't even Catholic.

She studied Father Kenny. If he had word of any destruction, she wouldn't have known by looking at him. His face was reverent and joyful when he passed her bench row as he processed along the small center aisle. Two altar boys from the orphanage preceded him. One carried the thurible and swung it gently to release the rich aroma of incense. She inhaled the delicious scent and watched Father Kenny. Inspired by his focus on the transcendent, she gave her heart over to God and the ritual of the Mass. She felt joy when Sister Rose presented Ben and Cornelia as confirmation candidates after the Gospel.

During Father's homily, Josefa vowed to make the new beginning and rebirth that he urged all to consider as they embraced the risen Lord. She felt strong and cleansed, able to push back against doubts...and emboldened to find and examine the reasons that fueled any uncertainties, hers or others, about her choices and plans.

Father turned toward the now-standing Ben and Cornelia and conducted the ceremonial renewal of their baptismal promise. Josefa was proud of Ben's strong responses and the simple dignity he and Cornelia exhibited as they knelt for the laying on of hands and the anointing. It was as if the Holy Spirit filled her as well as them.

Mass resumed, and Josefa bowed her head and knelt with the other Catholics when Father lifted the host and said the Eucharistic Prayer. When she rose to get in line for Communion, she was surprised to see that many worshipers of other denominations had also knelt out of respect. Persimmon Hollow was such a special community. She was glad she would still live here after she and Oswald married. If they married. She channeled her thoughts back to the Mass and to receiving Christ into her heart. But she was conscious of Oswald's absence before she bowed her head again. The fact of his nonattendance was as loud as the whisper of the Holy Spirit was soft.

* * *

"I feel like a new man," Ben said to Josefa and a circle of others outside the orphanage after Mass. "To be honest, I wasn't expecting much. But there's something to this Holy Spirit business."

"Uh-oh, don't turn into some brimstone and fire preacher or whatever they're called," Polly said. Billy snatched her bonnet, which as usual had become untied.

"Hey, give it back!" she hollered and ran after him, trailed by Bight children and curious orphans.

Josefa's heart did an odd flip-like flutter as Ben's slow smile radiated warmth. "I don't see myself as a preaching man, no," he said in the direction of the now-vanished Polly. He pushed his hat back a little on his head and faced Josefa. "No, this man has other plans."

She sensed his air of expectancy. He watched her, and waited. Who'd speak first?

"All right, I'll take the bait," she said. "If you're not going to be a preacher, what are you going to be? Will you continue traveling from town to town wherever the work is?"

He looked surprised.

"Would you care if I did?" he asked.

"Well, of course," she said. "The entire grove family would. You fit right in, and you would in town, too. Persimmon Hollow is your kind of place."

"You. I meant you. Would you miss me?"

The day went still and quiet on her. Shifting shade and sun filtered through the high pines around the building and played off the angles of his face. The blue of his eyes was intense.

Yes, she cried inwardly. *You know I would.* But her lips didn't form the words fast enough. The moment vanished in a jumble of youthful laughter as Polly, Billy, and the others stampeded back and surrounded Josefa and Ben with loud boisterousness.

Ben took a step back, and Josefa saw the brightness of his eyes dim. Quickly, his expression regained its good-natured amiability at the high spirits around him. Sister Rose reopened the doors to the entry foyer, and Agnes and Lupita were a step behind her.

"Come in, everyone. Refreshments are ready in the orphanage dining room," Agnes called. Her wide mouth, so often curved into a smile, settled into an uncharacteristic downturn.

"The Palatka church," Josefa said as soon as she saw Agnes's face. She gave Ben's arm an urgent tap. His expression was opaque as he turned toward her.

"Come, you must hear this," she said and started toward the door with him. "Something fearful has happened at Father Kenny's church in Palatka just when he saw fit to come celebrate Easter here."

"What? And how bad? When did you hear?"

"Just before Mass."

A larger-than-expected crowd had gathered for fellowship, but the celebratory mood of Easter morning dampened as word spread of the damages in Palatka. The Bights, the orphans, Polly, and Billy were put to work to make sure the seats and tables accommodated everyone. Lupita enlisted Josefa to assist with serving.

"Bye," she mouthed to Ben and took the apron Lupita held out. She tied the apron strings around her waist as she trotted after her aunt.

"Have you heard anything more?" she asked as they reached the kitchen. Lupita shook her head.

"I only know it isn't good. Right now, we need to get the food out. Father believes the information will be easier to stomach if people eat first. Then he will talk. *Dios Mio*, what is this world coming to?" She didn't wait for an answer but busied herself in setting out ham and biscuit sandwiches on one tray and cut carrots and celery on another.

"More sandwiches?" Josefa asked more than an hour later as she carried another tray into the dining room from the kitchen. She set it on the sideboard near the table where Agnes and Seth sat with the sisters, Father Kenny, the Alloways, Clyde, Ben, and, oh, how nice, Esmeralda Penn. The seamstress appeared slightly distracted. She darted her gaze this way and that around the room.

"Do you think I could have a few extra of those, dear?" she asked, turning in her seat as soon as Josefa set down the food. With quick movements, Esmeralda got up, took four sandwiches, wrapped them in a large linen napkin she pulled from her pocket, and slipped the bundle into a canvas bag she carried. She sat down as though nothing had occurred. No one else at the table had noticed. *What a lot of food for a small woman,* Josefa thought before she started back to the kitchen for the fresh coffee Lupita kept brewing. Bad news surely made the people of Persimmon Hollow hungry.

After another hour had passed, her feet ached from the unaccustomed waiting at tables and running back and forth to the kitchen. To think her aunt wanted her to do this kind of work full-time for relatives in a distant state. Josefa longed to be in her room, finishing the fancy hem work on the tea gown she was making for her trousseau. Or working on the green silk gown she secretly hoped to have reason to wear to something special, like a reception for the president or dinner at Oswald's or maybe even at the Stetson mansion. Now that would be grand. She could—

The decanter nearly slipped from her hand as she heard Oswald's voice. "I think we should organize a vigilante committee with the men in that town of Palatka and put the fear of God into the lawless."

Just when did he get here, she wondered. It certainly hadn't been in time for Mass. She glanced at him through lowered lids. Then at Ben, Seth, her uncle, and the other men to gauge their reactions. Ben's gaze met hers for the briefest of moments.

Oswald pulled out a chair and sat down uninvited at the already crowded table where the Taylor Grove families had gathered. He turned the chair so its back rail leaned against the table. He straddled the seat and gripped the top rail with fists as he advocated for rough justice.

"No. No violence," Father Kenny said. His quiet tone was in obvious contrast to Oswald's assertiveness. "Your offer is of course appreciated, sir. But it would be best for me to work with the lawmen in town and let them do their job. The culprit or culprits may be rebellious or ignorant youth in need of guidance, not harsh treatment. Let's talk of other things. The Lord will find a way for us to continue worship in Palatka. Today we celebrate our risen Lord and the seed of faith planted in Persimmon Hollow."

"I insist. I don't take no for an answer," Oswald said.

"Neither does anyone else at the table." Seth said before the priest could respond. Seth's eyes sparked with a prick of annoyance. Josefa inched closer and stood a few paces behind Oswald's chair so she could hear better.

"If you want to help, reckon you could check with those friends of yours you telegraphed and see if they know anything," Clyde said.

Oswald shifted in his seat but didn't answer. He caught Josefa gaping at the table from behind him.

"Ah, the little señorita," he said in a tone as smooth as the sheerest silk cuffs and collars in her sewing box. His gaze lost its hard edge, and his pale blue eyes glittered. He stood up and bowed. "Please, join us."

"Yes, please do," said Ben, also rising from his seat halfway around the table. He indicated she should take his seat.

Oswald shot Ben an incredulous look. Ben held his ground.

"I, uh, I…" Had she suddenly lost the power of speech? And movement? Josefa couldn't take a step. How could she choose whose seat to take? Especially because she wanted to take the one Ben offered. But then what about Oswald?

Agnes took pity on her. "Here, sit here," she said, pulling a chair from the next table and positioning it next to Oswald. Josefa plunked down the decanter of coffee and plopped into the seat with a glance of thanks to Agnes. She looked down at her hands, which she folded in ladylike fashion in her lap. Fatigue started to sap her.

"It's been a long day for you," Ben said as he sat back down. "Rest with us for a while."

"No need to be shy around me, Miss Josefa," said Oswald, taking his seat again and ignoring Ben. "I'm honored to be seated next to the most beautiful woman in Persimmon Hollow," he added in a voice loud enough for all to hear.

Josefa could feel the eyes of probably everyone on her.

"Or should I say, the most beautiful women in Persimmon Hollow," Oswald amended with a nod toward Agnes and Lupita, who bustled up at that very moment, wiping her hands on her apron.

Lupita looked surprised for a moment, then suspicious, and then flattered.

"You may say that again, loud enough for my *esposo* to hear," she said. Then, louder to her husband, "Alfredo, did you hear what our neighbor has said of your *esposa?*" Alfredo was seated a few tables away with the Bight family, where he was talking with Toby Bight.

"That man says nothing I did not already know," Alfredo called back, smiling at Lupita over his shoulder. Oohs and aahs echoed through the room, and people returned to their private conversations. Josefa felt her breath loosen.

"How much longer does he have to stay in the wheelchair?" Father Kenny asked Lupita.

"Not another day if he can help it," she said. "He already uses the cane and crutches more than the chair. But even he admits the chair is useful to him."

"We'd have been lost without the ramps Ben built, especially the hinged one that enables Alfredo to roll in and out of the low cart," Agnes said. "Thank you again, Ben." As she spoke, Agnes turned from facing Father Kenny to facing Ben's seat.

Ben's chair was empty.

He must have slipped away when their attention was on her aunt and uncle, Josefa thought, as she looked for him in the crowd. She saw him just about to walk out the door and wanted to go after him and bring him back into the warmth of the fold. They'd hardly had a chance to talk. She wanted to ask him about getting indigo to grow faster, and whether there were less messy ways to make dye from it, or if another plant could produce a blue color. She wanted to—

"Josefa?" asked Oswald.

Josefa reluctantly gave him her attention.

"Did I mention I have been invited to the Stetsons'? And asked to bring a guest?"

He dangled a gem in front of her, for sure. So why did she feel cornered? She waited for what she hoped would come next, an invitation. Talk around the table had quieted. A look of feral anticipation grew in Oswald's expression.

"Would you join me outside for a short walk?" he asked Josefa. "Just out front," he added at her slight hesitation.

She glanced at Lupita, who gave an almost imperceptible nod. Josefa allowed Oswald to take her arm and escort her out. She heard footsteps a discreet distance behind and hid a smile as she guessed Lupita had used the same slight head nod to send either Polly or Billy out as a shadow.

Outside, the day had developed into a perfect blend of breeze, warmth, and sun. Vivid splashes of magenta azaleas and white jasmine starflowers bloomed in bold outline against multiple shades of green.

"Such a beautiful day," she said as they strolled along the sandy trail that formed a U shape in front of the orphanage before converging into a single lane.

"Too muggy," said Oswald.

She laughed. "No, muggy would be the heat of that kitchen I just ran around in."

"Doesn't befit you."

"It's Easter, Oswald, and we're sharing food with neighbors. I don't mind the work at all. I enjoy the day's celebration and helping make it special."

He cleared his throat.

"Josefa, you do understand that a lady doesn't concern herself with such things. Servants handle those matters. Furthermore, ornate religious worship observances won't be part of your milieu. You will quickly forget this emphasis on superstitious religion that exists around here."

Josefa stopped walking. "I don't understand."

He exhaled. "You will spend far more time on entertaining, making calls, and hosting and attending dinner parties and civic women's events than you will on church, particularly papist doings. This constant concern about prayer and ritual devotions will fade. You'll look back on this and realize how fooli—how childish your behavior is."

The day's exertions suddenly caught up with Josefa. Every step felt forced. So did the discussion.

"Oswald, my faith is a part of my life, not something I wear only on Sunday mornings."

"Yes, yes, faith is important. It's the kind of religion I speak of."

"There's nothing wrong with the one I have. My religion is an ancient one, rooted in—"

He stopped midpace, causing her to do the same, and put a

finger to her lips. They were halfway down the drive. As they turned to go back, she saw Billy seated on the orphanage steps and drumming his fingers on his knee.

"You have a lot to learn," Oswald said and moved his finger. "More than I expected."

I've displeased him in some way again, she thought. His behavior confused her. How different could their worlds be? He asked the unthinkable if he expected she'd forgo the Church. For the first time, she had a tiny doubt about whether she could adapt to the lifestyle he depicted.

"You have the looks," he said. "The style. The fashion sense. But you have to learn how to act in society, not just look like you belong."

He assessed her from head to toe. "If I take you to the Stetson dinner, you'll have to follow my every move. If I use a certain fork, so will you. If I drink from a certain wine glass, so will you. You do want to learn how to act in society, I presume?"

She nodded. She did, in fact, want very much to learn.

"Fine," he said as they neared the building. The day felt chill to Josefa all of a sudden.

When they got inside, Oswald again exuded a warm ease.

"My dearest señora," he said to Lupita and bowed low over her small figure as she rested in a chair next to Agnes. "I beg your permission to escort your lovely niece to dinner with the Stetsons at their mansion. A beautiful house, but I'm certain the interior would never meet your standards of cleanliness and order."

Lupita's gaze was opaque. She didn't smile.

"Señor, we missed you at Mass," she said.

"Something I deeply regret," Oswald replied. "I didn't feel well earlier this morning." He placed a hand over his stomach.

Stony silence.

Surely, Tia won't deny me this chance, Josefa thought and cast a pleading gaze at her aunt. Maybe Oswald really had been sick. He hadn't eaten anything since he arrived.

She detected the slightest softening of Lupita's shoulders.

"Only if you follow my conditions, which we will discuss later," Lupita told Oswald.

"Whatever you decree," he said. "On that positive note, I'll be going. I'm still slightly under the weather." He glanced around at the group. "Good day, all. I'll see myself out."

"Good, because no one else will," Polly muttered under her breath.

Agnes had the look on her face, the one that alerted Polly whenever she spoke out of bounds.

"He asked you to the Stetson dinner?" Agnes asked as Josefa sank down into the chair.

"Yes, sort of…I don't know when it is. He didn't say when."

"Don't fret," Clyde said. "I'll find out from the greengrocer. The Stetsons are certain to put their order through him."

"Thanks," Josefa said. "I don't fully understand Oswald's ways. He acts differently. Superior, sometimes."

"He, his family, his kind—they're just people," Agnes said. She held out her arms as Cornelia came up with a sleepy baby Seth and gently placed him in Agnes's arms.

"He may have more social skills than any of us, but it doesn't give him a right to belittle you for lack of knowledge," Agnes added. "If anything, just the opposite. Josefa, remember your Gospels. Luke tells us that Jesus says, 'A disciple is not above the teacher, but everyone who is fully qualified will be like the teacher.' You can grow to become wise like the teacher, but that teacher has no right to put on airs."

"That Oswald is a bit of an odd duck, if you ask me," Clyde said.

Eunice Alloway Williams tapped her husband's arm lightly. "Now, dear."

"Just saying."

A knowing smile passed between the two of them, newlyweds in their mature years. Josefa saw the closeness between them. She yearned to feel that with Oswald. Maybe in time it would come.

"I'm not certain about his sincerity," Lupita said. "How sick was he that he missed Mass but managed to visit now?"

"I'm trying to be charitable, so let's give him the benefit of the doubt," Agnes said. "Perhaps he doesn't fully feel welcome here yet."

"You find the good in everyone," Seth said. "I'm reserving judgment just yet."

"What about what I think?" Josefa blurted out. She felt her cheeks flush. A jumble of exasperation, fatigue, confusion, and impatience churned inside her. She didn't even know herself what she thought.

She was tired and just wanted to drag herself home to her small room and lie down for a spell. She hadn't felt this low in a while. She had mourned for so many months after her family's death that at times she'd feared the darkness would never lift. Since crawling out of that, she had felt alive again. She didn't want to slide back.

There was no denying the symptoms clawed at her. She felt increasingly distant from the lighthearted gathering that took place around her. Her mother, father, and sister should still be alive to enjoy the day here, to celebrate Easter, nibble on cakes, and drink coffee. They should still be here.

"Excuse me," she said, rising to stumble off.

Lupita started to go after her, but Agnes held her back. "She might be better left alone for a little while."

Lupita shook her head. "This is alarming. She hasn't had one of these spells now for many, many weeks. I had dared to hope her grief had lifted."

"Me, too," Agnes said. "Let's see if she recovers without us making a big deal. She was so happy when she finally started feeling better."

Lupita sighed. "*Sí,* true."

"It's that stupid Oswald," said Polly as she cut a corner from the block of cake still left on the table.

"You're not making things better," Agnes said to her.

Polly shrugged. "She's never happy after spending time with him, is all." Her words hung there, and Lupita and Agnes exchanged worried glances.

Josefa left via the inside door, for she wanted to snatch off her apron and leave it in the kitchen. There, she ran into Sister Rose, who took one look at her face and set down the washcloth and pot she had been scrubbing.

"Josefa, is everything all right?"

Josefa's face contorted. "No. Yes. No. Out of nowhere, I had this stab of grief, of wanting my family back. Sister, when will this ever end?" She sat down at the table and leaned her head down atop folded arms.

The wood chair squeaked as Sister Rose sat near her. Josefa didn't look up.

"It's never easy to lose loved ones, especially when they go at healthy stages of life. But they're still with us because they're with God, and with the communion of saints. Think how many saints make up our Catholic family. We are never alone, Josefa. We may not be as close as we wish to be. But God is always near. His blessed mother is with you, too, especially in times of sorrow. Remember the apostle Paul's words: We're all one in Christ. Especially today, when we celebrate everlasting life. Pray to Jesus, and seek intercession from Mary. Pray to the saints. Ask them to ask God to help heal your soul."

Josefa lifted her head. "I will," she said. "Thank you."

"No thanks needed," said Sister Rose. "Now would you like to help me finish these pots?"

Josefa's look of alarm brought a bright laughter. "I see that if nothing else, you can be shocked out of your mood," Sister Rose said. "I jest. But I am serious in suggesting you might want to go back to the dining room. I'll be along in a few minutes. Father and I have a big announcement to make."

Chapter 9

*J*osefa slipped back into the family group at the table and poured herself a cup of Lupita's good, strong coffee. Sister's words had heartened her, and curiosity about an announcement had taken the edge from her lethargy.

"I thought you were going to rest," Agnes said while Lupita kept a keen eye on Josefa.

"I came back for the announcement," Josefa said.

"Announcement?"

"If anyone knew, I'd have thought it would be you, Agnes! Sister Rose said she and Father Kenny had something to tell us."

"It must be about the troubles at Palatka," Agnes said. "Father finished eating a while ago and left—said he had something to attend to with Sister."

Alfredo wheeled back over to their table. "It's settled. Toby is firm on having the family move to town permanently at the end of the year. He'll have enough furniture stock built by then to fill a small showroom. He'll sell them outright while he fills orders."

"Yes, Sarah told me about it," Agnes said. "She's proud of her husband and is doing all she can to support him."

"That's so sweet of her," Josefa said, clasping her hands over her heart.

"Marriage is hard work, not always kisses and hugs," Lupita said. "The Bights have had their share of hardships. Do not let your romantic dreams get in the way of reality."

"Actually, Aunt Lupita, I'm not," Josefa said with a maturity that caught the others by surprise. She knew she had to decide which was more important: a husband she bonded with or a man of means who could provide every comfort in life that she could imagine. Except perhaps true love.

"We'll see about that," Lupita grumbled. Her bottom lip started to protrude.

Sister Rose swept into the room.

"Attention, attention," Sister called. "Father has an announcement. Attention, attention."

It took a few moments, but the clink of china and murmurs of talk and laughter quieted.

Father Kenny had come in and now stood beside Sister Rose. Josefa saw a sadness in his eyes, and his face reflected weariness. Yet he also appeared serene and at peace.

"My brothers and sisters, as you heard earlier, St. Monica's Church has been vandalized. I ask for your prayers, both for our church recovery and for the misguided soul or souls who brought destruction to a house of the Lord. I stand before you, however, not to talk about that sad situation, but to bring you good news."

A ripple of surprise ran through the room.

Father Kenny waited until the room quieted again. He smiled, and this time it reached his eyes.

"I am happy to announce that the building fund for the Persimmon Hollow Catholic Church is healthy enough for construction to begin—as soon as you are ready."

"What a glorious Easter gift!" Agnes cried out. She gave the baby to Lupita, jumped from her seat, hugged the still-seated Seth, and then ran to the front of the room and embraced both Sister Rose and Father Kenny. She stepped back. Her trademark wide smile lit her face, and tears pooled in her eyes.

"No one has worked harder than you, Mrs. Taylor, to make this come true," Father said.

"Hear, hear!" Seth hollered. Amens mixed with applause. Josefa noted the mingled love and pride on Seth's face.

"No," said Agnes. "It was the work of the Lord and of everyone in Persimmon Hollow. I'm just the instrument. But Father," she turned to face the priest again, "I think I speak for everyone in saying we'd rather donate the funds back to you for repairs at St. Monica's."

The room was so silent Josefa imagined she heard a swoosh from the flames in the small votive candles that illuminated the statue of St. Isidore in the corner.

"Thank you, but no," he said. "We are an established church in Palatka. You are forging a path in missionary territory. The money goes here."

Seth rose. "Thank you," he said simply. "And thank you to the Alloway sisters whose father set aside land for churches when he founded Persimmon Hollow. You two," he indicated Eunice and Fanny, "are more than generous to bequeath a parcel for our needs."

Eunice's naturally stern-looking face softened, and Fanny waved her fan in furious swishes as her plump face colored pink.

"I guess all I need to add is that ground clearing will commence… tomorrow," Seth said. He sat down amid a round of applause. So soon! Josefa squeezed Lupita's hand in joy. Sister had been right. She was glad she'd stayed.

"I will see you all at benediction this evening?" Father said, his face awash in hope, as people started to rise and gather their belongings. The Catholics in the room nodded. Others looked at each other, their hands, the floor, or the remnants of cake on plates.

"Thanks but no thanks, reverend," Eunice said in a light tone. "Don't think we don't know you're trying to convert us all."

"Wouldn't be doing my job if I didn't," he replied with equal good cheer.

As people departed, Josefa knew she wasn't the only one to feel the shared warmth of fellowship.

"We are so blessed," Agnes said as the grove family walked the short way back to the main compound. "When I think of what I hear and read of anti-Catholic activity in other places, we're lucky to be surrounded by good people. Nothing like what happened in Palatka could ever happen here. I'm sure of it."

* * *

The next morning, Josefa dragged out her trunk and pulled two valises from under the bed. She heaved, pushed, and pulled them to the center of her room. *At Oswald's, a servant would have collected the luggage,* she thought. *Would have packed everything too.* She sat down on the trunk. *You, Josefa, are the servant here*, she could hear Aunt Lupita remind her. In truth, no one ever expected her to act as such, not even her aunt.

Josefa was too excited about the start of her apprenticeship to mull over her situation in life. There was nothing wrong with being a servant. She just didn't want to be one.

Hawks called in the near distance, and squirrels, mockingbirds, parakeets, and blue jays chirped and chattered at the sound.

Josefa loved to hear the sounds of birds and animals, to sit and admire flowers and trees, and to walk through the orange grove. She felt a kinship with creation every time she perched on the padded kneeler Alfredo had made for her and tended her dye plants. She looked forward to exchanging fabric dying tips with the dressmaker.

Josefa hadn't had a chance to say goodbye to Esmeralda yesterday or let her know what time she'd arrive in town today. By the time Father Kenny had finished speaking, the tiny dressmaker had gone. She had slipped away during the applause and comments. *She and her hidden sandwiches,* Josefa thought. She wondered what that was about and hoped she'd eventually find out.

She rose at the sound of cart wheels rolling over leaves. Billy was right on time to take her to town. A quiver of movement on her dressing table caught her attention. Her butterfly box! A slender, multicolored, fragile creature had emerged from the chrysalis spun on one of the branches. Now it clung to the branch. Josefa drew in a breath. Right at Easter season, this new life had shaken free of its cocoon. She was loath to leave the delicate creature here, even though Polly had promised to tend and guard the box. Could she transport the box with the newly hatched butterfly in such a delicate state? When was she supposed to set it free? It wasn't really moving yet. She wished Ben were here to witness this miracle with her.

"Hey, Josefa, you ready?"

"Yes, you can come and get the suitcases and trunk," she called out the window in response to Billy.

Two sets of footsteps, not one, thumped across the porch and into the house. Moments later, not only Billy, but Ben, too, walked in.

"Ben! Look!" she said and pointed toward the dressing table. "The butterfly is out!"

"Perfect," Ben said in a quiet, reverent voice.

"It's so beautiful," Josefa marveled. "Look at the colors. I could design a dress of these colors; they are so bold and bright and yet in perfect harmony."

Heads close together, Josefa and Ben bent over the box. She had a heightened awareness of his clean scent, a mix of pinewood and the outdoors. Of his solid presence. She worked to keep her breathing even. You two are friends, she told herself, friends sharing a moment between them. Nothing more.

"What do I do with it?" She almost whispered.

"Set it free," he said.

"Just like that? Put the box outside or something?"

He shook his head. "Right now that butterfly is drying its wings. After that, it will fly off and settle on a safe spot to gather strength."

Neither of them moved.

Billy shoved in between them. "Lemme see. Wow! You didn't manage to kill it, Josefa. Ha, ha." He scooted away before she could react.

"C'mon, you ready?" Billy added. "Ben and I need to load this stuff up so he can ride you to town."

"I thought you were taking me."

"Nope," Billy said. "Too much to do here, and Ben doesn't know the full routine yet, so I'll be quicker. He's working full-time here now, did you know? Old Oswald kicked him out. What'd you say, Ben? He was grumpier than a bear yesterday afternoon after leaving here?"

"Yeah, something like that," Ben said.

Josefa's and Ben's gazes met. She looked away, flustered at the intensity of his look. She reached to pick up the box. He put a hand on her arm. She went immobile as though locked into place.

"Better not to disturb it right now," he said. "If you like, I could come back and get it, make sure it gets a good start on freedom. Not sure bringing it to town would be the best plan."

She nodded. "Ok, thanks." Somehow, Ben always knew the right thing to do, the thoughtful thing.

"C'mon!" Billy repeated.

Billy and Ben each picked up a valise in one hand and an end of the trunk in the other, and maneuvered out of the room. Josefa stayed behind a few moments longer, listening to the bumps and steps and thud of the luggage being hoisted into the cart. She stared at the butterfly, ready to embrace a new world and way of life. And felt just a tiny bit like the newly born creature getting ready to test its wings.

* * *

"I am more than excited," Josefa said to Ben as they neared town.

"It's a good opportunity, for sure," Ben said.

"For me, too, if Josefa makes me some new clothes," called out Polly from the back. "Right, Josefa? You think that embroidery thread I'm picking up at the shop is for me to use? Fat chance."

Polly was allergic to sewing of any kind. Josefa settled back in the seat, comfortable despite the plainness of the wood seat and backboard. Nothing could dim the day.

"Polly would be more at home helping build the church than sewing the altar linens that will go in it," she told Ben.

"Everybody has a place in life, is the way I figure it," Ben said. "Just got to find it. Hey, there's an osprey nest atop that snag." He craned his neck and peered at a blob at the top of a dead tree that had lost most of its branches.

"Cardinals are nesting in the holly that grows near where I do my dying," Josefa said. "That reminds me. Do you know of any other way to make indigo dye? The process is so messy and smelly I had to go clear to the edge of the property to let the leaves ferment. I only did it once. Never again."

"Must be why it's so expensive," Ben said. "All I know is the standard procedure. Cheaper chemical dyes are starting to come on the market. Could be an option for you."

"Nothing produces that same deep purple-blue," Josefa said.

"I prefer nature's colors, too," Ben said. "Maybe try something different? You can get a nice red from bloodroot and the inner bark of the wild marsh plum. Not sure if bloodroot grows this far south, though."

"My aunt said an insect named cochineal is used in Mexico to make a red color."

"I could talk for hours about this kind of stuff," Ben said as the cart rolled to a stop in front of the dressmaker's shop. "But we're here. Do you want me to take the luggage to the Alloway House for you?"

"I'd appreciate it. Polly, tell Fanny I'll be there at lunchtime."

"OK," Polly said and scrambled out of the cart. "Be right back, Ben. I'm going to grab that thread." She went into the store.

Josefa stayed where she was. She didn't want to end the ride, not yet.

"Do you think—" she started to say.

"Would you like—" he started to say at the same moment.

They both laughed. "You first," she said.

"If you'd like, we could work together to expand your dye garden and experiment with different flora and plant more of your favorites as well. I can tend it while you're in town during the week. I'd be mighty proud to partner on such a project."

"I would love that," Josefa said, her thoughts already imaging fabric she could dye in clear, pure colors. "We could even attempt to find a substitute for indigo, although I don't think one exists."

"You got it," he said.

"Ben, I'm so glad we met," she said on impulse before climbing out of the cart.

"Not more than I am," he said.

His smile touched her heart.

* * *

"Welcome, welcome, here you are." Esmeralda flitted around when Josefa trailed Polly into the shop. "My, that conveyance is quite a bit different than the one you came in last time, Josefa."

Josefa looked out at the boxy lines of the utilitarian cart pulled by an ox. Funny, she hadn't noticed during the ride how plain the getup was. It was clean, strong, in good repair, and had been filled with good people and a comfortable atmosphere. Unlike another recent journey, when the sleek smoothness of Oswald's barouche had been the only truly pleasant aspect.

"We have a nicer one at home, but this one is the everyday cart," Polly piped up.

"And it was a wonderful trip," Josefa added.

Esmeralda nodded. "Glad to hear. Here you go, my dear." She gave Polly the embroidery thread and a few cents change. Polly and Josefa embraced, and the younger girl left. "I miss you already!" Polly cried after she stepped halfway out the door.

"I'm right here!" Josefa called. "Not far away at all." She followed Polly out and waved until the cart turned the corner toward the Alloway House. Not far away at all. She swallowed trepidation as her link to home turned the corner and vanished from sight. She was only two miles from the safety and security of the grove. She was in the heart of a welcoming town and would board with one of its most upstanding and warm-hearted citizens. All will be well. She would keep telling herself that.

Chapter 10

Tell me again, Josefa, why you wanted to do this, she asked herself two weeks later at the end of yet another day of some of the most boring needlework she had ever had the misfortune to apply herself to.

She shifted in her seat in her work area at the shop and gazed out the window. April was fast slipping by. Breezes already carried the hint of heat that warned of high summer. April was one of her favorite months, and she was spending most of it indoors.

She adjusted the fabric as she guided it under the sewing machine needle. Darn! She had stitched an extra layer of fabric to the sleeve when it folded over. She withdrew the fabric, picked up her sewing scissors, and began to snip out the thread. Tension pricked her forehead, and she forced herself to relax the muscles in her face, neck, shoulders, and arms. Lupita sure had been right when she warned about the reality of the work.

Still, Josefa was surprised at how tired her eyes were by the end of each day, and how cramped her fingers sometimes became after hours of sewing, far more than she ever did at one time at home. And she had sewn quite a lot there.

A sigh escaped her as she set down the scissors. At least she had a pleasant little working corner. The top-of-the-line Singer treadle machine, a pleasure to operate, faced the plate glass window so she could take advantage of natural light. The view gladdened her even when endless alterations of dresses didn't. She might scream, she thought, if Esmeralda gave her one more corset expansion. People just needed to eat less or get a little busier so they wouldn't grow stout.

"Tsk, look at the time!" Esmeralda jumped up from the machine she sewed on. "I need to run out for a bit, Josefa. Do mind the store for me. I'll return within the hour." The shop owner scooted behind the counter, picked up the canvas bag she carried to and from the shop each day, tied on her hat, and hurried out.

Josefa set down her sewing and stared at the empty space Esmeralda had just occupied. Again, the dressmaker had left. Every day it was the same thing. Josefa glanced at the clock. At nearly the same time, three o'clock. Esmeralda even used a variation of the same words each time she went on her daily mission. Where did she run off to every day? And why?

Josefa had a good mind to follow. But she couldn't because Esmeralda always asked her to mind the store during her absence. Josefa stood, stretched, and took a break for a few minutes. She immersed herself in the intricacies of the warp and weft, design, coloring, and other aspects of the bolts of fabric that filled the shelves. Some were imported from Italy, France, and even India. She ran her hand over the large remnant piece of fabric Esmeralda had given her to make a tea gown for the Stetson dinner.

Sometimes she wanted to pinch herself. To think she'd be dining at the Stetson mansion—for that's what everyone had taken to calling the house—in, what, another week? Yes, third week of April, is what Oswald had said the day he came to visit, looked around at her workspace, informed her of the date, and left. She hadn't seen him since. That was just fine. Working on the tea gown by the light of kerosene and candle at night, after a day of hard work, was almost too much sewing even for Josefa. Sleep came quickly when she collapsed into bed each night.

She retrieved the sleeve of the latest alteration, matched it to the bodice fabric, eased the two pieces together, and stitched the seam. Then she did the same with the other sleeve. She stopped the treadle, and the needle stilled. Josefa was drained and couldn't deny the strain the toil had on her. She was determined, though, to see things through and honor her commitment.

She took a few minutes to close her eyes and dwell in prayer. She hadn't prayed as much as usual since leaving the grove. She missed the small shrine to Our Lady of Guadalupe that Lupita had set up in their house. She never felt alone with Our Lady watching over her. She knew she was still here with her, but...sometimes Josefa got so busy that Our Lady seemed far away.

Josefa opened her eyes and looked around again at the yards of dry goods, the ginghams, seersucker, lawn, flannel, alpaca, silk, satin, brocade, even a bit of cashmere. Esmeralda had arranged all by fabric type and color. Surrounded by so much beauty, Josefa thought of the psalm about a wedding that spoke of a princess "decked in her chamber with gold-woven robes." When she was a child and heard that psalm, she used to imagine herself in a gown of gold, her hair flowing down her back, on her wedding day. Except the groom's image was never clear. It still wasn't.

She turned her attention back to the dress alteration. If she finished quickly, maybe she could spend some time on her own gown. Foot on the treadle, she started to pump. The thread broke. Josefa leaned forward, rested her forehead on the sewing machine, and decided to call it a day.

The shadows outside already had started to grow along Persimmon Boulevard. Esmeralda was taking longer than usual today. Josefa sat in the customer chair by the window to catch the remaining light while she leafed through the precious Bloomingdale's catalog. It had become her fashion bible, and she dreamed of a day she'd open a new edition and see one of her own fashions featured in the etchings.

A few moments later, Josefa's eyes widened at the catalog description for a ladies' trousseau. A person could order an entire ready-made trousseau. She was astonished, both at the concept, and at the price—$12.50. Who had that kind of money? She didn't.

She read the list to be sure her own chest of garments—the ones she'd been working on for a few years—was adequate according to the heights of fashion. Other than the quantity, she measured up fairly well. Her homemade bridal set was three pieces, just as this one was: gown, chemise, and drawers. She thought of the day when she would finally get to wear the fine muslin set, highly decorated with lace and detailed embroidery, for her new husband. Maybe she would add a band of lace to her hair, or fresh flowers, or—

The door flew open, and Esmeralda rushed in. "The time just flew. I didn't realize it was so late. You go on now, Josefa. Off with you. I'll see you in the morning."

She was flustered and flush, and more anxious than usual.

"Can I help you in any way?" Josefa asked. "Let me fix you some tea or coffee."

"No, no, you just go now," Esmeralda said. She hurried over to the counter where she kept her shop paperwork and started rifling through a pile of invoices. "Where in heavens could it be? I must find it! I knew this day would come. And here I need to get home to help..." she muttered to herself.

Josefa didn't know if she should stay or go. Something clearly was amiss.

"Is everything OK?" she asked.

"Yes, yes," Esmeralda replied, still bent over her task.

"Esmeralda, why don't you come back to the Alloway House with me for dinner this evening? It would be a nice change for you."

Esmeralda looked up as though surprised Josefa was still there. "Oh, no, dear, no, I really can't. Not right now. You go now." She came around front and shooed Josefa toward and out the door, and then closed it behind her. The "Open" sign flipped to "Closed." Josefa peered back in through the window. Esmeralda picked up a huge pile of paperwork and headed with it toward the stairs and her upstairs living quarters. God made us each in our own special way, Josefa reminded herself, and set off for the Alloway House.

It felt good to walk, to be in the open air on such a glorious late afternoon. Too good, in fact, to go right back indoors. Judging from the afternoon shadows, Josefa figured she had enough time to walk out to the church building site, three blocks past the Alloway House, check out the progress, and return in time to get ready for dinner.

The building site was quiet, with no one around. Josefa sat down on a large fallen pine. The property was already fairly open and airy and was adorned with tiny spring violets and tall, slender toadflax blooms. In the central, cleared building area, gray-white sand and clumps of overturned ground covers and grasses created small waves of soil. A lumber delivery was off to one side, covered with canvas. The sharp orange-pink of some late-blooming azaleas peeked through the understory in the far corner of the lot. Squirrels skittered up and down the pines.

Josefa flexed and squeezed her fingers and wrists to relieve the ache of repetitive needlework and absorbed the beauty around her. She sank into the peaceful stillness, and yet she was lonely. She wondered who was doing what at the grove this very minute. She missed them during her weekdays away. Despite the kindness and mentorship of Esmeralda, the warmth and care of Fanny, and the busy clatter of life in a boarding house, Josefa yearned for the extended family of the grove. Just as Lupita had warned, she had already discovered that too much time spent crouched over a sewing machine was as bad as doing no sewing at all.

She had six more weeks of the apprenticeship's grueling schedule to fulfill. After her commitment ended, she would find a way to do dressmaking that fit her schedule and her life. She rose and took one last look at the building site, imagining the new church with worshippers joined in praise inside.

Josefa strolled back to the Alloway House with spirits lifted by the day's beauty and the promise of the new church. So when she saw Oswald's barouche in Clyde's mercantile yard across the street from the house, she tried to ignore the hazy gloom that clouded her euphoria.

"Mr. Heller will join us for dinner this evening," Fanny said as Josefa entered the house. Oswald stood, bowed, and kissed her hand as usual. She had an odd sensation of going through motions of some kind of game. He sat back down. Fanny was more fluttery than usual.

"I'll go up and freshen for dinner," Josefa said. Her breath felt constricted, and it wasn't from exertion or excitement.

"Why don't you sit with Mr. Heller for a few minutes while I go see if Estelle needs any help," Fanny said and made haste to leave the room. "The other guests will be down soon, and perhaps they can entertain Mr. Heller while you take your toilette." She hurried out but made a point to catch Josefa's attention to flash a smile of anticipation.

Josefa sat down. Did she start talking? Or wait? Maybe it was weariness from the strenuous and unfamiliar workdays of late, but she was in no mood to second-guess herself about Oswald's social protocols.

Oswald slapped his gloves on the booted foot he had crossed across his other leg. He stood.

"I'll get right to the point. I'm honored to say your uncle has given his approval...uh, his blessing...to my request for your hand. We will start the planning process immediately."

Josefa stared at him, flummoxed. Was that a proposal? Didn't she have to accept first, before planning began? Or was his behavior normal for people of his station? Most of all, where was the flush of excitement and happiness she expected to feel at this moment of her life? This wasn't unfolding the way it did in her dreams. She was a step closer to her goal. She should be soaring. Yet her rapid heartbeat was more panic than passion.

"I see you are at a loss for words," Oswald said. "Don't worry, that's to be expected."

Josefa pressed her lips together. Marriage proposals didn't arrive on silver platters, nor did they show up every day. There was no one else on her horizon, certainly no one of Oswald's stature. She'd be a fool not to grab the opportunity. Especially when her aunt and uncle approved.

Yet part of her balked. She ached to feel love and closeness with the man she would tie her life to. Instead, she faced formality. Josefa wondered how Ben would react to the news...no, she would not think of Ben right now.

"I'm just...surprised," she said slowly. "It's so sudden."

"I'm a man of action," Oswald said and smiled. "The wedding will be at my home in the North. You will travel there with me. My family will see to the arrangements."

She felt a chill. She felt as though he were talking about her, not to her.

"Oh, no, my family will wish to bring me and—"

"No, Josefa, listen to me. Your relatives from this, er, town will be uncomfortable in the surroundings I envision."

Dread struck at Josefa. This wouldn't do. How could her aunt and uncle have agreed to such a plan?

"Of course they won't be able to leave here, not when grove and agricultural duties consume so much of day-to-day life," Oswald added, a bit hastily, she thought. "Your guardians have approved of our union. I'll take you off their hands. You'll no longer have to live on their charity and the grove owners' beneficence."

This should be one of her happiest days. Instead, she was numb with indecision and ambivalence.

"Your wedding gown will be jeweled, and you'll wear the family pearls," he said with a calculated gaze. "Brocade, silk, satin, whatever women wear on such occasions. You will outshine all of them. A matched team of horses will draw the carriage, with liveried footmen. The wedding will be in the church where my family worships."

Visions of the grandeur started to swell in Josefa's imagination.

"We'll honeymoon in Europe," Oswald pressed on. "Then you will be at home in my mansion in Philadelphia."

The dreamy interlude vanished. "I thought we would live here." Her voice was small, too small.

"You can't be serious," he said. "The land and house are investments, nothing more." He changed the subject as some of the winter boarders started to file in for pre-dinner talk. "Your family is well, I presume?" he asked Josefa, as though they had been discussing nothing deeper than the weather.

Dinner at the Stetsons, grand houses, fine clothing, servants, plenty of money, travel. All of it kept flashing through her mind in rapid bursts. The pictures were almost perfect. But the edges were jagged, and sharp enough to wound. Oswald treated her as though she were a thing he would acquire, like land or a house.

"I need to freshen up," she said, picking up her skirt to clear her shoes and running up the stairs. What was happening to her fairy tale?

* * *

Dinner at the Alloway House was served family style. Everyone else was seated when Josefa came in and slipped into the chair Oswald drew out for her. She placed her napkin in her lap and nodded a greeting to the other boarders. She could hardly remember the names of the two couples and single woman who made up the five boarders still in residence. The men were brothers, the single woman was their sister, and the other women their wives. The family members looked alike.

Oswald drew the couples into conversation as though they were long acquainted and was more at ease with them than he usually was with her.

Fanny passed the breadbasket and bowls of grits, spinach, and a pea and carrot mixture after Estelle placed the main course on the table, a tureen of aromatic chicken and dumplings.

One of the married women, seated on the other side of Oswald, let out a laugh. "I will make a point to see the exhibition when we return North. Too bad you won't be there to provide additional commentary. I feel as though I've seen some of the works already, just from your descriptions." She then turned to her husband on her other side and continued chatting.

Josefa was ravenous. Sewing all day made her hungry. And by focusing on her food, she was able to avoid conversing, or trying to, with Oswald.

After dessert was served, Oswald stood. "I'd like to make an announcement." The table talk quieted. He waited until he had everyone's attention. Josefa set down her fork and intertwined her fingers on her lap. He was going to announce their betrothal? Before they had a chance to go to the grove and share the news there?

"I think we should tell the family first," she exhaled and whispered to him.

"I'm not certain this would matter to them," he said in an undertone, before returning his attention the group as a whole.

Josefa pursed her lips. Perhaps he was right. No one at the grove had apparently objected to the idea of their getting married in the North. Or living there, something she wouldn't do willingly. She began to question long-held assumptions about her place in the family. No wonder her aunt wanted to ship her out to Texas. The hard truth was that she was alone, the odd person out at the grove.

The grove consisted of tight units of family—the Taylors, her aunt and uncle, the Bights. Even the orphans and the sisters were a family. She was the outsider. Oh, they loved and embraced her, but how long could she fool herself into thinking she could stay there indefinitely as a permanent, dependent guest? Josefa supposed she should be grateful to Oswald for pointing out the reality of her position. But all it did was make her sad. Good thing she had started to take responsibility for herself.

Fanny, at the head of the table, sought Josefa's gaze and gave a nod of encouragement. Josefa mustered only a thin smile, and she saw a question arise in Fanny's eyes. Not wanting to give anything away, Josefa turned toward Oswald

"As some of you may know, Emma Juch is one of the finest sopranos ever to grace the stage," he said. "Her opera is ending its winter tour of Florida, but she has agreed to perform a private recital at the Stetson mansion in this very town. A select few of the Stetsons' friends will dine with her beforehand. Any of you still here at the time are welcome to join us afterward for the performance."

The winter boarders all started to talk at once. Fanny and Josefa exchanged surprised glances.

Oswald cleared his throat. "Yes, I had something to do with the arrangement, if any of you were wondering." He sat back down.

Josefa was now bewildered.

"I thought you were going to tell them about our—" she started to say.

"I prefer we keep that between us for now," he quickly cut her off.

Between us and the grove, she thought. With the news common knowledge there, it would soon be in the ears of everyone in town. Including Ben's. The dumplings she'd eaten became leaden in her stomach.

Oswald looked at his watch and then clicked the case closed. "I leave town early in the morning on business. Until next time." He rose and bowed in a gesture that took in everyone in the room, then gave a deeper, knowing nod to Josefa.

She watched him depart, tall, authoritative. She wished she knew how to approach the world with similar assurance. It was one of the things she wanted to learn from Oswald. So far, all he'd done was tell her how to act in society. She stabbed her fork into the sliced strawberries that remained on her dessert dish.

Chapter 11

*H*e asked you to marry him?" Agnes stopped stirring the strawberries she was preparing for preserves. "Oh, Josefa!" She set down the ladle and ran to embrace Josefa but then stepped back, still holding Josefa's arms, to look at her with a penetrating gaze. "Where's the happy bride?"

Josefa wasn't inclined to go into details. "You mean my aunt didn't tell you about the proposal?"

Agnes's brows drew together. "No. I must be losing my touch. Maybe she wanted to surprise me. She's in the greenhouse. Let's go find her. She didn't think you would get back here so early today."

Josefa set down her weekend satchel on the table bench and untied her bonnet. Agnes called Polly to take charge of the stove until they returned.

"Have you set the date?" Agnes asked. "We have so much to do to get ready! Of course you'll have the wedding here. You know, I wasn't sure at first you two were an ideal match, but if you are happy, so am I." Josefa couldn't get a word in as they walked at a fast clip to the greenhouse.

"Lupita! How could you keep such a secret from me?" Agnes demanded as she pushed open the door, feigned a frown, and then let her smile take over her face.

Lupita looked up, an armload of fresh-cut rosemary sprigs in her arms. Ben turned from the back garden workbench, where he was potting what looked like okra and eggplant seedlings, waved a hand in greeting, and went back to work. The greenhouse burst with plants in various stages of sprout, seedling, and transplant size.

"*Dios Mio*, what did I not tell you?" Lupita asked.

"Something good, by the sound of it," Ben called.

"About Oswald's proposal to Josefa!"

Lupita stared at them as though they were unbalanced, and then her face started to fold into lines of disapproval. Ben dropped his trowel and made haste to pick it up and get back to his task, keeping his back to them. Josefa willed him to turn around again, but to no avail. *Please,* she pleaded inwardly. *Let me explain.*

"He did not seek Alfredo's and my permission." Lupita started to glower.

"But...he said he did," Josefa said.

Agnes's excitement dimmed. "Could Alfredo have forgotten to mention it?"

"Forgot to say what?" Alfredo called from outside the greenhouse. "What does my wife say I do wrong now? Me, a hungry man who comes seeking a bite to eat so I can make it until dinner. Josefa, look at these fancy new crutches your friend Ben made for me now that I'm getting around better and better."

Alfredo entered on his crutches nearly as smoothly as he normally did when walking on two legs. "He's a good one with the wood. The Lord above, he provides, no? With Toby so busy making furniture for his new store, it's good we have Ben to lead the church building."

Ben kept his back to them.

"Alfredo, you gave Oswald Heller permission to ask for Josefa's hand, and you don't say anything to me?" Lupita's voice started to rise.

Alfredo pulled himself up as straight as he could stand. His smile faded.

"I have not seen our fancy friend in days, maybe weeks. I did not give my blessing, and I would not give my blessing until he and I sit down to a long talk. There is much different between his world and ours. I would want to make sure our Josefa was in favor of him. That he would not take her away from us to somewhere distant. And, *mi esposa*, such a final decision would be for you and me to make together. But men such as that one, they do what they want, eh? They think they own the world. Bah!"

Alfredo stalked out, slapping the crutches on the ground with each step.

"And they say what they want, apparently, whether it is true or not," said Agnes, her hands on her hips. "I don't know what to make of this, but I don't like it."

"Me either," Lupita agreed. "I also wonder about that silver tongue he has been using with me lately."

"He acted as though all had been discussed, and agreed, and...I was surprised—and disturbed—when he said the wedding would be up North, and that we would live there, not here," Josefa said. "I thought...he said...he made it seem you would be happy to see me go."

"*Dios Mio! Dios Mio!*" Lupita cried and pulled Josefa into a hug and kissed her. Agnes encircled them both.

"This is your home," Agnes said. "Forever, if you want it. And let me say, you may want to marry this Oswald, but he will have to go around me and your aunt first. He'll have to do some fancy explaining to us, and some man-to-man talking with Seth and Alfredo."

"Your uncle and I have not given this man our blessing," Lupita said. "As far as I am concerned, there has been no proposal. And certainly no permission."

Josefa's confusion gave way to a joy of belonging, but then to a kind of despair over Oswald. Lupita's grave expression softened. "Come, tell us everything," she said as she stepped back from the embrace so that she could study Josefa. "You are happy with this turn of events he started? Then why do I see these?" With her hands, she pressed the tips of her fingertips to the outside of Josefa's eyes, where tears had started to pool. Josefa squeezed them back. Just nerves, she told herself.

"Come, we'll go to the cabin. Your uncle is waiting there, I'm certain, and hungry." Lupita took Josefa's hand and led her out.

"I'm going to finish the preserves and feed the baby," Agnes said as she walked out with them. "Come over to the house when you're ready. Please let me help sort through this."

"Yes, we'll determine where it is going," Lupita nodded.

It's going straight to a house in the North, Josefa thought as she twisted to pull the greenhouse door closed behind them. Ben still hadn't turned around. And he wasn't working any longer. Just standing there, with his hands gripped on the edge of the worktable.

As if he heard her gaze, he finally turned. "Hey, Josefa, before you go. I'll have some time to help you start that dye garden tomorrow, if you want."

Her gloomy anxiety lifted a little. Ben's steadiness was just what she needed right now.

"I would love to," she said.

"Good, I've got some plants started here."

"Let me see." Josefa went back in. Ben pointed out young seed-lings of indigo, cuttings of blackberry, and fernlike transplants she didn't recognize. She crouched down to look more closely.

"Marigold," Ben said.

"The regular garden marigold?"

"Yeah, should produce a yellow-orange dye color," he said. "Look, over here, I have some more."

They walked to near where Lupita had been gathering now-forgotten herbs.

"Josefa?" Agnes called in after her.

"Got to go," Josefa said to Ben. "But thank you. More than I can say."

"Anytime," he said, and the way his lips curved into a crooked smile melted her heart.

"Tomorrow after Mass? It's a week when Father Kenny stops here," she said. "The weather should be perfect. I'll be glad to get outdoors after all those hours of sewing."

"I'm ready," he said. "Whenever you are." He bent down, gathered up the rosemary sprigs Lupita had dropped, and held them out to Josefa. Their hands brushed when she took them, and she had an urge to grab hold of the strong firmness of his grip, instead of the pine-needle-like sprigs of the strong-scented herb. They stayed in mid-transition far longer than was necessary. *Why,* thought Josefa, *couldn't she feel this way when standing close to Oswald?*

"Josefa!" Lupita called this time.

She walked out immersed in dreams of a blooming dye garden and Ben's smiling warmth, a feeling of rightness, and a happy glow because he wouldn't be leaving soon. She couldn't figure why Lupita and Agnes met her with such curious expressions.

* * *

"I wish we could magically make them grow and be in full bloom," Josefa said the next day. She and Ben sat on the wooden bench at the edge of the dye plot and admired the half-day of work. The small square was laid out in neat rows of transplants. Wooden stakes at the end of each row were labeled with plant names.

"In due time," he said. "That's what my Dad used to say when I got impatient about a plant growing. Only in my case, it was usually trees, not coreopsis or blanket flower."

"You planted trees with your father?"

"Not really. He was a plant explorer and taught me everything I know about botany and nature."

Ben grew silent. Josefa considered how far she could—or should—probe. Oswald grew prickly and overbearing any time she asked even the slightest personal question.

"Did you go plant exploring with him?"

His eyes had a faraway look in them. "Hardly. I was young, and he went on expeditions to remote places in Asia."

A mockingbird's warble and trill filled the long moments of silence.

"He died in China."

"Oh, Ben!" Josefa placed her hand on his arm and wanted to hug him. "I'm so sorry."

He gave her a sad smile. "It's OK, really. He died doing what he loved. I've always wanted to follow in his footsteps. To explore and unearth new discoveries. A couple of species of rhododendrons are named after him. It's an honor in the field, to have a species named after you."

"Ben." She hesitated and then plunged in. "I sensed your passion for plants since the day we met. Can I ask, why are you a carpenter?"

"Employers aren't knocking on doors asking to hire plant explorers," he said. "The jobs are in more practical fields. Like carpentry. I don't have the money, education, or connections needed for exploration. Dad did. But he died young, and the family struggled. My dad's family has never been much help. They weren't happy when he married a peasant girl he met in Mexico, even if she was half-American. I'm the man of the house. It's up to me to provide for my mother and sister. Someday, though, I will get out on the trail of new plant discovery."

"You're part Mexican? Ben, that explains it!" she said. "When we met, something about your nose and the angles of your face were familiar to me, but I couldn't say why. Now I know. I can see traces of your heritage. Our heritage." She could sense it, too, she thought, in his steadfastness.

"Have you told my aunt?" she asked. "She'll adopt you!" Josefa peered at him. "Most people would never guess, though, to look at you. Not with those blue eyes and fine hair."

"I know," he said. "I get those from my father. My sister's coloring is a little darker than mine. My mother's maybe not so much. And, no, I haven't brought it up to Lupita. I don't really pay much attention to that kind of thing. It's not important."

To some people, it is, she thought. Obviously, to his father's family, it mattered. It mattered to her aunt. Oswald's family, in fact, might object to her.

"I'm glad we put the indigo at the edge," she said, wanting to redirect her thoughts away from Oswald. "It'll grow bigger than the rest."

"And stay in place," Ben said. "I want to harvest only some of the leaves each time, so that the plant continues to grow. That way, we can experiment with different dye techniques at different stages of growth. Weather permitting, it should work."

"The St. Francis statue in the middle is perfect," Josefa said.

"Your uncle has the hand of an artist. I couldn't believe when he carved that out of a fallen branch."

Josefa's forehead furrowed. "Uh, I just thought of something, Ben. I'll be back at work at the dressmaker's starting tomorrow morning, and I guess you'll be at the church site. Who will tend this in the meantime? It'll need watering every day for a week, at least, unless it rains."

Ben put his arm on the back of the bench. "Already thought of it, Josefa. I'm paying Billy to take care of it."

"Paying him? He should offer to do it for free."

Ben shook his head. "He already does a man's share of chores. This will give him some pocket change. All young men need such."

Josefa started to protest again, but Ben just shook his head no. "It's not much, Josefa. I can afford it."

"How can I thank you?" she asked.

"No thanks needed. From one friend to another."

She had a desire to lean against him and only kept herself upright by force of will. She stood up and started to walk between the newly planted rows. She stopped midway out and turned to face him.

"I know!" she said as the idea formed. "Ben, let me make you a new shirt. You're going to be doing dye experiments for me, and you helped with this, and I suspect you'll tend it every chance you get."

He frowned, got up, and came out to meet her. "That's a lot of work, Josefa."

This time, she got to silence his protest.

"Just a simple shirt, a work shirt."

"In that case," he said, "sounds like a fine plan."

A scream rang out.

"Look out! Boots! Boots, come back here! Boots!" Polly yelled. Her cat bounded into the garden, sprang upward in surprise at the soft dirt, did a rolling tumble, popped up, and started to dig and paw the earth.

"Boots!" Polly came running. Close behind was Lumpy, trailed by a racing Billy.

Lumpy skidded into the garden and collided with Josefa, who lost her footing and fell atop Ben, who landed sideways at the sudden poundage on him. The cat leapt up and over them and barreled a perpendicular path of destruction across the garden. Lumpy, quickly over his surprise, barked and ran after Boots. His big paws splayed the path of ruin over a wider area and showered Josefa and Ben with dirt.

"I had no idea Lumpy could still run that fast," a panting Billy said as he stopped at the edge of the garden, winded, with hands on his knees.

"He's never chased Boots before. They're buddies!" Polly called as she sprinted after the animals. "Last I saw them, Boots was sleeping atop his head!"

"Boots woke up and started play-biting his ear!" Billy yelled and ran after them.

"Good gosh, what just happened?" Josefa rolled off Ben, in full knowledge of how much she hadn't minded the closeness. She scrambled up and brushed dirt off her hands, skirt, and hair before she realized much of it landed back on Ben, who was still down on the ground, already fixing plants.

He was amused when he looked up. "What's a little more dirt, you know?"

She gurgled with laugher. He looked so ridiculous, as though he wore more dirt than was left in the garden. She knew she likely looked the same. There was a freeing lightness in not worrying that every hair was in place and fabric wrinkles smoothed out. She knelt down beside him, and together they made quick work of uprighting the trampled plants.

"We're lucky," Ben said. "Most of their paw prints landed between plants. We only lost a handful."

"Yes, it could have been so much worse," she said. They finished and helped each other up.

Seth ambled up. "I take it you're not going into town with us," he said to Ben.

"Not if you can get by without me today," Ben said and shrugged with a helpless air. Seth scratched his head under his Stetson hat.

"Stay here. Alfredo will go. We're bringing some produce to the Alloways. The two of us can handle it."

"Much obliged," said Ben, and Josefa saw him and Seth share a grin that had some kind of understanding in it.

Ben and Josefa finished tidying the grounds. She wiped down the statue, and Ben gave the restructured plants a fresh drink of water. Josefa knelt to pull out a stray weed that had escaped notice next to the statue and saw a shadow fall over the garden. She looked up. Oswald stood there.

Chapter 12

Josefa brushed the dirt from her skirt. Ben continued to water the plants at a slow, steady pace. As he strolled to and from the rainwater barrel to refill his bucket and pour measured amounts around each resettled plant, he moved as deliberately as the caterpillar she'd watched eat leaves.

"Oswald!" Josefa exclaimed. She reached out her hands to him but saw his slight recoil. She glanced down. She still wore the old gloves she used when working outdoors. They were caked with dirt and mud.

Oswald watched her peel them off. "Playing in the mud, I see."

She had been braced for a snide remark about proper behavior. It was gratifying to see his apparent enjoyment, for once, of the simpler joys of life.

"It's hard not to enjoy being in the midst of God's plenty," she said, her arms spread wide to span the area. She was giddy with the day's perfection, the new dye garden, even the mishap with the pets. She felt...alive.

"If you say. Are you finished? Could I have a word with you? We'll talk as you walk back to change." Oswald looked at Ben, who gave the appearance of not paying attention. There was nothing left to do with the plants, but he hadn't yet stopped tinkering. In fact, he started rewatering the whole lot of them again.

Talk. *Yes,* she thought. She and Oswald did have to talk, starting with his lie about her aunt and uncle's approval. But she wanted to savor a few more moments of sunshine before plunging down that road.

"Yes, of course," she said. "But do take a look at our dye garden first, and enjoy this gorgeous day." She wanted, no, she needed, him to see who she really was.

"I've been indoors too much, even for me," she continued. "It's so good to be back at the grove. Everything reminds me of one of the Scripture passages Agnes shared just before I came out here to work:

But ask the animals, and they will teach you;
the birds of the air, and they will tell you;
ask the plants of the earth, and they will teach you.

Oswald crossed his arms over his chest. "True. But, Josefa, remember, you'll have servants to do this type of work for you."

Josefa sobered. She supposed she would have groundskeepers. She hadn't sorted through the details of her future life yet.

Ben plunked down his bucket. "Some folk here are mighty interested in having a word with you, Heller," he said. "Something about plans that hadn't been cleared with—"

"None of your concern," Oswald said, his tone breezy but his eyes, Josefa saw, narrowed and cold. "An oversight, is all."

Ben shrugged. "Interesting how you knew what I spoke of right away." He started to whistle and went back to the now-depleted rain barrel. He glanced in and then walked to the nearby well.

"Sure hope we get some rain," Ben said and looked straight at Josefa. "This well here is about run dry. Funny, ain't it, how you think something's full and you find out it's nothing but an empty vessel."

Oswald stiffened. Josefa wondered why Ben had suddenly affected a countrified manner. And why he had directed his last comment to her. She wasn't stupid. She knew she and Oswald didn't have much in common. He wasn't empty. Just different, with his emphasis on appearance, behavior, and his...forgetfulness. Fingers of anxiety crawled up her spine, making her neck and shoulders tense.

"Look out! Coming through again!" Billy's call preceded the return of the miniature stampede by seconds, just long enough for Josefa to jump out of the way, Oswald to step back, and Ben to stay put at the well. Boots the cat, Lumpy the dog, a disheveled Polly with her bonnet hanging loose down her back, and a shouting Billy come tearing through. The animals missed the garden plot by inches.

"We had 'em, but Boots got away," Billy shouted over his shoulder as he raced by. The thud of the herd faded until they heard Polly shout, off in the distance, that Boots had jumped in the window and was safely inside the house.

Josefa instinctively met Ben's glance. "Good news," he said, grinning.

"You can say that again."

Oswald stayed silent and, Josefa thought, showed remarkable restraint given what she'd come to know of him so far. Perhaps there was hope for them after all.

"If you are finished here..." he indicated the garden and Ben with a sweep of his arm.

"Yes, there's been enough mischief and work here for more than one day," she said. She knelt to collect her garden tools and place them in her palmetto basket.

"Coming back to the house with us, Ben?" she asked.

He shook his head. "Going to check on the new farm acreage. I want to make sure schedules are ironed out before I head in to start work on the church tomorrow." He ambled off, not actually snubbing Oswald but not including him in the farewell, either.

Josefa rose and balanced her basket on one arm. "Would you like to escort me, gallant knight?" she teased. She reached out her arm in its dirt-smeared sleeve in her best imitation of coy.

Oswald, who had been three-quarters turned away from her, whipped back to face her. The even-tempered man of the past twenty minutes was suddenly impatient.

"Enough of this foolishness, Josefa," he said. "Act like the fashion luminary you float around trying to be."

Josefa was so surprised she nearly dropped her basket. "You're mistaken, Oswald. This girl here, now, is as much me as the young woman of fashion I also am. I like to dress up, and I like to sew, but I'm tough enough to do outdoor work, especially in my dye garden. It all goes together. Like a family has to do on a grove or farm. Every hand does its share."

"Spare me the moral lecture," he said. He stepped close, too close, and she had to squash an impulse to move away.

"Listen to me, for your own sake," he said. "You need to act every inch the lady, at every moment. For that is how you will act as Mrs. Heller. You do want to be Mrs. Heller?"

Josefa watched him with wary eyes.

Without giving her time to reply, he continued, pacing back and forth in a small path as he spoke. "I think we should wed soon. En route to the ceremony in the North. I don't want to wait. Don't blanch. We'll still go through the motions to appease everyone."

"Oswald, you have to talk to my aunt and uncle."

He brushed the idea aside with a wave of his hand. "What are they going to do, say no to a Heller?"

Josefa's shock was almost overcome by a snicker of laughter. He obviously had never come up against the twin pillars of Lupita and Alfredo united in opposition to something.

"They'll be glad to be rid of you," he said. "But, as you wish, I will speak to them."

She stamped out the needle of uncertainty that pricked her. Everyone at the grove had made clear that she was loved, was at home, and was an integral part of the family. But then again, there was her aunt's Texas plan. The dreary idea took root. Perhaps she really was in the way. People sometimes said one thing but believed another. The problem was, no one at the grove acted that way. While Oswald...

"Oswald," she said, suddenly weary of his pretentions. "Please remember I still have six weeks to finish on the apprenticeship."

"You're determined to see that dalliance through to the end?"

Dalliance, her foot. She stood straight and put on as dignified a face as she could, given her work attire and general air of dishevelment.

"To the very end," she said.

"If you insist," he said. "You are not yet my wife and not yet fully subject to my wishes. You'll do well to understand how matters will be in the future. We'll adhere to the Heller way."

Josefa actually felt a little shaky, standing her ground with him as she was. The apprenticeship had been the first bold move she'd taken on her own. It still felt new, like a stiff piece of overly starched collar that hadn't yet softened through wear. Asserting herself with a beau was even more of an unfamiliar fit.

He didn't take her arm as they moved toward the house.

Alfredo was gone to town with Seth, but Lupita more than adequately gave Oswald a dressing down. She had been lying in wait, in fact, and was out the cabin door almost before they reached it.

Josefa was startled to see Oswald accept the mixture of Spanish and English that poured down on him as though it were his due. He pled "unpardonable omission" and "the ignorance of oversight," and blamed his unacceptable actions on his eagerness to wed the beautiful Josefa. He was ever so polite to the small, thunderous woman who made clear she stood poised to ship Josefa off to relatives who would make sure she went from home to church and back again, courted with family present, and wed according to custom.

When it was over, he merely asked for Lupita's blessing and permission to seek Alfredo's approval. Lupita opened and closed her mouth like one of the bass the men pulled from the river. Josefa recognized that something serious was churning in her aunt's mind. But what?

"You'll get my blessing if Alfredo agrees and Josefa is certain she wishes to accept your offer," Lupita finally said.

"I'll take that," Oswald said. He bowed to her and then to Josefa and didn't stick around a moment longer.

"That man has more masks than a mockingbird," Lupita said as they watched him snap his fingers at Bernie and get in the barouche.

"Why did you give in after berating him?" Josefa asked.

"The rich act however they want," Lupita said. "I almost said no, but then I considered. If I said no, it might make him more determined. Tell me, my *sobrina*, does he promise you great things—clothing, jewels, things like that?"

She frowned when Josefa said that yes, he did, and that he also spoke frequently of his wealth, her future as a society lady, and her instability as a guest at the grove.

"Josefa, I see what he offers for your future. But do you understand what it'll mean to step into his society, a way of life so unfamiliar? One that may not accept you? He pushes too hard and is in too much of a hurry to wed. What does his family say? Look what happened to Ben's family. Yes, he told me about it, so sad it is. I said a prayer for his mother, bless her. You must think about all these things, Josefa."

"Oh, I'm sure Oswald's relatives will be fine," Josefa said. "He says he is his own man. You should hear what he told me to expect for my wardrobe and my, what did he call it, my boudoir— my sleeping quarters. Not just a room, but a suite of connected rooms."

Worry lines creased Lupita's forehead.

"Come with me." She took Josefa by the hand, and together they walked to the main house and went inside to find Agnes sewing in a window seat and baby Seth asleep in a cradle by her side.

"No one knows the Bible better than you," Lupita said.

"Actually, Sarah Bight does," Agnes said and smiled, without looking up from her stitches.

"This Oswald pushes too fast for a quick marriage and tries to sway Josefa with his smooth words. What do you say about someone who talks only of his wealth and promises great things?"

Agnes stopped sewing and lowered her embroidery ring to her lap. She picked up her well-marked Bible, which she always seemed to keep near.

"Yes, that's what I wanted," she said in a lowered tone after she searched for a certain place in the book. She looked back at the two women.

"God speaks plainly on this matter. Actually, he warns us. In the book of Esther. Listen."

She began to read, "And Haman recounted to them the splendor of his riches, the number of his sons, all the promotions with which the king had honored him, and how he had advanced him above the officials and the ministers…" She stopped and glanced up. "And we all know what happened to Haman."

Josefa couldn't remember at all what had happened to Haman, or if she had ever known. She knew she would look up the passage herself the minute she retreated to her room. Which, a glimpse of her reflection in the wall mirror told her, should be right about now, before dirt became permanently embedded in her clothes and skin.

* * *

A snifter of brandy by his side, Oswald sat at his rolltop desk and updated his American Protective Association counterparts on his efforts. "Your colleague continues his stealth inroads to make the world safe from Papism," he wrote.

He provided details of his joke of a courtship with the lovely señorita. "I have succeeded in making her think I will marry her," he wrote. "As I expected, she is easily led by the lure of riches. Once I seduce her, she will be ruined, and no other man will have her. That will prevent one more Catholic from breeding, by my way of reckoning. This aspect of my work is most agreeable, despite the girl's inferior class. I have decided to take her as a mistress, and to that end have added urgency to the supposed plan for marriage. It will enable me to secure her alone much sooner.

"Less to my liking is what I have learned through courting, namely, the continued progress among the Papists to build a church in the heart of town, the intrusion of more Papists to the colony, and the welcoming attitude extended to them by many others. I will continue to apprise you of the situation to thwart the rise of superstition among rational men."

Chapter 13

*J*osefa didn't have a chance to look up the story of Esther and Haman until one night at the boarding house early the following week. After poring over the Scripture by the light of twin candles, she understood that in the end, the wicked Haman didn't win. She would ask Father Kenny to elaborate next time he visited and the grove families joined him for Bible study. He always helped her interpret Scripture and apply it to life.

Josefa blew out the candles and crawled under the quilt, cotton bedcover, and clean white sheet, happy about being part of such a strong community of faith. It especially helped when her personal life was in disarray, like now. She looked forward to the first Mass in the new church. Maybe tomorrow she'd go check on the construction. Maybe Ben would be able to break from work. She could bring some cake and lemonade. She felt certain Esmeralda would grant her a longish break. The dressmaker took one every afternoon, didn't she?

Her employer's mysterious absences continued to gnaw at Josefa's curiosity. Maybe she went to pray by herself. But then why would she be so vague about what she did? This thought and so many others floated through Josefa's mind as she snuggled under the bedcovers and felt the night breeze drift through the room. Persimmon Hollow didn't have harmful night vapors like places near water. *Another reason to never leave,* she thought dreamily before falling sleep.

* * *

"How beautiful." Josefa stared at the circular, stained-glass window divided into flower-petal-like panels that depicted images of Jesus and the Nativity and scenes of Mary, Joseph, and other saints. The center circle showed the Eucharist in a monstrance.

"It'll go right there." Ben pointed upward to what was currently open air between the wood framing of the church's short spire. "Just a little above head-high so people will be able to look up at it when going in and out of church. Daylight will shine through and cast colored rays right through the building, up toward the altar."

The window's edging was encased in thick layers of paper, and the large, round glass was placed flat on the ground in a protected corner of the construction site. Ben hoisted it vertical so Josefa could see how sunlight sparkled on the colored pieces that made up the images. He eased it back down on the ground.

"It was delivered just this morning," he said. "I didn't realize it was coming. No one did. One of the new Catholic families in town donated it. Seth talked to them. They thought Father Kenny had told us, and Father Kenny must have thought they had announced it. Nobody knew that nobody knew." He looked at it again. "Adding a window like this is worth the extra work we have to do to make it fit."

He had tied a bandana around his forehead under his hat, which he took off. He wiped his arm across his head. "Another warm one today," he said.

"That's why I brought some lemonade and cake," Josefa said. She picked up the small basket she'd set down while she admired the window. "Do you have time for a break?"

"For you, always," he said. The words sounded natural and unaffected coming from him.

They sat in the shade of a sweetgum whose light green leaves wore the fresh brightness of spring. Josefa set out small plates of pound cake and poured cups of lemonade.

"Yeah, it'll be nice to have good food like this, regular, from now on," Ben said.

"How so?"

"I have to put in some long hours on the church if we're going to meet our deadline of a June finish. Agnes hopes to have the first Mass on the feast of St. Anthony, or if later in the month, St. John the Baptist or St. Peter. The workaround for the window is just part of a long list of things that need to be done. So I'm to board at the Alloways for, oh, a month or so, to be closer to the job site."

"That's wonderful! It'll be like the grove, almost. Although I'm usually so tired in the evening I don't join in much of the conversation or singing or games. Some boarders play cards. Others read or talk. Sometimes someone plays the piano. It'll be fun, Ben!"

He watched her with a curious expression, a little grave. He finished his cake and drank the last of the lemonade, then sat for a while. He leaned against the tree, knees up with his arms resting across them.

"Fun for a while. We'll see. Fanny told me the only space she had was in sleeping quarters attached to the barn, so I won't actually be staying in the main house."

"Yes, several boarders extended their season so they could stay in town for the president's visit," Josefa said. "I take up another room, and Fanny isn't quite finished redoing the two that are empty. Wow, the church and the president's visit, both in June. It's going to be a busy month."

"Between you and me, I don't see how we'll get everything finished here by June. More likely early July. I'm throwing everything I have into it, though, so we'll see. Could have the major work done in June. I'm sure going to try."

"Well, I still have several weeks to go on my apprenticeship. After that, I'll have more time to help with the altar cloths and vestments and other items needed for the sacristy and priests."

"And tend the dye garden." He nudged her with his knee. "We got to make sure no critters go loping through it."

The slight pressure of the touch made her feel far warmer than the day's sun did. Josefa's breath caught in her throat as she struggled to keep the moment light.

"Sure do!" she said brightly, to cover her confusion. She got busy and gathered the plates, jug, and mugs, and paid more attention than needed to their placement in the picnic basket. She stood up.

"I'd rather stay, but I need to get back," she said. "Esmeralda's probably waiting for me. Did I tell you she leaves every afternoon about three o'clock and is gone for about an hour? Every day. And won't say what she does. It's very odd."

"I've seen odder in my time. Probably takes a nap or something," Ben said.

"Hmmm, I never thought of that," Josefa mused. Then she shook her head. "No, she always takes a sack with her, with something inside it. I think food."

"Maybe she's hungry at that time of day."

"You are so practical, Ben. I'm over here dreaming up ideas of her meeting a secret paramour, or hiding a big animal like a panther that eats a lot."

"I'll take the practical. It's gotten me this far, and I don't expect it to fail me in the future." Ben put his hat back on and gave Josefa one of his open looks backed by calm, yet alive, eyes.

"We balance each other out," she said. "You do the practical, and I add the layer of dreaming."

"I know about dreaming, Josefa. I just don't let it get in my way."

She pursed her lips.

"That's why I need you to do it for me," he added. "For both of us."

"A deal," she said. "See you at the Alloways'!"

He nodded and went back to work. Josefa dropped off the basket before continuing on to the dressmaker's for the late afternoon wrap-up. She was stirred by their chat. She could dream. And dream big. For herself. And everyone else.

* * *

By the end of the month, Josefa and Ben fell into an easy pattern of evening camaraderie at the boarding house.

"It's Friday," Fanny announced after dinner as the week drew to a close. "No sewing, letter-writing, or reading tonight. Let's make it a special evening to launch into a busy weekend for just about everyone."

She looked around the parlor where everyone had gathered. "You're going to the grove, correct, Josefa? Ben, you mentioned you'd work all weekend. Tsk. A man needs rest." Turning to the group of five who did everything in a pack, she asked, "And you are still going on the river cruise on the St. Johns down to Enterprise?" They nodded. "Make sure to stop at Blue Spring. You know Coleridge wrote about that spring? Now, where was I? Oh, yes, let's make tonight special. How about a game of charades!"

No one volunteered to go first. Ben finally stepped forward. He pantomimed a man bent, as though carrying a weight on his back. He plodded around the room, keeping his head and gaze lowered toward the ground.

"Elephant!" cried out Imogene Gold, one of the wives. Ben shook his head.

"No! No! Pack mule!" said her sister-in-law, Mabel Gold.

Ben shook his head again. He squatted and pretended to pick up something from the ground and inspect it, and then placed the imaginary item into his pack.

Josefa looked around. Blank stares reflected back at her.

Ben straightened a little and gazed up, with his hand to his forehead, as though searching in the distance for something.

"Christopher Columbus!" someone called out.

Ben grinned and shook his head again. He made moves as though removing a pack, opening it, and drawing out two objects. He then squatted again, peered at the ground, and made as if writing something down.

One of the male guests jumped up, either Wallace or Theodore Gold. Josefa could hardly tell them apart. "I've got it! Dr. Livingstone!"

"No, you're wrong! He's either Lewis or Clark," said his brother.

Ben opened his eyes wide, tilted his head as though considering the suggestions, and then shook his head no again. Everyone started talking at once. Fanny signaled a time-out.

"Our rules say only five guesses, and that was actually six. Do tell, Ben."

He straightened and stuck his hands in his pockets.

"You were close. I was a plant hunter, like Joseph Banks or William Bartram."

"We certainly were close! I say we get some points, right, Theo?" The Gold brothers both jumped up. Josefa saw that Theodore was slightly taller than his brother, Wallace.

"Perhaps half a point," Fanny said, and the others agreed.

Imogene then mimed a geisha pouring tea, Mabel pretended to be a dance hall girl, and Theodore acted as if he were one of the new electric light bulbs—to which Josefa and Ben objected, as they hadn't actually seen one yet. Fanny called a halt for refreshments.

Josefa noted that Penelope Gold was the only one who hadn't joined in the fun. She'd sat quietly, sketchbook closed on her lap, mentally miles away. Her relatives never pushed her to join in anything. They let her sit in her sadness, but they all seemed to protect her.

"How did you know Imogene was a geisha?" Ben asked Josefa, pulling her out of her reverie about the silent young guest.

"I saw a picture in a fashion history book at Esmeralda's," she said. "Just yesterday, in fact. The timing was great."

"You're up next, you know."

"I know. I'm thinking." Josefa was stumped. What could she choose that would challenge such a knowledgeable group?

Darkness had draped over the house by the time they began their second round. Josefa got up and moved to the center of the parlor. She made a sign of the cross, lowered her head, and placed her hands in prayer position. Then she made as if she were petting an animal. She reached out one hand and with the other made a gentle movement as if she had something balanced on the outstretched arm and hand. Finally, she gestured toward the window, where the rising quarter moon hovered in perfect frame.

"Uh, night, animals...," someone muttered in thought.

"But she was praying too," said another.

Ben jumped up. "Animals. Prayer. St. Francis!"

Josefa smiled and curtsied.

"Wait, what was that about the moon?" asked Penelope, the first indication she'd even paid attention to the game.

"St. Francis believed we are all one with everything God created," Josefa said, thinking of talks she'd had with Agnes and the sisters.

"Is that so? Huh, interesting," said Theo.

"I had no idea," said his wife. "Everybody knows of St. Francis. We always just think about his taming animals."

"He didn't tame them as much as respect them," Ben said. He looked at Josefa. "I've been receiving my Sunday school lessons from the Sisters of St. Francis, remember?"

He really did listen, she thought, and not just to her. And he cared about what he heard.

The group called it a night after a few more rounds and a lot more laughter, especially at Wallace's imitation of a pelican flying and catching fish in his beak. That night, Josefa dreamed she was caught in a fishnet and struggling to breathe. A face moved in close. It was Oswald, and there was nothing funny about the laughter on his face.

* * *

Before she knew it, Monday arrived, and Josefa was back at her sewing machine in the dressmaker's shop. Her back protested, and she stretched and straightened her shoulders. Thank goodness it was May, the second of her two months on the job.

"Is everyone at the grove well, dear? Did you enjoy your time there this weekend?" Esmeralda asked from the other side of the room, where she labored over a particularly difficult bodice alteration.

"Yes and yes," Josefa said with some emphasis on a bright tone. She couldn't say she'd had to drag herself back to the shop. The glory of being a dressmaker had dimmed considerably now that she was at the halfway point of the apprenticeship and had a better understanding of what the job entailed.

She removed the skirt panel she'd just stitched and started to thread the cording through the narrow casing she'd sewn, quarter-inch by slow quarter-inch. It had never seemed so tiresome when she worked on her own items or on clothing for a family member. She'd much rather design a gown, make it once, and then move on to something new. Alterations were pure drudgery.

"Oh, I do have some news," Josefa raised her head up. "Oswald came and sat with us Saturday evening. The Stetson dinner is this Friday. This Friday! I thought it'd never get here after the date was pushed back to accommodate the singer's schedule. But now I'm glad for the extra time it gave me."

"Do you have your gown finished? We must get you ready. Oh my, dinner at the Stetsons'!" Esmeralda, who had settled down from her frenetic mode of the first couple of weeks, flew into a circle of concern. "What hat will you wear?" She studied the row of millinery samples on one of the shelves. "This one. No, maybe this one."

"I don't need a new or fancier hat than what I already own, do I?" Josefa asked.

"Of course you need a fancier hat. You will remove it, you know, with your wrap after you enter the house. But you must enter in full attire. There are certain standards, my dear, when you dine at the Stetson mansion."

Butterflies rose in Josefa's stomach. She was excited, but nerves had already started to mount. And it was only Monday.

"I know what," Esmeralda said. "I'll make a schedule. We'll have you fitted, finished, and ready to go with plenty of time to spare. What is on your alteration pile right now? What needs to be finished soon, and who is coming for a fitting this week?"

She spoke as much to herself as to Josefa and started to sort through the orders from clients.

"Oswald said he'd stop by the boarding house tonight or tomorrow to give me, uh, what he termed 'instruction' for how to act."

"Humph. I and Fanny Alloway can provide that for you just fine. Does he think we are backwoods bumpkins? I'm from Philadelphia, too, same as he is. And Fanny moved in the best circles before and during her missionary days."

She continued to study her ledger. "Let's see, I can move this fitting back a day. Yes, then we can do a full dress rehearsal for you." Esmeralda looked up. "You'll get ready here and then go to Fanny's where your gentleman friend will call for you. Will your aunt be assisting?"

"She's a little worried about me attending at all. Says no good can come from someone mixing with people of different stripes. Agnes thinks I can handle myself well with anyone. My aunt says it's not me she's concerned about. But they're both confident of Miss Fanny's chaperonage and will allow me to go and return from the Alloway House. They'll both probably want to help me dress, though."

"Yes, of course. Now hurry, hurry. Finish the day's work as quickly as you can. Where is the dress? How much more is left to do?"

Josefa carefully unfolded the rich fabric of the nearly completed tea gown. She and Esmeralda managed to fit in a few hours' work on it by the time the dressmaker literally ran out of the shop at ten minutes past three. Josefa stared after her, shook her head, and resumed work. She had too much to do to worry about Esmeralda's strange habits, at least today.

Chapter 14

The next evening was the second in a row that Oswald joined the boarding house group for after-dinner recreation. He sat on the sofa, crossed one ankle over his thigh, shifted in his seat, switched legs, and tapped his fingers on the armrest as he and Josefa waited for the others to join them.

"Must we sit with these people again for the entire time? I prefer that we make our excuses as soon as possible," he said.

"It would be poor manners for me to get up and leave," Josefa said. "Besides, the only way my aunt permitted this arrangement was if I stayed close to the boarding house."

"She'd never know."

"I would," Josefa said. "And so would Fanny, which means my aunt would eventually know."

Considering how little she and Oswald seemed to have in common, she preferred to stay within the circle of warmth that had developed among the housemates over the past few weeks. Most of the winter tourist activities had abated, and the out-of-state visitors were eager for company, except for the quiet Penelope. But even she always came downstairs and sat with everyone.

"I can't endure another round of charades and sing-a-longs," Oswald said in a low voice as footsteps signaled the arrival of others.

But there wasn't another round of singing or charades. In fact, Fanny closed the piano lid that had been open, sat down in her favorite parlor chair, and started to pour a round of tea after Estelle brought in the tray. Fanny hummed a little under her breath, glanced around at everyone, smiled to herself, and took her time with the tea.

Oswald shifted again, and again uncrossed one leg, crossed the other one, and upped his tapping to a drumbeat until Josefa gave his hand a pointed look.

"I have a surprise for us all," Fanny said. She picked up her fan from the side table and waved it around her face and neck, then placed it down. "I nearly burst all through dinner from keeping it quiet."

The winter guests exchanged questioning glances. Ben and Oswald looked at Josefa, who shrugged. She looked at Fanny.

"In a minute, in a minute," Fanny said. Her eyes sparkled. "I thought we first could get caught up on the news we didn't have time to discuss at dinner, while we wait for Miss Penn to join us and for Eunice and Clyde."

Estelle, who had left, returned with a small cloth bag that she handed to Fanny.

"Here's what you've been waiting for," Estelle said with a knowing smile, clearly in on whatever Fanny had brewed up.

"Ah, thank you!" Fanny said as she took it. She made no move to open the bag. "Estelle, did I hear you say earlier that progress has been made on land for the school?"

"Yes'm," Estelle said, and her face relaxed into lines of satisfaction and anticipation that had nothing to do with a drawn-out Fanny Alloway surprise. "Mr. Seth, Miss Agnes, the good sisters, and folks at Garfield agree the piece of land that rests between our settlement and the edge of Mr. Seth's property is the ideal location for our schoolhouse. Mr. Seth wants to purchase it and sell it to us for one dollar. We'll be trustees of the corporation that buys the land. A blessed day it'll be when our children have a school to call their own."

"I don't understand," said Josefa. "What school? Where's Garfield? And what about the Academy?"

Estelle cleared her throat. "Well, Garfield is my folks' settlement just south and east of town. Miss Fanny can best explain about the Academy."

Fanny's perennial cheerfulness dampened momentarily.

"Josefa...much as Eunice and I would prefer it to be different, laws in this state right now force the races to be educated separately. The Sisters of St. Francis at the orphanage have offered to help start a school for the children of color in the area."

Oswald exhaled next to Josefa, uncrossed his leg, and lowered his foot with a thud that was drowned out by the sound of Esmeralda entering the house, followed a few moments later by Eunice and Clyde.

"Good news, Eunice!" Fanny called out. "The land next to the grove will house the St. Rita's school the sisters and Estelle's community plan to build."

"I'm trying to place the exact location," Ben said to Estelle. "Mr. Heller's land adjoins Seth's where the railroad tracks curve north before cutting east again. Do you mean the land on the south side of Seth's?"

Estelle put her hands on her hips and pondered for a moment. "Yes, that's right, it is. The land with the old Indian mound on a hill that rises up from the spring on Mr. Seth's land."

"What about that land? Is there other land with mounds on it? Surely you mean another piece of land?" asked Esmeralda sharply as she removed her bonnet. She was a bundle of nerves, more so than usual, Josefa thought.

Everyone turned to look at her.

"Here, let me take that for you, Miss Esmeralda," Estelle said, taking the hat. "I'm certain that's the land Mr. Seth spoke to us about. He and the sisters and the bishop are in the process of contacting the owners and working through legal aspects, I believe."

"Oh, this will never do, not at all," said Esmeralda, but it was as though she spoke to herself. When she realized all gazes were on her, her eyes rounded in surprise.

"Oh, silly me, I must be thinking of some other property. I heard superstitions, is all, you know, about ghosts that might haunt the old Indian property." She laughed, but it was a brittle, high sound.

Josefa didn't believe her excuse for a minute. She had come to know her employer well enough to detect strain behind the attempt at normalcy. Something had upset Esmeralda, and it appeared to be connected to the school land. Josefa had seen her deal with enough demanding customers, torn fabrics, complex clothing constructions, and impossible deadlines to realize that she wasn't the type of woman who upset easily.

"Come, sit with us here," Josefa said to the dressmaker and patted the open spot on the couch next to where she sat with Oswald, who let out another puff of exasperation.

"I'm delighted to hear the school will soon become a reality," Eunice said to Estelle. "We have extra furnishings at the Academy that would probably fit nicely, if you care to have them."

"That's kind of you, Miss Eunice," Estelle said, and then she untied her apron. "Now I know Miss Fanny has cooked up a surprise, but I'm ready to call it a night." She left amid a round of good-byes.

"Just one more thing before I get to the surprise," Fanny said, and the four talkative winter guests protested in unison from the corner of the room where they sat clustered together. Penelope remained impassive.

"Tell us, Ben, how is church construction coming?" Fanny asked, laughingly ignoring the boarders with a cheery wave of her fan at them.

"What, pray tell, is he doing here again tonight?" Oswald leaned over Josefa's shoulder and asked in a voice so low she had to strain to hear it.

"He boards here," Josefa whispered back.

"Here? A single man here in the same place as you, a single woman boarder here alone?"

"Oh, stop," she whispered. "There's no impropriety. Fanny wouldn't permit it. What are you implying?"

Fanny glanced at them with raised eyebrows. Josefa flushed. Oswald looked the other way.

"Ben?" Fanny asked again, and Josefa noticed that Ben had angled himself toward her and Oswald and appeared to have heard everything that occurred between them.

"As good as if God were guiding my hammer, and maybe he is," Ben said. Oswald stood up.

"Stretching my legs," he said in response to the room's unspoken question. He walked over to the window and looked out at the darkened street.

"Whatever happened to the street lights that were to be installed," he asked in an irritated voice as he walked back and sat down.

"Need to check with Mr. Stetson on that one," Clyde answered. "Right now I believe we are hearing about the church. Right, Ben?"

Ben leaned forward and propped his elbows on his knees as he rattled off building lengths, lumber information, and construction progress. Josefa loved how his enthusiasm shone in his eyes. It made them seem even bluer, as if that were possible. His brown hair had streaks of gold from working in the sun, and his lean body looked fit and strong as he gestured to illustrate lengths and distances.

She leaned forward herself, in his direction, as though drawn by an invisible force. She saw Fanny watch her watch him and then glance at Oswald. Josefa straightened and followed the line of Fanny's gaze. Oswald met her eyes with a narrowed set of his own. She leaned back and felt as though air were being let out of her.

"And finally," Ben wrapped up, "we received an incredible, and I mean incredible, oval stained-glass window from one of the new Catholic families in town, and it is going to be a highlight of the entire building. Josefa, tell them. You've seen it. Isn't it grand?"

She leaned forward again. "Oh, you have no idea," she said to the others. "It has pictures of Mary, Jesus, the Holy Family…"

"…that are examples of fine workmanship…" added Ben

"…in the most beautiful colors…" Josefa said.

"…that do the Lord justice when the sun sends its rays on it," Ben finished.

Their gazes met, and a sense of warmth and wonder filled Josefa.

"Sounds like the Catholic community has something to be proud of," Fanny said. "Why, it's something all of Persimmon Hollow can be proud of!"

Oswald stood up again. He bowed to Josefa and then to the room in general. "Please accept my apologies. I recall that I left some business unattended, and I should get back to it."

"Oh, but you'll miss the surprise!" Fanny cried. "Wait, here it is." She opened the little cloth bag that had sat on her lap the entire time, and pulled out a book.

"You got a copy of *A Study in Scarlet* here in tiny Persimmon Hollow?" Wallace Gold exclaimed. "By Arthur Conan Doyle? How did you manage that? I heard about it when it came out last year, but I haven't even read it yet up North."

Fanny nodded, enjoying his astonishment and sharing the moment with Eunice and Clyde. Ben and Josefa looked at each other and shrugged. Esmeralda only paid half-attention, and Oswald gave in to irritation and started to open the door.

"Oswald, will you be coming into town again tomorrow or...?" Josefa started to ask, but the look on his face stilled her. His eyes reflected anger. Not at her, she realized. Not really at anyone in the room. Yet it was there to see, plain as could be.

"I will be here to escort you to the Stetson dinner Friday evening as planned, and sooner if possible," he said. "Good night, all."

After he left, the others settled down as Fanny began to read. Josefa rested her head against the back of the sofa and tried to listen. But her mind soon wandered, to her outfit for Friday, the perplexing question of Esmeralda's behavior, the altar cloths needed for the new church, and the new information about a school for children who couldn't attend the Academy.

Fanny was a good reader, but Josefa's eyes soon drooped. She closed them and then felt something draped across her lap. She opened her eyes to see that the afghan from the back of the couch now covered her lap. Ben was re-seating himself as she looked, and she caught his friendly "oops, caught me" look and his warm smile before closing her eyes again. She lingered briefly in that suspended space between wakefulness and sleep, and then sank into the security of her surroundings.

She awoke with a start.

"Sorry, Josefa...I tried to be quiet." Ben was walking through the now-darkened, empty parlor.

"How long was I asleep? Where is everyone?" she asked. She sat up, surprised, and heard the grandfather clock chime three times.

"You were sleeping so soundly that Fanny said to leave you," Ben said. "Everyone turned in hours ago. I was asleep but woke up hungry and couldn't settle down again. I came back in to get something to eat." He held up a napkin-covered plate filled with shapes she couldn't discern in the dark, and a cup.

"It's such a nice night I'm going to eat on the front porch," he said. "Now I've gone and woken you. Go back to sleep. I'll be quiet."

"No, no, that's OK," Josefa said. She stretched her arms above her head and released the hold with a shrug of her shoulders. "I must have been more tired than I thought." She yawned. "I know Fanny was excited about that book, but I guess I needed the sleep more than the story."

"It was actually pretty good," he said. "Detective story about a character named Sherlock Holmes."

Fully awake now, Josefa got up. "Mind if I join you outside?" she asked after she looked out the window. The nearly full moon flooded the yard and the quiet town with shadows and light. "It's a pretty night."

"Sure is and sure would like it," Ben said and held open the door for her.

She sat down on the porch swing, and Ben settled in beside her after placing the cup on the small round side table. He put the plate on his lap and pulled the napkin off the top.

"Carrots?" Josefa laughed. "I expected cookies or maybe a slice of pound cake."

"End of the season for these," he said as he picked one up and took a crunchy bite. The snap rang through the night. "They're so good right from the garden, and once these are gone, we'll have to wait months for the weather to be right again. Everything tastes so good right from the ground, you know?"

"Uh, I never really thought about it," Josefa admitted. She was more than happy to dwell on it now, though, to take her mind off him, his closeness, sturdiness, solidness, the way she wanted to slip closer, the way she wanted him to set aside the plate and put his arm around her and pull her to him.

Josefa put her hands up to her face to cool the flush she felt there despite the balm of the night's gentle breeze.

Ben stayed focused, too focused, on the food.

The night wrapped around them in shades of silver, gray, and white. The shadowed streets were empty. Only the buzzes and croaks of crickets and tree frogs broke the stillness, until a cross between a long chirp, whistle, and hiss merged into something akin to a cry, in a nearby tree. Within seconds, a responding call sounded from another tree.

Ben stopped crunching, carrot stick in midair. Josefa craned to look at the tree from which the first sound emerged. The calls had become a chorus, and the distance between them closed.

"Found 'em! Right there." Ben pointed with a carrot toward the outstretched limb of a longleaf pine several feet from the side of the porch. Josefa made out the silhouettes of two owls, side by side.

"Owlets," he whispered. "That's their fledgling call. It means they're hungry and want food. The parents are teaching them how to find it on their own."

"Just listen to them," she said. "And look how they stay together."

"Yeah, they're young," he said. "Haven't yet struck out for their own territories."

"I never would have found them if you hadn't pointed them out," Josefa said. "I wouldn't have been out here at all, probably." She hugged herself. "Glad I am, though. It's so beautiful, so quiet, so different than in daytime. The porch has become like another world. Just ours. Well, ours and the owls'."

"Maybe they caught the scent of the carrots." He chuckled.

"Right," she said drily and laughed with him.

Then she added, "Shhh. We'll wake everyone, especially Fanny. Her bedroom is only a couple of rooms away. I'm kind of surprised she's not awake already."

"OK, I'll be quiet," he said cheerfully.

They rocked and listened to the night sounds.

"Ben, how did you learn so much about the natural world?"

"My dad," he said.

She touched his arm. "I'm sorry. I remember you said he died when you were younger."

With his foot, he pushed against the floor and propelled the porch into a harder swing.

"Sure you don't want any before I set it down?" He held out the plate to her, and she took a carrot stick. The cool, sweet flavor and crisp texture woke up her mouth.

"This is a new one. I'd have never thought I'd be snacking on raw vegetables in the middle of the night on the porch swing," she said. *With you,* she didn't say.

"Some of my favorite times of day and night are the off-hours," Ben said, placing the plate on the table. "You can be alone with your thoughts, with the world, with God. At least I can. Feel close to God, I mean." He trailed off, keeping up the steady rhythm of the swing.

"I learned the most from my dad at times like that," he added.

"You miss him."

Ben nodded.

"Mind if I ask more about how he died? Had he been gone long on his trip?"

Ben shifted so that he halfway faced her, but he kept his hands on his thighs. The swing slowed to a gentle rock. Josefa clasped her hands in her lap in a tight hold, as though afraid they would reach out for his on their own volition.

"He would often be gone for months when an expedition set out," Ben said. "Other times, he would be home for months and would give lectures, write, that sort of thing. He hadn't been feeling well before the last expedition, but didn't want to pass up the chance to search for new species in China. The expedition was cut short after he died."

Ben grew quiet again, and the porch glided to a halt.

"I had looked forward to going on expeditions with him. I guess that's why I won't rest until I can someday follow in his footsteps. I can feel what drew him with such intensity, and I have to try it for myself."

Josefa swallowed hard.

"You're set on it, aren't you? It's that important?"

He shifted some more, and moonlight cut across his face in a way that picked up the gleam of excitement in his eyes.

"There's such a freedom to it, Josefa. A man feels alive. He's one in nature, forging a new path, and with some luck, making a discovery at the end of the trail. Or discoveries. Pushing the borders. Finding new boundaries."

This time, Josefa was the one who started the swing in motion.

"Don't you ever want a home and family?" she asked.

"Someday, I guess." He looked at her with an almost questioning expression. "Not sure I want to put a family through what mine went through, much as I loved my dad, and as much as my mom and sister loved him. Love him. We all still do. Always will. It was a life of uncertainty a lot of the time. Anyway, I don't have anything to offer a wife right now."

Except yourself, she thought.

"I admire how you look after your mother and sister," she said.

"Thanks. I appreciate it."

The swing stilled, and Josefa felt a little shiver of excitement. How she could love him, if only. If only he...no, stop, she told herself.

"I appreciate you, too, Josefa," he said in a lower, quieter tone.

She kept her gaze down. She didn't trust herself, afraid that if she looked at his face she'd give away feelings she wouldn't acknowledge even to herself. She couldn't. There was no future here with him, him and her together. He'd just said as much himself. Said what she knew already. Part of her wished Benjamin Stillman had never walked into her life. Another part of her knew that was a lie.

She stared at Ben's square, strong, capable hands. He held them palm down, resting on his thighs, fingers splayed apart. Strong, a little rough, with some nicks and scratches, but clean, with nails clipped short. Hands that could carry the weight of anything she would ever need to place in them.

Then she looked at her own. Small, slim, with neatly groomed oval nails and narrow wrists. And right now intertwined as though able to squeeze out the angst in her heart.

Suddenly, one of his large, strong hands lifted from his thigh and moved to cover her own. Completely covered her two clasped hands. Her head jerked up, and she heard her breath catch in her throat—and prayed he hadn't noticed.

She tried to form words, but nothing came through. Her lips were dry as she opened and then closed them and swallowed.

Slowly, as though time had slowed in the middle of the silver night, Ben raised her entwined fingers to his lips and gave them a gentle yet hot kiss. He set her hands down just as gently, but kept his hand atop them, and the slight pressure burned into her.

She followed the movement with her gaze. Even the owls had quieted, and the breeze faded. Only the crickets and frogs kept up their background calls.

Josefa closed her eyes and sat as still as the silent town, unwilling to move, unsure what to do next.

A groan escaped Ben. He shifted, and without warning, his arms were around her shoulders, and then down her body, and she was in his arms, and his mouth was on hers. Her hands came up instinctively, and she ran them over his chest, his muscled arms, his back. Her fingers combed through the curling edges and up the length of his hair. Her lips responded with a will of their own as she yielded to his pull and folded herself into the delicious sensation of his mouth, his body, and his scent.

Long moments later, the kiss drew to a silky close that left them both breathing hard as they broke apart and stared at each other. Something had shifted. A new intensity had surfaced, a subtle but strong shift in the balance of what had been a growing friendship and what could be a passionate love.

His gaze burned with a hunger she hadn't seen before. She yearned to lean into that feeling and explore where it could take them.

"You are one special woman, Josefa," Ben said.

"And you. You're a special man, Ben."

He stroked her hair lightly and trailed a finger down her face as she let her fingers splay across his chest. Shifting shadows overtook moonlit spaces as clouds drifted and tumbled above them.

"We have to forget this ever happened," she forced herself to say for reasons she didn't want to think about.

He nodded and didn't contradict her. But his Adam's apple went up and down in a noticeable swallow, as though she'd said something distasteful.

"I should apologize," he said. "But I'm not sorry." He squared his back against the seat and drew her close next to him.

"Me either. It was special. Just between us." She rested her head on his shoulder, and his arm around her tightened.

"Yeah, just between us."

The screen door flew open, and Fanny stood there, hands on her hips. "What in mercy's name is going on out here?"

Josefa and Ben jumped apart as though a fire had been doused with a bucket of cold water. Fanny stood there in astonishment, a wrapper hastily secured around her ample middle, her face reflecting shock and disappointment.

"Uh, er, nothing, Miss Fanny," Ben jumped up. "I…"

"Well, I never! Whatever has come over you two? I left Josefa asleep on the sofa because she was so exhausted, but I never in all my life expected…were you embracing before I came out? I declare! You, Josefa, so involved with Mr. Heller…and you, Ben, such an upstanding young man with big plans for a future. Oh dear, where is my fan?" She looked around, but none of her fans were anywhere in sight.

Josefa and Ben shared one quick glance before Josefa stood up.

"Get inside now, Josefa, this minute," Fanny said and shooed her toward the door before she could explain anything. "Your aunt left you in my care and you...you disregard my good intentions. Oh, mercy me."

She turned her attention to Ben. "You, off to the barn. Now." She waved him away.

Josefa scooted inside followed by Fanny, who tut-tutted at every step. Once inside, she patted the sofa as Josefa made toward the staircase.

"Not so fast," Fanny said. "Not only am I shocked at the behavior I witnessed, I'm upset that you betrayed my trust in you."

Josefa wondered just how much Fanny had seen and heard.

"Now," Fanny continued, "I want to hear exactly what is going on. The two young people I just saw together were as close as only courting couples should be when near marriage. I could feel the...uh...emotions all the way across the porch. When I see you with Oswald, you are stiff and he is proud, and I sense distance between you. My dear, you mustn't toy with men or your family and friends. You've led us all to believe Oswald and his grand life is your preference."

Josefa felt her misery hang in her eyes. Her heart ached. She hadn't wanted to cross that chasm of friendship with Ben. And also had wanted to, with a fierceness. Now it had happened. Crossing it forced her to face the coldness of Oswald and his barely concealed disdain for Persimmon Hollow, her religion, and her family. He was remote, and her likely future. Ben was warm, intense, and bound for places unknown and fortunes uncertain. He hadn't offered anything to hold on to, nothing at all. Just the opposite, in fact. Yet there was something so real there, as real as her time with Oswald felt forced.

Was she wrong in this plan of hers? Was God trying to tell her something by putting doubts in her way? Did a woman have to give up her heart to ensure she would be cared for in life? Was the alternative a life of endless work at a sewing machine? Young as she was, Josefa knew people couldn't live on love alone.

She pushed away the confusion, already agitated by the night's events and unable to cope with the burden of questions she couldn't answer. She focused instead on Fanny's worried, concerned face.

"I'm not sure what to think or what to do," she whispered.

"I know, honey. I can tell. But you must be careful. Men can get carried away, quite quickly."

Josefa shook her head. "Ben didn't take any liberties, or try to take any. That kiss surprised him as much as it did me."

"You kissed?" Fanny put a hand to her chest. So she hadn't been standing at the doorway the entire time, Josefa noted.

"Uh...just a small one," Josefa said. "It just happened. I welcomed it, Fanny."

"Have you kissed Oswald?"

Josefa stifled an involuntary shudder, but Fanny saw it. "No."

Fanny's sharp gaze forced her to acknowledge that kissing Oswald wasn't something she looked forward to. She was more interested in the clothes he spoke of her wearing, the jewels, the... Josefa felt small and superficial.

"You have some thinking to do, Josefa, for your sake and everyone else's."

"I know."

"Now get up to bed. We will talk more later, when the sun is shining."

"Fanny, can I ask you a favor? Please don't tell Agnes or especially my aunt about this, at least not yet. I need to think. Please give me some time to sort this all out."

Fanny pursed her usually merry lips. "You know I dislike keeping secrets, and a matter of this magnitude begs for the wisdom of all the older women you love and trust. You are too important. Marriage is too important. Why this request for secrecy?"

Josefa took in a long breath and told her the true reason, if not the entire one.

"It's only for a few days. Just until after the Stetson dinner. I want to see how that night turns out, to see how I...we...Oswald are in such a setting. Sometimes I feel Oswald is inconsiderate of me. Yet he dangles fancy homes, clothes, security, travel, everything in front of me. I've heard that women sometimes marry for reasons other than love. I'd just like to think and pray about this and then talk with Lupita and Agnes."

Compassion crossed Fanny's face.

"The trials of young womanhood can be heavy indeed," she said. "That's why Lupita and Agnes are exactly the people to whom you should speak. Since the dinner is only a few days away, I'll honor your request. But immediately afterward, we will march out to the grove and air the linen, so to speak."

Josefa opened her mouth to protest.

"Don't even try," Fanny said and patted her arm. "Go get some sleep. It's already almost dawn."

* * *

As Josefa had napped on the sofa, Oswald had ridden bareback out of town at a rapid clip. The night air was cool, and the stars dim against the bright moonlight. He slowed only after he reached the shanties near the river. The door was ajar on the largest one at the end. Shouts, laughter, and the clink of mugs spilled out from inside. He dismounted, entered, and strode through the thick cigar and pipe smoke that hung in the murky light of the kerosene lanterns. He waded through the men and assessed the faces of the ones standing at the bar, shooting pool, and playing cards. He finally stopped at a lone figure at the end of the bar. The man was nearly as wide as he was tall.

"Are you the one named Barrel?" he asked.

"Depends on who's asking, boss man," the man answered.

"You fit the description. Let's go outside. I want to talk to you, and I don't intend to shout over the swill in here." Oswald pointed with his thumb toward the door. Without waiting for an answer, he strode out through it.

"Fine with me, boss man," Barrel said and followed after him. "Stench in here is rank, anyway."

Oswald waited in the shadows.

"I have a job for you," he said.

"I figure you can pay handsome by the looks of you, but I aim to see cash first," Barrel said. "I ain't no fool. What kind of job you talking about?"

"Can you be trusted?"

"I'm a man of my word, yes sir. What about you?"

"Don't have the temerity to question me. Listen and listen good. I want you to accidently make sure a fire takes down the Papist church that's being built in town."

"The one them Catholics are putting up? After all them bake sales and benefits?"

"Yes, that one."

"I dunno. Don't feel right, messing with God's house."

"You are a coward?"

"I ain't no coward!" Barrel bristled. "It ain't just that it's a church. It's a church being built by folks I done wrong to in the past. I dunno. Don't seem right."

"You expect me to believe you have developed a conscience?" Oswald asked.

"Things got mixed up last time. I didn't like the way the job messed with women and children. Now this here job is kinda gonna mess with them again. Ain't ya got something better? Like maybe you want me to lift some fencing, do some cattle rustling?"

"I have no idea what you are referring to by 'last time,' nor do I care. I will pay you one hundred dollars cash to make sure a fire accidently starts and burns that infernal church down. Make sure the round window melts."

Barrel's eyes widened at the dollar amount. The two men squared off and took one another's measure.

After long moments, Barrel shifted his gaze away.

"It's the church being built with money raised by that school-marm who married the guy who has an orange grove, ain't it?"

"That's an apt description," Oswald said.

Barrel shook his head. "It's a sad day when I turn down cold hard cash, but I tell you, this don't feel right. No. I'm through messing with the wrong stuff. No jobs involving women or children. Nothing involving God. I got my standards."

Oswald stared at him. "You refuse?"

Barrel looked mournful. "I reckon I do."

Chapter 15

*E*smeralda fixed the Closed sign on the door and turned to the expectant faces crowded around her.

"Now we can really begin!" she said and ushered Agnes, Lupita, Fanny, Polly, and Josefa to the small back room sectioned from the main workspace by a curtain.

Josefa thrilled anew at the sight of her gown on the body form. "Isn't it the most beautiful dress ever?" she asked.

Esmeralda swirled into action before anyone answered. "Now, as I see it, we have"—she glanced at the clock—"two solid hours to get you dressed, make the final tucks and stitches, do up your hair, and have you practice walking again in the shoes. Then we'll have to get you around the corner to Fanny's without any dust or sand marring any aspect of this magnificent outfit. What time is that man calling for you? Oh, yes, at seven. I remember. All right, first, Josefa, try on the dress so I can do the final inspection. Then take it off and give it to…"

She looked at the assembled women. "Do any of you know how to press this delicate fabric?"

"I did many an ironing at the orphanage I grew up in," Agnes said and fingered the richness of the gown. "With so many people, we had to iron daily." She brushed a hand across the gown. "What is this fabric?"

"Silk satin brocade," Josefa said. "I couldn't believe when Esmeralda brought it out of a storage trunk as 'just a remnant' that would transform me into a princess for the Stetson dinner."

"Like Cinderella," said Polly. "Do you turn into a pumpkin after midnight?"

"She is to be back by or before midnight, or she doesn't go," Lupita huffed. "A dinner in Persimmon Hollow lasting past midnight? What kind of people are these?"

"They're important," Josefa said.

"In their own minds," Polly said, low, but not so low that Josefa couldn't hear.

"Stop! Don't begrudge me this fabulous opportunity."

"I don't!" Polly protested. "I just don't see what the big deal is. Why not just wear one of the dresses you already have? They're pretty. You already have more clothes than anyone I know. It's like you have to impress those people. Why? People are people."

Agnes and Lupita exchanged glances while Josefa stood near the gown covetously.

"It is indeed beautiful," Agnes said. "But the person who's going to wear it is the true beauty—the body and soul beauty."

Josefa only half heard. She was too busy imagining the entrance and picture she would make in the Stetson mansion. To think, she would be inside that grand house, larger even than Oswald's.

"Are you in love with the dress or with the person who will escort you when you wear it?" Lupita asked.

Why, oh, why did her aunt always have to force an issue? Josefa didn't want to think about it. Couldn't they just focus on the dress for now?

"Ladies, just wait until you see Josefa in this garment," Esmeralda said, taking charge again. "She truly looks like a princess. Let's get started." She scurried to collect pins, needles, scissors, and measuring tape. She put two flat irons atop the small laundry stove on the other side of the room.

Josefa stepped behind the three-panel screen. She changed into a clean chemise and drawers and put on the stiffer corset Esmeralda had laid on a chair. She stepped out.

"Lace it as tightly as you can," she said to Agnes and Lupita, who adjusted the stays.

"Tighter," Josefa said.

"You know, I fainted once because my stays were too tight," Agnes said. "When I hardly knew Seth—and at his house, no less. We were bringing Billy back after he stayed with us at the Alloway House. I hardly knew anyone in Persimmon Hollow yet."

"I remember that day," Fanny said. "You gave us quite a scare. We had brought a picnic lunch and were eating outdoors. Hmm, yes, I remember, too, thinking that day how you and Seth looked so good together. When you were standing, that is."

"The point is, Josefa, you don't want to faint at the dinner," Agnes said.

"Horrors," said Polly.

Agnes tightened the laces a bit more and tied them off.

"Won't they go any tighter?" Josefa asked.

"That's tight enough," Lupita said. "Let's see this dress on you."

Esmeralda tied on the bustle and then helped Josefa step into the dress. The dressmaker pulled, tweaked, draped, and adjusted folds of the ivory fabric and made a few stitches to further hold the silk tulle that accented the neckline, cuffs, and bodice.

Josefa stepped into the heeled satin slippers and did a twirl.

The room went silent.

"*Dios Mio*, you really do look like a princess," Lupita said. Fanny dabbed at her eyes. She was unusually quiet, and Josefa suspected why. Her heart did an unexpected skip when she wished Ben could see her right now.

"I was about to say that dress looks like it was made for you," Agnes said. "But it was." She pulled Polly into a hug at her side. "The ivory color makes your skin glow."

"I like the fern pattern in the fabric," Polly said. She broke free of the embrace. "I like how you have to look close to even see it. But, still, it's just a dress."

"It is more than that!" Esmeralda said. "We designed it based on a dress by Monsieur Worth himself that we saw in *Harper's*. Josefa will outshine every other woman at the dinner. OK, now, out of the gown," she said to Josefa. "Put your robe on, and let your aunt fix your hair while I make the final stitches and we press the folds one more time."

An hour later, Josefa strolled back and forth in the room to get a good feel for the shoes, the dress, and the unaccustomed topknot and ringlets. Esmeralda placed a delicate hat on her head at an angle.

"I guess I'm ready," Josefa said, wishing her insides felt as fixed and solid as her outside did. For all her excitement over the impending evening, she couldn't settle the small knot of nerves.

"You march out there and act as though you dress like this all the time," Esmeralda ordered.

"Agreed," Agnes said. "And carry the love of the Lord with you. We are all one in God's eyes."

"You stand tall. No one is better than my Josefa," Lupita pronounced.

"But let's hurry," Fanny said in a rush as she looked at the clock. "He'll be calling in fifteen minutes. We must get to the house."

Esmeralda wrapped a duster around Josefa as the others picked up her day dress and shoes and made haste to leave. "Have a perfectly wonderful evening," the dressmaker called after them.

Josefa's stomach knot grew as they entered the Alloway parlor, where the two Gold brothers were deep in a game of backgammon. Their wives weren't with them, but their sister sat off to one side, sad and quiet, her sketchbook closed on her lap and her gaze fixed on something beyond the window. Josefa, who felt every inch the sovereign, felt sad for Penelope and made a mental note to ask Fanny if she knew the reason for the young woman's melancholy.

The brothers looked up, and in their haste to rise and bow to Josefa, they knocked over the game board. Josefa wasn't accustomed to such a reaction. And was unsure whether she liked it. She felt a little bit unreal, as though a different Josefa had formed along with the exquisite dress, by far the most elaborate she had ever worn. Esmeralda had helped her apprentice create a couture masterpiece.

"It's just me," Josefa said to the brothers, who continued to gape. Penelope looked over and nodded a hello, but the sight of Josefa only seemed to make her more pensive.

The awkwardness ended with the knock on the door. Fanny opened it to see Oswald. As if by prearranged signal, Agnes, Lupita, and Polly scooted into the kitchen but left the door slightly ajar.

"Come in," Fanny said and stepped back as he entered. Josefa felt Fanny's gaze on her as she glided forward to meet Oswald.

He gave her outfit a once-over, raised his eyebrows in appreciation, and bowed lower than usual.

"Quite nice," he said and then held out his arm, stiffly formal.

"Quite nice? Is that all he can say?" huffed Polly as she peered through the slight crack in the kitchen door. "I'd rather see her go with Ben than him."

"I don't believe Ben was invited to the dinner," Agnes said from where she sat at the kitchen worktable with Lupita. "Josefa is stepping out into Persimmon Hollow's high society."

"And I pray she doesn't lose herself there," Lupita said softly. "Dear Lady of Guadalupe, please watch over her and guide her."

"Yes, please," Agnes murmured. She took Lupita's hand and beckoned to Polly to join them. Together, the three clasped hands. "Mother Mary, protect and guide our fragile butterfly Josefa. Keep her in your heart, watch over her, and above all guide her toward your Son, that she may know and remember what is true and important in life, and what is false."

"Amen," Lupita said.

They heard the front door close. Fanny came into the kitchen moments later.

"I'm worried for her, that she is blinded by his wealth and stature," Fanny said as she sat down with them.

"So are we," Agnes said.

"Now you see why I tried so hard to send her to Texas," Lupita said. "I should have pushed more to make her go. She will be lost if she looks to things of the world for happiness. And that man does his best to make her think she needs only money and things. I don't have a good feeling about this. Even the apprenticeship is trouble, although the reality of the work has opened my niece's eyes somewhat. But she spends less time with us at the grove. The sisters and orphans miss her. She used to join them for prayers every day, and now she is here in town all the time." Lupita heaved a sigh. "I miss her."

They were startled by a knock on the kitchen door that led to the back yard.

"Who is it?" Fanny called. "I'm not expecting anyone," she whispered to the others.

"Oswald Heller."

Lupita and Agnes sat up to attention, and Polly bounced out of her chair as Fanny bustled over to open the door.

"Pardon my intrusion," he said. "I must be quick, as Josefa awaits me in the carriage." He was in front of Lupita in a few steps.

"I have something to bring to your attention because of my regard for your niece," he said, the soul of concern. "You may wish to know that she resides here"—he glanced at Fanny for a moment—"with an unmarried man as a fellow boarder. That is all. Good evening." He half-bowed and left them with their mouths hanging open.

Fanny sputtered as she sat back down. "Well, I never! How dare he impinge on the propriety of my house."

"Is a single man staying here?" Agnes asked.

"Ben has taken to boarding here temporarily," Fanny said. "But he stays in the sleeping lean-to attached to the barn, not in the main house. I allow no shenanigans in my house."

But her face flushed as she spoke.

"Oh, we know that," Agnes said and reached for her hand.

"No, no, you don't," Fanny said and started to get out of breath.

"That man brings nothing but trouble, and I don't mean Ben," Lupita said. "He should go back to Philadelphia or wherever he is from. All the same, I will bring Josefa back to the grove right away tonight when she returns. We all saw what an angel she looked like. It's not Josefa I don't trust, but she's too young and too immature to know how to handle certain situations. She should live at home."

"She's not gonna like that," Polly warned.

"Too bad," said Lupita. "I don't like this."

"Fanny, are you feeling well?" asked Agnes. Fanny's face had grown pinker and pinker, and her fluttering fan made little difference despite stirring up a breeze brisk enough to send tendrils of her short curly hair flying around her face.

"Oh, I am about to burst!" she declared.

"What?" Agnes asked. "Tell us."

Lupita laid a hand over Fanny's arm.

"We're here," she said. "Are you feeling ill? Feverish?"

Polly looked from one to the other, perplexed.

"I don't understand grownups," she said to no one in particular.

Fanny let out a puff of a sigh and set down her fan.

"I promised Josefa we would tell you together tomorrow, but I must break that confidence. Oh, I feel awful. Oh, that poor child."

Lupita's concern turned to alarm. She rose and inhaled.

"What has my niece done?" Her lips were taut and eyes wary.

"Oh dear, oh dear, oh mercy." Fanny set down her fan and twisted her hands in her lap.

Now Agnes was up, and she started to pace.

Polly's eyes grew larger and rounder with every passing minute.

"I found them—" Fanny began.

"Who?" Lupita interrupted. "Josefa and Señor Heller?"

Fanny shook her head. "No." She inhaled again.

"I woke up the other night and came out to refill my water glass. It was past three a.m. I thought I heard noise on the porch but wasn't certain. You know my hearing has been growing troublesome."

"Yes," nodded Lupita with impatience. Agnes kept up her small oval pattern of pacing.

"And I found...I found... Josefa and..."

Lupita blessed herself and started to pray aloud in a voice that overwhelmed Fanny's. "Dear Lady, prepare me to receive and carry my cross no matter the burden..."

"I found Josefa and Ben embracing in the front porch swing!"

Lupita closed her mouth. Agnes stopped pacing. Polly grinned and glanced upward.

"You can imagine how taken aback I was," Fanny said. "Rest assured I reprimanded the two of them soundly and shooed Ben out of the house."

She relaxed back into her seat a few inches. "Mercy! I am so relieved to be rid of that secret. It has burdened my soul these past few days."

She leaned forward toward Agnes and Lupita. "Let me assure you they weren't in a tight embrace, and frankly, I believe I stepped onto the porch before anything occurred. They were seated very closely together and sprang apart as soon as they heard the squeak of the door. They did, uh, mention a kiss."

"This is a surprise," Agnes said and flopped down in a chair. "It could have been worse, I suppose. She knows better than to let herself...how did they both end up there, anyway, at such a time of night?"

Lupita drew her brows together. "What night was it? When did it happen?"

"A couple days ago, midweek." Fanny fleshed out the details of the encounter, including Josefa's plea for Fanny to remain silent long enough for Josefa to go to the Stetson dinner.

"Humph," grunted Lupita. "That's because she knows I would have withdrawn permission for her to attend." She crossed her arms over her chest. "To think, she has been spinning dreams about this Señor Heller. *Dios Mio*, he has even asked for her hand."

"Did she actually say yes?" Polly said.

Lupita and Agnes looked at each other.

"I think it's a matter of, she didn't say no," Agnes said slowly, as though in thought.

"If you ask me, she's in love with Ben," Fanny said. "I've watched them during evening parlor gatherings since he started staying here. She doesn't seem to admit it to herself, and neither does he."

"As Lupita has already said, I'm beginning to think Josefa is in love with the idea of Oswald Heller and his wealth, and not with the man himself," Agnes said.

Lupita tapped her fingers on the table. "I will wait here. The minute she walks into this house she is being carted back to the grove."

"She may be out rather late," Fanny said. "The Stetsons keep fashionable hours. I don't believe the dinner even starts until eight, at the earliest. Then there is the musical recital afterwards."

Now it was Fanny's turn to pat Lupita's hand. "No need to fret, Lupita. I asked Bernie to be eagle-eyed and -eared, and to make sure Josefa is never out of his sight when being escorted to and from dinner by Mr. Heller. Other than when they are inside the mansion, I mean." Her cheeks regained their normal pinkness.

"You are welcome to stay," she told them all. "But I'd be happy to bring Josefa out to the grove first thing tomorrow morning."

Agnes glanced at Lupita, then shook her head. "I recognize the set of Lupita's lips," she said to Fanny. "Josefa will step out of the carriage, into the house, and straight into the immovable block of an angry aunt. I'd like to stay, but the baby will need me soon. Polly and I will have to return to the grove long before Josefa's night ends."

"Have some tea first," Fanny offered. She got up and moved the teakettle to the warmest place on the stove, then checked the wood box. "It'll only take a few minutes to heat up. Estelle banked the fire before she left, but there are plenty of embers. Did I mention that Bernie's enthusiasm over the new school in his neighborhood is infectious? So many people are excited about it, although I've had to explain a number of times about the laws of this state and why we need a separate school. If women had the vote, I'm sure we wouldn't have such nonsense. How close do you think the land purchase is to being completed?"

She prattled on as she set out teacups, sugar cone, tongs, tea tin, and strainer and started to slice a lemon.

"I don't know," Agnes said as she helped Fanny set out some leftover slices of pie from the pie safe. "There seems to be some question about ownership of the land. We may have to find another parcel, although that one is in the ideal location. It appears someone filed and proved a claim on it a while ago."

"On that parcel of dense woods? Anyone can see with their own two eyes that there's been no improvement, at least not recently," Fanny said.

"Billy saw somebody there," Polly said from the other side of the room, where she inspected hanging rows of dried datil peppers. "At least he thinks he did. He wasn't too sure. Especially cause he could of sworn the movement and noise was up in a tree."

Agnes frowned. "We don't swear in the Taylor household."

Polly gave an exaggerated sigh. "I mean he was surprised."

"Perhaps the men should go take a close look out there," Agnes said.

"Anything to help move the school project forward," Fanny said. "There is a dire need for that facility."

Lupita didn't join in the exchange. Rather, she talked to herself. "It is one misstep too many," she muttered. "Alfredo has to come around to my way of thinking, this time." She glanced up at the others. "I knew I was right from the beginning. Josefa will be on her way to relatives in Texas before the new moon rises."

Agnes, Polly, and Fanny all started to protest, but Lupita shook her head. "You see how headstrong she can be. I fear for my beloved niece. She is on the road to trouble. I must stop her and protect her."

Chapter 16

*O*utside, Oswald climbed back in the carriage. "Just wanted to check what time I should have you back," he said smoothly to Josefa's questioning look as he signaled for Bernie to start driving.

"They set your curfew at half past midnight," he lied. "Although I pressed for a later hour. It shows ill breeding to leave before the hostess signals an end to the evening."

Josefa's nerves tightened again. There was much to know about how to act. Esmeralda had drilled her in dinner etiquette and social niceties for the past week. Oswald had issued instructions whenever he visited. When to speak, when not, which fork to use, when to use it, when not to eat, how much to sample…everything rattled in Josefa's head as she tried to remember it all. Worse, she had to pretend the odd rules came naturally to her.

"Be aware of the status of the home and people we're visiting," Oswald said. "This isn't a church social."

He wasn't helping her nerves.

But she was to dine at the Stetson mansion! She really did feel a little like Cinderella. She sank into the plush carriage seats and fingered the delicate lace on her cuffs. So why didn't Oswald feel like her Prince Charming?

She silently rehearsed etiquette tips for the rest of the ride and was glad Oswald wasn't talkative. The carriage rounded a curve, and the mansion loomed up in front of them, three stories of lighted windows. The exterior torchlight played with the Moorish curves and accents on the wooden structure. Josefa stared, mouth agape.

"Try not to gawk. It doesn't become you," Oswald said.

His house was large, but this was bigger and grander. It was larger than the Academy, and that was an entire school. She was impressed. At the same time, an inner voice nagged: *Why does one family need so much space?* She thought of the seven Bights squeezed into the orphanage's caretaker quarters. The mansion before her was one family's second home—a winter getaway. There were things about this upper class, as Oswald called them, that didn't make sense to her.

The carriage rolled to a halt in the curving drive, and Bernie came around to help her get out. She took his hand and met his gaze.

"Keep your head up, and you'll do fine," he said in a low voice as he helped her down. His quiet confidence in her buoyed her. She willed her unease to lessen before she set foot inside the door. She looked ahead and then whirled back to share her amazement with him, but by then Bernie had stepped back to stand by, impassive and eyes averted, while Oswald exited as though Bernie weren't even there. It was Josefa's turn to feel irritated. She disliked the way Oswald made himself out to be better than others. Oswald needed reminding that every person's human dignity deserves respect. Such reminders were part of a wife's duty, to help her husband stay on a righteous path, and she fully intended to exercise that right.

Those thoughts flew from her as the door opened and a butler stepped out to greet them. Instantly, Josefa immersed herself in the brightness shining behind him, where a chandelier glittered. How many candles did they use to make it glow so brightly, she wondered. She hurried forward until she felt Oswald's hand on her arm, restraining her to a more sedate pace.

The butler bowed, took her shawl and hat and Oswald's hat, and ushered them through the foyer and into the waiting room as he announced their names. Josefa looked upward and around. There weren't any candles. Anywhere. The room filled with upholstered seats, a fireplace, a piano, and end tables was illuminated by... some kind of magical means. Josefa did her best not to stare as a regal, coiffed woman in impeccably tailored silk came forward with her hands outstretched.

"Welcome. I'm Elizabeth Stetson, and I'm so pleased you could join us this evening." She ran an almost imperceptible assessing gaze over Josefa before meeting her stare and giving her a warm smile. "Please join us in the ballroom until dinner is served." She led them into the adjoining room.

Josefa was glad Oswald was by her side, for she wasn't sure which way to step, turn, or sit or who to talk to. At least ten people mingled in a room that was a good five times the size of the foyer and waiting room combined. It, too, was lit by something other than candles or gas, and there wasn't a kerosene lantern in sight. Most of the other people were older than she, all were poised and stylish, and all seemed to shine as much as the polished wood floors.

Ben would like to see the intricate design work in this flooring, she thought when she noticed how different tones of wood formed symmetrical patterns that were oddly familiar. She calculated the price of the rich upholstery of the sofas and plush seats scattered around the room. She reckoned the material alone cost more than Ben made in a year. She pursed her lips and looked around for something else to take her mind off places she didn't want it to go.

Oswald had released her arm. Worse, he had abandoned her.

She searched and found him bending over the only other young woman in the room. Josefa didn't recognize her but instantly felt diminished by the confident grace, laughter, and demeanor of the comely dark-haired lady. Even her dress rivaled Josefa's, which Josefa hadn't thought possible. She was in a copy of Worth, for heaven's sake.

The woman glanced her way momentarily in response to something Oswald said. Her face pouted into dismissiveness as she examined Josefa's gown from afar. There was something greedy and harsh in the look. The woman's eyes glittered with an envy she kept wiped from her expression. Oswald followed the line of sight, nodded at Josefa, and resumed his conversation.

Josefa felt hot, then cold, then her inner ear heard Bernie's words, the same advice everyone had given her before Oswald picked her up. Yes, she was out of her element here, but she'd do her best to ensure not a single one of these people would figure that out. She checked her posture, keeping her head up and neck straight.

"My dear, allow me to bring you some refreshments," a polite older man appeared at her elbow. "John B. Stetson, at your service."

She was grateful, and she saw a look of kindness in his eyes as he took her arm. "This way. I noticed you studying the chandelier when you entered. This is the first house in Persimmon Hollow to be wired for electric light, thanks to my friend Edison. That's him over there. He winters in Florida too, only farther down the coast." He pointed out another middle-aged gentleman whose graying hair, like his host's, had thinned at the top.

Oswald re-emerged as Mr. Stetson handed her a glass of something. She sipped at the bubbly liquid and stifled a cough at its strange taste and prickly texture.

"We're celebrating electricity, my boy," Stetson said to Oswald, who already had a glass in his hand. "Next up will be the streetlights for town."

"Oh, I heard about that," Josefa piped up, happy to be able to contribute to the small talk. "Everyone is excited."

"As you might expect in a place like this," Oswald added.

"All set to go tomorrow night," Stetson said. "Persimmon Hollow will be the envy of every city in Florida. It's the least I can do for the memory of my late friend. If he hadn't founded the town, I wouldn't have purchased this grove, built this house, or gained a fine winter getaway and investment. Ah, excuse me," he said and headed off to speak to a guest who'd signaled his attention.

"Don't gulp your champagne," Oswald murmured. "It's meant to be sipped."

After another half hour of awkwardness that she assuaged by drinking another glass of the bubbly liquid, Josefa had to use the water closet. No one had prepared her for such an emergency. Did she leave and go use an outhouse? Surely a house like this had indoor water closets. She cast surreptitious looks in several directions, to no avail.

Josefa did what she could to forget the pressing need. She admired the artwork. The polished wainscoting. The intricate design on the beams. The Moorish trim on the wood-frame indoor wall of windows. She nodded and smiled at whatever Oswald said that sounded as though a response was required. And she grew more and more uncomfortable.

Finally, she saw Mrs. Stetson momentarily alone checking refreshments on a sideboard. Josefa left Oswald's side and sought out Mrs. Stetson before she started to mingle again.

"Ma'am," she began.

"Elizabeth."

"Yes, Elizabeth, do you, uh, please, I would like to freshen up before we dine."

Understanding dawned almost immediately in her eyes.

"Of course. Right this way." She escorted Josefa back through the waiting room and foyer and into the hallway. "Up the stairs and then to the end of the hall," she said, giving Josefa a smile that put her almost at ease.

Josefa was coming back down the stairs when she met the other young female guest going up. Like Mrs. Stetson and the other women, her attire was exceptional and her hair fashioned in a complex arrangement of curls. Josefa knew her own more mature hairdo suited her face, but...she tried not to compare herself to the woman as they each stopped mid-step.

Josefa's lips curved a tentative smile.

"The servants' stairs are on the other side," the woman said, and Josefa saw her eyes glint in the shadowed stairwell. "Oh, silly me. I saw you in the ballroom," the woman simpered. "Forgive me, but with your skin...this light...my mistake is understandable." She drew her dress to the side as she continued up the stairs, as though to avoid touching Josefa's. No introduction. No small talk. Just inexplicable rudeness.

Bit by bit, Josefa unglued her hand from its grip on the railing. She wanted to walk down the rest of the stairs and out of the house, and tell Bernie to take her home. Home, where people loved her. Home, for that's what the grove was, no matter how much Oswald hinted that she was little more than a poor relation.

But that would be admitting defeat. *Dim lighting, my foot,* thought Josefa as she listened to the other woman's footsteps in the second floor hallway. Both Mr. and Mrs. Stetson had been gracious. Who cared what some idle guest thought. But Josefa did care. She carried the hurt when she returned to the ballroom just as Mrs. Stetson called everyone to the dining room. Still, she maintained her poise as she laid her arm on Oswald's, and they proceeded to the dining room.

The bubbly beverage started to make her head ache, and the house, though beautiful, was stuffily warm. The dining room wasn't as large as she had expected, and the press of people made the space close in around her. Someone's strong, lily-scented toilet water assaulted her nose. This was not shaping up to be the magical evening she had anticipated.

The seats around the dining room table were pushed close together to accommodate the number of diners. Another heavy chandelier hung low over the table, which was crammed with place settings, cutlery, wine glasses, and floral centerpieces. Josefa was seated between Oswald and a vacant chair. Her empty stomach, starting to roil from the champagne, lurched when she realized the only person not yet at the table was the woman from the staircase. Who obviously would sit right next to her.

Josefa studied the cutlery. What was that tiny fork for? Butterflies fluttered again, and she rehearsed what she'd learned. If all else failed, she had only to look at what the hostess did and follow her lead. Josefa was on the edge of a personal battlefield, and her mission was to navigate through the meal without making a faux pas. Oswald was oddly remote, despite being right next to her.

"Well, let us begin. I'm sure our late guest will be in shortly," Mrs. Stetson said after waiting almost too long. She signaled to the servants to begin the first course. As the two men placed small bowls of a cold soup in front of each diner, the missing young woman flounced into the room.

"I'm so sorry," she said but didn't sound remorseful or appear rushed. All the men rose as she took the seat next to Josefa. They sat down again once the woman was seated. Mrs. Stetson's smile was hard.

"How nice of you to join us, Adelaide," she said.

Adelaide proceeded to dominate the dinner discussion with Oswald, talking over and around Josefa, as soon as she learned who he was.

"The Hellers of Philadelphia and Charleston!" she exclaimed with a coy glance after hearing his full name.

"One and the same," he said.

Worse, Oswald rose to her bait, Josefa noted. He basked in the flirtatious remarks and bantered with the woman's inane comments. Josefa kept her own counsel with the myriad plates, forks, spoons, butter knives, and foodstuffs smothered in sauces and gravies. She may as well have been invisible, for all Oswald and Adelaide included her in the conversation. Talk around the table was lively among other seatmates, but Josefa didn't know how or whether to join in.

When Adelaide tittered at yet another bland witticism from Oswald, who never conversed with her, Josefa, like that, she gritted her teeth and rose.

"Why don't you just sit here," Josefa said to Adelaide and gestured to her own seat. The room chatter ceased. Mrs. Stetson's eyes widened. Oswald scowled. The diners stared at Josefa, who knew within seconds she had blundered, badly. *What,* she thought, *were people at these affairs meant to just sit and suffer through whatever?* She lowered herself to her chair, dabbed the corner of her mouth with her napkin, and didn't meet anyone's eyes.

"Ladies, shall we? It's time we retire to the ballroom so the men may enjoy their brandy and cigars before the musical entertainment," Mrs. Stetson intervened. "We will enjoy coffee and tea as we await the arrival of Emma Juch."

Elizabeth Stetson laid her napkin aside and stood up. "This way, please." She led the women out as though Josefa's comment had been appropriate and perfectly timed, and not done when dessert cake remained half-nibbled on plates and fruit untouched on platters.

* * *

"So who is your family?" Adelaide pushed next to Josefa and spoke loudly as the women seated themselves in the chairs and settee grouped around the fireplace. "Where are they from, and what do they do?"

Esmeralda had warned her someone might ask about her background. "You have nothing to be ashamed of," Esmeralda had told her, sounding very much like Lupita and Agnes.

That sentiment was all well and good at the dressmaker shop, Josefa thought. *But it didn't translate to a room the size of her entire house, with polished wood floors, fine art and tapestries on the walls, brocade drapes, and carved wood furniture that gleamed in the light of stained glass lamps.* She felt as though she were playing dress up.

Josefa grappled with the emptiness of no reply. Nothing at all came to mind. All the women in her life would advise her to tell the truth. But Josefa couldn't bring herself to say that her "people," as Adelaide termed it, were of the same class as the woman who carried in the silver tea set. She studied the unfamiliar blond woman holding the tea service and decided she must be one of the servants the Stetsons brought with them from their Northern home.

"Did you not hear me?" Adelaide asked. She patted her glossy curls and spread out her skirt so far on the settee that Josefa was pushed up against the armrest. Adelaide turned her face full forward to Josefa, who caught herself just before she gasped. Adelaide had paint on her face. Two spots of color. Something dark rimmed her eyelids. Josefa had never met anyone who used cosmetics. She tried not to stare.

"Tea, dear?" Elizabeth Stetson held out a cup for Josefa. "As soon as we're settled, I'd like to show you and the others my quilts. Perhaps you noticed the floor designs resemble quilt patterns? Done at my request. And please accept my compliments on your gown. Is it a Worth?"

Josefa brightened. "No. I mean, it's patterned after a Worth. But I made it. With the help of a dressmaker, I mean."

"Indeed," Elizabeth said and studied the garment with a keen interest.

"You admit to sewing your own clothes?" snickered Adelaide.

Elizabeth shifted slightly in her chair. "Tell me, Adelaide. What brings you back to Persimmon Hollow? Didn't I hear your family sold the Land Hotel and moved back to Chicago?"

"Oh, no, they kept the hotel but hired a manager so they wouldn't have to fuss with it so much," Adelaide said. "I came down when I heard the president was coming to Florida. How exciting! You know how chilly it still is in Chicago. I was delighted when Mother said she'd write to you. Will you really be able to secure me an introduction? I am a relative, after all. Why, you and my mother are practically sisters!"

Elizabeth's smile seemed stiff to Josefa. "If you consider third cousins sisters, then I guess we are. However, you overestimate the level of my importance, I'm afraid."

With that, she turned to her other guests. Adelaide frowned and then pouted. Josefa was glad she had a teacup in her hand because it gave her something to do. After endless minutes, Elizabeth got up and went to an armoire. She opened it to reveal several folded quilts.

"Would anyone like to see these?"

Josefa thought she was never going to ask.

Chapter 17

The clock chimed once before Josefa and Oswald even started to take leave. Josefa alternated between trying to act sophisticated and tamping down worry over arriving home late. Adelaide's simpering didn't help matters.

"Oh, Mr. Heller, I do hope we meet again," she said in a voice that oozed charm. "I know you appreciated Miss Juch's singing as much as I did." Which Josefa hadn't. She had grown bored fifteen minutes into the forty-minute recital.

Oswald cast an appreciative look at Adelaide.

"I'd be honored to meet a lovely lady like you again," he said. He kissed her hand, and even lingered at it.

"Why, perhaps in the next few days?" Adelaide refused to stop flirting. "I do so admire a man of action and determination, and that's what I've always heard of the Hellers."

Josefa stepped closer to the door. Oswald ignored her. Her temper rising, Josefa opened the door herself, while the butler tarried and waited for Oswald's signal. Her action got Oswald's attention, and he was beside her in two long strides.

"Oh, you will escort your fiancé home after all?" she said, tired, irritated, and unable to hold her tongue.

"Jealousy doesn't become you."

"I'm not jealous," she snapped, then drew a breath. "It's late. We said our goodbyes to the hosts some time ago. I'd appreciate it if you would take me home."

His gaze was indecipherable, but he accompanied her out.

"You'd do well to emulate Miss Land. She has breeding, class, and sophistication."

And ill manners, thought Josefa, remembering the meeting on the stairs and the pushiness in the ballroom. *Why would she want to model herself after someone rude, aloof, and enamored only of herself?*

"Why didn't you mention our betrothal?" she asked.

"I told you we will keep it quiet for now when out in public."

"Why?" She tilted her chin up. Josefa knew she was naïve, but she wasn't a ninny. How long could she continue to deceive herself that marriage to Oswald was the answer to her uncertain future?

"I, er, decided we should wait for the most appropriate time. As I've said, we could skip the formalities and have a simple wedding. A small ceremony somewhere out of town."

Josefa leaned her head back against the seat, closed her eyes, and let her body fall into the rhythm of the swaying carriage. She was tired from having had to make small talk for hours, from drinking too much champagne, and from acting as though she were someone else.

"I'll engage the services of a minister, set a time and place, and then you and I will slip away and return a married couple," Oswald said.

Had he taken her silence as acquiescence? She opened her eyes and looked, really looked at him. At his handsome profile, visible even in the darkness of the gray night. His straight, assured posture, even when seated. She didn't know this man, and wondered if she ever would.

"I'm glad you agree," he said, a note of approval in his voice.

"But I don't."

"You will."

He turned his head away and purposely, she imagined, refused to either look at her or continue a discussion she had no intention of pursuing either. She was too weary to argue. Tomorrow she would spill her heart to...whom? The saints, that's who. She would bring her heavy heart to the communion of saints.

Josefa felt far from the young woman she'd been before Oswald showed up, and before her aunt's mission to direct her future toward Texas. Josefa had drawn comfort and support from the hours spent at St. Isidore's small chapel when she'd first arrived in Persimmon Hollow, grieving, lost, and lonely. She'd shared in the suffering of Christ's passion and felt close to Mary and the other saints whose triumphs over adversity had helped her bear her own losses. Now she had no time for the orphanage, or for extra prayer, or for learning from the saints. *What had become of her,* Josefa wondered. *Is this what Oswald's definition of ladyhood meant?*

She knew the answer as soon as the question arose. Agnes never forgot God, ever. Lupita considered Our Lady of Guadalupe part of the immediate family. The sisters never let anything interfere with daily recitation of the Divine Office. Fanny Alloway's Bible was always out, open, and in use at the boarding house, where Estelle hummed spirituals that she told Josefa made her heart feel close to God.

No, thought Josefa, *she was the one who was lost.* She didn't need anyone to confirm that for her. An image of Ben crossed her mind, his face with its ready smile. She felt a tug at her heart and a wish that Ben, not Oswald, were seated next to her. *Yes, she was lost, in more ways than one.*

The boarding house came into view not a moment too soon. The entire lower floor was lighted. *Not a good sign*, thought Josefa. Someone had waited up, and here she was more than an hour beyond curfew.

Oswald was coldly attentive as he helped her down and escorted her to the door. The magnificent dress that had made her feel like a princess now weighted her. The hardness of the walkway pressed against the thin sole of her beaded slippers.

"Good night, then," said Oswald the minute they reached the porch. She didn't ask him in, and he didn't linger for an invitation.

The door flew open before she turned the knob. An angry Lupita stood there. "I hope you have a good explanation, young lady."

"I tried, Aunt Lupita," said Josefa. "I did all in my power to secure our departure but...but they don't live like other people. They're still there, most of them, getting ready to view stereo-scopes and watch a demonstration of something called a recording machine. The singer might even perform again. Oswald was annoyed that I wanted to leave. It was..."

Misery coursed through her. It was a horrible night, is what she almost said. That disappointment was greater than having to deal with her disapproving aunt.

Lupita's face softened, to Josefa's surprise. She pulled Josefa inside, put her arm around her, and led her to a chair.

"There, there, my little one, sit. Tell me about it." She eased Josefa onto the sofa and sat beside her. Fanny came in, and the worry that creased her face changed to relief.

"Praise the Lord. I thought we would have fireworks, it is so late." As she spoke, the clock struck two.

"No, Josefa is sad." Lupita stated the obvious. "This was not as it should have been, this night?" She turned Josefa's face to hers in a gentle pull before letting her go.

Josefa shook her head mutely. She was determined not to cry. She was a young woman. No tears.

Fanny settled in a rocking chair. "Whatever happened? My dear, you look positively deflated. You glowed when you left here."

Lupita rose. "I knew no good would come of this. Josefa, there are many problems. I am here for more reasons than the lateness of the hour. No respectable young woman stays out so late."

Not now, Aunt Lupita. Please. Josefa wanted only to climb the stairs and crawl into bed.

"Can we talk about it tomorrow?" she asked, letting her eyes convey mute appeal that usually softened her aunt.

"We will have plenty to talk about tomorrow," Lupita said. "Like the way you will return to the grove immediately." She held up a hand at Josefa's confused expression. "No arguments. I heard all about you and Señor Stillman's inappropriate behavior on the porch."

Fanny picked up her fan from a side table. Josefa almost asked to borrow it.

Lupita continued. "And this nonsense of trying to become Mrs. Oswald Heller III when your background and his are too far apart. All must come to an end, Josefa. I see the sadness in your entire body. The time has come to try my plan."

Josefa started to protest, and anxiety overcame fatigue as Lupita's words sank in.

Lupita waved her arm at Josefa. "No. It is your turn to listen. I agreed against my better judgment to let you go on this adventure. It is clear it isn't working. That was our agreement. Now you live up to your end of the bargain."

"I never agreed to anything," Josefa protested. "You decided I did."

Fanny rose. "Ladies, ladies. It is two in the morning. We need to rest. Let the good Lord's sun rise on this before we go any further."

Lupita and Josefa just looked at her.

"I insist," said Fanny, her chubby face reflecting a determination she rarely expressed. "Upstairs, both of you. Ben brought the rollaway bed to Josefa's room for you, Lupita."

She took each by the hand. "Please, for me, no more discussion tonight."

"I am tired," Josefa admitted. She also felt more than a little like a drooping flower. "I'll take the rollaway bed, *tia*. You use mine."

"*Si*. I am tired too," Lupita said. "Come, precious one."

"I have news of my own to share in the morning," Fanny called after them as they started up the stairs. Josefa glanced back. Fanny's cheeks creased in a smile of girlish delight. "You won't want to miss it," she added.

Chapter 18

"W ho is that with Ben?" Josefa held back the lace curtains and peered down into the yard of the Alloway House, where the early morning sun shone on an animated Ben in conversation with a slight, white-haired, bespectacled man.

The man gripped a walking stick and was anchored by two large, battered suitcases and a giant trunk. Ben seemed almost in awe of the older gentleman, and whatever they were discussing had enthused them both.

She was unable to drag her attention away. Ben had a way of movement that was so natural and assured, yet unassuming. Nothing forced. No airs. He was focused on what was in front of him, and his interest made his face bright with intelligence.

Josefa leaned her palms down on the windowsill and took a deep breath, then pressed her lips together. Dreaminess for a future with Ben that wasn't to be would get her nothing but a dash of cold reality. She sighed.

"What is wrong?" Lupita came over and looked out just as Ben gestured toward the house and picked up the stranger's luggage.

"Ah, that must be Fanny's guest. Yes, I told her it was all right to give him this room since you're coming back to the grove with me this morning, right after breakfast."

She turned a sharp eye on Josefa.

"Has Ben said anything about his plans for after the church is finished?" Lupita asked with feigned attention on an imaginary hair out of place in Josefa's braid.

"No," said Josefa and moved away from both her aunt and the window. She picked up her hat and her aunt's scarf, handing Lupita the silk square. "And you know what's wrong, Aunt Lupita. Dragging me back to the grove like I'm a child. I have an obligation to Miss Esmeralda."

"And you will see to that obligation," Lupita replied. "By traveling from and to the grove each day, for the, what is it, three weeks you have left. Then we will discuss your next steps and maybe take a trip."

"I'm not going to your relatives in Texas or Mexico or wherever," said Josefa. She flipped her braid over her shoulder instead of winding it around her head. "I can't leave my dye garden." It was the first excuse that popped into her mind, after, of course, the unspoken and unwanted thought that she hoped to keep open any chances with Ben.

"We'll see," Lupita said, watching her closely. "Ben can tend to it for you, like he has been doing."

"Ben will leave and head for who knows where when his work here is done," said Josefa, but her words came out as more of a wail than a statement. She sat down on the side of the bed with a plop.

"If he goes, then it is *Dios's* way of saying something wasn't meant to be," Lupita said in a gentle voice. "Perhaps that other man in your life isn't meant to be, either. You are tense and distraught, Josefa, not the excited girl who left the grove weeks ago. I am concerned for your health." She sat beside Josefa and put her arm around her waist. Josefa gave her a sad smile, placed one hand over her aunt's, and closed her eyes.

"Put your worries in the Lord's hands, little one," Lupita said. "Young love can be confusing. That's why marriages are best arranged by those who know and love you, and who can select a good man for you. My cousins in Texas know of a..."

Josefa let another exaggerated sigh escape. "It is almost the twentieth century, Aunt Lupita. Would you please stop trying to arrange a marriage for me!"

She got up from the bed. "Can we go eat breakfast before this talk of arrangements makes me lose my appetite?" But she said it with a smile.

"Ah, you are so young, my little one. Come, let's go."

The others were seated and drinking coffee when they arrived in the dining room, where the smell of the warm, rich brew permeated the room. The new guest at the head of the table commanded an attention that exceeded his unprepossessing appearance. Ben was like an overeager puppy. Fanny bustled to and fro between the kitchen and dining room with a flushed face and distracted air that was almost euphoric. The winter boarders were rapt in their attention, at least the two brothers were. Even their wives and sister paid quiet respect to the guest.

Lupita sat and reached for the pot to pour coffee into the mugs at her and Josefa's place settings, but Josefa headed for the kitchen.

"I'll see if Estelle needs any help," Josefa said and went to find out exactly who this stranger was, this man who impressed everyone.

"Miss Fanny's beau from her girlhood," Estelle said before Josefa even asked. The cook handed Josefa a platter of scrambled eggs. "Put these out on the table for me before they cool."

"You're kidding! I have to hear the whole story." She took the platter.

"Miss Fanny, she'll tell it," Estelle said.

"But why is everyone else staring at him too?" Josefa asked.

"Oh, he's a famous plant man, botanist, I think Fanny said. Travels all over for some fancy college. Yes, he sure has caused a stir among folks here."

Josefa's heart thumped, and a touch of gloom seeped into her. A plant hunter. That's who was making Ben look and act like a man who had reached an oasis after a trip through the desert.

She returned to the dining room and set down the platter on the table. Estelle followed with a bowl of grits and plate of bacon, caught Josefa's eye and smiled, and left.

"Lupita, Josefa, let me introduce Dr. Archibald Smithson," Fanny bubbled and fluttered from one part of the room to the other.

"I'll thank you to call me Art," said the man in a cheerful voice. "And I'm not a medical doctor, so you can leave off that, too."

"He's only one of the most famous men in the field of botany," Ben said. His eyes were alight with admiration.

"Man with weak lungs has to do something to earn his way," Art said.

Fanny finally settled in a chair near Art and snapped open a fan that she waved around her head and neck.

"If I had only...I...wait until Eunice hears that it's you," Fanny blubbered. In another minute, she would be crying, Josefa predicted. And they would be tears of joy.

"You know each other?" she prodded, as if she hadn't heard.

The glance that passed between Art and Fanny warmed the chill that still soaked Josefa from the previous evening's disappointments. Art patted Fanny's hand on the table. Lupita's eyebrows rose so high Josefa was surprised they didn't arch above her hairline.

"It's a long story...we go way back," Fanny said, looking around the table before gazing again at Art, who smiled right back at her.

"To think, after all these years, an Indian mound brings us together," Art said.

Josefa waited for the explanation.

"Mind if I take a look at some of your books?" Ben asked, clearly uninterested in whatever personal history Fanny and Art shared. Which, Josefa noted, they weren't exactly rushing to explain. They were so happily basking in each other's presence that the past seemed an afterthought.

"Wait until I show you the town Father built," Fanny said to Art. "You will be amazed."

"Well, then, let's be on our way," Art said. "We're not getting any younger. We have to make up for lost time." He rose and held out his arm to her. Fanny blushed to the roots of her curly silver hair. "Oh, Art, no joshing."

"I'm as serious as the day I did my orals," he intoned, then broke into a grin.

"Uh, okay for me to..." Ben broke in again.

"Look at as many books as you'd like and take as long as you want with them, son," Art said. "I'll expect repayment in the form of regional plant lore to supplement my research. The fossilized flora in those mounds may speak volumes of history to us."

"You're studying the plants of Persimmon Hollow?" Josefa asked.

"In a way," Art said. "I drew the short straw when one of my colleagues, the professor Fanny and her sister wrote to about the mounds, couldn't make the journey here as arranged.

"My colleagues await my assessment of the site's worthiness

for full-scale exploration. Professorial expectations are low, else others would have jumped to trade places with me. But I've partnered on my share of archaeological enterprises, enough to expect surprises. I'd relish proving the others wrong."

Such a large voice from a small man, Josefa thought, as Art and Fanny left and the rest of the party started to scatter. The boarders headed out for a game of croquet, with boxed lunches from Estelle.

"Josefa, you have no idea how famous he is. I mean, really famous." Ben said. "That he's here is…it's like a chance of a lifetime for someone interested in botany. I sure hope he's staying awhile and that I get to do some work with him."

He rattled off discoveries, research, lectures, and awards that distinguished the professor.

"But what is he to Fanny?" Lupita asked. "They act like long-lost friends."

"Estelle said he was Fanny's former beau," Josefa said.

"Ah, that explains that liberty he took at the table," Lupita said.

"I kept waiting for them to fill in all the details," Josefa said. "I want to know the whole story!"

"Save that for another day," Lupita said. "Right now, it's time to head out to the grove." She glanced around the dining room and at her vacated seat. "I think I left my scarf upstairs. I'll be right back."

"The books he's written are the best in the field," Ben continued, hands in his denim pants' pockets as he and Josefa went into the parlor. *Honestly,* Josefa thought, *was she the only one interested in the love story?*

The professor's trunk was opened to reveal numerous books and papers. Ben dug in with a balance of reverence and glee. "Lookee here, Josefa, at this one!" He held up a leather-bound volume labeled *Plant Life of the Americas* for a few seconds before leafing through it.

"Let's see, the days are getting long. I can do six or seven hours on the job site, depending on how the materials come in, and still put in three or four with him if I time it right." He spoke without raising his eyes from the book.

And spend no time with me, thought Josefa selfishly.

Ben slipped more and more away from her with every passing minute. At the same time, his hold over her grew ever stronger. She watched him, unobserved, as she waited for Lupita to come back downstairs. The intensity of his interest made his unassuming facial features coalesce into an attractively handsome whole, lit from within. His already-bright blue eyes gleamed with an eager joy. The way he absentmindedly pushed back shocks of his hair that fell forward because he never got around to a haircut only added to his appeal.

He half knelt with one knee on the floor and the book in hand and was oblivious, she knew, to the figure he cut—toned, fit, and fine. She had to push back an impulse to lean over and run her hands down his broad shoulders and back, embrace him, make him turn and kiss her again…

The brisk passions she'd witnessed all around her this morning made her own unsettled state more obvious in her mind. She knew how it felt to be so excited about doing something that hours faded and workarounds were developed for any possible obstacles. That's how she felt about designing, sewing, and creating special dresses tinted with the rich colors from plants in her dye garden. When absorbed in real fashion, not alterations, mending, or darning.

She saw the excitement in Ben, had felt the bond between Fanny and Art. They had the liberty to explore and reach for new or rekindled dreams. Ben because he was a man, and Fanny and Art because they were elders who bore the wisdom of age and knew how to use it. Her choices were limited: marriage and motherhood; a tough road as a woman of business; the veil of the convent; or spinsterhood and life as a dependent.

Much as she loved the sisters and orphans, Josefa knew the convent wasn't the right future for her. Marriage and motherhood she expected without question. She had thought, maybe, a small dressmaking shop could be a place of her own, to keep her close to the finer fabrics of life when the calicos and muslins of everyday use weighed her down. But Esmeralda worked herself to the point of weariness and had little to show for it. The poor woman even resorted to taking extra food from gatherings.

The ache traveled to Josefa's temples.

"You ready to go?" Estelle came through to ask just as Lupita came down the stairs. "Ben, get your nose out of the book and help with their bags, would you please?" Estelle asked.

Ben looked up as though he'd been time traveling to another world. "Huh, what? Oh, sure!" He got up and replaced the book with utmost care to the exact spot from which he'd lifted it. The grin he shot Josefa melted her.

"Bernie's out back with the wagon," Estelle said. "He's ready anytime you are, Miss Lupita."

"He's not working for Oswald today?" Josefa asked.

A thunderous look came over Estelle's face. "I don't like to speak ill of your beau, Josefa, but let me just say I'll be glad when we get the school built so Bernie can teach and not have to bow to that..."

"It's all right," Lupita said. "Mr. Heller is now on my bad side, too, and Josefa's. What did he do to Bernie?"

"Fired him for protesting how he treated his horses. Then tried to get him to come back. Then got mad when Bernie said he already told me and Miss Fanny he'd run people around for us today. Told Bernie to get out of his sight. And don't you know he'll be right back in his face in a day or two needing a driver." Lupita clucked in shared disapproval.

The ache that had hovered around Josefa's temples threatened to throb. She might be headed toward a sour life if she allowed the courtship to continue. If she broke it off, her aunt would follow through on her plan to send her away. She felt like she had to choose between the lesser of two evils instead of a bright star of contentment and joy. It just wasn't fair.

Chapter 19

*T*hat's right, life isn't fair, my little one." Lupita was on a sermonizing streak as Josefa helped her fold clean towels and sheets in Seth and Agnes's bedroom at the grove early that evening.

Breakfast at the Alloway House seemed like it had been days ago instead of hours. Josefa couldn't shake the lethargy that had settled over her since their return. Nothing interested her. Not her fabrics, or her dye garden, or Polly's updates on her chicken with the wavy feathers, or Billy's pride in his marksmanship, or anything, really. Even baby Seth's gurgles and coos helped only a tad. Ben wasn't around. He was in town. Oswald had made a brief, stiff call earlier in the afternoon, but it had dragged out interminably. Even the thought of returning to the dressmaking shop again sat on her like a burden.

Agnes came in with a lantern to keep away the falling dusk just as Lupita made her comment. Agnes set down the lantern, studied Josefa, and pursed her lips.

"Can I help?" she asked and sat down on the bed next to Josefa's droopy figure. She started to fold the nearest towel.

"I don't see how," Josefa said. "You have the perfect life. How could you understand?" Josefa knew the petulance she heard in her tone was inexcusable, but her inertia made cheerfulness a distant, unreachable target.

"Try me," Agnes said. "I only make it look easy."

Josefa shrugged. She was entangled in an odd courtship, in love with the wrong man, pricked by the realities of her dressmaking dream, and snared by her aunt's antiquated notions. Everybody around here knew all that. What else was there to say?

"I tell her to do for others when she is low in spirits, but she doesn't want to listen to her aunt," Lupita said. "She could hem washcloths and stitch bed covers for the mercantile's collection bin for the needy. The orphans would benefit from lessons in needlework. It's not like Josefa to be so low. It is this Oswald. I know. "

In her fog, Josefa registered the unusual note of worry in Lupita's usually commanding voice.

"The word of the Lord can be a tremendous help in times of trouble," Agnes said to Josefa in her gentle, calming way. Josefa restrained from rolling her eyes over how Agnes thought Scripture cured everything. *Not this time, Agnes,* Josefa thought.

Agnes rose, lifted the Bible from her dressing table, and sat back down. The thin pages being turned made a soft ripple of sound.

"Ah, here, Josefa, listen: 'Your light shall break forth like the dawn, and your healing shall spring up quickly…you shall call, and the Lord will answer; you shall cry for help, and he will say, Here I am.'"

Then Agnes said, "God always answers, always guides us. Sometimes the answer isn't what we ask for, though. You have to trust in God."

"And in his Holy Mother," added Lupita and blessed herself. "Have you spent any time in prayer lately with Our Lady of Guadalupe?"

Josefa shook her head.

Agnes looked back down at the Bible's pages.

"Read Isaiah. He was a wise prophet. Look, he could be speaking to you right here." She put her finger to a line on the page: "Arise, shine; for your light has come, and the glory of the Lord has risen upon you."

"God's light will always shine," Agnes said, and Lupita nodded in agreement.

Josefa jerked her head up.

"Oh, no!"

She looked at Agnes and Lupita's surprised faces, and pressed her hands to her cheeks.

"I forgot! Lights. You said light, and it reminded me!"

Josefa jumped up.

"Whatever are you talking about?" Lupita asked as she finished folding the last sheet.

"The street lights. The ones Uncle Alfredo and Seth have been so excited about. The ones that will light part of Persimmon Boulevard. The electric lights."

"Yes, but what about them?" asked Agnes.

"They're going to be turned on tonight. Mr. Stetson and Mr. Edison were going to alert others in town today. Last night at his dinner, Mr. Stetson asked me to be sure to tell everyone here so we could be there for the big moment."

"Tonight?" Agnes exclaimed. She glanced outside at the matte tinge of early dusk and nearly flew out of the room.

"Seth! Alfredo! Billy! Polly!" Agnes's footsteps kept pace with her calls for the others.

Lupita, muttering in Spanish, took off after Agnes. She stopped long enough in the doorway to turn to Josefa.

"*Dios Mio!* Don't just stand there. We have to go! I hope we are not too late!"

So did Josefa. Agnes certainly had been right. God indeed had something to say to her. It sounded a lot like a friendly reminder that life didn't exist for her experience alone.

Outside, Seth and Alfredo, who was back on two feet, prepared two wagons, Billy yelled and hallooed as he ran toward the orphanage to alert the sisters and orphans, Agnes fussed with baby Seth's clothes, and Lupita carried out cloaks, capes, and blankets for everyone to sit on. She handed them to Polly, who quickly stacked them in the wagon bed in which she already sat. Josefa ran to help.

"Get in," Seth called. "We'll ride down and overtake Billy and pick everyone up. Alfredo, you fit all the orphans and the sisters with you. I'll take the Bights. Agnes, Lupita, you sit up front with me."

Daylight dwindled faster than any of them wished as they set out. At the orphanage, the horses hardly came to a halt as the passengers scrambled aboard.

Josefa bowed her head and prayed they wouldn't be late.

* * *

"You made it!" Clyde hollered from the excited crowd that milled in front of his mercantile. He stepped out to meet the wagons and walked alongside as Seth and Alfredo guided the horses around to the store's back property.

"Eunice was getting worried. Almost reckoned you weren't interested. Can't say as I'm clear about whether this lighting is a blessing or a curse. Folks have mixed feelings. Been getting an earful. You will too."

It was the most Josefa had ever heard the laconic Clyde utter at once.

"Wouldn't miss this for my life, my man," Seth said. He tossed the reins to Billy, who tied the horses to hitches and gave them water.

In record time, the grove contingent quick-stepped to the storefront along Persimmon Boulevard.

"There they are!" Billy pointed to Mr. Stetson and Mr. Edison, dressed in suits and talking with workers in overalls. A crowd clustered around them by a pole with a glass appendage at the top. The pole was almost at the corner of the main intersection. Nearby was a steam-powered contraption and other equipment Josefa couldn't identify.

Seth, Alfredo, Clyde, and Toby Bight headed over to confer with the men. Billy grabbed Polly. "C'mon, let's get a close-up look. I heard the lights are going to shine as bright as thirty-two candlepower!"

"Oh, no, you don't!" Agnes proclaimed. She held baby Seth in one arm and reached the other out to restrain Polly. "We don't know if those things are going to explode or what. You both stay here."

"It's bad enough your father is over there," Lupita tsk-tsked. "And Toby, too, he with five children. And Alfredo!"

"Nothing's going to explode," Billy exclaimed. "That's Thomas Alva Edison. The famous inventor. He knows what he's doing. He's put his lights in big cities!"

"I know who he is," Agnes said. "Just stay here. You're close enough."

Josefa glimpsed Ben and his newfound mentor Art emerge from the crowd and greet Seth and the other men near the central pole. A moment later, they were swallowed by the swirl of people and the hum of movement. Then she saw Fanny, *Fanny!*, right there next to Art near the new contraptions. Eunice also stood near.

Sarah, Agnes, Lupita, Josefa, and the sisters herded the Bight children and the orphans a few steps in the other direction.

"Oh, there's another one," Agnes said, stopping. Another pole, apparently already equipped to accept the electricity Josefa knew would course through it, stood about halfway up the block. At the end of the block, another pole rose.

"Let's stay right here," Agnes said and ushered the group under the awning of the shoemaker's shop, equidistant between the first and second poles.

Billy took small steps away and watched for an opportunity to escape.

Agnes gave him the look.

"Aw, Agnes, you ain't gonna make me stay here with y'all are you? C'mon."

Her face softened. "You stick close by Seth, you hear."

Billy was off before she finished her sentence.

Polly was on his heels.

"Agnes, please let her go," Josefa interceded as Agnes opened her mouth to call the girl back. "Even Fanny is over there. And Eunice. I'll watch Polly from here. Should the slightest spark smolder, I'll spring to get her in an instant."

Agnes shifted the baby to her other arm and nodded. The sisters put the orphans on a buddy system and allowed them to inch closer to the action.

Lupita shook her head. "If the good Lord wanted the night to be bright, he'd have made it that way."

"It is kind of exciting, though," Josefa said. She caught the hum of anticipation as the workers started to put down their tools and step away from the equipment.

"I'm of a mind to agree with your aunt," she heard Estelle say nearby. The cook and a group of her neighbors had joined the throng and settled next to the grove women. Josefa wondered if Oswald was somewhere in the crowd. And Esmeralda. She hadn't seen either. The dressmaker's shop and upstairs living quarters were dark. She didn't think anyone would want to miss such a historic event.

"I'm not exactly sure why we'd want light at night," Sarah ventured.

But Josefa saw the future.

"These lights—they'll be like extended daylight," she enthused. "Like we have gained extra hours in the day!"

"Oh, I don't know," Sarah said, looking at the night sky. "That light will dim the magnificent stars. Look. Just look at them."

They gazed at the uncountable twinkles of stars huddled together in dense patches that blanketed the sky.

"Helps remind one how small we are compared to the grandeur of God's universe," said Sister Rose.

A thump of a hammer on an iron wagon wheel silenced the chatter and titters of excitement. "Ladies and gentlemen, we are about fifteen minutes from the big moment," called out Clyde. "We are witnesses to history!" Cheers erupted, and the sisters, Lupita, Agnes, Sarah, Estelle and her companions murmured prayers next to Josefa.

Ben loped out of the horde near the main-corner light and crossed over to Josefa.

"I knew you'd be here. I knew you'd be interested," he said and took her hands in his. "This town is going places, Josefa! It's amazing! Just look!" He released her hands, and they stood side by side, shoulders almost touching, and surveyed the throng.

Then stay, Ben, Josefa answered in her heart, while she outwardly responded to his enthusiasm—it was impossible not to. She extended an arm to draw in Polly and other youngsters who were running back their way, then to the corner again, and then back again to the women on the sidelines.

Lupita stopped her prayers, glowered at Ben, and advanced toward him. Josefa maneuvered herself between the two.

"She knows about the porch," mouthed Josefa as the baffled Ben's greeting to Lupita faded in the face of her peeved expression. "The kiss," Josefa whispered.

Even in the darkness, Josefa saw the creep of a blush along Ben's neck. He stumbled, then caught himself. She gulped back a gurgle of a laugh as he tripped over his own feet before he managed to right himself. He came to a halt directly in front of Lupita.

"Señora, I…"

"Uh-oh, she has that look on her face," Polly said. By silent accord, Polly and Josefa moved to bookend Ben. Josefa noted that despite Lupita's glower, Agnes and Sarah watched with what appeared to be bemusement.

"Señora, I want you to know that I respect Josefa and—"

"Yet you attempt to ruin her reputation?" Lupita asked. "I could insist on marriage for your shameful behavior."

Josefa's spirits plummeted at the alarm that crossed Ben's face before he wiped his features into respectfulness.

"When the day comes that I can…I mean when I have a home… when I'm able to support…I mean…"

"You mean that isn't now, correct?" Lupita filled in the words for him.

"Yes ma'am."

"Then I suggest you keep your distance from my niece."

No, thought Josefa. *My aunt cannot keep dictating my life. She keeps forgetting we're almost to the twentieth century.* Josefa couldn't bear the thought of not seeing Ben.

"Lupita, perhaps we can talk this over." Agnes said, stepping forward, and Josefa wanted to kiss her. "You have every right to be concerned over the breach of propriety." She gave her own look of dismay at Ben. "He surely should have known better."

Lupita harrumphed. "As should Josefa, too."

"Ben is our master carpenter at the church. He helps at the grove, and there is bound to be interaction," Agnes said. "If he expresses remorse, I believe he means it. Perhaps you can search your heart for forgiveness?"

She turned to Ben. "I also recommend you avail yourself of the sacrament of confession the next time Father Kenny makes his regular mission visit. You too, Josefa."

Agnes spoke next to Lupita. "May I suggest you consider that they meet only when others are with them? Ben has shown himself to be trustworthy on many occasions."

Lupita continued to frown. Josefa held her breath. Polly watched with avid interest. Ben appeared miserable and stiffly formal. Agnes was patient. Everyone else had inched closer to the main intersection.

"Josefa, count your blessings that we have such an angel of mercy as Agnes," Lupita said.

"You have my assurances it'll never happen again," said Ben. He gave a stiff bow to Lupita, turned, and stalked off toward the crowd. Josefa could almost see the tenseness of his shoulders and neck.

"Ben, wait." She started after him. She didn't care who watched or how unladylike she appeared. "Wait." She reached him in moments, glad to be in the sliver of middle zone between the grove clan and the larger town gathering.

The eyes he turned toward her were so troubled and intense she halted in midstep.

"Josefa," he said, but her name sounded strangled. "I can't..." He shoved his hands into the pockets of the work denims he still wore from the long day on the construction site.

"I can't give you what you need. What you want. Not right now. Not for a long while. If ever. I don't have the means, and I can't settle without them. Won't settle without them—even if I did have a piece of land to call my own. Which I don't. I already support a family, and can't let go of the dream to chase my father's footsteps. I'm giving all I can right now, Josefa, and I know it's not enough."

She turned her face up to him to catch every emotion in the glow of starlight.

"Your aunt thinks I'm some oaf with wrong intentions," he said. "I'm not. You know I'm not."

"My aunt likes you," Josefa said, grabbing at the only part of the discussion that gave her solid ground to balance on. "She just gets excited over things. She worries about me."

"With good reason," Ben said. "You're a beautiful woman, Josefa. So beautiful, and you don't even realize how much. Naturally beautiful. You think I like to see you with that boorish Oswald? You think I'm not aware I can't claim a tenth of what he has?"

Ben barked a laugh. "Make that a hundredth."

He put his hands on Josefa's shoulders and pulled her so close she almost moved in for a kiss. Another part of her awaited the stalking steps of her aunt, who was only several yards away.

"I love you, Josefa," Ben said. Serious. Low. Full of emotion. "I love you so much I won't ask you to wait for me. It's not fair. To you, or to me."

He dropped his hands and put imperceptible distance between them in physical space but miles in emotional connection.

"I won't ask if you love me. Because I don't want to know your answer," he added.

"You already know what it is, Ben." Josefa surprised herself at the tenor of her claim. She stepped forward and closed the inches between them until they nearly touched.

His eyes glinted, and a hard sheen came over them as his hands encircled her waist and she gripped his arms.

"So what do we do, Josefa?" Every word carried heat.

She wanted him to kiss her; that's what she wanted. She wanted to feel that swell that had come over her on the porch, that sensation of both falling and floating.

His face lowered over hers. The normally relaxed, amiable Ben became a man who knew what he wanted and decided to claim it. Josefa closed her eyes and pursed her lips. She, too, had a claim to stake.

A brilliant white flash bathed her eyelids. She shrieked and jumped back, and simultaneously opened her eyes to see a startled Ben. They soon were drowned in a cacophony of cheers, yells, comments, and laughter. Three odd pools of eerie bright light glowed in large, elongated circles around each of the poles. The result was a town with splotches of unnatural glow and resultant long shadows that stretched off buildings.

Josefa and Ben's isolated moment was lost in the swirl around them. He grabbed her hand as people around them applauded the illumination, and pulled her back to the safety of the grove group, now clustered in front of the mercantile. Josefa couldn't stop staring. Half the night that surrounded her was bathed in partial daylight. She didn't know what to make of it. She gripped Ben's hand like a lifeline. She looked at the lights with wonder. He studied them with interest and intrigue.

"Mercy, it's so bright it will wake up my rooster!" Fanny popped out of the crowd. "Land sakes alive, we are part of the future! But my rooster!"

"Ah, it'll be just fine, Miss Fanny," Ben said. "You wait and see."

"How could I not see?" she exclaimed. "Mercy!"

Even in her awe, Josefa couldn't shake her awareness of Ben's presence. Just then, Oswald strode from the jumble of townsfolk to her section of the street. He reached for her arm with a proprietary air that no longer made her feel special. She suspected he did it only for show. Ben took note and stepped back although he kept his gaze on her. In the artificial daylight, she saw a dare in his eyes that bore into her. *Who will you pick?* he seemed to ask. *What do you want to do, Josefa?*

Just what kind of question was that, unspoken or implied? Josefa thought, a trifle irked. She hoped the glowing lights conveyed her irritation. Ben had closed the door before it barely opened, and now he issued her wordless challenges?

She shook off Oswald's hold and moved toward Ben. The night's excitement, her aunt's drama, and her conflicted feelings bubbled and merged into an exhaustion that fueled an irritability in her.

"Don't you look at me like that, Benjamin Stillman," she said, and almost poked a finger into his chest. "You laid out the boundaries nice and clear, and I don't see any room there for me."

Without giving him a chance to reply, she twirled and stalked back to an astonished Oswald, eyebrows raised at her bold movements.

"And don't you tell me what I'm supposed to think or say or do," she said to him. She left plenty of space between herself and him, turned around, and glanced at the equally confounded Ben.

She crossed her arms over her chest and kept her head high. Off to the side, Agnes nudged Lupita and smiled.

"My *sobrina*, she is growing up," said Lupita and dabbed at the corner of her eyes.

Chapter 20

Josefa straightened up in the dye garden and set aside the hoe. She reached her arms over her head and stretched from side to side. Only one more week to go, she thought, as her body responded to the freedom of movement after long workdays bent over the sewing machine. She'd been exhausted upon arrival at home last night. The daily commute to and from the heart of Persimmon Hollow, on top of the workload, wore on her.

Her gaze caught the fullness of the indigo bushes, and she judged them likely ready for harvest. It'd be nice to have Ben help with the dye process, to be sure. But she no longer thought that was such a great idea. She adjusted her wide-brimmed bonnet to block the sharp rays of May sunlight, picked up the hoe, and attacked weeds. She wouldn't ask Ben. She couldn't be around him for any length of time, not if she wanted to protect her heart.

The indigo would have to wait or just go to seed. The dye was expensive because of the laboriousness of the process that transformed the plain little plant into pressed cakes of rich blue-purple coloring. She could live without purchasing or manufacturing it. There were plenty of other dyes, and more and more cloth was available in marvelous colors all the time now. Esmeralda had shown her an entire new world of fabric.

Fatigued as she was from the apprenticeship, Josefa wouldn't have missed the experience. She had learned much from Esmeralda. So much...but not what pulled the seamstress away from the shop on a schedule of clocklike precision each afternoon.

Josefa leaned on the hoe handle. She had tried everything but direct questions, which she felt weren't appropriate for someone in her position to utter. The mystery nagged at her. She remembered Ben's calm, rational guesses about the seamstress's whereabouts, but Josefa preferred her own imaginative scenarios. They added to the mystery.

She shook her head. Again, Ben had floated into her thoughts. She hadn't seen him since the big night when the lights went on in town. She'd been deliberate in avoiding the church building site and the Alloway House when she expected he'd be there. He hadn't come to see her either, not at the dressmaker's or at the grove. She hoed with renewed vigor, as though she could clear her mind of Ben the way she removed clover, pepperbush, and Spanish needles.

A thump, bump, and snort—the standard Lumpy greeting—interrupted her reverie. She stopped to pet him and looked for Billy. He invariably was never far behind the dog that spent as much time at the grove as at home at Clyde's Mercantile. Polly often made up the trio. And sure enough, there they were.

"Want to come fishing with us?" Polly asked. "It's the only thing we could agree on 'cause I won't go hunting and he made a face when I suggested fern collecting. We're going to see if any of the Bights want to go, too. C'mon, it'll be fun."

"No, you run along, I'm enjoying my time here," Josefa said.

"Oh, wait. Here, Ben dropped this off for you." Polly gave her a folded piece of paper she pulled from her pocket.

Josefa lost her grip on the hoe, and it thudded into the sand.

"When?" She took the paper and started to unfold it.

"I don't know, maybe a half hour ago. He came by to talk to Seth, something about the church being almost finished. They left pretty quick."

"Come fishing," Billy said. "For once I got to escape a harvest. Alfredo kicked me off the crew when the Wilson boys showed up asking for work."

Josefa was momentarily distracted from the note. "Who?"

"The Wilsons, you know, from out in the woods," said Polly. "They always look kinda ragged anytime I see them. We're going to give them half of what we catch. Let's go, Billy. We have to get back before they finish picking and leave."

"Sure you don't want to change your mind?" Billy asked. Josefa shook her head. Not on her life. She watched Billy, Polly, and the tail-wagging Lumpy set off at a brisk pace. Only then did she look down at the paper clenched in her fist.

She picked up the hoe, set it against a tree, and moved to the bench in the shade. She sat down and opened the note.

"*Josefa, Found this in the professor's papers and copied it out for you. And to think he is asking me to teach him about Florida plant lore! I bet you can make some special fabric colors from these plants. See the descriptions and properties he lists for each of them? Figured you'd be interested. The man is amazing. You should hear him tell stories about his travels! Wow, makes me keen on going. I keep hinting that I'd be an able assistant. Ben.*"

She had no wish to hear stories about the professor's travels. Stories that made Ben long to trek to hinterlands and beyond in search of elusive new plant species that were always just over the next mountain.

Josefa knew she shouldn't malign work that meant so much to Ben. But knowledge and emotions lived in different places in her body. Ben had said he loved her. But he apparently didn't love her enough to stick around.

She prayed for help to bottle the sourness of not having her own way. Instead, she forced her attention to the dye plants, inhaled the earthy scent of freshly turned soil, and watched bright cardinals, parakeets, and blue jays dart among the trees and shrubs. The spicy raspberry scent from the roses against the kitchen garden fence drifted to her on the day's heat.

Josefa considered how the bright reds, greens, and blues of the birds could translate to a delicate embroidery with instant impact, on a table runner or pillow edge. She mentally formed the stitches and pattern as she gazed. And in doing so, she was reminded of the subtle understanding that prodded her every time she got lost in a spell of sewing or designing. She didn't know a thing about plant exploration, but she knew how total absorption grabbed hold of a person. The lure of new species consumed Ben the way the appeal of a fresh design did her.

But there was one big difference. Her passion wouldn't take the two of them away from each other. Whereas his would.

She looked at the paper again. Ben was right. It was indeed amazing. She had no idea that some of the flora he listed could serve as dye plants. Well, acorns and elderberry, yes, she knew that. But she'd no idea the roots of cedar could yield a purple dye, or that dog fennel would provide yellow, or fleabane a gold or green depending on the mordant used. She pored over the plant properties and growth habits. Cedar grew all over Seth's land, and dog fennel was wild on roadsides. Fleabane required closer searching. She looked forward to dye trials with all of them.

She hummed as she finished hoeing the small patch of ground. Her fingers itched to hold a needle, sit in the shade, and embroider a piece of snowy fine linen with bright, bold colors.

She cleaned off by the outdoor well and headed to the Taylor house, resigned to a possibly tense encounter with her aunt. If Lupita were still wedded to her most recent resurrection of the Texas travel plan, nothing would deter her. Still, one could hope.

"Need any help, *tia*?" she asked as she entered the kitchen.

Lupita shook her head as she kneaded a massive hunk of bread dough.

"Almost ready to shape this into loaves," she said. "After the second rise, you can help me carry them out to the brick oven. With it so warm already, I don't want to heat up the kitchen."

She and Josefa looked out the window at the quiet yard where the brick barbecue with a side oven stood empty and, presumably, unprepared for the job.

"That Billy!" Lupita grumbled. "He was to get the oven ready. Where is he? Nowhere to be found, I guess."

"He and Polly and possibly some of the Bights went fishing."

Lupita kneaded with an extra burst of energy.

"They plan to give half their catch to the Wilson boys."

"Ah," Lupita said, her face reflecting satisfaction. "They learn the lessons of our Lord and take them to heart."

"I'm sure Billy just forgot to stack the wood and kindling by the oven," Josefa said.

As I hope you forgot your renewed mission to send me away, she thought as she lined up the loaf pans and seasoned the inside of each.

Lord knew Josefa had prayed, and prayed some more, to every intercessor she had ever relied upon. To each, she had prayed with similar intent: *Please send my plea to Jesus, that Aunt Lupita will understand the best way to guide me toward the future.* Josefa figured the saints knew full well she meant for that future to not include Texas.

Lupita divided and shaped the dough, and tapped and patted each loaf into the correct proportions. "I'm making extra, just in case. In case the church is finished enough for us to have Mass tomorrow. Soon we will have Mass in our own church! Praise *Dios*! The day can't come soon enough!"

Josefa doubted the first Mass would be said the next day. The grove would have been in a frenzy of preparations. She suddenly wished she had gone to visit the building site over the past week. She both anticipated and feared the building's completion. They'd have a Catholic church right in town. But that very church would no longer need the hands that built it.

"We will want to have a potluck after the first Mass, of course," Lupita continued. "If Seth and Agnes come back with news that we can celebrate a Mass tomorrow—tomorrow, I can hardly imagine it, and of course it probably will not be so, but—I want to be ready with the bread."

She shrugged. "It will not go to waste, in any case. I'll send the extra home with the Wilson sons. In fact, I think I will do that anyway. I can't imagine the first Mass could be tomorrow."

"Aah, Aunt Lupita! The loaves and the fishes."

Her aunt looked at her, surprise in her eyes. "What? Oh! *Si!* No, I hadn't thought of that! But now that you mention it...the Lord has his ways, does he not?"

"Yes he does," Josefa nodded in agreement. And dared breathe. "I'll get the fire started for you," she offered.

"*Si, gracias,*" said Lupita. "That will give me time to bring lemonade out to your uncle and the men." She gestured to the large jug on the main table. "I'm sure by now they drank everything they carried out before."

Outside, Josefa saw that Billy had cut and stacked the needed wood and kindling. He just hadn't carried them from the woodpile to the brick oven. She rolled up her sleeves, brushed the inside of the oven clean, and placed inside enough wood for the hot fire needed to heat up the oven in time. Once lit, she closed the iron door and made sure nothing blocked the built-in vents. Then she settled down for a spell in one of the rocking chairs on the small back porch of the main house.

The thump, thump of a galloping horse reached her soon after she threaded her needle and took the first stitches. The horse, with Oswald astride, soon pranced into the backyard courtyard work area. She rose. Oswald waved at her to sit back down. He dismounted and covered the short distance to the porch in three large steps. He stood despite her invitation of a seat. She stopped in mid-stitch and left the needle tacked into the cotton, which was caught in a smooth circle by her embroidery ring. She looked up.

He paced, small, quick steps in a tight circle.

"I've given this all the thought it requires," he said and stopped in front of her. "We have had enough discussion on the matter. You and I will leave and have a quiet marriage ceremony in Orlando. I have family friends there and will send word for a justice of the peace to meet us at his office. I cannot wait any longer, Josefa."

She stared at him. Was he out of his mind? First he spoke of grand ceremonies in Philadelphia or wherever, then of a small ceremony, and now of being married in a place of business. With each passing day, the image of herself as a rich, fashionable Mrs. Oswald Heller III appeared more and more a fairy tale with an unhappy ending.

She set down her sewing. *Our Lady of Guadalupe, give me strength*, she prayed.

"Did you wait for my aunt to leave for the fields so you could ride up here unannounced? Were you out there, watching?" She had no intention of gracing his ridiculous proposal with an answer.

"Suppose I was," he said.

"I just wondered, Oswald. Because you know my aunt will insist we wed in church. Holy matrimony is a sacrament. It is important to me, to her, to the entire family, and to the church. We have to talk to the priest first, together, and prepare to receive the sacrament. If my aunt heard what you just said, she'd chase you out of here with a broom."

He waved a hand in annoyance. "Fine. We can go through the Papist motions if you insist. Afterward. We'll do it later."

"You mean have two ceremonies?"

"Yes. If you insist."

"We would have to have the wedding Mass first."

He paced again, stopped, and looked at her with heat in his eyes. "I said I'm ready to do this now."

"Holy matrimony is the only way I will consider myself to be married."

He scowled. "You are challenging my decision?"

Yes, she supposed she was. She kept silent.

"Are you?" he repeated. "I expect a wife to do my bidding without any backtalk."

That wasn't how Josefa thought of marriage. She thought of Seth and Agnes's marriage, of her aunt and uncle's. Neither of the men would order his wife to do something she strongly resisted. The couple would talk and find some kind of middle ground or other solution. Nobody ordered anybody around. Nobody had absolute authority. Each respected the other's special strengths and offset the other's weaknesses. They really listened to each other. The way Ben listens...she let the thought trail off.

She felt a calm reserve settle on her.

"I am not your wife, Oswald," she said.

"And you may not be," he said.

And perhaps that's as it should be, she thought, but didn't say.

They stared at each other. The birds had quieted as the morning rose toward noon. In the stillness, she listened to Lupita's lumbering steps that grew from faint to firm as her aunt returned from the fields. The screen door squeaked open, then closed with a light thud.

"Josefa?" Lupita opened the door to the back porch and peered out. "Ah, Señor Heller."

Josefa noted the absence of any offer of refreshments.

Oswald gave a bow so slight it was almost an insult.

"Good day, ma'am." Without a word or look at Josefa, he left the porch, mounted the horse, and rode away in a cool, deliberative manner.

Lupita came the rest of the way out, looked at Josefa's face, and sat down in the adjacent rocker.

"You know, my little *sobrina*, sometimes the devil can wear an attractive face. He makes false promises and lures with bright trinkets. Sooner or later, though, he can't help but show his true self. "

"I think I'm beginning to understand what you mean," Josefa said.

"Good. That is good. Then maybe you will also see that after the church celebration and after the president's visit…you will accept that I feel the need for you to be among our own."

"In Texas," Josefa said flatly.

"It would be for the best."

Josefa closed her eyes and leaned her head back. Maybe it would.

Chapter 21

"I can't believe tomorrow is my last day," Josefa said. She basted a ruffled border to the edge of a skirt and measured again to make sure she eased the cambric plaid into place evenly. "The time passed so fast, it's hard to believe it's early June. It seems like yesterday I first came in here." She snipped out a few stitches, realigned the fabric, and repinned it.

She set down the scissors and pincushion and glanced up at Esmeralda, who was seated across the room in front of a dress form on which she draped muslin with one hand and pinned with the other.

"I know, dear, and I hope you plan to work a few days a week for me until this crazy time of fashion mania ends. I never cease to be amazed. Every woman in town wants to impress the first lady. As if they will even get close to her. To think I wanted to be back home by now." She pinned with a briskness that increased with the tempo of her voice.

"I can lend a hand," Josefa said and resumed the hand basting. The ruffle had been troublesome from the start, because no matter how much Josefa tried to focus on the task, her mind wandered to Ben, to Oswald, and to her aunt's intentions.

"The president won't be here for another couple of weeks," Josefa said. "How much do you have left to do?"

Esmeralda lifted her arms into a gesture that swept the room. "You have no idea. The more the papers report on the trip, the more every woman decides something has to be turned out, let out, refitted, or dyed, or she wants a new hat, or ribbons or new feathers. Feathers! You know how I am about the senseless slaughter of birds so that fashionable ladies can adorn their hats with feathers! I will not use those feathers, and women will just have to find them someplace else because it won't be from me."

She quieted momentarily as she wrapped a measuring tape around the dress form in various places and then jotted down the dimensions. Josefa bit back a smile. She had become fond of the excitable little seamstress and her streams of nervous chatter. Esmeralda had a good heart.

"Why, I even had to refuse Mrs. Stetson when she asked that I replace the egret feathers on the hat she plans to wear. You know, of course, that the Stetsons have been invited to the main presidential reception. 'Why, Mrs. Stetson,' I told her in my best voice, 'you know the society ladies in Boston have a campaign against using such plumage.'

"Always remember, Josefa, be careful how you say no to important clients. I made sure to guide her toward thinking like a leader in society on the matter. She said she had no idea so many birds died and thanked me for telling her...

"But then she added that while she may give up plumes, she would not give up the idea that you, yes, you, Josefa, would make her dress for the reception."

"What?" Josefa could hardly get a word in.

"Yes, she said her seamstress wasn't able to make a special trip here, and that Mr. Stetson was set on staying long enough for the big visit, and she just had to have a new gown because didn't I know she never dreamed to bring such an item in her trunks to the wilds of Florida."

"I'm still digesting the fact that she asked specifically for me," Josefa said.

"She was mighty impressed with what you wore to the dinner," Esmeralda said. Her face shone with approval.

"You'll keep all the proceeds from the job, of course. This could launch you on that haute couture dressmaking business you came in here dreaming about. I already told Mrs. Stetson you'd be happy to fashion a garment for her. She'll be in tomorrow for a design consultation and fitting."

Josefa couldn't tamp down her surprised delight. One of her wildest dreams was coming true.

"No more apprentice after tomorrow," Esmeralda said, busy now at the fabric shelves where she pulled out bolts in various shades of blue. "I'll be proud to announce that you are a trained dressmaker ready to hang out her sign. You were near that point before you came in, but I think you learned a little here."

Josefa laughed. "I learned a lot! How can I ever thank you?"

"By staying long enough to help me with the ladies in a furor over seeing Mrs. Cleveland."

"If you'll help me with advice and counsel on the Stetson gown."

Esmeralda nodded her head with vigor. "Consider it done."

Their chatter was soon replaced with the whirl-like hum of their sewing machines. A while later, Josefa lifted her gaze when she heard the pace of Esmeralda's needle slow and then stop. The dressmaker scurried over to the counter, took a package, and left with a quick "I'll be back soon."

Josefa stopped sewing and leaned back in her chair. She didn't even have to look at the clock to know it was three in the afternoon. She had learned a lot here over the past two months, but she hadn't learned where Esmeralda went every day. She had become so fond of her mentor that she fretted more and more over the mystery. What if Esmeralda were in some kind of trouble? Maybe she had to pay ransom money. Or pay to keep someone quiet. Yes, that would explain why she had to steal food when no one looked. Because all her money went to…

Josefa's daydreams darted this way and that as she imagined ever more fantastical reasons for Esmeralda's odd behavior. Maybe she should be blunt and forward and just ask Esmeralda. But she couldn't get comfortable with the idea. Esmeralda was her elder and her supervisor in business, not a relative or close personal friend.

She drummed her fingertips on the sewing table. She had only one more day to find out. Tomorrow was her last day of regular work hours at the shop. What to do? She sat bolt upright. She had it! Or did she? Did she dare follow Esmeralda tomorrow? At a discreet distance. Josefa tossed the idea around in her mind. It seemed silly. Then noble. Then silly. Certainly nothing she'd ever attempt alone.

The longer Esmeralda was gone, the more Josefa warmed to the plan. Billy and Polly would jump at the chance to go with her. But Josefa knew whom she really wanted as an accompanying presence. Ben. Calm, level-headed Ben. If Ben went along, she'd feel both safe and as if she were on an adventure.

Yes, she admitted, she also wanted to see Ben for reasons that had nothing to do with his common sense. She needed to see his frank smile and warm eyes. She wanted to feel that sense of lightness and rightness that surfaced only when she was with him.

Josefa decided to head over to the church site as soon as Esmeralda returned. She could thank Ben for the letter about dye plants and request his assistance on discovering Esmeralda's secret. And maybe bring him up to date about the celebration Agnes was organizing for the day of the first Mass in the new church. It was only a few weeks away.

Josefa picked up the completed skirt with its three tiers of ruffles at the hem and snipped loose threads. She was halfway through ironing when Esmeralda returned, and she felt a tad guilty about her plan. But only until she saw Esmeralda's face. Esmeralda looked drawn and worried. *That's it,* Josefa decided. *If she's in trouble, townsfolk need to know so they can help.* Persimmon Hollow was a place that cared. Sometimes people needed a little push to realize they needed some help.

* * *

"You're not serious?" Ben pushed his hat back and scrunched his face.

"I am indeed," Josefa said, pacing back and forth along a short, invisible row in front of the church doorstep.

"Could be it's none of our business," Ben said, and he resumed hammering nails into the door trim.

"Could be it is! Could be it's Persimmon Hollow's business, Ben. Just like last weekend. Alfredo sent Billy off the harvest crew so the Wilson brothers could earn some money, and then Lupita baked a double batch of bread on the pretext of hoping the church opening would be the next day. She knew it was too soon. That left her with a full day's baking to share, and guess who she shared it with?"

"The Wilsons?"

"Yes. And if anybody had gone to them and asked if they needed help, they'd have said no. You know folks don't like to take charity. Sometimes you have to find other ways to get help to someone."

"You think following Esmeralda to see what's up is the best approach?"

"I honestly can't think of anything else. Trust me when I say I can't outright ask her."

"Why not?"

"Because she would have said something about it by now if she felt comfortable sharing the information. It's impolite for me to barge forward with a personal question. It'd be rude. I wasn't raised that way. And I'm pretty sure no one else knows of her strange habit."

"I don't think sneaking after people is proper, either," Ben said and stopped hammering. "But I have to admit you've got my interest up."

"Then you'll come?"

"Somewhat against my better judgment, yes." His grin widened. "Billy and Polly are our chaperones on this journey?"

She blushed. The memory of their kiss, his words, and the challenging look that had gleamed in his eyes the night of the street lighting rushed the blood to her face.

The heat in the air suddenly grew thick, especially in the gap between them. Space seemed to compress, too. Ben's gaze on her was intense. She was drawn into its depths and took a step closer.

Then she came to her senses and shook her head.

"No."

"No, what?" Ben asked.

"Just no. Stop looking at me like that. Stop making me feel, Ben. Stop making me fall in love with you!"

"Why?" His gaze now had shifted in tone and was more calculating.

"Because you don't plan to stay."

"A man has to be able to provide, Josefa. For himself. His family. Believe me, I would stay if I could. It's not that easy."

"Instead you will break my heart."

She saw the pain cross his face.

"No, Josefa, I don't want that. You're right." He stepped back and increased the distance between them. She yearned to bridge it.

"Can we just enjoy the time we have together?" His voice sounded strained.

She shrugged. There weren't other options right now.

But then he reached out and smoothed a stray lock of hair that had escaped her thick braid. She put her hand up to grab his, met his gaze, and granted him a small smile that spoke of other wishes.

Ben might be duty-bound to a path of responsibility that led him far from her, but he was going to travel it with her memory attached. As attached as his had become in her life, through which she now moved with an awareness of him always on the periphery.

"Hey, Ben, you done with this door? We're ready to paint," one of the crew members called out to him.

"Go ahead. I'll be right there," he yelled back, then redirected his attention back to her.

"Two more weeks, and we'll probably be done even before that," he said.

"Agnes is deep in celebration plans," Josefa said. "Are you staying for the festivities?"

"I plan to," he said. "Then I've got to get up to St. Augustine to check on my mom and sister."

She nodded, despite the ache in her heart. She wished she'd been able to shield her heart from him right from the start. She wished she could drum up this much emotion about Oswald. She felt a twisting in her stomach, like she had eaten something heavy and sour. There in the bright sunshine in front of a church, the falseness of her relationship with Oswald was a thorn. The closer she came to the reality of being Mrs. Oswald Heller III, the more it pricked at her.

"So...what time do you want to go on this, er, expedition tomorrow?" Ben asked. Around them, the other workers had circled from the far side of the building to the near side by them. White paint glistened on the boards of the building as they brushed on thick layers.

"She goes exactly at three o'clock. I mean, to the minute."

Josefa ran through mental scenarios.

"I'll be at the shop," she told him. "Could you meet me there? I'll tell Billy and Polly to do the same. The three of you should get together first. And watch! Keep an eye on her direction when she leaves. When she gets far enough away, signal to me. I'll run out, and we can follow."

Ben nodded.

"You're sure you want to do this?" he asked again.

"Absolutely," said Josefa.

"Okay, I'm in. Partly because I don't want to see you get into any scrapes."

"I think what we're doing is right," she said. "Till tomorrow." She waved goodbye and left. Ben picked up a paintbrush and went back to work.

Once she solved the Esmeralda mystery, Josefa thought, her mind and soul would be more at rest. She'd be better able to determine how to resolve the uncertainties that swirled around both Ben and Oswald. Her fixation on becoming the fashionable Mrs. Heller had started to appear childish and immature, whereas it had once been so firm she had redecorated his house in her mind.

Meanwhile, her delight in friendship with Ben had given way to more complex emotions that surprised her as much as they seemed to do him. She still dared to dream that a future with him was somehow possible. Yet that's all it was, a dream.

eep her in sight!" Josefa said in a loud whisper. She, Ben, Polly, and Billy trailed Esmeralda, who strode like a woman on a mission. She carried the same bag Josefa had seen her grasp from under the counter every time she left the shop for her three o'clock journey.

"We don't want her to see us!" Polly replied in the same loud whisper.

"Geez, you two, she can't hear us," Billy pointed out. "She's almost a quarter mile ahead."

"Ouch!" Josefa stumbled over a tree root and put out a hand that Ben quickly grabbed to steady her.

"Careful," he said.

"I don't want her to turn around and see us," Josefa said in the same dramatic whisper.

"We could just say we're out for an afternoon walk," Ben said, keeping a hand on her elbow. "That's probably all we're going to get out of this adventure anyway."

"Really, Ben! As if I have time for a stroll around the neighborhood. You wouldn't believe the complexity of the gown Mrs. Stetson has ordered, and I have such limited time in which to complete it. I mean, it is...oh, look!"

Ahead, Esmeralda had paused and turned toward a tree and its thick understory at the side of the road. Then she disappeared.

"Hurry!" Josefa said and lifted her hem so she could pick up her pace. "Or we'll never find where she went into the woods."

"Good thing, because if she'd kept going at that pace she would have ended in the lake or on Taylor Grove land," Polly said.

"Hey, I think I know where she's going!" Billy exclaimed. Gone was the blasé attitude he'd adopted in the wake of the rational reasons Ben suggested every few minutes as they trailed the dressmaker. "That's the way to the property my dad's trying to buy for the school, the one Estelle and the sisters want to build."

He sprinted ahead of Josefa, Ben, and Polly, then waited for them to catch up at the point of Esmeralda's entry. "Yup, I'm sure this is the property," he said. "I've explored out here."

Palm trees, scrub oak, palmetto, and pine fronted the road and formed a solid wall of tangled vegetation. If they hadn't seen the dressmaker vanish into the wilderness, they'd have never guessed she'd gone that way.

Josefa blew out a puff of air.

"I haven't come this far to stop now. It's my last official day at the shop. We have to figure this out, or I won't be able to rest for fear that Esmeralda is in some kind of trouble."

No one argued. Ben studied the twist of shoulder-level branches and squatted to inspect the ground. Billy followed his lead. Josefa wiped sweat beads off her face and unpinned, retwisted, and repinned the braid atop her head. She had fled the shop so fast she'd forgotten her hat. Polly plucked at the Spanish needle seeds that clung to the lower inches of her skirt.

"Here," Ben said. "She went in here." Sure enough, evidence of footprints were visible in the way the leaf mold compressed in a narrow trail that appeared at first glance as a mere break in the foliage.

He waved them to get in line behind him. "Small steps, no talking, be as quiet as you can."

"I'm holding my breath, even," Josefa whispered.

"Don't worry about us," Polly said quietly. "Tustenuggee taught me and Billy how to walk in the woods like he does."

"She means with no noise," Billy explained and then rolled his eyes when Polly scowled at his commentary.

"Where in heaven's name is she going?" Josefa wondered aloud before they stepped in. "And every day, no less. No wonder she always seems tired when she gets back. How far have we walked?"

"I'd say close to a mile," Ben said.

"So she's been going almost two miles each day," Josefa noted. "No wonder she hoards food and is still so small and skinny."

"This is becoming a stupid adventure," Polly said as she squeezed between the spiky swords of palmetto bushes. "If a rattlesnake jumps out of these palmettos and bites me, you guys are gonna be mighty sorry when I die."

Josefa stopped mid-step and looked at Ben.

"We're probably all right, but it pays to keep alert, as always," he said. "Esmeralda came this way minutes before us, so any snakes are likely long vanished. And, see, the path widens up ahead."

Indeed, once behind the border vegetation, a fairly wide path wound through the woods.

"I have my knife, and Billy has one too, if we need them," Ben said.

Curiosity propelled Josefa forward, and she kept close behind Ben as he led the way. Sure-footed but cautious, he was quiet yet covered ground quickly.

After about ten minutes, they entered an inner clearing that was formed by a tree-lined circle. Esmeralda stood on the far side, at the edge, and talked to a tree.

Ben stopped short, and Josefa collided with his broad back. She let out a loud breath, covered her mouth, and moved to Ben's side. Polly and Billy peered from behind them. Together, they watched Esmeralda gesture and talk. Her voice was audible, but she was too far away for her words to be heard with any clarity.

Josefa gripped Ben's hand. "Oh, that poor woman," she whispered.

Ben squeezed her hand in return. "You can say that again."

Billy and Polly gaped, mouths open.

"Golly, you'd a never thunk she's a crazy woman just from talking to her in town and stuff," Billy said.

"It's think, not thunk," Polly corrected him.

"Oh, brother."

"Hush," Josefa's silencing word was sharp. "Say a prayer for Miss Esmeralda instead of bickering."

"You okay, Josefa?" Ben asked, releasing her hand. "Sit down, here, in the shade. You look pretty shaken. I know, it sure is sad. What a surprise."

Josefa stayed upright but leaned on Ben as she watched, yet couldn't believe, what was in front of her. The competent, talkative, nervous sprite of a woman was off her rocker. That was about the only thing Josefa hadn't dreamed up to explain the daily absence. She was beginning to be sorry she'd followed. Ben had been right. This was none of their business.

She was mournful as she turned to Ben. "Should we step in and offer her some help? I feel like I should do something."

"We might startle her," he said.

"Yes, but I don't want to leave her here alone. Whatever drew her to this spot has addled her so much she can't even function properly. We must do something."

She bit her lower lip and tried to come up with a solution. From the way he stood there with his arms crossed, she knew Ben, too, was stumped.

Suddenly, the branches of the oak tree that was Esmeralda's conversation partner started to shake and rustle. Leaves rained down, followed by the appearance of booted feet, then legs, and finally a torso and head. Esmeralda reached out and helped a man land on his feet.

Josefa gasped so loud it drowned out Polly's half-shriek, a "Holy Cow!" from Billy, and Ben's "Eh?"

The man snapped his head in their direction and advanced on the four of them, who now huddled together. Ben stepped forward to shield them.

"I see ya, I seen ya coming in from half a mile out!" The man shouted. "Quiet, you were. Good woodsmen!"

Esmeralda twirled around. Her mouth opened in shock, and she put her hands up to her cheeks.

Josefa flushed and called out to her. "Are you hurt? We're here, Esmeralda. All will be OK."

Esmeralda stared, horror in her eyes. She opened and closed her mouth. The man drew closer to the little group with heavy steps that plodded through the grassy clearing with determination. The same determined step, in fact, that Esmeralda used, Josefa thought a bit wildly. The man's grayish-brown hair was bushy and tangled, with leaves and twigs in it, and his brown eyes were large and bright, and she couldn't see his mouth under the unkempt beard.

"Now see here, sir," Ben began.

"Let me shake your hand, my friend," the man said. "It's not every day I get folks come to visit. Come in, come in." He grabbed Ben's hand and pumped it. And pumped it some more. And didn't stop.

Esmeralda was beside him in a few swift movements. "Now, you let go of your new friend's hand so he can visit, y'hear, Ralph," she said in a soft voice that Josefa had never heard her use.

"Yes, yes, of course. Yes," he muttered and shook his head as if to clear away confusion.

Polly and Billy took a few steps back and continued to gape.

"Thank you, sir. I'd be honored to step in," Ben said.

Josefa moved forward. "Me too." She gripped Ben's hand, and he hers.

The man tilted his head back and roared with delight. Josefa jumped in fright, then squeezed Ben's hand and shifted closer to him.

"Mighty glad you finally brought your wife," the man said to Ben. Then he stopped talking and seemed momentarily lost.

Ben and Josefa's gazes met. Esmeralda appeared to be on the verge of tears.

"Ralph, why don't you show Ben your collection of dried flowers, and I'll visit with his wife," Esmeralda said, regrouping and using the soothing tone.

"All right, then," he said and waited for Ben to accompany him. As they moved toward the tree where Esmeralda had been standing, the dressmaker turned to Josefa.

"I'm sorry," Josefa said before Esmeralda could say anything. "We followed...I thought...Esmeralda, I thought you were in trouble or needed help or...how could I not notice that you left the shop every day, every single day, at three o'clock and were gone for so long and then always seemed tired and anxious upon return."

Esmeralda's shoulders sagged, but her hands were balled into tight fists. She shook her head.

"No, it's...I guess it would have become known at some point," she said to Josefa and glanced at Billy and Polly, who had stepped back a little farther but were within hearing. The dressmaker's usual vitality had drained, and she looked wan and faded. Josefa's heart went out to her.

Esmeralda looked at the tree, where Ben and Ralph squatted over some point of interest on the ground. She turned back to Josefa.

"Ralph is my brother. I bring food to him each day because otherwise he would starve." Esmeralda said. "It's not what you think. He's forgetful, is all."

She watched him for a few minutes before she continued.

"Ralph was smart, a businessman, who did well for himself. But his mind...he fell off a ladder he had climbed to change a wall sconce. He hit his head against the corner of a counter. We thought he had died. He was unconscious for two days, and it was a miracle when he woke up. At first he seemed OK, but his eyes were unfocused. Yet he seemed to get better, at first. Then we noticed he wasn't acting quite right. It became apparent the fall had affected his memory in some way. And his behavior, too, but not in a frightful or dark way.

"He walked out of his house and went to live in a nearby wooded area. We were quite perplexed, Josefa. No one in the family could get him to stay in our homes—or in his own. Winter was closing in. He and a partner had homesteaded land here several years previous, and Ralph held on to his claim after his partner moved on. We had a family council and packed our bags for Florida—we being my parents and me, since I'm a widow and my children are grown.

"We held out hope Florida's climate might bring him back to his old self. You can see that didn't happen."

They all watched Ralph deep in discussion with Ben. At intervals, Ben nodded and inspected the flora Ralph showed him.

"My elderly parents didn't like Florida, and their health started to fail. They soon returned North. Now my sister needs help with their care. So I'm moving back, and trying to convince one of my children to come down and stay awhile. Maybe even build on the land here to keep an eye on Ralph. He lives in a tree house and won't go elsewhere. He seems to have found a measure of peace. But he's forgetful. He forgets to eat, for example."

"I knew it!" Billy piped up. "I knew I saw suspicious movement in the tree the day me and dad came out here to check out the land. I knew it wasn't a bird or squirrel."

"The land isn't for sale," Esmeralda said.

"You're the legal holdup?" Understanding dawned in Josefa.

"Yes." Esmeralda nodded. "Ralph is happy here. He proved up enough in the early days to secure the land. He stopped working it after a freeze damaged his grove and a storm blew down the shack he'd built. Went back North to earn his living. Even if the land were for sale, I'm not sure anyone could get him to leave, without forcing him off."

"What if we offered him another tree house on another piece of land?" The idea sparked in Josefa almost as she spoke the words.

Esmeralda looked at her with a quizzical expression.

"I'm thinking aloud," Josefa said. "If there were a place he could go that would be closer to people who could help...you and your family wouldn't be compelled to shoulder the burden alone.

He'd be closer to caring people, and Estelle's community would have a school nearby."

The idea took shape as she spoke.

"Money from the sale of the land could be saved and used for his food and other care."

She knew her proposal was presumptuous, but she also knew Ralph could find a sheltered home site at Taylor Grove, and that enough people there and in town would make sure he got along all right.

Ben and Ralph rose and walked back to meet them.

"I was just saying, Ralph, that perhaps you might be interested in moving to a new tree house," Josefa said. Ben's glance darted to her, and his eyes held questions that gave way to understanding, and then, admiration.

"Ah, missy, now why would Ralph do that?" He leaned in toward her and peered at her, lips pursed and eyes squinted with interest.

"Just an idea," she said. "That's all. Maybe we can talk about it later."

"Yes, later, later. Essie, I'm hungry. Did I eat today?"

"No, Ralph, but I brought you a sandwich." She opened her bag and got out the food. Ralph sat down in place and started to eat.

Ben caught Josefa's gaze and raised an eyebrow and shoulder in the direction of the path back out toward the road. Josefa nodded yes.

"Esmeralda, we're going to leave. I'll come back to town Monday, pick up my things and work out a schedule for Mrs. Stetson's gown," Josefa said. "In the meantime...my aunt and uncle, and Agnes and Seth, are wonderful at finding solutions. Let me see what they suggest about Ralph, and if they think my plan has any merit. In the meantime, if you'd like, we can bring food to Ralph over the weekend. It's not that far from Taylor Grove."

The dressmaker was seated now on a towel she'd spread on the ground next to her brother. She shook her head. "Thank you, but no. I've grown accustomed to these visits. He has, too, so we'd best keep things on their normal routine. But, thank you so much."

"Nothing to thank us for," Josefa said. "You're the one who deserves the accolades."

She and Ben, Polly, and Billy started back through the woods. The return journey was somber, with even Billy and Polly's normal exuberance subdued.

"Life is so fragile," Josefa finally said as they were halfway to the main part of Persimmon Hollow, where Billy had parked the grove cart in Clyde's mercantile yard.

"Never know when something's going to happen," Ben agreed.

"But love is so strong," Josefa said. "Real love." She felt wiser than she had at the start of her apprenticeship—but especially since the start of this very day.

"Listen to our prayers, oh Lady of Guadalupe," she murmured. "Help us in our needs. Help others in their needs. Help that family through their trials. And help us help them."

She looked at Ben, at Polly, and at Billy with eyes anew. The day had become a reminder of how much they all needed one another and how much stronger a community was than a lone person trying to steer through life unattended.

* * *

It was a quiet, reflective group that gathered in the living room after dinner that evening. The kerosene lantern pooled its light on the open pages of Louisa May Alcott's *Jo's Boys* as Seth looked for where he'd left off reading aloud the previous night.

"What happened to the bookmark?" he asked.

"Hmmm," said Polly and picked up fluffy Boots from her lap, where she had been brushing her. "I think we might have the culprit right here. The ribbon on the top of the bookmark was too much for her to resist. I found it lying on the kitchen floor earlier today."

"That cat belongs in the barn," Billy said.

"Nuh-uh," said Polly. "She's a house cat. She stays inside. Sleeps with me at night, too."

"Shhhh," Agnes said. "I just got the baby to sleep." She checked the blanket over him in the cradle.

"I'll put the two of you in the barn if you wake the baby," Lupita said as she started to stitch a patch onto a pair Billy's work pants.

"If Uncle Alfredo's snoring doesn't wake him up first," said Josefa, pointing toward her uncle. "Look." His head nodded on his chest.

"Ah, here we are," Seth said. "Ready?" He glanced around the room to make sure he had everyone's attention. All except Alfredo and baby Seth, that is.

"I'll keep it short tonight," Seth said. "That debate about Ralph took longer than I expected."

"And no firm solution yet," Agnes said. "Although Josefa's suggestion gives us a good base to start from. It could work—especially if we can determine that his eccentricity can be guided. We have a sewing circle meeting at Fanny's in a few days, and we'll see if any more ideas emerge. Please read to us, even if just for a short while."

"At your service, ma'am," Seth said, and Josefa saw the love in his glance toward Agnes. "I know a certain someone in the family wouldn't be able to sleep without a story update," Seth added and looked at Polly. She bobbed her head so hard in eager affirmation that her curly ringlets bounced.

"Thought so," he said. "Chapter 11. Emil's Thanksgiving. The Brenda was scudding along—" Suddenly a loud rap on the front door startled them all. Alfredo jerked awake. The baby smacked his lips in his sleep.

"I'll see who it is." Billy jumped up. He opened the door, and everyone saw Oswald framed against the starry skies. "Oh, uh, hi, won't you come in…"

Josefa moved to head off Billy's invitation and to stop Oswald before he strode in, took over the room, and disrupted the evening's tranquility.

"I'll take it from here," she said in a quiet but firm voice to Billy. "Let's go to the porch, Oswald, so we don't disturb the others."

He trailed her outside, where she positioned herself directly in front of the window. Everyone inside would be able to keep her in view.

"I came by the shop twice today to see you," he said. He seemed both annoyed and bored, and his gaze wandered from her to the yard to the acreage beyond, and back again.

"We were out…visiting," she hedged.

"It'd be nice if you made yourself more available," he said.

"Oswald, I've been thinking…about you, me, our future." If she had a future with him. "I, ah, I must insist—if we decide to move forward, that is—on a long engagement, in keeping with my family's traditions. And a Catholic wedding."

She took courage from his silence. "Actually, I question whether our future together is meant to be. I beg you to allow me time and space to pray about this…and I ask that you accept my wishes if I feel our companionship and marriage plans should come to an end."

There. She'd said it.

"Yeah, yeah, whatever," he said and checked his watch.

She crossed her arms over her chest in an attempt to appear collected. His quick acquiescence raised her guard. Oswald hadn't ever been so readily agreeable. She resented his cavalier attitude and apparent indifference to her concerns. She had put her heart into her words, while he—she allowed herself to see, as she hadn't in the past—was engrossed in himself. She wasn't even sure he'd listened fully to her.

"Well, then," she said, "I'm glad you understand. The time apart will help us determine the truth, to know if we are meant to spend our lives together."

His eyes glittered in the pale light that spilled from the window.

"Time will disabuse you of whatever silly notions others have put in your head, Josefa. However, I will make allowances for your youth. But don't try my patience too long."

He glanced around again, looked at the seats, pulled out a handkerchief and wiped the porch railing before leaning against it.

"I didn't come over here to discuss wedding plans. I'm here to tell you I finagled invitations to one of the presidential receptions. Of course you will attend with me."

"Oh!" Josefa couldn't tamp down her elation. She gripped her hands together. "That's so exciting!"

Oswald's eyes gleamed. "I knew you'd be dazzled."

"I'd get to meet the first lady?" She'd dance to his tune, to an extent, for such an opportunity. He'd been quite agreeable, if distant, to her request. He wouldn't abuse their understanding.

"Meet her? Possibly. At the least you'll be in the same room."

First, an haute couture dressmaking commission. Now, a chance to be presented to the best-dressed, most fashionable woman in the United States. Perhaps she'd be noted as the designer of the dress Mrs. Stetson was wearing to one of the gala events.

Josefa's dream burned brightly.

Her euphoria deflated a bit when she saw the self-satisfied smirk on Oswald's face.

"I'm...greatly appreciative to you for this opportunity," she said. "I'll understand if you wish to withdraw the offer due to my request for time and reconsideration of our relationship."

"Think nothing of it. The offer stands."

She wondered if perhaps he did have a magnanimous side. He certainly was being generous. Not many men would accept the introduction of doubt into a relationship with such equability and then turn around and extend an invitation of such magnitude. Part of her was tempted to think he didn't care what she said or did about anything. But that made no sense. He cared enough when she committed the social stumbles he called faux pas.

"I don't know how to thank you," she said.

"By getting rid of whatever ridiculous chaperone your guardians cook up for the trip," he said and grinned. "We'll likely stay overnight in St. Augustine or Jacksonville."

She almost laughed aloud, relaxing her arms and letting them hang at her side.

"That, Oswald, will never happen." And for once, Josefa knew she'd be in full agreement with whatever her aunt dictated regarding propriety for the occasion. Lupita would insist on at least one appropriate chaperone, if not two.

"I see," he said and glanced at his pocket watch again. "The night grows late. Good evening, Josefa."

He didn't bow or kiss her hand or step inside to exchange courteous good-byes. He was gone as quickly as he had arrived.

Josefa was too tired to ponder his behavior long. The day's

exertions had taxed her. Her eyelids were heavy as she went back inside, where Seth's strong voice held the audience rapt.

She'd already missed much of the storytelling. She didn't want to interrupt their pleasure with her own news. It could wait until the morning. She yawned and waved a goodnight instead of rejoining the group. Her tidy bed in the Gomez cabin beckoned. As did the dreams that swirled through her head.

Chapter 23

So what did you decide?" asked Fanny, stopping her needle mid-stitch.

"Well," said Agnes, "Tustenuggee lives in a chickee on the homestead, so why can't Ralph live in a tree house. We certainly have enough land at the grove. Esmeralda said he's eccentric but harmless. Quite friendly, in fact. The cause of concern is his memory problems."

"Who's gonna build the tree house?" Polly asked in her first show of interest since she, Josefa, Agnes, and Lupita had arrived at the Alloway House for the sewing circle meeting. Polly sat on the sofa in the parlor, apart from the others at the table, and stitched halfheartedly on a needlepoint until finding an excuse to put it down and hold baby Seth. Josefa was pretty sure Polly had been laboring on the same small sampler for the entire year Josefa had been part of the family.

"We'll let your father and the men decide those next steps," Agnes said. "But I'm sure they'll welcome your opinions," she added.

The baby was quiet, so Polly gently placed him in the cradle Fanny kept in the house. Then she moved over to the table.

"Josefa, how many layers of...that scalloped stuff are you

putting over the skirt? Is that the dress for Mrs. Stetson for the president's event?" she asked.

"Yes, and 'that stuff' is called tulle. It will almost cover the pleated skirt. Then I'll add a few bows of velvet ribbon, probably black, as accents against the deep rose of the skirt and the lighter pink of the over-drapery. The bows will match the small velvet jacket. Vest, really. It'll be sleeveless."

"The outfit is shaping up beautifully," said Agnes.

"What are you going to wear that day?" Polly asked.

"That day?" Fanny parroted. "Josefa, are you also going to see the president?"

Josefa nodded but didn't glance up.

"My word! Tell me all the details."

Her enthusiasm was as great as was Josefa's, though Josefa had mixed feelings. While the idea of the trip and reception was exciting, the reality of her escort wasn't.

"Honey, what's wrong?" Fanny asked in a gentle voice.

"I'd look like that, too, if I had to go anywhere with Oswald Heller," said Polly. Even Agnes's frown didn't dissuade her from giggling at her own comment.

"An invitation to a presidential reception offers you superb opportunities to meet women who can afford high fashion," Fanny said.

"Josefa is having second thoughts about her place in Señor Heller's life," said Lupita. "I for one breathe easier for it. Each day I grow more convinced they are unsuited to one another in temperament, in what each expects from a spouse, and in matters of faith."

Josefa only half heard her. She had begun to spin her dream web again until it glistened in her mind. She saw herself dancing at the presidential reception, surrounded by people and finery of exquisite taste, with herself in...oh...maybe her green satin dress, the one with the gold embroidery and accents of lace. People would ask where she got her dress...and would ask did she know who dressed Mrs. Stetson and...

"Josefa! Come back to earth." Polly tapped her arm.

"Oh, what did you say?" Josefa asked and felt her cheeks grow warm. She was acting just as she'd done with the Stetson dinner. Her dreams glittered and then reality proved stark. But this time, she'd get to see the first lady's fashions. Surely that made everything worthwhile.

"Nothing. Your aunt was talking about Oswald. But I want to say that this dress makes me realize I'll never be able to sew like you."

"Oh, it's a special dress, that is certain. I'm taking extra care. You know, perhaps it could lead to more commissions. Things I could do from home. Not life in a dressmaking shop."

"I know of no man who wants his wife to run a business instead of a home," Lupita said.

Except Ben, Josefa thought. *Ben wouldn't mind.*

She looked at Agnes. "You can and create specialties and confections for the tourist store while being a wife and mother. And didn't you continue teaching for a while after you and Seth married?"

Agnes nodded and stopped sewing. "Yes. It is a lot of work, but I believe in using the talents God gave us. The jams and jellies are some of our most popular items at the store. I couldn't do it without the assistance of Lupita. But Seth and the baby and Polly and Billy are more important, and they always will be. Family comes first, Josefa."

As if on cue, baby Seth woke up, started to fret, and then began to howl.

"He doesn't know where he is and doesn't see you!" Josefa exclaimed, but Agnes was already out of her chair. She picked him up and checked his diaper.

"A call of nature," she said. "Excuse me, ladies, for a few minutes."

"Use my bedroom," Fanny called as Agnes held the baby in one arm and picked up her carry bag of baby items.

"Polly, take a few turns with the needle on the shirtwaist for me," called Agnes as she left.

Her comment made Josefa remember her own dear, departed mother, and how they had sewn together for many happy hours. Sewing always made her feel close to her mother. How she wished she and her immediate family were together, gathered at the table right now. The pain underneath the healing scar still throbbed at times.

"Yes, family matters," Josefa said. "Aunt Lupita, you know that's why I don't want to leave you and everyone at the grove and Persimmon Hollow. But maybe it's the best thing I could do."

She looked up, her eyes huge in her face. She had been so certain of everything, only a few months ago. "Maybe I should stop fighting and just go to your relatives. Stop fighting and practice acceptance."

"They are your relatives, too, *mi sobrina*," said Lupita, but she didn't appear overjoyed that Josefa might be living with them instead of with her at the grove.

Fanny tut-tutted and poured more tea for them all. Polly jumped up and hugged Josefa from behind, but otherwise the room was so quiet the call of a mockingbird from a tree outside the window carried through the house and settled around them.

Lupita let out a heavy sigh. "I don't look forward to you leaving."

"*Tia!*" said Josefa. "Then why have you been talking about it for weeks? Months?"

"Because I love you, Josefa, and I want the best for you. I want a good marriage for you, with a man deserving of you. I was never convinced about the worth of Señor Heller, despite his attempts to win me to his side. He is a smooth talker. But now I sense your doubts grow larger each day." She waved a hand in the air. "We'll talk about this again after the church celebration and after the president's visit. That is what we decided, no?"

Josefa set down the mass of tulle, got up, and hugged her aunt, who turned in her chair to return the embrace. Fanny dabbed at her eyes. Even Polly appeared moved. By the time Agnes returned with the gurgling baby, everyone was misty-eyed.

"What did I miss?" she asked as she sat down with the baby in her lap.

"Seeing just how much we love one another and how important family is," said Josefa, and she slid back into her own chair.

"And how great that Josefa will be around Persimmon Hollow a while longer," added Polly. "A long while, I hope."

"Good, because things might get a little exciting soon," Fanny said. "Art has determined the shell mounds out by the river rail bed merit much closer attention. He plans to stay the summer and do preliminary work. He's recommending that his colleagues— along with himself—conduct a full archaeological dig next season or possibly the year after that. Who knows what they'll find!"

"Would this be the professor who was your youthful beau?" Agnes asked, though all at the table knew the answer.

"Oh, pshaw," Fanny said, coloring. She fanned herself. "No one was more surprised than me when he showed up."

"I'm happy for you, Fanny," Agnes said. "A scientific study sounds compelling."

"Why is everybody so bothered about the mounds?" Polly wanted to know.

"You best ask Billy when we get back," Agnes said. "He knows quite a bit. He says Tustenuggee told him many of the mounds that dot the river valley contain sacred items, and in some cases are places of eternal rest for his ancestors. We can learn more from Tustenuggee."

"Ben is also intrigued by the mounds," Josefa added.

"I remember, Fanny, how you pointed them out to me on my first day in Persimmon Hollow, when we went past the railroad construction," Agnes said. "Everything was so strange to me that day."

"Hard to believe now, isn't it?" Fanny asked.

"It's an example of how God provides, but we don't always see the direction right away," Agnes said in a quiet voice. "I was in agony from homesickness when I first arrived here. I didn't understand what God was telling me at all."

She glanced at Josefa. "That's why we persevere. Even when the road's direction isn't clear or to our liking, at least at first, and especially if we're unable to change it."

Josefa knew she had questioned God plenty in the past year. She didn't want to talk about duty and accepting God's will today. She readjusted the pins in her fabric now that she was ready to attach the draped tulle to the pleated skirt.

"Agnes, have you decided what to do for the final benefit for the church's building fund?" Josefa asked. She wanted to get the focus off her, her wishes, her wants, and her hopes.

"I have a few ideas," Agnes said, turning toward Fanny. "What's your opinion on doing a bazaar or a theatrical?"

"A play!" said Polly.

"A play!" echoed Josefa, thinking of the costumes she could create.

"Bazaar," said Lupita.

"I'm a bit torn," admitted Agnes.

Fanny looked at them for a moment. "Why not both?"

"Why didn't I think of that?" Polly wondered.

Fanny warmed to the idea. "But not now," she said.

The women all looked at her.

"A play and bazaar take months to execute properly. Plan that for next season, perhaps to benefit the orphanage. For now, what about a box luncheon? We could pull it together quickly and have it before the winter boarders all leave. They'll be gone soon after the president's visit. But while here, they likely will participate or at least donate. We'll have plenty of time afterward to dream up the theatrical and everything that goes along with it—rehearsals, a set, costumes."

Fanny's option was so perfect everyone murmured immediate agreement. But mention of the boarders brought to Josefa's mind the sad young woman.

"Fanny," she asked, "why is Penelope Gold always so melancholy?"

Fanny sighed. "It's quite tragic. Her sister-in-law told me Penelope made the journey to Florida unwillingly. The family ordered her to go, to keep her away from an unsuitable beau. I understand he's quite unsavory."

"Hmm, yes, that is sad," Josefa agreed. "She appears to find some peace in art. She sketches and paints beautifully."

"She does," Fanny agreed. "She's quite nice when you sit and talk with her. I'm certain she'll contribute to the benefit."

Josefa began to mull over her box lunch. Maybe Oswald would bid a nice price as a donation to the church. He'd told her about his family's philanthropy. Cooking wasn't her strongest point, despite her aunt's pointed comments about reaching a man through his stomach. But she always got compliments when she made fried chicken, thanks to Lupita's tutelage.

By the time the group prepared to leave, the plans for the box luncheon were in place for the following Saturday, a little more than a week away.

"The timing is perfect," Agnes enthused as they gathered the baby's things and their sewing supplies. "With only one week between the lunch and the first Mass, we'll generate a lot of excitement about the church dedication."

"Look, here come Clyde and Eunice," said Fanny as she ushered the women to the porch.

The Alloway House was near the main thoroughfare, Persimmon Boulevard, and faced the large, enclosed rear yard of Clyde's Mercantile. Clyde and Eunice had been living just across the street from Fanny in the mercantile's attached living quarters since marrying.

The women watched Eunice and Clyde march over from the mercantile yard and up the walkway toward the Alloway porch. The two almost looked alike, tall, spare, gray-haired, except Eunice wore spectacles and Clyde didn't. Right now, they shared the same tight-lipped expression.

"Hello!" called Agnes. "Say hello, Seth," she said and helped the baby lift his arm and wave as she and Josefa, Lupita, and Polly stepped off the porch and started down the walk.

Eunice patted the baby but hardly broke her stride as the two groups passed on the walkway. "I'm sorry we don't have time to tarry," she said, her gaze sharp. Clyde gave a stiff nod as he passed.

Josefa turned and looked at their backs as they climbed the steps to the porch. Fanny was still in the doorway, but her smile faded as they approached. She gave one last, short wave to Josefa before hurrying inside after Eunice and Clyde and closing the door.

"Should we stay and make sure everything's all right?" Josefa asked Agnes.

"They certainly appear vexed," Lupita said.

Agnes massaged small circles on the baby's tiny back. "No," she said slowly. "They would have called us back if we were meant to hear...whatever they are in such a hurry to discuss."

Josefa saw a mixture of concern and hurt in Agnes, who was like a daughter to the middle-aged, childless Alloway sisters who had spent years as missionaries before helping their father settle Persimmon Hollow.

"Must be mighty serious," said Polly. "I never saw them act like that in all the time we lived with them. Did you, Agnes?"

"No," said Agnes as she shook her head. "But whatever it is, it's in God's hands."

"*Si,* the business is between them and God, not us, at least not right now," agreed Lupita, and she urged the little group out toward the road and across the street to their horse and buggy in the mercantile yard. "They will tell us if and when we need to know."

Josefa said a silent prayer that all would be well. But she was uneasy. The looks on Clyde's and Eunice's face were ominous. Exactly the opposite of everything Persimmon Hollow was about.

Chapter 24

Seth guided the team off the roadway, and the wagon rumbled down to the shore of Blue Lake. Josefa felt the buzz of excitement stirring the crowd there. People were more animated than the lake itself, which was alive with the ripple of mini-waves from the day's breeze.

"Wow. Something more is going on than just a box lunch," Polly said. "I need to find out."

"Just a minute, young lady," Agnes halted her. She turned from the front seat and with her free hand grabbed Polly's sleeve before she had time to stand up in the wagon bed.

"We're as anxious to know as you are," Lupita said. "That crowd is louder than the carpenter bees when I hang laundry near one of the holes they drilled in the line post."

"We'll walk together," Agnes added to Polly.

Josefa and Polly climbed out of the back of the wagon, and Billy handed them each their neatly packed box lunches. Alfredo assisted Lupita, and Seth took the baby while Agnes descended. Then he handed the baby back to her.

"Thanks for making my sandwiches for me," Polly whispered to Josefa, quietly enough that Agnes and Lupita couldn't overhear. They were focused on settling the baby once Seth got the perambulator out of the wagon. The mosquito netting draped over the baby's buggy was decorated in delicate embroidery by Josefa.

"Next time, you have to help with the preparation!" Josefa chided her gently. "You have to learn!"

"Where's Ben?" Polly asked. "Why didn't he come with us? He was at the grove talking to Seth just before we left."

Josefa wondered the same but refused to ask. She didn't want to care where Ben was.

"He wanted to check something at the church first," Agnes answered. "He's so dedicated. I like that. He said he'd be along later, before the auction begins."

"Maybe he'll bid on your lunch, Josefa," Polly said with a side-long glance at Josefa, who toyed with the embroidered tea towel she used to cover the wicker basket that held the chicken.

Josefa saw Agnes watch her with a thoughtful look on her face. "You know, Josefa, the men who make the best husbands are sometimes hidden under exteriors less fashionable than expected," she said.

"Who said anything about husbands?" asked Josefa, who started to feel quite cross for no reason at all. "Can we go find out what the excitement is about and forget about my courtship status for a while?"

"Halloo, halloo!" Fanny detached herself from the crowd and came huffing up to meet them. "Did you hear the news? This is unbelievable!" She fanned herself, her cheeks pink despite the day's perfect weather.

Fanny fell into step with them. "President Cleveland and his wife plan to make a stop in Palatka! Can you imagine! So close! A journey of only a few hours! Dears, now the entire town is ready to make the excursion. I mean, we had excitement before, when everyone thought the closest stop was St. Augustine or Jacksonville, but Palatka? You will be going, won't you?"

"Fanny, I don't want to take this little guy on such a trip," Agnes said, gesturing toward the baby. "Too much noise, dust, and crowds."

"I will stay back too," Lupita said. "These feet are not up to such a day of pushing through crowds."

"Seth hates crowds," Agnes added.

"Alfredo isn't fond of them, either," said Lupita, and the two women laughed.

Josefa had already left the conversation. She was lost in a daydream. They were all at the train station in Palatka, and Mrs. Cleveland had just exited the train from a door mere steps from where Josefa stood. The first lady looked around, and her gaze settled on Josefa. *What a lovely dress, dear, who is your seamstress,* the first lady asked Josefa, who curtsied and—

"Josefa! *Dios Mio,* are you hard of hearing?" Lupita asked.

"That would be me, and I heard you just fine," Fanny said. "Josefa must have her mind on someone—er, something—else."

Lupita looked at Josefa under lowered brows. "Come help us set up."

The group found an open spot in the crowd and arranged their blankets and baskets as Fanny went to see about the order of the auction.

Soon after, she was back by their side and ready to start.

"Agnes, do you want to do the announcing, take the cash payments, or help keep the young ladies and their lunches in order?"

"I'll work with the girls," Agnes said. "I'll join you in a few minutes. I need to feed the baby first."

Fanny nodded and started to walk off. "Oh," she said and stopped. She turned back toward the little group, and she no longer smiled. "I have something more sober to share, afterward, that you'll want to hear," she said. "Remind me, Agnes." She cast a quick, uncomfortable glance at Josefa before she left.

"What was that about?" Josefa asked.

"We'll find out later," Agnes said. "Too much going on right now." She was distracted, opening a small container of food she had mashed into a pulp for the baby to digest. Josefa again felt a tiny pang in her heart as she watched the baby and Agnes's tender care of him.

"Your turn will come," Lupita said to her and pulled her close for a hug.

For once, Josefa didn't pull back as she was apt to do when someone came too close to knowing her heart. She hugged her aunt. Lupita then took over the feeding and shooed Agnes to the picnic tables being used as a staging area.

"Attention! May I have your attention!"

Billy had the loudest mouth in the state, Josefa sometimes thought.

"The box luncheon to benefit the building of Persimmon Hollow Catholic Church is about to begin." He stepped down from the orange crate that served as a makeshift podium, and Fanny, Agnes, and Eunice took over.

"Ladies, please line up here," Eunice pointed with authority to a space at the right of the two tables piled high with box lunches.

"As your name is called, pick up your box, walk here next to us, and let the bidding begin. Bidders, when you win a box, please provide payment to me—I'll be sitting right there—before you sit down to dine with your luncheon date."

Eunice stepped away to her cash post, and Fanny stood up.

"Do I have any volunteers to go first?" she asked.

Silence. Never had a crowd become so silent so quickly, thought Josefa. But it lasted only a minute.

"I heard Lupita Gomez brought her rice and beans," a man yelled.

"Heard the same," shouted another.

"Yes, we did make one exception to the rules," Fanny said. "Because this is such an important benefit, we allowed married women to participate. Husbands, we expect you to bid on your wives' food!"

Lupita waved at them to go ahead without her. Agnes brought up Lupita's basket.

"Fifty cents!"

"One dollar."

"One dollar and a quarter!"

Clearly, Fanny's rule was being ignored, Josefa thought, as she looked around. Lupita was famous throughout Persimmon Hollow for her rice and beans. She'd brought enough today to feed at least ten people.

"Do you accept pesos?"

Alfredo had the crowd's attention. He gave a wide smile.

"My tired brain couldn't determine the exchange rate!" Fanny protested.

"In that case, I bid five dollars," Alfredo said.

"Sold!" called Fanny. "But I understand Mrs. Gomez brought quite a supply with her. She wishes me to say that anyone who wants to buy a bowlful may do so for twenty-five cents. She and Mrs. Taylor will assist you."

Josefa was called to the front halfway through the auction. Suddenly shy, she walked up and stood with her box.

Oswald called out a bid almost before she reached Fanny at the staging area.

"Two dollars."

Really, Josefa thought. *Couldn't he bid a bit higher?*

"Two dollars fifty cents."

She looked to see who had outbid Oswald. Oswald did the same. Her heart did a quick skip when she saw Ben. He stood a little ways off from Oswald, but had they been on opposite ends of the lake, their differences still would have been apparent.

Oswald was a portrait of a country estate owner, as far as she could tell from comparisons to etchings she'd seen in *Harper's.* He wore a pressed white shirt with starched collar, fitted breeches, and riding boots. He even had on a cravat. He looked a little bored, and definitely out of place in Persimmon Hollow. His pale blue eyes were expressionless.

Then there was Ben. His work pants were a bit rumpled and hardly new. Her practiced eye knew they had been dyed with bark of oak. His shirt was clean but of common homespun with ties instead of buttons like Oswald's. He wore brogans, not riding boots. His hair was, as usual, somewhat disheveled but clean. But he was robust, sturdy, and alive with a spirit and interest in the proceedings that Oswald lacked. Ben's eyes were bright and as warm as his expression.

He looked like exactly what he was, a country boy. One with a big heart. One who made her think of kisses by the light of the moon.

She knew in her heart who she hoped would win her lunch.

She watched as Oswald gave Ben a once-over and then turned his glance away with an air of dismissal as he snapped his fingers in the air.

"Three dollars," Oswald said and brushed an imaginary speck of dust from his sleeve.

"Three-fifty."

There was a gasp from the crowd. Oswald darted a look of annoyance at Ben, who stood still but tall and firm. Josefa again noticed his air of quiet assurance. Ben didn't look at Oswald. He kept his gaze fixed ahead, toward Josefa, but without meeting her gaze.

"I don't have time for this," Oswald said. "Four dollars, and let's be done with it."

Josefa saw a brief expression of distaste cross Fanny's face before she ignored Oswald's comment and looked toward Ben to see if he would increase his bid.

Ben did meet her gaze then, for the merest moment, and Josefa felt her own eyes widen at the depth and love she saw there. Ben was quiet, she thought, but he was no simpleton, and anyone who thought so seriously underestimated him.

"Four-fifty."

She was stunned. She knew how much Ben's family relied on every cent he sent them. Why was he doing this? For her? For the church? To get back at Oswald for some reason?

Oswald's face grew impatient, and he smoothed his palm across the front edge of his hair, being careful, Josefa noticed, not to muss it.

"Ten dollars. Let's see the country bumpkin top that," he said.

Fanny's mouth fell into an O. As did Josefa's. And Agnes's. As, Josefa was quite certain, did everyone else's. Bidding ten dollars on a box lunch was unheard of. She'd never known of one to go above five dollars. Even those were topics of conversation for weeks. Invariably, those couples courted and wed.

Ben was silent.

Fanny recovered first.

"Well. I guess you have earned the right to eat lunch with Josefa," Fanny said to Oswald, somewhat more stiffly than was her norm. Josefa sent a slight smile toward Oswald, who didn't return it. She looked away in confusion, just quickly enough to see Ben's shoulders dip ever so slightly before he pulled them back and straightened his posture. The movement was so subtle she would have missed it had she not looked directly at him at that moment.

She felt a yearning, a stirring inside her. She wanted to go over and thank him. No, she wanted to kiss him and be wrapped in his arms. She wanted to tell him there was plenty of chicken at the house and that, in fact, the family planned to have chicken that very evening for dinner. And that she hoped he would join them, that she knew he would be welcomed.

All that raced through her mind. But none of it made it to her lips. Her legs didn't move toward him, either. Her duty was to courteously dine with Oswald.

Oswald paid Eunice and started toward Josefa. Moments later, he had a hold on her elbow, tighter than she thought was appropriate. She looked down at her arm and frowned. He loosened his grip but kept her in a firm grasp.

"I hope this is worth it," he said and held up the boxed lunch in his free hand.

Josefa thought the exact same thing.

Oswald steered her away from the family picnic blankets and toward a small group of picnic tables under a cluster of laurel oaks. She twisted slightly and tried to see where Ben had gone, but he was no longer within sight. She did, however, see Agnes talking with the sisters, the orphans, and the entire Bight family.

"Look, Oswald. Everyone from the orphanage is with my family and the Taylors. Wouldn't you like to eat with them? You could get to know them and—"

"No."

"But..."

"I would rather give you my complete attention."

They walked in silence to the tables.

Oswald set down the lunch and used his handkerchief to brush away the few leaves scattered on the table. He used the same handkerchief—made of fine linen and monogrammed, Josefa noted—to open the box lunch. The rich aroma of fried chicken reminded her stomach she hadn't eaten in a while.

"Do you care for a piece?" he asked her.

"Gosh, yes. I'm starved."

Oswald looked at the chicken, then at Josefa. "Ladies never admit to hunger, at least not in front of a man."

With the handkerchief, he removed a small wing and handed it to her. Josefa reached into the box and removed one of the two tea towels she had packed. She sat down and spread it on her lap, accepted the food, and savored a bite.

Oswald watched her without expression, or at least without an expression she could read.

"Here," she said and gave him the other towel. He took out a drumstick, bit into it, chewed, and swallowed. And said nothing.

Josefa knew her fried chicken was good. It wasn't that she expected a compliment, but...no, she would not ask him if he liked it. She cast about for something else to discuss.

"When you are my wife, you will dine on caviar and pâté," he said.

Josefa swallowed in surprise.

"I, uh…," she began and stopped. "You do recall our conversation and my request?"

He frowned and tossed his nearly whole piece of chicken into the brush under the trees. Josefa winced at the waste of food.

She tried again. "I've been flattered by your attentions, Oswald. But each day I grow more certain of our incompatibility."

"Once I get you away from here, you'll understand that I'm just trying to help you become presentable," he said.

Josefa became very still. Whatever she had once told herself she felt for Oswald faded even more.

"I guess you haven't changed your mind about not living in Persimmon Hollow?"

He laughed, but the sound lacked lightness.

"You guess correctly. We'll live in Philadelphia and winter in Charleston."

"You do know that my future—no matter where I am—includes caring for my aunt and uncle when they cannot work any longer." She spoke it as a statement, not a question.

This time, he snorted. "I don't run old-age homes."

Josefa looked down at the wing she'd savored moments ago. She no longer had an appetite.

The sudden arrival of Polly broke the tension. "Josefa! Josefa, hey, do you two want to go canoeing?"

Welcoming the distraction, Josefa greeted Polly as she skipped up to them. "C'mon, you, me, Billy, Ben, and most all the Bights are going," Polly said. "Uh, and you're welcome to join us too, Mr. Heller."

"That would be fun," Josefa said.

"Certainly not," Oswald said. He stood. "I've had enough fun for one day. As a lady, Josefa, you would do well to think twice of the company kept on such excursions. Good day."

The parting words did nothing to improve Josefa's mood.

"I used to fear I'd do or say something wrong around him," she said when Oswald was out of hearing range. "That I didn't know how to act around a man like him. I now see otherwise, thanks be to God, as my aunt might say."

"You mean you see that you should always be yourself," said Polly. "And that you're happiest with those of us who appreciate Persimmon Hollow instead of looking down our noses at it...at least, if you want my opinion." She smiled as if to say she'd have offered it anyway. Which was true.

"Yes, I know, but..."

"Did he like the chicken?"

"He never said."

"What an oaf. Talk about no manners." Polly put her hand up to her mouth. "Uh-oh, now I sound like my mom. Anyway, Billy talked Ben into buying my box, but then we all shared it together, and Ben said it was the best sandwich he'd ever had, and I told him you made it, and he said he thinks you are one of the best cooks of any woman he knows."

Josefa was silent as she let that comment sink in.

"You know people are whispering about a love triangle, after the bidding war over your lunch," Polly added.

"They should stop wasting their time," Josefa said. "Ben told me he...he has no immediate prospects. Plus, Polly, he has a dream. One that's as strong as mine, if not stronger."

Polly's mutinous look, familiar to all in the grove family, crossed her face. "I don't believe you two won't find a way around all that. Love finds a way, isn't that what we hear time and again? At home, at church, at the orphanage?"

Josefa nodded in agreement but had no reply. As she and Polly gathered the rest of the chicken, the box, and tea towels, she could see Oswald in the distance as he neared his horse. The animal stood out from among the tired mules, oxen, and other horses, just as Oswald stuck out in Persimmon Hollow.

"He won't accept that I want to back out of our courtship," Josefa said.

"Who? Ben or Oswald?"

"You know full well who I mean."

"He'll understand sooner or later. Everyone else will be glad."

"You're sure of that?" Josefa asked. They strolled back toward the larger group. She soon halted.

"Look," Josefa said and pointed. Oswald had stopped and now spoke to someone who looked like, yes, it was, Ben. Both were stiff as they faced one another. Oswald pointed his finger into the open palm of his other hand repeatedly as he emphasized some point. Ben interrupted him. Oswald laughed. Ben stood closer and spoke again.

"They're not going to fight, are they?" Polly exclaimed.

"No, I don't think so, but they certainly aren't exchanging pleasantries."

Oswald shook his head, then spoke again. Ben stepped back as though in surprise. He then came forward again and seemed to question Oswald. But Oswald's posture suddenly took on a relaxed, confident air. He leaned against a tree trunk and folded his arms across his chest. Ben, who had not removed his hat during the encounter, took it off now, raked his fingers through his hair, and plopped his hat back on. He stopped talking, turned heel, and walked off as though he couldn't leave fast enough. Oswald straightened, moved away from the tree, and went toward his horse. He'd gained a swagger between the beginning and end of the encounter.

"I wonder if we'll ever find out what that was about," Polly said as she and Josefa resumed walking.

Josefa turned the incident over in her mind but didn't have a chance to immediately tell any of the others about what she and Polly had witnessed. When they reached the picnic blankets, Agnes was in a serious discussion with Fanny, Eunice, and Clyde, the kind that no one interrupts.

"I almost told him that we don't want any of his kind in this town, but then he'd know I did some checking up. I wasn't fixing for an argument right then or listening to him claim I insulted his respectability," Clyde said. "Don't think I don't aim to confront him though, and soon. First, I want to round up support, especially another buyer."

"Agnes, I was shocked at his actions," said Eunice. "So brazen in his certainty the group would accept his offer. Surely he knows we'd realize, eventually, the type of people they are. As if we want to harbor hatred in Persimmon Hollow."

"You're right, and Lupita and I need to discuss this with Seth and Alfredo," Agnes said. She glanced at Josefa and Polly as they neared the group. "And with Josefa before the relationship goes any further."

"What group? What people? Who's hateful?" The questions bubbled from Polly as she plunked down the basket. Josefa felt a knot of dread. She'd heard enough to inform her that the topic of conversation most likely involved Oswald.

"None of your business," said Agnes in the sharpest tone Josefa had ever heard her use. Polly was so surprised she closed her mouth at the same time her eyes went wide.

"Help us clean up," Agnes urged more gently. "Then go find the rest of the family and get ready to leave."

"But we want to canoe," protested Polly. "Billy and Ben and me and the Bights and Josefa. Fancy pants left. What's the big hurry?"

Agnes and Fanny exchanged glances.

"Mr. Heller left?" Agnes asked.

Josefa nodded. "But I think Ben has left too. Polly, I'll skip the boating, if you don't mind. My heart's no longer in it, not today."

"If the Bights are staying longer and agree to bring you back, you may go, Polly," Agnes said. "Go ask. But return immediately and leave with us if they're unable to accommodate you."

Polly ran off. Soon, the splash of canoes and oars in water indicated the answer. Josefa wished she wanted to join the fun, but she felt weary and far older than her years.

"You were referring to Oswald, weren't you?" she asked Agnes, who nodded but didn't explain.

"I told him, more than once, that I have doubts about our suitability," Josefa said.

The older women exchanged glances. Seth and Alfredo had rejoined the group, and they and Clyde carried a load of supplies to the wagon.

"Can you tell me what you were discussing about him?" Josefa asked.

"When we get to the grove," Agnes said. "We don't want it to be the talk of the town."

Agnes laid a hand on Josefa's arm. "We know you've had your heart set on the idea of becoming his wife. Just remember you can always find comfort in the Lord, no matter how deep the hurt or serious the concern."

Before Josefa had a chance to tell them she'd come to her senses about the idea of being a high-society lady, her aunt spoke up.

"Tell your sorrows to Our Lady," Lupita said. "She will always guide you and intercede."

Whatever had happened had shaken her aunt and Agnes, Josefa thought. They could all benefit from some time with Lupita's peaceful home shrine to Our Lady of Guadalupe. Josefa wished she were there right now, surrounded by the flickering light of the small votive candles they lit during prayer. It was a small statue, atop an equally small corner table draped with lace-edged linen. Yet its ability to help her feel closer to God far exceeded its physical size.

Chapter 25

*Y*ou still plan to attend the president's reception with him?" Ben frowned as he talked to Josefa later that day. "Even though you've decided against a future with him? I don't understand."

The afternoon sun cast long shadows over the dye garden, rich with lush plant growth from summer's warmth. After spending quiet time in prayer by the small home shrine, Josefa had strolled out to the garden bench with hand sewing. She had been surprised to find Ben already seated there, dirt on the knees of his pants, and the garden weeded and watered.

She sat down next to him. He rested but appeared anything but relaxed.

"Like I just explained to you, Ben. I've told him, more than once, that I think we're incompatible," she said, trying not to feel defensive. "He knows the presidential reception is important for me, for dressmaking reasons. He was magnanimous to let the invitation stand after I said we likely had no future together."

Ben blew out a long, low whistle. He straightened from a slouched position, leaned forward, and let his forearms rest on his thighs. He gripped his hands together.

"That's not what he told me at the box lunch," Ben said. "We had...words out by the wagons and horses. He claimed you two will be married within the month."

Josefa put her hand on his arm in unconscious reaction.

"Ben, no! That's not true."

Ben turned his head so that their gazes met. His conveyed a mixture of love, concern, hesitation, and a hint of sadness.

"You two obviously have different understandings then."

She removed her hand, her mind awhirl at Oswald's audacity. She and Ben sat in silence and listened to birdsong, tweeps, chirps, and insect buzzes while Josefa attempted to get her thoughts around Oswald's unpredictable behavior.

Ben stood. He put his hands in his pockets, then took them out. He stood in front of her, then walked to the edge of the garden, then came back. He stopped in front her.

"God's honest truth, Josefa, I love you. You know I love you. And I think you love me."

A yellow-and-black-striped butterfly hovered over the passion-vine flowers that bloomed on a trellis near the end of the bench. Another alighted inches from the first, and the two soon did a dance of delicate flutterings, swoops, and contacts.

Lips parted but silent, Josefa reached out and rested her hands on his arms in a move as light yet as determined as the butterflies neither of them looked at. She rose, her head tilted up so that her gaze locked on his. Her sewing slid off her lap unnoticed. They were face-to-face, inches apart, unsmiling, separate, yet locked together by the force of their feelings. She traced the outline of his firm mouth with her eyes and remembered how his lips tasted when covering hers.

Josefa swallowed, licked her lips, and longed to see a clear path through the yearnings of her heart.

"Ben, I...I love you too," she said softly, the words almost a surprise to her—almost. "But we have walked this path and reached this fork in the road before. You say you can't offer me what I need."

There. She'd said it, released the concern into the open air. Without a resolution to the weight that dragged at any chance of a future together, they'd be at a standstill.

"Not yet," he corrected her.

"What are you saying?" A faint hope leaped in her.

Ben stepped back again and did a small pace before coming to rest by her.

"Josefa, can you be happy without all the riches Oswald promises? The mansions, houseful of servants, a wardrobe large enough to dress the entire orphanage."

"Of course I can," she said.

"Because even when I can provide, and I hope and plan to provide well, I doubt it'd ever reach the level of his wealth. You need to know that up front."

Josefa recalled the glitter of the Stetson dinner, and the odd emptiness she experienced during it and afterward. As though she had expected to find something miraculous amid the opulent furnishings and sparkle of champagne, but had instead found them empty vessels. She remembered anticipating her apprenticeship, but then experiencing the strain of being away from family at the grove and of being tied to long hours of shop work.

She had begun to realize she was happier amid the everyday joys of life with people she loved, and that she savored her visions most when she intertwined them with the warmth of home. She had always intended to attain her goals without leaving Persimmon Hollow.

"I've come to understand, more than ever, what's most important, Ben," she said. "The people I love and who love me, and the community in Persimmon Hollow. But I can't shake free of my wish to stitch finery of my own design and see others happy to wear it. You, of all people, I think, know what I mean about having a dream."

She gestured with her hands.

"These fingers itch to make beautiful clothes, Ben. Sometimes I feel the grace of the Lord guiding my needle. I feel the Holy Spirit because sometimes I look at the creations that emerge from my hand and I know they wouldn't—couldn't—have existed without inspiration. So how could I turn away and not use this gift from above?"

Ben listened, intent on her words, in a way Oswald never did.

"But," Josefa continued, "I also learned at Esmeralda's that I couldn't focus only on a dressmaking business that would claim all of me. I want a home and a family, a husband and children... and I want to design and make clothes. Sometimes I just get confused about how to find a balance. My aunt has her own ideas for my future and believes she knows what's best for me. Which makes me even more uncertain. Then Oswald comes along with an easy way for me to have it all. Or so I thought."

She raised her arms in a gesture of supplication. "I have no answers, Ben. I just know that you understand me more than anyone else. I just know that...I love you."

She saw love and desire in his face as he reached to put his hands on her shoulders but then drew them back as if just remembering his hands were grubby from gardening. He took a step back.

Josefa laughed, and her anxieties eased. "Ben, I don't care a whit if a little dirt gets on my dress." She moved in close and settled into his embrace as he wrapped his arms around her and rested his head atop hers. A flicker of fire sparked in her, and she listened to the mingled heartbeats that voiced what neither one of them spoke.

"Will you wait for me, Josefa?" He spoke low, in her ear. "Will you untangle yourself from the man who is all wrong for you and wait for the one who is right?"

She looked up and met his lips, and let an urgent kiss answer. She sank into his warm, hungry mouth for moments that passed far too quickly. Finally she drew back.

"Yes, Ben," she said. "Yes, I will wait." The two butterflies flitted past them in a harmony of movement.

He smiled, the first time he'd smiled, she realized, since they'd come together in the garden.

"If my aunt doesn't send me to Texas, that is." She'd meant it as a joke, but the words came out seriously.

"Then I'd just have to travel out there and get you," he said.

She leaned in close again and sank into another kiss. He was so strong, so right, so everything. Together they could face anything. She smiled up at him and got lost in one more of his kisses.

This time when they broke apart, her heartbeat was as jumpy as the butterfly that alighted on her arm for seconds and darted off just as quickly.

"But, Ben…" she began as she tried to sort her restless emotions and tame the heat inside. "I'm still determined to go the reception. I'll get to see the first lady and be close to the most amazing fashions I'll probably ever see in my life." She let her hands lay on his chest. "You do understand, don't you?"

Ben lowered his head so that their foreheads touched.

"No, Josefa, I don't. But I love you. I see the spark when you talk about your aspirations. That, I do understand. I won't rest easy until you return. I have half a mind to go with you."

She placed a finger lightly on his lips. "No, Ben. You're more needed here. Esmeralda is going as chaperone. She and I have a single-minded fashion mission for this journey. There will be tons of people there, and we're coming right back the next morning. Oswald, for all his faults, is a gentleman and will provide any protection we might need."

"Except from him."

Josefa laughed. She could foresee no woes ahead for the trip, none at all.

⁂

"You realize, son, you need steady employment, prospects, and a home suited for a wife." Seth and Ben leaned side by side against the split rail fence that enclosed the large kitchen garden.

"I understand, sir. When I meet that criteria, I will have your blessing?"

"You already have mine. You need Alfredo's. And Lupita's. And Agnes's. Knowing this crew, you'll probably need Polly's and Billy's, too. And the Alloways's, and Clyde's, and Sarah and Toby's..."

"I aim to marry Josefa, sir, not all of Persimmon Hollow," said Ben, so serious he missed Seth's levity.

"Understood," Seth said and clapped a hand on his shoulder. "Alfredo will want specifics. Time, dollar amounts, assurances. Be ready with answers."

"I will, sir," Ben said.

"And stop calling me sir. You're almost one of the family."

⁂

"He's talking to Alfredo right now," said Lupita and shaped her tortillas with a happy slap.

"Oh, Josefa! What a joyous turn of events!" Agnes grabbed her hands and danced her in a circle.

"Not yet it isn't," said Lupita. "We wait to see if he is worthy."

"Oh, Aunt Lupita!" said Josefa. Then she saw Lupita's dimples, which showed up only when she was deeply happy.

"Will you set a date now?" Agnes asked as they stopped their twirl. "Or wait? Will you at least announce the good news to everyone? Oh! You could announce at the after-Mass celebration next week! Perfect timing!"

"And the bishop will be here, no less," Lupita added, a hint of excitement in her voice.

Josefa sparkled, swept up in the excitement. Her plan was so perfect. She took Agnes's hands again and did another twirl.

"No, we'll wait to say anything until after the presidential visit," Josefa decided. "It would look silly if we announced, and then I went to the reception."

Agnes released her hands so abruptly Josefa fell backward into a chair. The slap of tortilla-shaping halted suddenly.

"You're not still going to the reception with Oswald?" Agnes and Lupita asked simultaneously.

"Yes, I am," Josefa said. "You know how important it is to me. Ben knows. He's OK with it."

She looked at the two surprised women, whose happy faces had morphed into grim lines.

"Oswald knows our courtship is damaged and ending." Josefa omitted the part about his refusal to fully accept the idea. She would use the time on the trip to make sure they came to terms.

"Foolish," Lupita said and shook her head. The dimples were gone.

"You may want to rethink the journey," Agnes cautioned. "You are about to become informally betrothed to another man and—"

"And miss seeing the most fashionable woman in the whole world, and miss a chance to show what I can do as a dressmaker, to people who can afford my gowns, and miss a chance to pick up tips from just seeing the first lady's dress and the other people there?"

Josefa stood up and stalked around the room. "A betrothed man would be able to go, no questions asked. Why is it that only men can mix passions with home and family? Ben has dreams. You think he'll drop them to marry me? No, he will find a way to make them all work. Well, I can do the same. Ben understands me needing to do...to use... my God-given gifts."

"We don't always get what we want, but we...," Agnes started to say.

"You're going to tell me we get what God wants us to have," Josefa said. "But you also say that God helps those who help themselves. I'm helping myself."

"A woman's duty is to her husband and home," Lupita proclaimed with a firm slap of a tortilla on the counter.

"And the best way I can do that is to make sure I use and balance what God hands me to work with!" Josefa said.

"OK, we hear you," Agnes replied. "But those wishes have no bearing on this upcoming journey. Your aunt and I have misgivings."

"Oswald knows where I stand, and he kindly kept his invitation to the reception open. He'll know about Ben's and my relationship before we go. The reception is only in Palatka...not Texas." She cast a look at her aunt. "We'll be gone overnight, and you know that Esmeralda is not only happy to chaperone, she's as excited as I am at the fashions we'll get to see, not just on Mrs. Cleveland, but on the others there too."

Lupita started to knead dough and punch it down.

"I forbid it. Your uncle will forbid it too."

"It's too late," Josefa said. "The arrangements are made. It's only a few days away."

Agnes looked toward Lupita. "We have to tell her."

Lupita nodded.

"Tell me what?" Josefa asked.

"There's something you don't know about Oswald, Josefa," Agnes said. "We learned from Eunice and Clyde at the box luncheon that Oswald wants to sell his property to an organization known as the American Protective Association so they can use it for winter sessions and a vacation home for members."

Josefa shrugged. "So what?"

"The group's mission is to discourage and prevent the expansion of Catholic neighborhoods in rural and recently settled regions."

Josefa stared at Agnes.

"No! Are you certain? How could he be so forceful about wanting to marry me and...why, he even agreed when I insisted on a church wedding."

She remained silent about his other plan for a pre-church secular wedding in some judge's office. Had he merely toyed with her about the church ceremony? What a beast. But to mention the conversation now would mean a sure end to her anticipated journey.

"You listen to me," Lupita said. "You will not travel with that man, anywhere, no matter who is chaperone."

Josefa balked. She'd crafted a vision of the reception in her imagination that couldn't be thwarted. A layer of annoyance at Oswald simmered atop it. Yes, she most certainly would go. He owed the trip to her, whether he knew it or not.

This time, there'd be no sneaking around to get her way. She had matured beyond that.

"This is the last time I'll let him escort me anywhere," she said.

"We're talking about a man who woos a Catholic girl while associating with an anti-Catholic group," Lupita said.

"Yes, and the reception is his payment for being so deceitful.

Relax, Aunt Lupita. I have every intention of spending as little time as possible by his side throughout the trip."

Lupita's face was hard as she and Josefa stared at each other.

"I'll allow it only if you go and come back the same day," Lupita finally said. "You and Esmeralda can return on the river. Nighttime travel harms no one aboard the steamboat as long as you have the proper companions."

"I'm certain Ben would be at the river waiting for you, if asked," Agnes said. "I'm sure he'd go himself if he didn't feel so responsible toward last-minute construction duties."

"And you will find a second chaperone. I want two. At least," Lupita added.

"I am an adult," Josefa said. "You can stop treating me like a child."

"When you stop acting like one, I will," said Lupita, slapping and shaping more tortillas with renewed gusto.

"Ladies...," Agnes said. "Let me lead us in a prayer for all, even misguided Mr. Heller. Especially for him."

Chapter 26

swald glanced at his watch. Josefa checked and rechecked her luggage to make sure her reception gown wouldn't wrinkle and wondered how all of Persimmon Hollow seemed to have assembled in the kitchen at Taylor Grove.

Esmeralda flitted from one person to another to another. "I'm quite confident we'll be fine," she said. "Especially now with our return scheduled on the steamboat. Why, we won't even be gone twenty-four hours."

Ben leaned against the door, arms folded across his chest, directing a fixed stare at Oswald.

Lupita sat at the table, saying the rosary. Alfredo sat next to her with a cross look on his face. Fanny sat across from them, her fan in rapid motion. Art, seated next to her, was more intent on a field guide than on the conversation.

"You couldn't find even one other person to go with you?" Agnes asked for the third time.

"And do what? Sit in the carriage while we're at the reception?" Josefa asked. "The invitation list is closed."

"I'll go. I'll wait with Bernie at the carriage," Polly piped up.

"Bernie isn't going," Josefa said. "It's another driver, someone I don't know."

"That's a sweet offer, Polly, but hardly appropriate given the situation," Agnes said. "We hoped for an extra person with them at all times."

"I tried but..." Josefa began.

"Invitations aren't as simple to procure as they would be for one of your frolics," Oswald interrupted and again looked at his watch. "Time is growing late."

"With all due respect, it's you with whom we've grown apprehensive," said Seth, who leaned back against the work counter next to the sink.

"I am aware of that fact," Oswald said. "I didn't find it necessary to point out there are no grounds for such doubt."

"This is the opportunity of a lifetime for Josefa," Esmeralda said and then repeated variations of the comment as she continued to go from one person to the other.

"My niece forgets her place," Alfredo said.

Josefa sighed.

Eunice, standing near the door with Clyde, adjusted her spectacles. "Let's approach this from a scholarly perspective: We have three adults—one man, two women—who will travel together to Palatka in one carriage and attend an afternoon reception. Then the two women will return together via steamboat, and the man will return alone as he pleases. Perhaps we can set aside differences of opinion on the personalities involved and look only at the travel arrangements."

The room quieted.

"That's my Eunice, right to the point and always making sense," Clyde said and hooked his thumbs in his overall's suspenders.

"No one would ever guess you were a school principal," Agnes said to Eunice and smiled for the first time since the travelers had attempted to leave.

"Time is wasting," Oswald reminded them.

Josefa wedged between her aunt and uncle and put an arm around both.

"Your little *sobrina* is no longer a little girl," she said quietly. "All will be fine." Alfredo clasped a strong hand on her, but Lupita, who had completed her rosary, clung to the beads in one hand, hugged Josefa with the other arm, and let tears trickle down her face.

"I will pray the entire time you are gone," Lupita said.

Josefa kissed them both. Billy, who had been reading over the professor's shoulder, reached to grab Josefa's suitcase, but Ben got there first.

He picked up the bag, muscled between Oswald and Josefa, and started to escort her out. "Heed the lady's wishes the entire time," he said to Oswald, and there was an underscore of warning in his tone.

"I always do," retorted Oswald, who didn't step aside to give Ben any room.

"Especially the one about her wish for the future," Ben said.

"That's not your concern," Oswald said as they stepped onto the porch.

"It is now. I have her aunt and uncle's blessing for Josefa and I to plan our future together, a blessing you never bothered to secure."

Oswald halted for half a step, then resumed walking. Josefa saw a muscle twitch in his jaw. He strode to the other side of the carriage as if Ben hadn't spoken.

Josefa's own breath strained against her corset. She hoped the rest of the journey wouldn't be as dramatic as the leave-taking. She cast a wild look at Ben as he steadied her ascent into the carriage. She wished he were going instead of Oswald.

She reminded herself not to adopt others' fretfulness as her own. This was a simple journey, nothing more. All she had to do was make sure Oswald understood that her reflections affirmed the doubts she'd already voiced. They were incompatible. And her heart had been claimed elsewhere.

Ben squeezed her hand as she settled into the seat. She reached out to touch his cheek. "I love you," she whispered. His eyes warmed enough to soften the tense lines around his mouth.

"I love you," he said low, then turned and helped Esmeralda into the carriage. The carriage shifted and creaked as Oswald climbed up and sat atop, next to the driver. Ben's and Josefa's gaze met again, this time in mutual relief.

The men finished securing the luggage in place, and the horses took off with a jolt. Josefa waved until she could no longer see anyone. Then she leaned back.

"Esmeralda, I can't believe we're actually going!"

The dressmaker's eyes were huge with anticipation. "Just think what we'll see!"

"I wonder what Mrs. Cleveland will wear? Do you have any idea?"

"The papers have been speculating," Esmeralda said. "I saw, just last week in *Godey's*, a full report of her outfit at a charity function. Marvelous! She had on…"

And the strife at the grove was soon forgotten. Except by Oswald.

***

"Why are we stopping at this hotel?" Josefa asked Oswald when he dismounted in front of the smaller hotel in Palatka. "Isn't the reception at the Palatka Inn?"

Oswald nodded, lips compressed. "You will get ready here. And hurry. The reception begins in ninety minutes."

Josefa glanced at Esmeralda. "I won't leave your side, dear," Esmeralda said as they exited and went inside. A porter brought in their luggage.

"I'm sure we could dress at the reception hotel," Josefa said. "They surely have a room set aside for visitors such as us." She was uneasy at Oswald's clipped, withdrawn manner. But he didn't act inappropriately. He was more like a dark, angry shadow.

"The ladies shall use my room to dress," he told the concierge. "I will meet them here in an hour." He stalked off.

Forty-five minutes later, Esmeralda adjusted the placement of Josefa's hat as the final touch on her outfit. "You look beautiful!" she said and turned Josefa to face the mirror. A blip of satisfaction rippled through Josefa. The dress was perfect.

"You look lovely too," she said to Esmeralda. The dressmaker did a three-quarter turn to each side to inspect her own attire. Slightly less fancy than Josefa's, it still did the dressmaker's skills justice.

They hurriedly packed their travel clothes and rushed out to meet Oswald in the lobby with minutes to spare on their hour. He wasn't there.

Josefa drew her brows together. "He's punctual," she said. "And proper. There's no way he'd enter the reception late."

They looked around, asked the desk clerk, and then wandered outside where they saw the empty carriage and the driver's shrug, so they went back in and sat down. Josefa looked at the clock. "Only twenty minutes to the start of the reception," she said, worried.

"I'll go look out back," Esmeralda said. "We haven't checked there yet."

Josefa started to go with her, but the dressmaker shook her head. "We can't afford to miss him if he walks in the front doors.

You wait here. I'll be back in moments with or without him."

Esmeralda was no sooner out the back door than Oswald emerged from a side room whose door was half-ajar, grabbed Josefa's arm, and rushed her out to the carriage.

"Stop! What are you doing? Don't mess my dress! Slow down! We have to wait for Esmeralda!"

He pushed her into the carriage, hoisted himself in after her, and signaled the driver to go. They started bumping down the sandy street.

"Pull that top lower. Show some bodice," he ordered and attempted to make the change himself.

"No," she said, indignant. She shoved his hand away and readjusted her dress.

"When will you learn you have to obey me, your soon-to-be-husband," he said as a statement.

"No, that's where you are wrong, Oswald," she declared. "I tried to say this nicely, but you don't want to listen. We are not suited. I refuse your almost-offer of marriage. I tried to tell you in every way possible without offending you. As you never properly asked for my hand or sought my guardians' approval, I don't know why we're even having this conversation."

"No, my dear, you don't understand," he said in a cold voice.

The carriage came to a sharp halt in front of the Palatka Inn.

Josefa tried to calm herself. These nerves wouldn't do. With feigned boldness, she got out and told the driver to return and get Esmeralda. Oswald gave a curt nod, and the driver departed.

Oswald adjusted his cravat and took Josefa's arm. "We will appear the happy couple," he said.

Josefa gritted her teeth but said nothing. She focused on what she'd so long looked forward to. Her eyes widened as they entered the foyer and she glimpsed the shimmering fashions through the open doors of the ballroom. She adjusted her posture and prepared to make her own entrance.

But the guards escorted them to a smaller side room, not to the large ballroom. They were directed into a combination lounge-restaurant.

She looked at Oswald, who shrugged and went to the bar.

"Sir," she said to the official-looking man at the door. "I think we're supposed to be in the ballroom." He took her proffered invitation card.

"No, miss, you're eligible only for this room. Now don't you fret. We expect the president and first lady to stop in here first for a few minutes before they make their way to the main event. Shouldn't be long now. Isn't it a grand day!"

Too surprised to answer, Josefa looked up at Oswald with a question on her face as he returned to her side.

"I said a reception at the hotel, did I not?" he asked.

She didn't waste time on an answer. The room grew more crowded and hot, and her dress was crushed from all sides. Finally, she saw a frazzled Esmeralda in the doorway and attempted to wave her over to them, but could hardly move or make herself known.

Excited murmurs of talk swelled to a frenzy. The room grew even more crowded and cries of "They're here!" and "There they are!" flew around her. She couldn't see Esmeralda anymore and had even lost sight of Oswald. Taller people blocked her view. In desperation, she climbed onto the seat of a chair just as the presidential couple stood in the doorway, smiled, waved, and said a few how-do-you-dos.

Josefa watched in wonder. She had mere minutes to drink in the stunning fabric and styling of the first lady's gown, her perfect hairdo, and her exquisite hat. No wonder she was called the most fashionable woman in the world. And the president looked dashing in a suit of superior tailoring and quality fabric. She was actually seeing the president of the United States, right in front of her, and the first lady!

Then within moments, they were gone, escorted by an entourage out of the room and into, she guessed, the larger ballroom. She scrambled back off the chair. The packed room emptied as quickly as it had filled. Josefa felt herself carried along with the crowd, despite her attempts to find her companions.

She stumbled, felt a stranger help her steady herself, then found herself outside again, alone in the push of people. She managed to peer back inside. The doors to the big ballroom were closed, with guards in front of them.

Josefa deflated. It was over? Already? All that for...two or three minutes? Once again, Oswald had altered the way he delivered the facts. He'd led her to believe they'd be at the main reception.

As if her thoughts conjured him, Oswald materialized in the crowd. "There you are," he said. "Let's go."

"We have to wait for Esmeralda."

He didn't even answer, just hurried her along the street and around the corner to his carriage.

"Oswald, this is ridiculous. Please go back and find Esmeralda."

Once again, he made sure the two of them were alone in the carriage. This time, Josefa considered the option of jumping out before the horses picked up speed. Enough was enough. She saw that Esmeralda, bless her, had scooped up both their travel bags from the smaller hotel and put them in the carriage. She was glad, for they filled the space next to her and forced Oswald to sit across from her.

She was unprepared for the attack. He threw himself on her, grabbed her face and kissed her hard.

She fought him off and slapped him. "Oswald! Stop!"

He responded by pulling her atop him. She pushed back off.

"Struggle all you want, my little señorita. I considered a sham marriage, but why bother. We're on our way to a boarding house where I will take the liberties afforded me as a husband. And then señorita, I will return you, soiled."

As the import of his words sunk in, Josefa found a groundswell of courage she hadn't realized she possessed. She silently called upon Our Lady of Guadalupe, St. Francis, St. Theresa of Avila, and Jesus himself.

She let herself appear to relax, so that Oswald would loosen his grip on her. She even rested her head on his shoulder, distasteful though it was. He grunted in satisfaction. Then in a movement as rapid as the one he'd used on her, she bit his shoulder, jumped up, and pushed hard against the door as he yelled in outrage.

The carriage was still moving slowly in traffic. She tumbled out, landed on her bustle, and scrambled to her feet as the carriage stopped. Quickly, she dodged the other carriages, horses, and people on foot, and bolted for the sidewalk with the sounds of an angry Oswald close behind.

Was it coincidence that she had landed in front of St. Monica's Church itself? Josefa thought not and was inside the door before Oswald could grab her.

"Father Kenny! Help!" she shrieked as her eyes adjusted to the dimness and to a sudden halt of song. She ran toward the priest who was cleaning the temporary altar rail put in place after the break-in. "Help me!"

Father Kenny put down his rag and hurried to meet Josefa halfway down the aisle. He shielded her by stepping in front of her as Oswald stormed up and demanded Josefa.

"This is a place of sanctuary, my son," the priest said. "She is safe here." The choir, which had stopped rehearsing when Josefa burst in, watched the scene unfold. Oswald declared he wouldn't leave.

As a standoff evolved, a handful of choir members slipped out the side door. A short while later, the sheriff and a team of men entered. Once they heard the story, they arrested Oswald. Josefa felt a prayerful and immense relief as they led him away.

Then she realized she still had no idea where Esmeralda was, and that they both had to be at the steamboat landing in record time.

"Rest easy, my child," Father Kenny said. "Choir members will be happy to search the city for your dressmaker friend. The altar boys will jump at the chance to make a trip to the steamboat landing instead of continuing work on repairs. You and your friend will have a full escort, and I'm happy to lead the way. Now let us pray first. We always have time for God, do we not? Just as he always has time for us."

Chapter 27

The wind gust was just strong enough. The stove-box embers that smoldered in the doorway in a pile stirred and then leapt. They caught the next puff of wind, rode it to the doorframe, and latched onto lumber that had been dried to perfection before the first nail had been hammered. From there, the fire danced up and across the building's wooden frame, reaching for fuel with greed. The slender bell tower imploded. The small sanctuary folded inward. Main walls buckled into the wooden pews. Persimmon Hollow Catholic Church was gone before it welcomed its first worshippers.

* * *

Pray for us, oh holy mother of God, that we may be made worthy of the promises of Christ.

"Amen," whispered Josefa and made the Sign of the Cross after the final words of the Hail Holy Queen. She kissed her rosary and rolled her fingers over its smooth beads, letting the strand slip from one hand to the next. The room was quiet, as usual after evening devotions, but to Josefa the stillness had a rich silence. She savored the way everyone lingered, as though no one wished to inject reminders of pending duties into a shared sacred moment.

After the recent excitement of the Palatka trip, Josefa appreciated

Persimmon Hollow and Taylor Grove more than ever. She glanced at her aunt and uncle, at Seth and Agnes and the baby, at Polly and Billy, the latter two quiet for once. How she loved them all.

The only thing that could have made things better was if Ben had joined them for devotions. But he had been at the church every waking moment these last few days to make sure all finishing touches were complete before tomorrow's opening celebration. A few hours ago, Billy had returned from helping with site cleanup to say Ben had been called to a sudden meeting with Art at the Alloway House.

She remembered the joy she'd felt when she saw Ben waiting for her and Esmeralda at the steamboat landing. How good it'd felt to be in his arms, to tell the story from the safety of his embrace. How he was willing to let the law deal with Oswald instead of acting as a vigilante. And how he vowed he'd move mountains, by hand, if necessary, to do what needed to be done so they could wed sooner than they dared hope.

Josefa lurched out of her thoughts when Agnes rose and snuffed out the pinch of frankincense and myrrh incense she'd lit for prayers. Sudden notes of charred wood and smoke made a strident push into the room, carried on the breeze that resumed as dusk seeped into late evening. The heavy odors of the intruders soon overrode the lingering scent of the fragrant rosins.

"A woods fire?" Josefa asked.

"I hope that's all, and a small one at that," said Agnes, frowning. "Better a forest fire than something in town." Little Seth shifted in his cradle, awoke, wrinkled his nose at the harsh smells, and began to fuss. Polly picked him up and rocked him. "There, there, little man," she said in a singsong voice.

"That's no woods fire," said Seth, already up and almost to the door with Alfredo and Billy steps behind him. The men were gone before Josefa and the other women had time to call after them to mind their safety.

The clang of the town bell crossed the two-mile distance between the grove and downtown, and its repeated peal spoke of urgent need for every man to lend a hand.

"*Dios Mio,*" murmured Lupita. "I pray the fire doesn't destroy anyone's house."

"Especially not tonight," Josefa said. "Not with tomorrow being such a big day at the church."

Agnes took the baby from Polly and patted his back as she walked back and forth across the room. "We'll have no celebration if someone is mourning a loss. We'll ask Father to dedicate the Mass to them instead."

"Please, stop it, all of you," said Polly, and she stood up and put her hands over her ears and then on her hips. "Always thinking the worst! Everything will be fine. You saw how fast they raced out of here, and you know every other man in Persimmon Hollow did the same. They'll have the fire under control in no time." She shook her head, impatient with their fretting.

"If you ask me, we should all be there helping," she added.

Josefa stared at Polly. "I'm not a woman of action like you, Polly," she said. "But I would love to go see the completed altar linens and make sure the sisters don't need any help. Do you think they have finished the hems?" she asked Agnes.

"They're not only finished, but they already placed everything in the church. But let's go visit them anyway," Agnes said. She took charge of the small circle before nervous tension did. "They must be wondering about the fire as much as we are. Toby Bight and the older boys likely left with the others."

A sliver of ash landed on Josefa's sleeve as the women filed out. The unease she felt was reflected in Agnes's and Lupita's faces.

They were downwind from the fire, and the acrid odor made the sickly orange glow on the horizon seem even more threatening than it looked.

No one said what she knew they all had to be thinking. Fire was one of the biggest fears on the frontier, especially now at the end of the dry season and right before the near-daily summer rains started. The right combination of spark, wind, timber, and dryness could combust into a flame nearly impossible to contain. The worst scenario would be a building fire that jumped to other nearby structures.

"Let us pray *padre* does not have to say a funeral instead of a High Mass of celebration," Lupita said as they walked toward the orphanage. She blessed herself.

"You are always so dramatic!" said Polly.

"You mean realistic," said Lupita.

They knocked on the orphanage door instead of familiarly walking in because it was so late in the evening.

The sky's muddy orange glow had dimmed somewhat, but the air remained heavy with smoke. Agnes drew the edge of the baby's blanket loosely across his nose to help block the worst of it. Josefa felt a yearning as she watched Agnes look at the tiny face with love and protection in her eyes. Soon, she thought. Soon she and Ben would be married, and she would have a baby of her own to love. A baby to rock in a cradle by her side as she plied her needle whatever way best fit her life.

***

"Who did this?" The next morning Bishop Moore stood before the jumble of the smoke-darkened coquina rock foundation, wood ash, and charred logs. He stepped over debris and the foundation that formed a neat rectangle along the ground, and turned to face the citizens huddled in a misty rain that had fallen too late.

"Who in their right mind would do such a thing?" the bishop repeated.

Josefa said nothing, only stared. She was speechless. Not that he had asked her. The bishop had made a long, hard, special journey to consecrate the new church. Now he looked to Seth and Father Kenny for answers.

Seth didn't answer. Neither did Father. Nor anyone else. For the first time since Josefa had arrived in Persimmon Hollow, the leading citizens were at a loss for words.

Oswald was the first to find his voice. She started at the sound and stepped closer to her aunt and uncle, and again scanned the gathering for Ben and wondered where he was.

Why, Josefa questioned, was Oswald here, close enough for Seth's glare at him to start another fire. The last time she saw Oswald, he was being carted away by authorities in Palatka. He should be in jail. Instead, he was brazenly calling attention to himself here. The man's audacity knew no bounds. She swallowed a lump of unease.

"A man of his kind uses money to help authorities decide things in his favor," whispered Lupita.

"Which won't help him this time if we can prove our suspicions about the fire," Seth said in a low voice.

"Where is the builder of the church?" Oswald asked. "Note he isn't here. An odd absence. Could it have something to do with this terrible fire?"

Lupita hissed quietly. "He spreads poison." Seth clenched his fists and cut a look over to Clyde, whose lips were pressed into a frown, and at Alfredo, whose heated gaze belied an impassive expression.

What a monster, Josefa thought. She wrestled with a dark feeling, a new one. It pressed and tried to rise in her. *Jesus tells us to love our enemies*, she thought, *but how?* Anger simmered in her, not love.

She was glad when Agnes beckoned her and Lupita to leave with her, Polly, the sisters, and the orphans. "We'll prepare the chapel at the orphanage for Mass," Agnes said. "Then we'll have a quiet gathering and share the food we prepared." She spoke as though in a daze.

Thank goodness, thought Josefa, as she left with them. She needed the strength she always found at the chapel to remind her how to be a Christian.

At the chapel, Josefa vented her feelings with the assistance of a palmetto-fiber broom. On her third round of furious sweeping over the now-clean floor, Sister Rose walked over and placed a hand atop the broom handle to stop Josefa.

"It's not up to us to pass judgment," she said. "Especially on what we don't know for certain. We can pray for resolution, or better still, pray for whomever or whatever caused this misfortune."

Agnes overheard from where she stood positioning and repositioning the cruets. Her face was wan.

"You're right, Sister, and we give thanks for the reminder. But I think I speak for Josefa and myself both in saying how hard it is. You know how long it took, how many benefits, pinched pennies, and sacrifices on so many people's parts, to build the church. To have it go up in flames is almost too much to bear."

"To hear Oswald disparage Ben is too much to bear too," Josefa said. "And nobody can find Ben." She almost wailed the last sentence.

"We have to accept what happens, even that which we don't want or like," Sister Rose said. "Don't I know it isn't easy sometimes. It doesn't mean we don't take action to change situations.

We just try not to judge." She gave them a compassionate look.
"Do you wish to pray? We all wear the Miraculous Medal close
to our hearts. Draw strength from its testimony to patience and
forgiveness as we pray the Act of Charity."

The women knelt together and bent their heads as they prayed
forgiveness to all who injured them, and for pardon from anyone
they may have injured. Soon after they finished, they heard the
stampede of footsteps from the hallway and the sounds of horses
and buggies outside. It was time for the Mass they should have
been celebrating in the new Persimmon Hollow Catholic Church.

Bishop Moore strode in first. "A fine job, my sisters in Christ,"
he said as he glanced around the neat chapel with its framed
Stations of the Cross on the walls and its statue of the Holy Family
in one corner.

The bishop took one look at Agnes, placed his hand on her
head, closed his eyes, and murmured a prayer. "Thank you, your
Eminence," she whispered when he finished and stepped back.
For the first time in hours, she gave a slight smile.

Seth, Polly with the baby, Alfredo, Billy, and the orphans all
filed in after the priests. Behind them, the other Catholic families
and a crowd of non-Catholic townsfolk made their way inside.
The chapel became not only full but crowded. Eunice carried in
a small melodeon, set it up, and started to play as though on pre-
arrangement with the bishop.

"Welcome," said Bishop Moore. "Although we wish we were
gathered in a more celebratory atmosphere, we are always
grateful for the opportunity to worship our Lord as a community.
I especially welcome our non-Catholic friends and thank them for
joining us."

Josefa was soon immersed in the readings, the music, the Gospel
message, the sublime mystery at the heart of the consecration. She

appreciated the bishop's homily reminding everyone of the power of forgiveness and the importance of it.

Forgiving or not, a glum set of faces filled the orphanage dining room after the Mass. People picked at the deviled eggs, sandwiches, and beverages. Every time Josefa perceived movement near the door, she jumped to see if Ben had arrived.

"We plan to question everyone in town and find out who may have been passing near the church yesterday, and especially last night," she heard Seth say to a group gathered at a table. "There has to be a witness. Something overheard or seen."

Few people stayed long in the somber atmosphere, so unlike the Easter dinner in the same spot a mere two months earlier. Most remained only long enough to share condolences, offer help, nibble on a few refreshments, and say farewell.

"Uh, where is Ben, anyway?" Billy asked. "I got a question about the coop I'm building for Polly's chick with the strange feathers. I need him to help figure out Polly's weird design."

"It's not weird, it's special, like my chicken," Polly said.

"What? Did you say you are looking for Ben?" asked Fanny, who had drawn near to say goodbye. "Goodness, my hearing grows more faint by the day."

"Yeah, do you know where he is?" Billy asked.

"We haven't seen him all day," Josefa added, as tenseness coiled within her.

"Of course not," Fanny said. "Ben is gone. I thought everyone knew."

"Gone?" Josefa asked. "Gone where?"

"To the Bahamas."

Chapter 28

"Oh, dear," Fanny said, her face flushed. "What with my hearing...you know I don't want to bother anyone with it, but I do miss more and more especially in crowds. Yes, Ben is on his way to the islands, I forget which one. They left last night, almost as soon as Ben got to the house. I mean Ben left for the islands, but Art and Bernie drove him over to the coast so he could head south by water. Art was enthused about the chance to explore the flora between here and the Indian River."

She dug in her palmetto-frond bag. "Josefa, in the confusion with the fire and then rushing out here...I haven't been to the church site yet, you know. But in the bustle of everything, I neglected to give this to you." She handed Josefa a letter. "It's from Ben."

Josefa tore it open.

Dear Josefa,
This opportunity for fieldwork landed in my lap, and I can't pass it up. Professor Art's colleague wrote with immediate need of a helper for an expedition in search of endemic species of Epidendrum orchids on Andros and perhaps other nearby islands. Scientists think there are a number of them yet to be discovered. The pay is beyond

*what I imagined and will go into our marriage fund. Sorry
I'm missing the church celebration, but, Josefa, all I could
think was how this both inches us closer to independence
and lets me build my name in the field. I won't be gone
long. Two months. Will write when I can. Love, Ben. P.S.
I sent a note to my mom and sister. Soon as I get back,
we'll travel up so you can meet them. Maybe Lupita and
Alfredo can go too? I love you.*

Josefa read and reread the note. Two long months: the rest of
June, all of July, and even into August. It seemed interminable.
She felt a sharp insight into how it felt to watch your soul mate
run off to chase a dream. She had done the same, with disas-
trous results. She prayed his journey would be safe and a success.
He wasn't going to unexplored territory like his father had done
when he lost his life. No, he was going to a British colony. All
would be fine. Josefa would keep telling herself that.

She turned to her aunt, and then burst into tears.

* * *

Every available spare hand in Persimmon Hollow pitched in to
rebuild the church. Clyde donated the lumber. Toby Bight organized the carpenters; Agnes, Lupita, and Sarah Bight created a
food chart that rotated lunch preparation and delivery among
the women; and Fanny and Eunice organized the meal assemblies
at the Alloway House. Cornelia took charge of Polly, the Bight
girls, and younger orphan girls to make sure workers always had
beverages. Seth, Alfredo, Billy, Toby, and the older boy orphans
split their time between construction and their duties at the grove.
Ralph surprised everyone with his skill in construction, marred
only by intermittent confusion over what task to tackle after he

completed a duty. Josefa, Esmeralda, the sisters, and the most experienced orphans sewed and embroidered new altar linens. And in what all agreed had to be a miracle, the stained-glass window sustained only minor damage. Repair was minimal.

"We could be finished in a month at this pace," Seth said one workday. He, Alfredo, Billy, and Toby sat with the grove women and ate the Brunswick stew cooked for that day's lunch.

"Ben's in for a surprise when he gets back," Josefa said. She pined for him more each day.

"Excuse me, heard a man could get a job and vittles here," an unfamiliar voice said.

Agnes jumped up, mouth open in surprise. "How...I can't believe...what are you doing here?" she demanded.

Seth was by her side in an instant. "Answer the lady," he growled.

Josefa stared. The man was a stranger to her. He was as round as he was tall and had a squeaky voice. He shifted from foot to foot.

"I, uh, I beg your pardon, ma'am, I didn't realize..."

"Why aren't you in jail?" Agnes asked. "What is your name again?"

"Oh, I paid my dues, yes ma'am I did, and I aim to be a working man now. That's why I come here asking for work. Uh, my name is Barrel. I mean, that's what I go by." He eyed the food with a hungry face.

"You abducted me and my children, and you have the nerve, the absolute nerve to walk in here and..."

Josefa had never seen Agnes so agitated. Good God, the man must have been one of the kidnappers who snatched Agnes, Polly, and Billy a couple of years earlier. It had been part of a whole big plot. The men had been working for the railroad, which was trying to run Seth off his land.

Barrel stepped back from them. "I didn't know you was here. I'm going, ma'am."

"Just a minute," Seth said. "How did you know there was work here? I know you don't live in town."

"I live out by the river, and it's big talk out there, yes it is," Barrel said. "I didn't think that man would go through with it, but sure looks like he did."

"What man?"

"Uh, I don't know his name. Rich guy, fancy clothes, the kind that expects everybody to do his bidding. I told him right off that no, sirree, I wasn't interested, no way, in setting fire to no church. Wasn't me who did it. No, I'd rather go hungry than mess with God."

Seth described Oswald in detail. Barrel nodded. "Yup, sounds like the guy. I'd know soon as I see him."

"Good, because you'll be called on to say the same to the sheriff mighty soon," Seth said.

"Who's that?" Barrel had caught sight of Father Kenny hauling wood.

"A priest."

"No kidding? You got priests who do work?"

"We serve where needed," said Father Kenny as he walked by and overheard.

Barrel stood there, looking hungry for more than food.

Agnes closed her eyes for a long moment.

"Guess I'll be leaving," Barrel finally said in a disappointed voice.

"Can't hire you," Seth said. "Your presence would be too upsetting to my wife."

Agnes opened her eyes. "Have something to eat first," she offered. Seth handed him a bowl of stew from the tureen.

"I ain't lying when I say I changed my ways," Barrel said between rapidly spooning the stew into his mouth. "No sirree. I didn't like messing with women and children in that job, and I tried to tell my partner that, but he didn't want to hear it. Me and him parted ways after we got throwed into jail."

"I may have work for you at my church in Palatka," said Father Kenny, who had stayed close and listened to the conversation for a few minutes.

Barrel brightened. "Can I try going to church, too?"

Father Kenny nodded. "We can begin instruction in the faith if you are seriously interested."

Barrel squinted up at him. "Good a time as any to get right with the Lord, is how I figure it." He went back to eating. Seth gently drew Agnes away. She leaned her head on his shoulder, and he pulled her close. Seth nodded a thanks to Father Kenny.

* * *

Josefa marked the days on her calendar and focused her sewing activities on instructing the orphans. Two months never seemed so long. High summer moved in, with its regular afternoon showers. The rain lightened the humidity and left the air as sparkling as the raindrops that clung on leaves and glittered in the sun that burst through the clouds.

Then as she sat on the front porch one late afternoon, too warm to even pick up a needle, there he was. Ben rode up the lane on his horse. Josefa rose from the rocker, afraid the heat caused her to imagine him. But no. There he was, tanner, leaner, more serious, a bit...harder. She shrieked with joy and ran down the steps into his waiting arms.

"How I missed you," he said as he kissed her hair, her face, her neck.

The feel of his strong arms around her made her want to stay like that forever. But the rest of the grove got wind of his return, and the two were soon surrounded.

"Come, we all want to hear," Agnes said. "You will stay for dinner."

"And for the night," added Lupita.

Ben's familiar grin came back. "Much obliged," he said. "I've got some things to say."

He and Josefa stayed entwined as they wandered back into the house.

* * *

"So there you have it," Ben said as they all sat on the porch after dinner and spooned ice cream before it melted. "All it took was a taste of that life to make me realize I wanted to be in Persimmon Hollow. That my life here, with Josefa, came first, and the exploration second." He paused and pulled Josefa closer to him on the swing. She snuggled in, with no intention of moving.

"Before I came here this afternoon, I had a talk with Professor Art when I stopped to drop off my field notes. He wants to stay too—he's sweet on Fanny, it's plain as day to me—and he's close to retirement. So he was amenable to my proposal. But I need for the citrus expert to weigh in." He glanced at Seth and outlined his plan.

"You've hit on a winner in my book," Seth said. "Persimmon Hollow needs its own plant nursery, and you're a good man to make it happen."

"Me and the professor," Ben said. "He crowed about how he'd be the partner who put in the money, and I'd be the one to do the work. Said he had no intentions of being a silent partner either. He thinks the whole thing is a grand idea."

"Thank you, Holy Lady of Guadalupe," said Lupita. Josefa grinned. She was in heaven on earth. Ben, her home, her family. Everything. Because she'd learned, too, that a dream was nothing unless it included the people who mattered.

"Best of all," Ben continued. "Josefa and I won't have to wait as long to marry. I aim to be the provider she needs within a year."

"Or less," said Josefa, and everyone laughed.

"Or less," agreed Ben with a smile.

* * *

"You keep it, dear," Esmeralda said to Josefa a few days later as Josefa stood before her with the Bloomingdale's catalog in her outstretched hand. She, Polly, Agnes, and Lupita had come to help the dressmaker pack up her store.

Josefa's eyes widened. She had been loath to relinquish the treasured book, even though she wasn't going to plunge into a full-time dressmaking future. Esmeralda continued to fit bolts of material into boxes. "You might need that catalog. Just like I might need all this fabric back home, and I have no intention of opening another shop. Unless I move back here."

Josefa set down the book and started to pass fabric rolls to Esmeralda. "Thank you! You don't know what the catalog means to me. It's funny. There're so many different kinds of merchandise on the pages. At first, I cared only for the big section on fashion. Now I see how everything plays a role in a household. Everything fits together."

Esmeralda looked up from a box and smiled. Lupita, who had started cleaning the shelves, loudly gave thanks to Our Lady for her intercession.

"You're thanking the Blessed Mother for a catalog?" Josefa asked her aunt.

Lupita and Agnes exchanged happy glances.

"No, my sweet *sobrina*," said Lupita, and she walked over and swept Josefa into a hug. "I thank Our Lady for never giving up on you, even when I was in despair over your twists and turns over the past months."

"Our Lord and his mother never give up on any of us," Agnes said gently.

"Amen to that," said Polly.

Epilogue

March 1889

Josefa stepped into Persimmon Hollow Catholic Church holding tight to Alfredo's arm. He wore a look of pride as he escorted her down the aisle.

She saw the bold love, anticipation, and appreciation cross Ben's face as they neared the altar rail. She had poured her heart into her wedding gown, on which she had labored for months after first making Ben the finest linen shirt a man could want.

She soon forgot the shirt and the dress. All that mattered was Ben by her side and Father Kenny, who welcomed them. Every minute of the Mass, the ritual, the sacrament of holy matrimony was like a precious jewel.

"You may kiss the bride," Father Kenny finally said. Ben and Josefa faced each other, and everything else in the church fell away. There was no building, no other people, no anything but the two of them, encircled by love and commitment. His lips were warm, firm, and inviting.

"Let us all applaud the newlyweds," Father Kenny announced to the packed church. Everyone stood and clapped, and the choir harmonized as Josefa and Ben started down the aisle together, hands held as though neither ever wanted to let go. The joy they shared spread across the church as they passed each pew. Little Seth, now a toddler wobbling by Agnes's side, let out a happy shriek when he saw them.

Billy and one of the orphans opened the double doors so the newlyweds could pass through. Josefa and Ben stepped out into the dazzle of sunlight and stood for a moment on the top step. Josefa didn't want to let the moment go too quickly.

A flash of orange in a shrub a few feet away caught her eye, and she glanced over. When she saw what it was, she tugged at Ben to go have a closer look. As others exited the church, they saw Josefa and Ben, heads together, peering closely at a shrub.

"Two chrysalides," Ben said in a hushed tone. A bright orange fritillary unfolded itself from one. A fully emerged fritillary hung lightly from the other.

"New lives," said Josefa. She and Ben looked at each other. New lives, just like theirs.

~ THE END ~